NEW STORIES
FROM THE SOUTH

The Year's Best, 2002

The editor wishes to thank Kathy Pories, Dana Stamey, and Anne Winslow, colleagues whose talent, skill, patience, and tact are essential to this anthology.

She is also most grateful to the many journals and magazines that, year after year, provide the anthology with complimentary subscriptions.

Edited by
Shannon Ravenel

with a preface by Larry Brown

NEW STORIES FROM THE SOUTH

The Year's Best, 2002

Algonquin Books of Chapel Hill

Published by
ALGONQUIN BOOKS OF CHAPEL HILL
Post Office Box 2225
Chapel Hill, North Carolina 27515-2225

a division of
WORKMAN PUBLISHING
708 Broadway
New York, New York 10003

Printed in the United States of America.

ISSN 0897–9073
ISBN 1–56512–375–1

CONTENTS

PREFACE: HOME OF MY FATHER, AND GRANDFATHERS, AND GREAT-GRANDFATHERS
by Larry Brown vii

Romulus Linney, TENNESSEE 1
From *The Southern Review*

Dwight Allen, END OF THE STEAM AGE 28
From *The Greensboro Review*

William Gay, CHARTING THE TERRITORIES OF THE RED 55
From *The Southern Review*

Max Steele, THE UNRIPE HEART 73
From *The Washington Post Magazine*

Aaron Gwyn, OF FALLING 81
From *Louisiana Literature*

Dulane Upshaw Ponder, THE RAT SPOON 95
From *The South Carolina Review*

Andrea Lee, ANTHROPOLOGY 110
From *The Oxford American*

Doris Betts, ABOVEGROUND 124
From *Epoch*

R. T. Smith, I HAVE LOST MY RIGHT 146
From *The Missouri Review*

Brad Barkley, BENEATH THE DEEP, SLOW MOTION 158
From *The Virginia Quarterly Review*

Ingrid Hill, THE MORE THEY STAY THE SAME 183
From *The Raleigh News & Observer*

Kate Small, MAXIMUM SUNLIGHT 188
From *Nimrod International*

George Singleton, SHOW-AND-TELL 201
From *The Atlantic Monthly*

Julie Orringer, PILGRIMS 216
From *Ploughshares*

Bill Roorbach, BIG BEND 235
From *The Atlantic Monthly*

Russell Banks, THE OUTER BANKS 252
From *Esquire*

Corey Mesler, THE GROWTH AND DEATH OF BUDDY GARDNER 257
From *Pindeldyboz*

David Koon, THE BONE DIVERS 269
From *Glimmer Train Stories*

Lucia Nevai, FAITH HEALER 288
From *The Iowa Review*

APPENDIX 307

PREVIOUS VOLUMES 317

Larry Brown

PREFACE: HOME OF MY FATHER, AND GRANDFATHERS, AND GREAT-GRANDFATHERS

Cotton is opening now in Mississippi. The boys and men with their guns and their pickups and their four-wheelers on trailers are out in the road again, and I know that the bucks are beginning to scrape the velvet from their horns. The days and nights are turning cooler, and the grass in my pasture is going to seed. Twenty-two years have passed since I sat down to a portable electric typewriter in my mother-in-law's house at Yocona and began to try to create a novel from my imagination, a novel about a man-eating bear in Yellowstone National Park, a place I'd never visited, a novel that was loaded with sex and violence.

I did not know that I had entered into an apprenticeship of learning, or that the process of it had begun that first night. That realization came much later, after I had a few years in. I was simply writing, with very clumsy hands and a much clumsier mind, and trying to tell a story. I had some characters, and I had them set in a place where all the action would unfold, but I was so naive that I didn't even know you were supposed to double-space. I didn't know a lot of things. I didn't know that it might be helpful to write about places you actually knew, or that sex and violence weren't the only things worth writing about.

Writing stories and novels and essays and other things for a long time naturally results in a mountain of paper, especially if you're using a typewriter for twenty of those years. Now that I have a computer, I don't create reams of typed pages anymore, because now like everybody else I do all my revision on the screen instead of by hand, like I used to, with a pen or pencil, and I don't have to print anything out until I need to show it to somebody else. And I usually don't even have to do that, because now a piece for a magazine or a story or even a manuscript for a book can be electronically transmitted.

But in spite of all these changes in the revision process and the transmissions of the finished products, it's just words to me, whether they're on paper or on a screen, it's just people getting into trouble, and me following them around from night to night to see what they're going to do next. I don't have to do all that retyping to correct pages, which was a tremendous loss of time, and so perhaps I have more time to write new things, but all this electronic help doesn't change the fact that it's just making up things from your head and turning them into a story, trying to turn names on paper into living, breathing people who can get rained on or drive cars or eat ribs at midnight at Mississippi.

When I began I knew nothing, or almost nothing. I knew that I loved to read, and always had, and it didn't look like it would be that difficult a thing to be able to learn how to write. I wanted to write stories and novels of my own that I would enjoy as much as the ones I loved best.

As I see it, the apprentice writer enters into a contract of time with no defined boundaries, or only those that are self-imposed. Nobody can tell you how long it's going to take, or if it will ever happen, and by that I mean whatever measure of success the writer is seeking, whether it's the publication of a short story in a literary magazine or an article in the *Christian Science Monitor* or the writing of a five-hundred-page novel that gets on the bestseller list and rides it for weeks or months and then gets made into a blockbuster motion picture. My expectations were large at first, very naively so, and then when things started getting rejected, I had no choice but to reappraise my condition and my level of skill and the amount of determination and desire I possessed. I had to decide whether or not I was going to be in it for the long haul. And if I wasn't going to be in it for the long haul, there was no need in sitting down and ever starting another novel or story. I had no proof that I could succeed. But I just had a burning faith that if I kept writing for long enough, I would eventually learn how.

If you could go through all those boxes that are up in my attic, and out in my room, and see the stuff I wrote in the early years, say between 1980 and 1984, you would have to say that I had no talent. You wouldn't be able to form any other conclusion. It's that bad. But it's also proof to me that the average man or woman can learn how to write fiction if they try long and hard enough. My own experience is the closest proof I have and I don't know about anybody else's case, although I talk to writers sometimes who have been going at it for ten years with little or no success. But I've never encouraged anybody to stop, because I know that you've got to write X number of words before your apprenticeship period is over and somebody is willing to pay you money for something you've written. The only bad thing is that nobody can tell you how many words that X covers. It might be two hundred thousand. It might be a million. For me it was seven years until my first book, and I think it's safe to say that I've written a couple of million words by now. The thing is, it was all done one day at a time. One page a day begun on Thanksgiving produces a 365-page novel by the time the next Turkey day rolls around. I've found out you can build a house the same way.

So. Starting is fairly easy, publishing is hard at first, and being rejected is always hard. Maybe hardest of all is being able to put your innermost thoughts down in words, to be able to pull up out of yourself the deepest human feelings that make you who you are, and that define each individual writer's take on the world, and therefore the work. I figure that every story in the world has already been told, and that a variation of every bad or good thing that has ever happened to somebody who is alive this minute was suffered or enjoyed by some other people a thousand years ago and a thousand times over.

My personal philosophy on short stories and novels is that they have to start soon, as quickly as possible, with no messing around talking for three pages about the history of Aunt Helen's boyfriend Junior, who drinks too much and smokes dope, and *that* was the reason he was over at her house that day when all the hogs got out and ate either Granny or Cousin Lucille. I say come on; let's start the story on the first page with him staggering out into her yard from the pickup with his whiskey bottle and his champion coon dog and then let's roll toward the ending with a few thrills and laughs and some tension and understanding about why these things have happened along the way.

I sometimes hear from young or old writers about how hard it all is. I tend to say, Well, that's a fact, Jack, or to find somebody else to talk to on the other side of the room. Of course it's hard. It's supposed to be hard, and there are no guarantees. The rewards from writing are based on the time the writer puts into it and the perseverance and dedication and determination the writer possesses. There are years that have to be spent learning your craft, and I don't see it as being much different from studying with a master carpenter or a journeyman mason to learn how to lay out a house from the dirt up or to lay courses of brick up from the footing. Faulkner said that the only things worth writing about are the truths of the human heart in conflict with itself, and I've tried to follow that advice.

I've told my story over and over, about how I was working at the fire department, and wanted to write, and sat down and started doing it and wrote five unpublished novels and over a hundred short stories, for seven years, until my first book appeared. I've told the story so many times that I don't tell it much anymore. These days what I want to do is just keep writing, because that's the thing that makes me feel most alive.

I'm also much more aware, these last few years leading up to my fiftieth birthday, about the great and neverending circle of life in this world. I see it in the memories of my grandmothers' faces, and in the memories and pictures of my children's faces, who are now grown men and women. I think every story starts from the character, from imagining a person in a place with something going on. It might be something as simple as somebody looking at a dead dog on the side of the road. How they arrived there is the question. The rest of it is piecing those lives together, and staying with it night after night.

My regular thing is to get in my truck late in the evening just before dark, and ride down the roads around my house and listen to music, on the same old trails I'd ridden when I was an eighteen-year-old boy just out of high school, a boy who had no real direction in life, who only liked to hunt and fish and read, who was only hoping to stay out of a terrible war, but would go if he had to. I watch the ground being broken for cotton and beans in the spring, and the leaves coming on to the trees, and I watch through summer's heat as the green plants grow up strong, and then when the pickers and combines roll through the fields in the fall, I watch the hints of yellow and orange touch the hardwood ridges that shelter the turkeys and the deer, until some more time passes, and the leaves are all gone, and gray winter has finally set in, and there's nothing to do but wait for the bright first leaves of spring again. I set my people in this landscape, and I go home each evening to eat supper, and to write again, and finally to sleep. This is all that I have, this land called North Mississippi, home of my father, and grandfathers, and great-grandfathers, and luckily for me, it turns out to be always enough.

Larry Brown is the author of eight books, the most recent of which are *Fay,* a novel, and *Billy Ray's Farm,* essays. His books have won many prizes and awards, including two Southern Book Critics Circle awards for fiction and the Lila Wallace–*Reader's Digest* Writer's Award. *Big Bad Love,* a collection of short stories, has been made into a movie starring Debra Winger and Arliss Howard. He lives near Oxford, Mississippi, on family land.

NEW STORIES
FROM THE SOUTH

The Year's Best, 2002

Romulus Linney

TENNESSEE

(from *The Southern Review*)

Far down the aisles of the forest the enchantment held its wonderful sway, and she felt in her own ignorant fashion how beautiful is the accustomed light. When the horse's stumbling feet had ceased to sound among the stones, the wilderness without was as lonely and unsuggestive of human occupation or human existence as when the Great Smoky Mountains first rose from the sea.
—Charles Egbert Craddock, American novelist, 1885

One, traveler.

An old woman walked slowly through the woods. She stopped and stared at a waterfall. She was dressed in her black, handmade clothes, with a goat-wool blanket over one shoulder, to lie down on. Straw-white old hair, unbound and unkempt, stuck up and out. She carried a thick wooden stick, had a leather bag tied around her waist, and that was her. She stopped and looked at the waterfall gushing. With her stick she pushed aside brush, hacked down some brier. No mistake. Carson's Falls. She was upset when she remembered its name.

She pushed on. She stopped, poked around with her stick. The brush was thin, cut recently. Who did that?

She found the ruts of an abandoned trail. She shook her head, poked her way through thicker brush that had overgrown the hidden trail. Then she stopped, staring ahead at empty air. She had walked herself into a mountaintop meadow. It was a windswept bald. She was waist-high in timothy grass. Before her was a boulder and a bluff, a sudden, sheer end of the mountain and a drop-off that made her dizzy now as it had, she knew, made her dizzy before. The setting sun bathed her black dress in gold. She peered over the edge, then stamped around the boulder's edge until she kicked up two rotted planks, and looked at what was under them. Then she dropped them, turned around, and went away from the bald. Was there surely a house, off behind that range of sycamores that wasn't there? More brush. Behind it she saw that house, at the edge of a large cornfield. She knew if the house was there, and if she could find ruts again, she could find the tree. It took her a while, but she did.

It was a maple tree. It had many knobs and burls on it. Afternoon sunlight, leaf-dappled, poured down on her. The light hurt her eyes. She put her hands high on the tree. She found a burl, above her head. Something stuck out of it. She opened her leather bag, took out a barlow knife, reached up and cut into the burl. Something there. It was an old piece of glass. From a mirror. She rubbed it. She could see her face, old and lined, behind the scum.

Two, family.

A man and his son, tired and dirty, axes on their shoulders, were going home. A woman on a porch nursed her baby. She called out, Yoohoo!

The old woman heard that, and was bewildered. She jabbed her stick into the ground in frustration. Maybe they are over there. She moved off through the brush, but away from the cabin.

Supper, said the wife. Take a seat, said her husband. He flipped a crate on end for his son, shoved up a slat chair on rockers for his wife. He stood on his porch looking out over his land. Tell your mother what we did today. And his son said, Girdled trees.

The old woman walked away from the maple tree. She stumbled, sank to one knee, bent over, one hand on the ground. An old cowbell. She picked it up. She jiggled it. She staggered to her feet and rang it. It clanked, peaceably. Ordinary thing. She clanged it louder and listened to it, shaking her head, astonished. This can't be.

Daddy, we ain't got no cows near the bluff.

Some stray. Now sit down. They did.

This here is our estate.

The cowbell sounded closer.

This here. This land, creek, this house. Yours one day, son, if you want it and can stand me. Your babies and then more babies plain after them. By God, I aim to build out this porch half again this wide. Cut that brush, we'll be looking out over 159 acres! All of it cleared! All of it ours! Son, when you can go, you can go. But if you stay, you stay. Understand that?

The old woman clanked her bell. She had moved in a circle and now stood again by the edge of the bald, one foot on one of the rotten planks. Above her was a drift of darkening clouds, bellies hairy with dark vapor, but through them the sun came down in one shot of straight light. Beyond her were steel-blue mountains, one behind another, vast in their own company. It was only a view. There were many such.

She left it, as if suddenly hurt, holding out one hand behind her. She went toward the house.

The wife said, Split me some wood, I got to heat ever'thing up again. The husband said he'd get the damn wood, and he wanted his son to sit on that porch and think about what he wanted in this life. He went around back. The wife went inside. The boy sat there. How do you know what you want in this life?

Three, arrival.

The boy shaded his face with his hand. He saw a shadow move just beyond the yard. It was the old woman. She held the piece of mirror in her hand. It caught the sun's last light, which off a slant played on the boy's face.

He got up quickly. The dark figure walked out of the shadows of the brush.

Hidy.

Who're you?

Where's ever'body else?

What?

Let me figure this out. You're some boy I never seen before. You live here?

Since one year ago when my Daddy he bought this place.

Who from?

The county something. There was some old man living here, but he died.

Name?

Larman, I think it was.

I know that. I mean his first name.

Abner, I think it was. Ask my Daddy.

The boy jumped off the porch and ran around back.

The old woman looked around the place. Ab?

The wife came out of the house. The boy and the husband came around the back. They all saw the old woman.

Hidy. This your boy?

Yes.

Said you bought this place from a man named Abner Larman.

I bought this house and one hundred fifty-nine acre, but I bought it from the county. Mr. Larman died here, all alone.

There was two hundred. And the old woman walked away.

Hershel, it's getting dark. She'll fall down.

The husband went off his steps, caught up with the old woman. It's near dark. You live hereabouts?

About seven mile, over that west ridge.

Seven mile?

Three-day walk for an old woman.

Got somebody waiting on you there?

Nobody waiting for me nowhere.

The husband led her back to the porch. The wife pushed the slat chair forward. They helped her sit. The wife tried to take her cow-

bell, but the old woman held on to it. Then with a sigh she closed her eyes, sat very still.

The husband hunkered down next to her. You say you live seven mile from here?

In Tennessee.

Tennessee border's a good forty mile over the mountain.

Thought so.

Walked forty mile, from Tennessee?

'Bout seven. Three days 'bout seven mile.

A bird squawked. Her eyes came open, then closed again. Ravens still pester a man plowing?

Do. Where'd you stay last night?

There was a creek I knowed from somewhere. It comes down the mountain, undercuts the rock. Sandy and dry there a ways underneath the ledge. Made me a gig out of my barlow knife and a stick. Gigged two frogs. Keep my matches in my oilcloth. Four legs on a stick, breakfast. That was last night.

Where you heading?

Here. She opened her eyes. New post beams. Some of this floor is all different. Not much of a job; you do it?

Beams, not the flooring.

Ab wouldn't. Billy maybe. All gone now.

The old woman laughed, sudden and harsh. She got up, with energy. Place ain't rightfully yours at all. It's mine.

A raven, on the updrafts above those people, could see a split-log house and four people on its porch. It could see a white-haired old woman, dressed in black, begin to walk up and down while a family watched her. And another raven on those same drafts, sixty years before, could have seen that same woman.

Four, courtship.

When she was nineteen, she walked right there, on that porch. Her name was Samantha Larman, called Sassy. And to her came a man named Yawls Ridley. Rooster Ridley, men called him. He was big, always smiling, and full of satisfaction.

Will you marry me?

If you will take me to Tennessee.

I won't. We will live here in Carolina.

Then you are a damn shit hog.

And you are a woman powerful bitchy.

Yawls Ridley went. Hensley Edwards came. Tennessee. He went, cursing her powerful bitchy. More the same. Alone with her refusals she was then, having to listen to other voices on that porch.

Wild, said her mother. No way to talk to no man, said her father. Got to settle down, said one brother. Nineteen years old, said her sister. Who's gonna want you after you hit twenty? said another brother. Nobody, said a third. Be reasonable, said her mother.

Her father saw someone coming. Griswold Plankman, said the sister. See, Sassy, what you'll get? said a brother. Griswold Barrel-Bottom Plankman, said another brother. That's who, said the third. That man is a death worse than fate, said the sister.

All them Plankmans are crazy, said the father. Hello there, Griswold.

Griswold Plankman came into the yard. He stepped carefully, a dirt farmer toward a clean house. He took off his hat. He gravely addressed them all. He had his hesitating courtliness, but a pock-marked face lopsided from bad teeth and a body twisted by farming. He coupled each name with a bow. Mr. Larman. Mizzes Larman. Billy. Morgan. Ab. Rachael. Sassy.

Hello, Griswold.

This here is a pleasant day. Dead-dog silence. It is, said the mother. Dead-dog silence. Dogwoods out, said Griswold. Gums, too, said the mother. Cherries bright red and dogwood too. Fire-red in the gum trees, said Griswold. Dasn't forget that, said the mother, and Griswold said, With your sourwoods at color, no, indeed. What would we do if we couldn't have a birch maple?

Get this tree-talking fool out of here, Sassy said

I will talk turkey if you will talk squirrel, Griswold said.

She'll be pleased to, said her mother. Just don't do it here, said her father.

Five, proposal.

They walked down a road. Two ruts, dug by wagons.

You are as welcome here as the bastard at the family reunion.

They walked up from the road onto the bald. Moved near waist-high in timothy grass.

You know what made the river angry? It got crossed so many times. When is a door not a door?

Jesus Christ, Griswold.

When it's ajar. Why is a pig the strangest thing?

I don't know! I don't care!

A pig gets killed before he gets cured. Why is life the hardest riddle? Ever'body has to give it up.

They reached the bluff, timothy grass around a big outcropping of rock on the mountain's edge. The sharp ridge dropped away, became miles and miles of air and blue distance.

You wanting to be took to Tennessee? Griswold pointed to the world beyond them. That's Tennessee. Forty mile over hard mountain, and nobody much in them. But I am taking you at your word. If that is what you want, I will give it to you.

What could she say? Her word.

He took her back to her family on the porch of the cabin, and as formally as he came, he left.

Won't happen, Sassy said. No man'll sell Carolina bottomland for Tennessee slopes. He was talking to hear hisself think. Won't be back.

Six, wedding.

Griswold wore a threadbare black wool coat and a string tie off a collar sticking north and south. He held a little bunch of trailside wildflowers in one hand. He handed them to Sassy. She stared at him and took them in disgust. Then they turned to the preacher.

Well? said Sassy. Do you take this man for your lawful wedded husband? said the preacher. God damn it, said Sassy. Man and wife, said the preacher.

• • •

Seven, eat.

Banjos fiddles mouth-harps tub-drums. Chalk line for bass fiddles, four sticks for rhythm. Planks on sawhorses; eating the goat barbecue, the slaw, swiss chard, and the rhubarb pie. Men with pipes passing raw do-for-your-body corn, women sipping dainty plum brandy, do it for yours, too.

Sassy sat stiffly in the family's best mohair chair, Griswold standing deadpan beside her. Sassy for the first time fearful. Never left to go more than five miles away, not in all that young and scornful life. Then it all stopped. Like some signal, a sign given. Sassy shuddered. Her brothers brought up a wagon with a high-handed roan in front and a slouchy mule in back. Wedding presents. Griswold picked Sassy up and carried her to the wagon and set her in its seat. Then he climbed up next to his wife.

Momma? Poppa? Billy? Morgan? Ab? Rachael?

Bye, Sassy.

Eight, wedding night.

They got a little ways off from the house.

Wait! Stop! We lost a box. Sassy climbed off the back of the wagon. She went to a painted wooden box lying in the trail, broke open. Kneeling in the dirt, she picked over the spilled contents. My box of dressing things. Look! My mirror's busted!

You ain't going to need mirrors in Tennessee.

Sassy looked in the piece of glass. She saw her face, for the last time thinking, I am beautiful.

My hair's messed up.

Won't be noticed from a galloping horse. Stick it in that burl yonder.

Griswold got down. He took the broke-off glass from Sassy, went to a maple tree, and stuck the mirror into the burl so she could use it. Sassy fixed her hair. Then they got back in the wagon. There was a little sunlight still coming through the leaves. It caught the glass, and the mirror reflected it.

They hadn't gone five minutes more when Griswold stopped

the wagon again. He got off, said Come on, and walked into a meadow, toward a boulder and a big drop-off, waist-high in timothy grass.

The sun was setting, and Sassy saw what she'd always seen, where she'd played as a child. Beyond the drop-off, mountains. Griswold walked with her to the gray boulder. He brushed a place with his hand and sat her there, then sat beside her.

Dig with your feet.

Do what?

Slide them back and forth. Make places. So we will always have been here.

Sassy watched Griswold slide his feet back and forth. She had to do it too. The two of them pushed their feet back and forth like children.

Long, narrow ridgebacks slid away, one behind another. Now outcroppings of rock and earth, inside bones all stone. Now swirls of pine and balsam. Glittering lakes and dead gorges. Forest and brush fell away as the rock they sat on shoved them into the sky.

Silent air, with that huge, gaping hole below. But quiet they were too, above the world and close to it. Hear that cricket clear its throat? Feel big or little in the dusk, depends. Mountains change a body. So yes, make footprints. Then say it later. There I was, once. Know hard mountains, like all must. Live here, and accept death before it comes.

Don't see the black bat against a pale moon. Study no sign. Of good, or bad. Or both together, all at oncet, or now. Call life mountain gloom and mountain glory, and death will take care of itself. Live here like birds, from ravens to finches. Look here, look there, fly here, fly there, into the brush, the maple tree, and finally the sky, to come no more. Our miseries no different from anybody else's, just higher up. Try hard but not too hard; birds won't. Don't give a damn, and soon you won't. Slide your feet, and leave your trace, and let the mind alone whilst you brood over the eternal husks of our cruel and hard but, God damn you, piss-elegant mountains. Think kindly of men and women who live on them for a little while before they get old and die. *Z* is for Zack. He climbed up a tree. His good Lord to see. The tree was tall, he had a fall. And never seen his Lord at all. If you require no abundance, you can squander all opinion. And accept death before it comes.

Sassy and Griswold, two shadows, sitting on a rock. That black mountain night swallowed them like a frog does bugs. They got down from the rock. Their hands met. In the darkness Griswold pointed to the footprints they made.

You and me.

In the wagon, on a bridal bed made from her two best sheets, Sassy first submitted with teeth gritted. Then she realized she was not unhappy about this man. He took his time. But she was having the thoughts women have with men. Something to do with the past while enjoying the present, randy but also otherwise, as if the act of pleasure is done half with someone else, somewhere else. No, it was you, and your husband or your wife, and yourself. Thinking about what, while breeding?

If I can't be a tablecloth   I won't be a dishrag   if I'm too poor to paint   I'll be too proud to whitewash   tell me you love me   so I won't allow I hear it   I'm too proud to fancy you too vain to deny you   but I am married now   all that is over let it go   all my pride   all my days   times I recall when if it happen you pass   while enduring my time   I wonder me if over your ridge and down   far lands across   meeting who under a green shaddergum tree   all that is over   I made a bargain I'll keep it   whar all to

Then, for awhile, a river ran through their wedding night. It was deep, and Sassy was content with it. But there was that something else. She heard, jumbled, her brothers and her sister talking about her, and she saw her mother and father looking at her. Then it got late and very cold. Sassy and Griswold pressed themselves together and slept.

Nine, honeymoon.

Yiiiii! said Sassy.

They traveled.

How long is this going to last? We've been on these godforsaken trails past six weeks now. Ain't we done forty mile yet?

Then there was a store. No sign, just a never-painted, one-window shack maybe ten feet wider and deeper than a cabin.

You don't go in there. Women don't go in the store.

I did at home.

With your daddy and brothers. Here it's me and you. Good-looking woman. Think you're mean. Kind of man hereabout take after you, wish you'd never been born.

When Griswold came out, helping him load was the benastiest-looking man Sassy had ever seen. She shivered.

A day after that, Griswold stopped the wagon.

This is our place. Hundred two acre, from that sand gorge to a stand of gums, to six lindens somewhere yonder. There's a triple oak beyond where I see the top of that rise we own, and twenty acres over. We'll walk the boundaries tomorrow. Lay some fencing. I can commence clearing. Hush, hear the creek?

It's over there.

No, over there.

Ten, house.

Salt. Seed. Flour. Flour sacks. Hemp. Tar. Kerosene. Wicks. Lamp. Matches. Pipe tobacco. Strip leather. Nails. Broadcloth. Needles. Thread. Cord.

The first thing you do, with strip leather, is make a sling. You take it to the creek and drag rocks with it. That makes a chimney. And that makes a fire. Sassy and Griswold sat by their rock chimney with firelit faces.

For a strange man, your husband, plant corn and beans. Build a sled, hitch it to your mule. Slide it ever'where. Girdle trees, axe notched through the bark so they die. Cut them down dry, bring them home. Your walls won't warp. Build your cabin, one room, but a big one, center-beamed even, notched corners, a piece of porch wide enough to rock a slat chair on. Make your bed with the dry wood, some rope, your mattress with a flour-sack tick packed with wildflowers and pine straw until the first crop of corn, then husks. Later you'll have ducks, can sleep on feathers. Clear your land. Split-rail fence it. Plant more corn and beans. With a strange man, your husband, endure the rain. Treasure the sun. Fear the snow.

Griswold!

My daddy delivered my momma. Me and my sister and my brother. We lived.

Eleven, birth.

Sassy was in labor. Griswold knelt before her, holding her legs apart. He moved her hip sockets, to soften the bones.

How will you cut the cord?

With my knife.

Wipe it off, for Christ's sake?

I'll burn the blade. Cut the cord with a burned knife. Tie it off with burned string. Keep it covered with burned cloth. Cord will rot off, leaving a belly button clean and shapely, so I was told.

You don't know what you're doing. A midwife at least, or a granny woman, somebody!

Trouble is midwives don't keep things clean. I knowed one grabbing for the afterbirth herself with grimy hands, and the mother died. You ain't a-going to die. Baby's head's coming first, I can feel it. I mean, if you take about four crates and stack them, knock them together, and take out their bottoms and tops, and if you just slant them this way and that, then, my Daddy showed me how, you can push a rag dolly through it, and it comes out right. I been told it.

Agony came, in her shoulder of all places, and then the birth pain contracted her. It took her bottom and top, then went away slow, like rain stopping. Then came again.

The afterbirth was full and complete, leaving Sassy swept out and clean, Griswold calculated, like a clean, empty farmhouse on land good for an early crop. Griswold did cut the cord with his pocketknife, his eyeballs falling out of his head, but he did cut it, tied it off both times in the right place, so you have to say this much for the man—not only were his hands clean, but his rags were washed out and scorched black over the fire he kept going like a furnace. There was a shallow pine bowl he had whittled out, and ready he was to wash the baby in warmed-up water, and dress it himself.

Men here go to pieces, slip, slide, cut and run. It is like having a baby while your husband has a nap, and they have done that, too, terrified and unconscious. But Griswold went about midwifery calm and smiling. He held up their bloody creature, jiggled then whopped it alive. It was a girl. He washed her off, him whistling, her screaming, in the wooden bowl. He dressed her in more clean rags, not scorched, just warm. He gave the baby a spoonful of ginger-root tea, to clear that throat. Finally, the baby got to suck.

Griswold Plankman would not let his wife work for three whole days. Unheard of here, where most are up and washing in one.

Sassy said, Plain luck. Anything at all bad happened, a breech, or the afterbirth growing on her insides, what would he have done? She'd be dead, baby dead. She swore she would never again let him do this to her. But what she could not say was that there wasn't the living child in her arms, at her breasts sucking strong, a fat infant improperly but functionally born as if it really did slide down Griswold's stacked wooden crates, his harebrained idea of a woman's insides, bumping down and out slick and mannerly in a carpenter-smooth notion of the muckslide-bloodslide of birth.

Not only that, the baby grew up smartly, with a good disposition. Rachael Ann, their one happy child.

Twelve, four days.

About three months later, her husband in the field, she lay down naked on a cornhusk mattress, gave Rachael Ann her milk. Belched her, then laid the baby facedown betwixt her breasts, aspraddle, naked mother naked baby breathing smooth, blood thumping, asleep together.

Sassy woke to see Griswold standing above them. She thought she would tell her husband he could go to hell, she wasn't getting up, they were sleeping. But Griswold, before she could say it, turned without a word and went back to his field. That night he came wordless to his corn and coffee, got up from it, and sat the evening away on the footstep of the house, one hand clutching each knee, staring at something he had never suspected.

The second day he was worse. Not only did he not go that morning to the field, but he asked, asked, if he could sit quiet and just watch Rachael Ann suck, before she and Sassy slept another morning away. Sassy said, Yes, sir, he could, and he did. This was not manly mountain behavior. Griswold worked in the afternoon but got home way before dusk. He asked her to sit on the front step and not say anything while he cooked supper. After they ate, he went into the dark woods, came back an hour later with a piece of gum log he had bark-shaved and hollowed into a cradle. He put Rachael Ann in it, where she turned over once, and gone she was into that sleep that favored her as long as they could keep her.

The third day got worse. Griswold came home at noon, said something confused, took Rachael Ann in his arms, walked out the door and off into the brush. Sassy looked after him, exasperated and anxious, until she saw it.

It was a lunatic showing the world to a baby. That whole afternoon, taking a three-month-old baby here and taking her there, explaining in swallowed words, sounding as much like a cow mooing as a man talking, all sorts of things no baby could comprehend but maybe could feel.

This here is your leaf mold, Griswold said aloud, bending over and showing Rachael Ann some dirt. Up as high as we are, best stay below waterfalls with plenty of leaf mold or you'll grow one crop of bad corn, eat it, get sick, and have to move. Sometimes a fire'll do it, burn down through the leaf mold, and it's ruination. Can't have that.

God almighty, Sassy said.

Griswold explained in detail to Rachael Ann how his plow, harrow, scythe, great ax, and hoe all functioned, one different from the next. Then he went from tools to trees.

Rachael, this here is hickory. That there is oak. Your hickory is tougher. Locust over here, and it don't rot, so use it close to the ground. Careful what you cut. Some stumps are the devil, others come out like old teeth, but think twice about which will do what.

She ain't going to build no cabin, said Sassy. She's a baby and a woman, not a man.

It was as if he heard nothing, so intent was he on being, it finally occurred to Sassy, not so much a man being manly with a daughter instead of a son, but, well, a lordly, goodly, hostly man, generous in make-yourself-at-homeness. But this was with their infant daughter, for Christ's sweet sake, who lived there anyhow.

Griswold named every last tree on his land, in a mad obsession of fatherhood. Up one side of his property and down the other Griswold took that baby, it drowsy part of the time but big-eyed awake some of it, too, and even intent in her father's arms, as if listening closely to what he had to say. Sassy did not know whether to smile or worry.

Finally he took Rachael Ann into the house, to tell her where everything was.

And here will be a stove one day, and he laid down Rachael Ann in her gum-tree cradle.

Welcome. Then he went out to plow.

The fourth day ended it.

There was a sudden gust of dawn rain. After it came wind and a bright day, with all their trees blown sideways and back. Griswold had done nothing all that day. He had, it seemed, passed into some back of beyond in his own head and sat again on the porch steps, not moving except for both his hands, twitching, turning over and back, as if letting things go.

Have you given up farming?

Four days, said Griswold, and went back to the plow.

Thirteen, Malcom.

Go on, yell!

I'll die!

And a boy lay in her arms, clean, washed by Griswold in the wooden basin he'd carved for Rachael. Griswold cleaned his knife again, after he had cut her cord.

Sassy nursed their son. They named him Malcom.

Fourteen, time.

Slow. Fast. Fast. Slow.

All alone in the mountains of Tennessee. Husband. Babies. Farm.

Fifteen, visitor.

Sassy heard Griswold from the field, a noise that never came out of him before. When she got to him, he was on his knees, one hand holding himself off the ground, the other pressing guts and blood back inside his stomach.

Get me rags!

Sassy ran to the cabin, tore up some clothes, and came back fast as she could. Blood was streaming through Griswold's fingers. Tearing cloth, Sassy packed the wound.

I turned my back on my mule. Kicked me onto the harrow. Stuff that in!

Griswold and Sassy stanched the blood by packing the cloth in and around the wound, but it did not hold. Could he walk? Griswold tried to get up. His eyes shut, and he fainted. Sassy held her husband, a dead weight. She couldn't lift him. Blood seeped out around the rags. She tried to haul him and couldn't. The wound was wide open again. He would die.

A man appeared behind her. She had not heard him coming. It was as if he dropped from the sky.

Griswold tried to see who was there and couldn't. But he heard the man's voice. He said nothing. The man helped Sassy get Griswold on his feet. His arms gripped Griswold around the side, holding him upright, elbows packing in the rags at the same time. He walked Griswold into the cabin, where Sassy boiled water.

Griswold drank some corn whiskey, and they washed the wound.

Where's his saw?

The man went outside, sawed wood, came back with a contraption. It was like a big clothespin. They washed then clamped the wound shut with two slabs of wood and two bent nails. It was like a pair of pliers. They waited for one hour. Together they opened the clamp, stitched the wound with needle and thread like any sackcloth dress, and clamped it shut again. The wound was deep but clean. Griswold opened his eyes, conscious again, and saw the man. Much obliged. Don't say nothing about it. Griswold closed his eyes and seemed to faint again.

Now Sassy could look at this man, dropped out of the sky. Who was he?

Griswold moaned and twisted about. Then he was still, as if unconscious again, but he wasn't.

She was more aware of this man now. He was looking about her like a polite gentleman will when he wants a woman. Sassy wiped sweat from Griswold's face.

That night, when Sassy was asleep, Griswold and that man crept out of the cabin together. Feverish, aching every step, Griswold still got down to the river with that man, and in the moonlight by the creek they faced each other.

What are you doing here?

What are you?

Now, you'd think she'd'a seen. That something else. But she was charmed. Glad her husband was alive, and another man in the world to smile at her. You never know how close you are. To what's up a tree, looking down.

In the morning, the man was gone.

Sixteen, neighbors.

There was the call from the edge of their yard, and the powerful exchange of Hidys. They could see Griswold ponder them and decide if it was sooner or later, it might as well be now.

Spencer Shook said, Spencer Shook. Wife Abby, daughter Hester. This here is the Bladen family, this here the Wilders, and that there Mullins people. Live maybe three mile off.

Plankman, Griswold and Sassy. Babies Rachael and Malcom. Another'n on the way.

Calculate we are the closest souls anywhere near you. Got a poke for you in the wagon. Peaches, bee-gum honey, molasses, salted deer, and a few helpfuls.

Griswold Plankman jumped on that. He plain herded them out to their wagon, leaving Sassy behind, and told them the way it was, the way he wanted it to stay. The men agreed, and that was that. The women didn't like it, said so, said so twice, but took the peaches to Sassy.

Seventeen, friend.

It was some time later Hester Shook had a frank talk with Sassy Plankman. She was not your walleyed, spindly-legged, thirty-year-old castoff, where men low-rate women the day they hit sixteen. She was just twenty, and a better-looking woman you never saw. But there was bad trouble to it, disgraceful.

I can't be wild. I cannot abide a man naked. Coming at me looking like a tree with a stump sticking out of it that close to the ground. I live at home, and will forever. But I'd treasure a good neighbor.

Hester, give me your hand.

Hester did, and the two women stood there like men buying and selling, but that is not what those women were doing.

So we ain't alone now, Sassy said.

Hester swallowed and said no.

Eighteen, Giasticus bones.

This was when Rachael and Malcom were about eight and six, Sarah three. Sarah wasn't in it, just the older two. Sarah was asleep when Rachael and Malcom, playing, brought two old crates, covered with canvas, to their mother and father. Spring rains had undermined the creek-bank. They'd put what they'd found in the crates. Sassy laughed.

Giasticus bones—that's the bird with a ten-foot tooth and the fifty-foot wingspread, what carries off cows, she said.

Then a head they pulled out of one crate.

Jesus Lord, said Sassy.

Chilluns, said Griswold, what you found was some man who likely fell on creek rocks years ago, washed down in the spring rains, and got buried in the clay. This year's rush uncovered him. What's in the other crate?

Bones with clay still on them. And black stuff, said the children.

Cover his face, said Griswold. Go back down to the creek and dig a hole. Away from the water this time. Shovel's back of the house. Go on.

The children got the shovel and went to dig the hole.

That man saved your life.

I knowed the son of a bitch. His name was Goudy, killed a man named Pringle, I think it was. Would have us. I got him down to the creek, where my sickle lay upside the 'simmon tree.

You cut off his head.

And chopped him in pieces, and stuck him six feet down in clay. These rains dug him up.

Why?

He would have told you things before he killed you.

The children had dug the hole.

Younguns. You take these bones back down to the creek and shovel him in, ten feet this time, and let him be. Take the Bible out of the house, hold it, and say him something.

And the children did that while Sassy stared slack-jawed at Griswold and him at her. She'd once thought him just simple. He'd thought her just wild. But he was hard under his jokes. She was soft under her feistiness. Things move, in marriage. She was astonished at him. He was wary of her.

I had to kill him.
No you didn't.
Yes I did.

Nineteen, summertime.

It was sunup. Griswold and Sassy stood on their porch. Griswold had just hayed his fields. There was the smell of fresh grass around them. Griswold put his arm around Sassy's shoulders. They were at peace.

And God made the roads of this world so crooked, a man and his wife can't always tell if their life is going somewheres grand or jest coming back home. Weather is changeable, and marrieds can't always tell wet from windy. Back home now, sunshine in the morning, breezy and pleasant. There is always a squirrel in a tree somewheres.

They stood together, looking at the morning sun. Dog days came later, but right then it was summertime pleasant, and so were they to each other. Stretch, get warm, find sun. But Sassy felt, in her husband's arm around her, a hard hold, making her uneasy.

Twenty, rattlesnakes.

The Shooks and Ab Mullins carried Malcom into the yard. Sassy yelled for Griswold.

They laid Malcom down on a quilt on the porch.

Keep him on his stomach, said Spencer Shook. On his back, the poison moves faster.

Sassy did what was told. Griswold came running, as did Rachael behind him. He'd had her on his shoulders, plowing. They all gathered around Malcom. He had to fight for his breath; it was that bad. He had been playing with the Shook boys on the Shook place, in plain sight of Spencer Shook and Ab Mullins, who happened by.

In his shoulder, said Ab Mullins. Another'n in his jaw, jest over his throat. Twicet at once. I want to say copperhead, but diamondbacks is what they was. Tell by the marks. Around here, big as your arm.

Snakes? said Sassy.

Cut and suck him, said Griswold.

No good to it, said Spencer Shook.

Griswold had out his barlow knife. He found the bites. He cut an *x* on each place. He bent his head and sucked those wounds, first one then the other.

Spencer Shook watched him do it. Mr. Plankman. Griswold paid him no mind.

And in deed and truth, two diamondback rattlesnakes came off a waist-high ledge at Malcom. Both bit him the same split second. One hung long enough for Ab Mullins, on the run the minute he saw it happen, to knock the serpent down.

Griswold tried to turn Malcom over, on his back. Ab Mullins and Spencer Shook helped, shaking their heads. Griswold cut and sucked the wound on Malcom's jaw, spitting blood and poison. They stood there, watching what would be, and worse to come.

Can't hardly breathe atall now, said Ab Mullins.

Spencer Shook said, Griswold. Cutting and sucking for the diamondback won't do. Copperheads, adders even, but not diamondbacks. That venom's inside him.

He's black in places, see, said Ab Mullins.

You'll jest disfigure the boy, said Spencer Shook.

Malcom's groans turned into whimpers. Griswold cut again, deep now, above and below the neck and then again into his shoulder. Malcom screamed, bit his lip till blood came there too. Griswold sucked the cuts, spit, sucked again and again, then cut again. More screams, more sucking. It was like something awful in a whorehouse.

Sassy said, Griswold, no more!

He's commencing to swell up, said Ab Mullins. If he's lucky, what went into his leg and jaw will bust his heart. If not, take longer. That venom scalds open the veins. Fills your body with blood.

That's what's black, said Spencer Shook.

Painfullest way any soul leaves this earth, said Ab Mullins.

Griswold wanted to kill them both, talking like they were buying horses. But Sassy saw they were right.

Stop, Griswold.

And then that boy looked at his mother with the most peculiar look she had ever seen.

Can I tell her?

It was an argument they'd had, father and son, for a long time.

If you want, said Griswold.

No, the boy said, but he said it like a man.

I'll need to witness some kind of a yes from him, said Spencer Shook. It's the law.

Son? said Griswold. Understand?

Yes, sir, Malcom said.

That'll do, said Spencer Shook.

Kiss him, said Griswold, and Sassy did.

Can't be no bullets in him, said Spencer Shook. It's the law.

Make it a crime, said Ab Mullins.

Do what you was doing with your knife, said Spencer Shook. Only way my brother got freed from it.

Malcom screamed.

Venom, said Ab Mullins, is breaking down his veins.

Griswold hit Malcom hard on the head with the butt of the knife. Malcom's eyes closed. Griswold cut his son's throat.

Push on him, said Spencer Shook.

Griswold pushed down on Malcom's body, and a great gush of black blood poured out of the hole in his throat. He was dead soon.

Twenty-one, grief.

For many days, Griswold worked himself near death, ate hardly a mouthful of anything, then just sat sleepless. He wouldn't move. He wouldn't talk.

Who could blame the man, had to do a thing like that? Watch over him, see he don't do the same to hisself. Say, My God, this life, and get some tea.

Until Griswold said, God damn this, and went on like he'd never had a son, leaving Sassy to grieve alone, for the longest time.

Twenty-two, Rachael.

Time came.

Momma?

Sassy kissed her daughter, who went off to marry the Carson boy at what was said to be a Carson family celebration too far for her and Griswold to go to. Peculiar thing, that a woman so feisty when young didn't just get worse, grow old more of the same, but turned around and became so quiet and calm she'd said yes to a thing like that. She never saw her daughter again. Rachael melted into what Sassy always believed a far-off family. Rachael died young, a worn-out wife. Nobody told her mother. Some tried to, but couldn't. Sassy wondered and even asked a time or two why her daughter never came home. Then Sarah, the same.

There it was, and it stayed that way. Neighbors said nothing. They got old, died, some of them. Others would see Griswold come to the store for nails and coffee. Sassy stayed home, as always.

Twenty-three, anniversary.

Forty-five year in Tennessee, said Griswold.

And you did bring me here.

Yes, I did.

They both outlived their children. Griswold was eighty-one when he fell and cut himself on a sickle.

Twenty-four, widow.

When Old Man Griswold Plankman died, his wife, Sassy Larman Plankman, stayed up two nights sewing by her own hand a thick winding sheet of some quality. Then neighbors helped her bury him, in one of his fields.

And how could they tell her then? They should have. I mean, the man was dead. But it had just gone on too long, and they couldn't.

Old Maid Hester Shook went lots to keep Sassy company.
I'm powerful uneasy.
You're grieving.
Got the fidgets, bad. Go where? What for? I don't know.
Don't try to leave Tennessee. You could get lost.
But something is eating at me.
Stay where you are. Right here.

Twenty-five, joke.

So now you can see it all again like when they started, from where black ravens slide down updrafts, the two ridges, one from where the old woman came, the other where the family farms, where she tells them this life of hers, holding on to that cowbell, wheezing, coughing, can't stop talking because whilst they are listening and wondering, she is still traveling, this time in her own head, where, slow and cold as ice, comprehension comes slowly aborning.

I commenced little walks, said Sassy.

And she did. Never looked back. She was loose in country she'd never seen before that she had seen before. She was wandering in her pitiful old age, at the same time finding real places of powerful remembrance.

I was coming here, said Sassy.

That can't be, said the husband. Tennessee is forty mile off.

But they were all around her, in the woods and clearings. In mountain dusk, with the farm family on that porch, she saw them all again. Momma, Poppa, Billy, Ab, my sister Rachael and my daughters Rachael and Sarah, my son Malcom and my Griswold. I found this cowbell. On some cow, two days' walk, not hardly seven mile. I heared the waterfall! Carson's Falls. Where I played as a child. My daughter married a boy named Carson and left home to go far away and I never laid eyes on her again.

Then the tree. Sassy held up that piece of broken mirror. That tree, she recollected a 'simmon tree, but no, it was that maple, with a piece of mirror stuck in a burl grown all around it. Where her husband put it, broken, on their wedding day. She had looked at her face in it. Young bride, old woman. Two flashes of one mirror. Great God a'mighty.

She's loony, said the wife.

One day in Tennessee, and the next Carson's Falls? And the same road all overgrown. A road she ran down every day of her young life? Then she come out of the brush, into the clearing right over yonder. The house. The boy.

That man, said Sassy. That damn man.

They didn't see it. They were just watching her ring her bell and stamp her feet. They heard her say scoundrel and Goddamned bastard all in a pouring-out of hard feelings mixed up before them in whoops and a raging comprehension. It was the boy, the boy, who said it, before his father and mother, and said it out loud and to her.

He never took you to Tennessee at all.

God.

He put you in a wagon.

God.

And drove you around in circles, in these same mountains.

And settled where he meant to all along? said the wife.

On his own land? said the husband.

Seven mile off, said the boy. You never got to Tennessee at all.

Sassy looked at each of them in turn, seeing behind them her own husband and children, and her mother and father and her brothers and sisters.

You thought you were in Tennessee, but you wasn't, said the boy.

God. Were they all in on it? My dead son, when he was dying? My daughters, who walked off from me without hardly one word? My Momma, Poppa, seven mile away for fifty years? Getting me married, getting me gone! Griswold, you never told me what you done to me. You never would have told me! By God, you died without telling me!

She shook her head and stomped her feet and rang her cowbell. She got her breath.

Whoo, said Sassy. Shoo.

She looked at the family, on its estate. She looked at the cowbell and the mirror in her hands. She dropped the mirror and the cowbell at her feet and started off.

Give me the baby, said the husband. I'm hungry now. The husband took the baby and went into his house. His wife followed and shut the door.

The boy picked up the cowbell and the mirror and followed Sassy.

Twenty-six, powerful remembrance.

He was fearful of getting caught by darkness in the mountains alone, but it was almost a full moon, so he kept on, since he just wanted to.

She went to the bald. She sat there in dusk turning to night, on an outcropping of ridge rock on the edge of the bluff, surrounded by timothy grass gray in the moonlight. Under the shadow of falling night, the terraces of land spread in darkness beyond her for miles and miles, not in blue distance now but in darkness.

The boy saw that she was moving her feet back and forth. He sat next to her, and she let him. He set his feet to the ground with hers and pushed them back and forth. He knew about footprints; boys do. They make trails through the brush, saying, See, I am here too. In the dusk the boy could see his face in the piece of mirror.

If I can't be a tablecloth, I won't be a dishrag. If I'm too poor to paint, I'll be too proud to whitewash. If it happen you pass. Whar all to?

Mountains don't answer such as that. The boy saw his face dark in the mirror. Something like a raven flew across the moon.

LAURA CALLANAN

Romulus Linney is the author of three novels and many plays, produced throughout the United States and abroad. Stories have appeared in journals including *The Southern Review, Story Quarterly, Fiction, Shenandoah, The Missouri Review, Image, Pushcart Prize,* and *Antaeus* and in *New Stories from the South 2000.* In 2002 he was elected to the American Academy of Arts and Letters.

My childhood years in the Appalachian mountains near Boone, North Carolina, were never so alive as when I spent thirty days in Japan in 1955, a wandering soldier on leave from Hawaii. That is because I saw how Japanese artists, like the singers and fiddlers and storytellers of my mountain childhood, needed only very simple things: some sand, a rock, a reed, paper, a piece of cloth. I thought, perhaps, I could do something like that, with simple elements I cared about. My love for their Noh theatre was awakened when in North Carolina later I heard the germ of this story. "Tennessee" is Appalachian, but it is also like a Japanese Noh play: bone simple but spanning time. In a void its people come before us, where, as in the mists of the Smoky Mountains, they (and we) will appear and disappear.

Dwight Allen

END OF THE STEAM AGE

(from *The Greensboro Review*)

Thanksgiving, 1961. On the way home from the football game at the fairgrounds, my father suggested to his cousin Louis Mudge that we take a detour. Dad wanted to see a steam locomotive that was parked in the Louisville & Nashville yards, a 4-8-2 that the L&N, an all-diesel line by then, had borrowed from the Illinois Central for an anniversary excursion to Nashville. He didn't seem to notice that most of the day's light had fled or that cold mist fuzzed the air. It didn't matter to him that he'd be riding the excursion train a few days later; he wanted an early peek. I looked at the hair standing up on the back of his head, like a woodpecker's crest, and I thought that a person whose hair sat flat wouldn't have proposed a side trip like this.

Uncle Louis, whose brown felt hat was speckled with confetti, said that seeing the IC engine parked in the L&N yards would be like seeing a movie star in her house clothes.

My father said, "I'd pay full dollar to see Ingrid Bergman in dungarees."

My older brother, Harry, who was twelve, spoke up from the farthest corner of Uncle Louis's Ford sedan that smelled of tobacco and dogs and old newspapers. "Who's Ingrid Bergman?"

My father didn't answer Harry's question, perhaps because Harry had mumbled it, perhaps because my father's excitement at seeing the IC engine had made him deaf to voices from the backseat.

I watched a raindrop slide down the window and thought about a halfback named Perryman jittering through a confusion of pads and helmets and then flying free across stadium dirt. Perryman played for Male High, a school my father and his cousin had attended twenty-five years before, when it was all-boys and all-white. Perryman's shoes had been wrapped with tape to make it look as if he were wearing spats, like a drum major. The Manual High defenders hadn't had a chance.

Uncle Louis chuckled, maybe at the idea of Ingrid Bergman in dungarees, maybe at the earnestness with which my father expressed himself. Uncle Louis had been chuckling all afternoon, between sips of coffee from a thermos. Not too many months before, he'd been in Arkansas. I'd heard my mother say to somebody that he'd gone there to "dry out." I'd imagined him lying on a plank, baking in the sun. When I asked Harry about this, what "drying out" meant, he said, with a certain authority, "It means he needs to get some air. His bones are damp and achy."

Our father had driven his cousin to Arkansas. On the way back, Dad had spent a couple hours in the rail yards in Memphis, taking pictures of rusting, coal-burning locomotives and their diesel replacements. That night, he'd written his cousin a letter on Peabody Hotel stationery. The letter, which mentioned a "beautiful" 4-8-4 Dixie Line locomotive he'd seen that early autumn afternoon, had ended up in the rear seat of Uncle Louis's sedan. My father had signed it, "Devotedly, Bill."

Uncle Louis turned off Second Street onto St. Catherine. The L&N yards were toward the west side of downtown Louisville, near cigarette factories and distilleries, not far from where Ida, our maid, lived. She'd spent the morning in our kitchen, helping my mother prepare dinner, and then we'd driven her home on the way to the game. When we drove through her neighborhood after the game, I didn't see anybody on the streets, except for a man who was looking under the hood of a car.

"They're rolling up the sidewalks, Billy," Uncle Louis said. "Hardly any place for us boulevardiers to go except the rail yards."

My father said, "We'll make it quick."

When we got out of the car, the mist had become drizzle. Uncle Louis pulled down the brim of his hat; it shielded his glasses but not his birdy beak. He wore a long wool coat and baggy trousers held up by suspenders. Like my father's clothes, Uncle Louis's always looked as if they'd been tailored for his shadow, or for the person he might become if only he would eat three square meals a day.

My father didn't wear a hat or suspenders, but he bore enough of a resemblance to his cousin that they were sometimes mistaken for brothers. It wasn't just their noses or the glasses with the flesh-colored frames or their slightly stooped, unathletic builds. They'd grown up next door to each other, on a bluff above the river, separated only by an acre of lawn. After they graduated from Male High, they temporarily parted ways: my father went to college out east and Uncle Louis attended an art school in Cincinnati. During the war, when my father was back home, studying law, and Uncle Louis was painting landscapes that looked as if they'd been done by someone with an astigmatism, they'd served together in the Kentucky militia. They'd trained on weekends. "We were going to mow down the Krauts as they boated across the Ohio River on a Sunday afternoon," Uncle Louis said. He also said that the brigade's commander had described my father as the worst soldier he'd ever seen, and himself as the second-worst.

My father zipped up his plaid jacket and strapped his camera across his chest and led us toward the roundhouse, where he believed the IC engine was being kept. We passed between strings of freight cars that seemed to go on forever, into the gloom. Harry said, "This is boring." He kicked at the gravel. He was wearing basketball sneakers he'd scissored the tops off of because he thought he'd look cooler that way. Our mother had yelled at him for ruining a good pair of shoes.

Our father, who moved at a meditative pace when not around

trains, was traveling at a near-trot now. Uncle Louis said, "Billy, if the Pinkertons come after us, I'm not going to be able to outrun them." Uncle Louis had always moved as if tomorrow was a fine time to get somewhere, and his stay in Arkansas hadn't made him any faster. He stopped to light a cigarette.

My father turned around and said, "The Pinkertons are having Thanksgiving dinner now."

Uncle Louis said to me, "Your father is a model citizen, except when it comes to trains." My father was a judge. I'd seen him in his robes once, and I didn't think anybody standing before him was likely to quake.

The locomotive and its tender were, as my father had predicted, outside the roundhouse. Two diesel switchers pincered it. I'd seen a number of steam engines in my short life, mostly by the light of day, and I didn't think this one was more impressive than the others. Or less so. It had eight driving wheels and they were all taller than me by a foot.

My father hopped back and forth across the tracks, shooting pictures from different angles, trying to outfox the dark, which kept coming down, along with the rain. "I trust you opened your aperture wide," Uncle Louis said. He borrowed Dad's camera and had us stand in front of the engine, with its moon face and tarnished silver bell.

"Père et fils sans chapeaux," Uncle Louis said, fiddling with the lens. "Soaking up the atmosphere in the L&N yards. 1961: near the end of the steam age."

"Say it ain't so," said my father, who smiled through the drizzle.

Harry didn't smile. It was my older brother's policy to present a solemn face to the world, when he could manage it.

Uncle Louis put his hat on my head. For a second, I felt like I'd just walked into a warm, smoky room with big chairs to lounge in. My father asked Harry if he wanted to pull up the hood of his coat, but Harry said he was fine.

We walked back to the car and got in. When Uncle Louis turned the key, the motor made no sound, not even a click. My father, who sometimes complained about the corrosive effects of the internal combustion engine on modern life but knew little about repairing one, said, "Must be a wiring problem."

Uncle Louis said, "Could be."

"Maybe it's the radiator," Harry said. "Or the valves."

Uncle Louis said, "Could be, Harry."

We went to look for a pay phone. We didn't get far before Uncle Louis remembered that there was a pie in the trunk. Robert, the black man who kept house for Uncle Louis, had made it. Uncle Louis had intended to deliver it to a friend of his late mother on the way to the game.

Uncle Louis got the pie, and we walked out of the yards and along a dimly lighted street toward Broadway. My father led; he walked briskly, at close to his railyard pace. A skinny dog spotted like a hyena waited for us at a corner, next to a bus bench. Uncle Louis said to me, "If it's mean, we'll give it a slice of pie." The pie was pecan.

When we passed, the dog lifted its nose slightly. Otherwise, it showed no interest in us.

"It was hoping for banana cream, I bet," Uncle Louis said.

We turned up Broadway, which was better lighted but not any less deserted. We passed a vacuum cleaner store, a loan company, then a pawnshop whose window was full of knives and watches and medallions on chains. We found a phone in a White Castle, the kind of place my mother, who put wheat germ in our cereal every morning, might skin my father alive for taking her children into. There were two black men at the window counter, eating dinner.

I said we should call Ida. Maybe her son Alvin, who drove a garbage truck for the city, could come get us.

My father said Ida didn't have a phone.

"Duh," Harry said.

I flicked at his ear with my finger, but missed.

Uncle Louis ordered Cokes for me and my brother and a coffee for himself while my father called my mother. Dad said "Honey?"

and then explained where we were. Eventually he said, "We'll just hail a cab."

"Sounds like you're in the doghouse, Billy," Uncle Louis said.

Dad called a Yellow Cab and then bought a nickel carton of milk and sat down on a window counter stool between me and Harry. He wiped his glasses with a napkin. He always looked grim without his glasses, as if he were waiting for the next blow to fall.

The two black men finished their meals and lit cigarettes. One saw the purple Male High booster button on Uncle Louis's coat and asked if Male had won.

"Thirty-four to thirteen," Uncle Louis said.

"Perryman ran wild," my father added.

"That Manual coach don't have the brains of a housefly," one of the men said. They got up and went out the door.

A radio was playing in the back of the restaurant. It was tuned to a station that Ida sometimes listened to when she was ironing in our basement. I watched out the window for the cab. Harry sucked at the last drops of his Coke through a straw, as intent as a scientist working on an experiment. Uncle Louis sipped coffee and picked confetti off his hat. Then he asked me if I'd ever heard the story about the goat my father's family had kept when he was a boy.

I didn't recall any stories about goats. I was trying to listen to the song on the radio—some man trying to say how much he loved a girl. Harry sucked on his straw until Dad said, "Harry, that's enough now."

Uncle Louis said, "Well, your grandparents had a goat named Cyril. He was named after a fellow your granddad and my father played bridge with."

My father said, "That goat was the sorriest creature." The recollection seemed to have cheered him up.

"In the summer," Uncle Louis said, "Cyril liked to sleep under a car, where it was cool. Oil would drip all over him and he'd get filthier than he already was. So then he would decide he needed a bath and he'd amble over to our house and take a dip in the pool."

I didn't understand how a goat could decide it needed a bath, but I didn't say anything. I watched a man wearing a hooded blue windbreaker come through the door. The drawstring in the hood was pulled so tight you could see only a portion of his face. He went to the order window and asked for a hamburger.

"Just one?" the lady asked. Most people ordered six or seven at a time; one was about one bite's worth.

"Yes, ma'am," the man said.

"Anything to drink?"

"No, ma'am."

When she brought him the hamburger in a little white box, he asked her to put the box in a bag. She did, and just when she was about to hand it to him, he said, "Give me everything you've got in the register, except for the pennies and nickels and that kind of shit. Just put it in the bag, please." He was pointing something at her; it was hidden under the windbreaker.

My father and his cousin were laughing. Now they were talking about a dog Uncle Louis had owned a long time ago, a terrier, which somehow got trapped in a utility pipe and had to be extracted by a plumber.

"Don't give me those fuckin' quarters," the man in the windbreaker said. "They'll break the bag. Just the bills."

"Yessir," the woman said.

I tapped my father on the arm and said, "Dad?" I noticed that he had cut himself shaving, just above his Adam's apple. I glanced back at the man in the windbreaker. He was looking at me, at all of us. Only the center of his cold-reddened white face was visible, and each individual part was competing to be the meanest.

My father and Uncle Louis didn't stop talking about the terrier until the man in the windbreaker said, "Don't do anything dumb, mister." He sounded like somebody trying to sound older than he was, like my brother did, when he tried to explain to me a scientific principle like gravity, for instance. The man in the windbreaker was addressing a large man in an apron and a white paper hat. The robber was backing up toward the door, the hamburger bag with the money in one hand and a silver-barrelled gun held high in the other. The gun looked like one I no longer played with, a cowboy six-shooter that came with a tooled leather holster that had a thigh string. When the man was abreast of us, Uncle Louis, who was closest to the door, swiveled on his stool and said, "You don't need to hurt anybody. Just take your money and go." Uncle Louis was between me and the robber. My nose was close enough to Uncle Louis's overcoat that I could smell the whole day in it—that and my own fearful breath coming back at me. On the robber's nose, I saw a red dot, like a pimple or a boil.

Uncle Louis later said that his first mistake had been to open his mouth. His second was to open it again. He said to the robber, "Why don't you take this pie along, too? It's pecan." Then he reached behind him for the plate.

At Thanksgiving dinner six years later, my second cousin Gee asked Uncle Louis to tell the story that my mother sometimes referred to as A Series of Bad Decisions on Your Father's Part. My father took a drink of milk from a tall green goblet. Gee's mother, whose husband had died the year before, said, "Maybe we should save that for after dinner, Gee." Everybody in the family, even the second cousins' second cousins, knew the story—or parts of it.

Gee said that Martin might like to hear it. Martin was a high-school student from England who was spending the fall semester with us. He was handsome and self-confident, with smooth cheeks and a wide mouth that a steady flow of mockery had seemed to warp slightly. (To annoy me, Martin would refer to Ida as "your Negro slave.") It had taken Gee, who was two years younger than Martin and me, about five minutes to fall in love with Martin. Before dinner, she'd gone into the bathroom to make herself look more stunning than she was in her miniskirt and boots. Martin had said to me, "The lipstick is a bit whorish, but she's not bad for fourteen."

My father hadn't yet said the blessing. We were waiting for my mother to emerge from the kitchen with the turkey, which she was carving with a new electric knife. She wouldn't permit my father to carve the turkey, because she believed he would make a mess of it. She thought I had a future as a carver of meat but that my day had not yet come. I was sixteen and lacked finesse. Harry, who was at college out west, as far away as he could get, was not a candidate for other reasons.

My grandfather, my father's eighty-year-old father, jiggled the ice in his glass in the hope that more Scotch might somehow materialize. He'd had his limit, and unhappiness was growing like a weed in the fold between his white eyebrows.

Martin said, "I'd love to hear the story, especially if it's sordid and violent."

Uncle Louis lowered his chin to the napkin tucked into his collar and chuckled. Martin amused him, it seemed—a guy who didn't know jackshit about anything, except what he'd read in books or seen on the movie screen.

Granddaddy said, "Is this the story about Louis falling asleep at the Toddle House? In that plate of hash browns?"

"No, Dad," my father said, sitting a little taller in his chair at the head of the table, as if by doing so he might somehow absorb Granddaddy's question and cause it to disappear. "Why don't you tell Martin about Cyril the goat? He might enjoy that."

"God save us from goats," Granddaddy grumbled. The crease between his eyebrows deepened and he sank into silence.

Gee said to Uncle Louis, "I'll show you my etchings if you tell the story." She fluttered her eyelashes. They were long and swooping, worked on.

"Oh, Virginia," her mother said, using Gee's given name. "Don't be so silly."

Uncle Louis laughed more than was called for. His shoulders shook under his cardigan; the soft flesh under his chin vibrated. Perhaps, I thought, believing I was wise, he laughed to hide his disappointments. I'd learned a few things while leaning in doorways, skulking around the house. I knew, for instance, that Uncle Louis had forgotten to pay his taxes the last few years. I knew that he'd lost all but a couple of his private art students, and that an artist whom he'd rented space to in his house had made off with a box of heirloom silver when she moved out. I knew that my father had driven Uncle Louis back to Arkansas again, two years before. I knew that to help his cousin my father had commissioned a painting of a steam engine. (The result hung in my father's basement office, not being suitable, in my mother's view, for a more prominent wall.) And now I knew, as did everybody else at the table, that Uncle Louis had passed out drunk at the Toddle House, though whether this incident was post- or pre-Arkansas I couldn't have said. Tonight, anyway, Uncle Louis was drinking a Coke.

My mother said from the kitchen, "Go ahead and say the blessing. I'll be there in a minute."

Dad said, "We'll wait, honey."

My grandfather came swimming up out of his silence and, snorting derisively, said, "They caught him with his pants down."

It was unclear whom Granddaddy was referring to—possibly a politician, possibly somebody at the nursing home—but nobody made inquiries. My father told Granddaddy about the football game he and Uncle Louis had attended that afternoon. I'd begged off and had gone with Martin to see *Bonnie and Clyde* at the Rialto.

"Male is in decline," my father said. "Manual seems to have all the horses nowadays."

My grandfather considered this, lifting his chin above his ascot, and said, "You still have that dog, Louis?" I wondered if he meant the dog that had gotten stuck in the pipe.

My father said Louis had two boxers now.

"They're supposed to be guard dogs," Uncle Louis said. "But they act like pussycats."

"I wish that place would let me keep a dog," Granddaddy said. He meant the nursing home.

My mother came in with the platter of turkey, saying, "I don't see what's so great about an electric knife." My father said grace, his holiday version, which went on for a bit. Then Gee announced with her red lips that Uncle Louis would now tell the story of the time he offered a pie to the White Castle thief and nearly lost an eye.

"That again?" my mother said.

"I'll tell the expurgated version," Uncle Louis said, putting a scoop of stuffing on his plate.

Later that evening, after I'd taken Granddaddy back to the nursing home, Martin asked me to tell him the unexpurgated version.

We were in the den, watching a variety special on TV that featured Dusty Springfield and Burl Ives. My father and Uncle Louis were downstairs in the rec room, looking at slides of trains my father had photographed in Europe that summer. The women, except for Gee, were in the kitchen.

"The robber called Uncle Louis a 'fucking four-eyed faggot,'" Gee said. She giggled. Her bare thigh was within an inch of Martin's leg.

"'Fuckfaced,'" I said. "Not 'fucking.'" When the robber swore at Uncle Louis, I'd lifted my nose from the damp wool of his overcoat and turned to look at my father. Light bounced off the thick lenses of his glasses, the hair in his nostrils seemed to quiver, his Adam's apple rose and fell, but his mouth was shut tight.

"And then the bloke hit your uncle in the eye with the cap pistol," Martin said.

"He's my father's cousin, actually," I said. "We just call him Uncle."

"So the bloke hit your dad's cousin, right?" Martin said impatiently.

"Yeah." The robber had swung the gun, knocking Uncle Louis's glasses to the floor and opening a cut under his eye. The gun was a toy—or so we found out later—but its parts were metal. Cheap metal, but metal nonetheless.

"And then," Martin said, "the Negro bloke, the cook, descended from the flies like a deus ex machina and saved the day, right?"

In Uncle Louis's description, the cook, who was built like an icebox, wrestled the robber to the floor and sat on him until the police came. Under his paper hat, which fell off when he jumped on the robber, the cook was as bald as a genie. His skin was a purply black shade, the color of some vein of ore deep within the earth, a rich and fearsome color. When he had pinned the robber and the robber had stopped flailing, the cook said, "If you say one word, pus-head, I'll put my fist through your motherfuckin' face."

The cook's comment hadn't been included in the Thanksgiving table version of the story. Nor was Uncle Louis's confession, made to my father while holding a handkerchief to his swollen eye in the back of the police cruiser that took us home. He said he'd been so frightened he'd thought he was going to soil his trousers. My father, who had his arm around me and held the pie in his lap, said, "You deserve the Croix de Guerre, Lou." My father was shivering. Harry sat up front with the policeman, asking him questions, whether he'd ever been in any high-speed chases, for instance.

Martin said, "I love America. So violent and yet so sentimental." And then he began to flop around on the sofa like a rag doll, eyes popping and warped mouth agog, the way Bonnie and Clyde had done at the end of the movie, in slow motion, when the Texas Rangers pumped them full of bullets. When Martin was finished, he laughed in self-appreciation. Gee laughed too, of course.

I went outside to smoke and discovered that the crumpled pack in my pants was empty. I wondered if there might be a cigarette in Uncle Louis's car. He still smoked, as my mother would sometimes note when my father came home from a night of cribbage with him. I explored the front and back of Uncle Louis's Ford wagon, the car he'd bought to replace his old sedan. I looked on the dash and in the glove compartment and under the seats. I found an ice scraper from Grissom's Sinclair, a tin of peanut brittle, a thermos, some *National Geographics,* and an empty box of Parliaments. In the luggage space, there was a fifty-pound bag of dog food and overalls dappled with paint. In a pocket of the overalls, I found a pistol.

I sat in the backseat and looked at the pistol under the car's dome light. There were no firearms in our house, aside from the

BB gun my father had bought at the urging of my mother for the purpose of shooting at a Great Dane that ran loose in the neighborhood and sometimes attacked Judge, our dachshund. (The gun was in my father's basement office, still in a shopping bag.) The pistol had a pebbly grip and a short barrel that I couldn't quite fit my pinkie into. Had Uncle Louis bought it for protection? Perhaps the White Castle thief turned up in his dreams. When he'd told the story at the dinner table, he'd made a comedy out of it, cleaned it up the way he'd cleaned up stories about my father and himself in the Kentucky militia. He'd claimed he hardly ever thought about the incident, except when he drove past a White Castle. I didn't believe him. What else would have led him to buy a gun?

I pointed the pistol out the door at the dark. Then I put it back in the overalls.

I found a longish butt in the ashtray and smoked it down to the recessed filter. I went back into the house, through the rec room door. The slide projector was on, beaming a picture of an SNCF electric locomotive onto the stand-up screen. My father and Uncle Louis had gone down the hall, into Dad's office. I could hear them talking.

"Here it is, Lou," my father said. "I sometimes read this for consolation." I tried to think what my father read for consolation, aside from histories of railroads and the meditations of certain jurists. He attended church, of course, but mostly, I'd always assumed, out of duty.

Uncle Louis was silent. Then he said, "Some earnest fool tried to convert me at that drunk farm. I said, 'It's hard enough giving up bourbon. Don't make me give up my disbelief, too.'"

"Jesus was a wise man," my father said, though not with any fervor. He didn't have a future as an evangelist.

"But does Jesus know anything about sinking funds and outstanding debts?" Uncle Louis made an odd, gassy noise, like a chuckle spoiled by indigestion. Then he said he was thinking of selling his house and moving away, possibly to New Mexico.

"I hope you won't do that, old bean," my father said.

"I might, Billy. I might move out there and paint steer skulls, like Georgia O'Keeffe."

"I hope you'll paint more train pictures," my father said.

Uncle Louis didn't sell his house or come within five hundred miles of Georgia O'Keeffe. He did try to go out west for a month's vacation in the summer of 1968, but his dogs were stolen from his car at a diner in Missouri and then the car died in Kansas, so he gave up and came home, only to discover that Robert, his housekeeper, had had a stroke.

Not long after, Uncle Louis was hired to teach art at a girls' school. With my father's help, he was able to pay off taxes in arrears. He bought a new car and got a dog from the Humane Society.

By 1969, the year I left for college, he had acquired a new housemate, a young woman who did the cooking in exchange for room and board. Cora was from Floyds Knobs, Indiana, across the river. She was a teacher's aide and did volunteer work for a downtown jobs program. She was also a potter. Uncle Louis said to my father, "I don't think she's going to run off with what's left of the silver."

When I came home from college that November, my mother was laid up with a bug and Granddaddy was feeling too run-down to venture out of the nursing home, so it was decided that we'd have Thanksgiving dinner at Uncle Louis's. We'd take some dishes Ida had made in advance. Cora, whose virtues didn't seem to include good relations with her family across the river, had agreed to cook the turkey. Not that I'd be able to eat it. A month before, in a conversion inspired by some late-night reading, I'd decided to become a vegetarian. Harry would eat my portion—eat it and say something smart.

Even though I was an intellectual now and had lost interest in football, I went with my father and Uncle Louis to the Male-Manual game. (Harry skipped it; he didn't get up until noon anyway.) My father drove his gray three-on-the-tree Chevrolet sedan, a car so drab he hadn't bothered to have a rear-end dent repaired. The radio had only a tuning knob, no buttons. When Uncle Louis got in the car, he said to me, "It's good for the souls of our elected officials that they not ride around in style." Uncle Louis's own soul appeared to have departed him during the night; under his brown hat he was pale and drawn.

It was a bright fall day, a day that felt like the last warm breath of the year. Uncle Louis said Cora had kept him in the kitchen all morning, shelling chestnuts and crumbling stale bread for stuffing, when all he wanted to do was sit outside in the sunshine with a cup of coffee and watch for the pileated woodpecker that lived in the woods below his house. "You know all the trouble you have to go to just to shell one damn chestnut?"

My father let the clutch out too quickly as he turned onto River Road, and the car bucked a little. We drove in silence past the Pine Room and the KingFish and Mr. Grissom's Sinclair, the bountiful sunshine lapping at the car. Then Uncle Louis said, "I tied one on last night, Billy. Cora gave me a taste of her dinner wine and one taste led to another, as they say. I fell off the wagon onto my pitiful face." He turned around to look at me. "Did your dad ever tell you I'm a grisly old boozer?"

I saw that a stem of Uncle Louis's eyeglasses had been secured to the frame with a gob of electrical tape. Perhaps he actually had fallen on his face. I said, "No."

"Your dad is the epitome of discretion," Uncle Louis said.

Dad said, "You've gone a long time without taking a drink, haven't you, Lou?"

"A long time would be accurate if you don't count a number of episodes you don't know about."

My father told his cousin not to give up the ship.

"This old ironclad?"

On the way back from the game, my father took a route that led us past the railway museum he'd helped found a few years before. The museum, which was on a patch of once-industrial riverside, had just acquired an L&N steam engine—a 4-8-2 Baldwin that had carried passengers around the Southeast between the world wars—and my father wanted to show it to his cousin.

"It's on the homely side," Dad said, pulling into the dirt parking lot and stopping next to the chain-link fence that enclosed the museum. "We need to give it a coat of paint and polish up the cab." He asked Uncle Louis if he wanted to take a closer look at the engine. He had a key to open the gates.

Uncle Louis said, "I think we better get home and check on the turkey." There was confetti on his hat and raincoat. He'd sat stiffly in his seat for most of the game, sipping coffee. Late in the second half, he turned to me and said, "The problem with football is that there are too many discussions and too many people falling down too often."

As my dad attempted to put the Chevrolet in reverse, he ground the gear and then stalled the car. "Doggone it," he said.

"Give me an automatic any day," Uncle Louis said.

When we got to Uncle Louis's, my father remembered he needed to pick up the dishes Ida had prepared. He dropped us off and drove away, stirring up leaves, narrowly missing a boxy old Rambler parked beneath a sycamore. Uncle Louis didn't know whose car the Rambler was. It didn't belong to Cora, who drove a VW.

As we went up the cracking, moss-laden brick steps to the front door, we heard music, and then Uncle Louis remembered that Cora had invited a boy to dinner.

When we went inside, he said, "It's her only serious flaw." I thought he was referring to Cora's choice in boyfriends, but he meant the music. "I think she might have a tin ear." The music was "In a Silent Way" by Miles Davis. I owned the record myself; I found the sad, bleating trumpet consoling.

Uncle Louis laid his hat on a low wood chest that was long and deep enough to store a knight's armor, or so I'd imagined as a child. But when I'd lifted the heavy lid, it had contained only yellowing newspapers and an umbrella. Probably it still did.

We walked through the sitting room, where the hi-fi was, and into the kitchen. Cora sat at the table, peeling the skins from cooked yams. Steam rose from the yams, whose flesh was a dark, lush, underworld orange.

"So, who won the game?" Cora asked, after Uncle Louis had introduced me. Cora had long, straight, dark hair parted in the absolute middle of her head and sharp cheekbones that made her seem older than she probably was. She was pretty, in a country kind of way.

"Manual won," Uncle Louis said. "I believe we were the only white people there."

"Hmm," she said, pulling a strip of yam skin free. She had long fingers. I imagined her throwing pots, the wet clay rising, dilating, fluting.

Uncle Louis asked where Jacques, the dog, was. Cora said Jay had taken him for a walk.

"Jay? Did I hire a dog trainer named Jay?" Hatless, his gray hair matted, his stomach sticking out beyond the panels of his raincoat, Uncle Louis looked as if he'd spent the afternoon asleep in a movie theater. He went into the pantry.

"Jay's my friend," Cora said, glancing at me. "He's having dinner with us. Remember?"

"Yes, your friend. You told me about him. Though I could use a dog trainer, if he's available." A cupboard door, its wood swollen, scraped open. Glass clanked against glass.

"He's studying welding at JCTC," Cora said. JCTC was a local technical college. "But he likes dogs."

"A dog is man's best friend," Uncle Louis said. I heard the glug-glug of liquid flowing into a receptacle.

"I'm going to excuse myself and go take a bath," Uncle Louis announced. I watched his raincoated figure slip out of the pantry, tumbler in hand.

Cora said, "I think we may be all out of cooking sherry now, but I have some beer Louis doesn't know about, if you'd like one. Jay brought it." She was slicing the peeled yams, making wheels of them.

"I could go for a beer," I said. I would have to drink it before my father arrived. I wasn't legal—you could be drafted in Kentucky at eighteen, but you couldn't drink—and my father minded about such things. Even Harry, who was only a few months shy of legal, didn't drink in Dad's presence.

Cora spooned a sauce over the yams. It smelled lemony. Then she put the saucepan down and went into the back hall. When she returned with the beer, a silver can of Sterling, she saw me looking at the embroidery bordering the neckline of her thin white peasant blouse. I adjusted my gaze upward.

"Louis went down to the Pine Room last night," she said, "after I made the mistake of giving him a hit of wine. I didn't know he had a problem."

"It's not your fault," I said, pulling the pop-top.

The back door opened and Jacques entered, followed by Jay. Jacques was some sort of terrier mix. His ashy gray coat was stiff and harsh, and he had goatish chin hairs. Jay undid the leash, and Jacques shot out of the kitchen, as if he'd just seen a cat stealing through the sitting room.

Jay wiped his boots on the rug by the door. He had long hair and a patchy beard that didn't conceal a skin condition, and his eyes would have been visible through fog. I thought he might be stoned. I thought there was an unpleasantness in the fixity of his mouth. I also thought I'd seen him before, a long time ago. I was sure of it.

Cora asked me to carve the turkey. I said that I didn't think I should, since I was a vegetarian. Harry said, "But he wishes he wasn't." Then she asked my father if he would do the honors and he said, "I'll give it a try." While at home, fetching Ida's dishes, he'd put on a necktie, a blue one decorated with the Chesapeake & Ohio cat nestled in a quarter moon. It flopped against the turkey's browned skin as he hacked meat from the breast. Cora lifted the tie from the turkey, brushed it off, and tucked it inside Dad's shirt.

Harry stood back by the stove. He'd come with a girl he'd

known in high school named Libeth. He was clearly stoned. He was sucking a Life Saver, and kept touching his earlobe, as if its existence baffled him.

Jay stood by the refrigerator, drinking a beer, looking steadily at Harry's date. Libeth went to college out east. She was a serious girl, who was known to laugh in your face if you said something ignorant. Harry was a serious person too, when he wasn't drunk or stoned, and he must have liked the idea of having someone to laugh with at the ignorance of humanity. Three years on the East Coast seemed to have sharpened certain parts of Libeth's face. She stared back at Jay until he flinched.

Jay pulled at the collar of his flannel shirt and scratched his beard. He'd hardly said a word since entering the house. Then he said to me, "The last turkey I had was at Eddyville. It tasted like crap."

My father looked up from his carving. Eddyville was a state prison.

Jay opened the refrigerator and leaned in, as if he wished to escape from his confession, which was loose in the room like a bat.

Libeth said, "What'd you do? Knock over a store?" She was wearing a Peace Now button on one lapel of her blue-jean jacket and an Eldridge Cleaver button on the other.

Harry giggled. Too much pot made him giggle.

"Something like that," Jay said, refrigerator light washing over him.

Cora said, "Jay made a mistake and he paid for it and now he's doing fine."

When Jay shut the refrigerator and I saw his eyes again, the dark gleam of them, I understood why I thought I'd recognized him earlier. I believed he was the guy who had come through the door at the White Castle, eight years before, his face all but hidden under his windbreaker hood. I wondered if my father recognized him, or if the beard threw him off. Neither my father or Uncle Louis had testified at the trial; Uncle Louis had even asked that the assault charge be withdrawn. I remembered my father saying, after the White Castle thief had been convicted and sent away, that the boy who had done it was barely eighteen. But he'd had a juvenile record, and he'd been given a stiff sentence. The judge hadn't been moved by the fact that the weapon was a toy.

Had Jay recognized my father? When Cora introduced them, had the name Judge Dupree given Jay a jolt? Whatever the case, my father, a proponent of keeping the conversation flowing away from danger, started telling the story about Cyril the goat.

Cora stirred gravy. She had a busy, mistress-of-the-kitchen look on her face. The kitchen was very warm and I could see sweat building up under her blouse. "Goats are the most useless animals," she said, as if she'd had a lot of experience with them. "I don't know why anybody would want to keep one."

She asked Jay to get a basket out of the pantry for the rolls. He seemed happy to have something to do. I was relieved when she sent me upstairs to fetch Uncle Louis.

Harry came with me as far as the staircase. I said, "It's him, that guy, the one who stuck up the White Castle. I swear. Don't you recognize him?"

"No." His pupils had taken over most of his eye sockets.

"You're so fucked up, Harry, you wouldn't recognize yourself if you bumped into you."

"It's how I get through these family dinners." He grinned. If there was a positive side to Harry's increasing use of drugs and inebriants, it was that it had made him more amiable. He was happy when he was high. He said, "Last night, Libeth and I made it. Even though she has a boyfriend in Boston. Even though I could hardly get near her in high school. It was so great. I couldn't believe it was happening. What'd you do last night, Morgan?"

Jacques lay on Uncle Louis's unmade bed, his tail whisking the headboard. Uncle Louis was in the bathroom. The door was open a crack. Water dripped into the tub.

I said that dinner was ready.

"The turkey has been burned to a proper crisp?" I heard him rearrange himself in the tub.

"Dad's carving it," I said, studying a framed black-and-white photograph on the dresser. It was of my father and his sons—*père et fils sans chapeaux,* soaking up the atmosphere in the L&N yards, November, 1961. The picture was grainy, a bit underexposed, but my father's happiness was evident.

"Tell him to save a drumstick for me," Uncle Louis said.

"I met Cora's boyfriend," I said. Jacques regarded me with terrier ears upraised.

"Is he a vegetarian like you or a dirty old meat eater like me and your old man?" He farted, rippling the water like an outboard starting up. *"Excusez-moi."*

"Meat eater. And an ex-felon. He told us the last turkey he had was at Eddyville."

"Cora has an ex-felon for a boyfriend?" Uncle Louis seemed less shocked by this revelation than by her taste in music—or perhaps it only confirmed something about her taste in music. "What'd he do?"

I saw him again, the cold-reddened center of his face. "He looks like the guy who popped you at the White Castle."

"Is that right?" He sounded almost amused. Then he said, "Are you sure? I thought that boy's name was James. James Becker. Or Beckett. Something like that."

"Maybe I'm wrong." I didn't recall Cora having mentioned Jay's last name.

"It would spoil dinner if you're right," Uncle Louis said.

Water sloshed as he moved in the tub. "I hope you won't ever find yourself in a situation where you have nothing to drink but cooking sherry. It's god-awful. And you have to drink a gallon of it to feel the least bit giddy." He chuckled. "However, it's probably better for you than aftershave or Sterno juice."

Though I'd never tried aftershave or Sterno juice, it seemed probable to me that I would turn out more like Uncle Louis than my father, who never drank anything stronger than a Coke, who didn't take the Lord's name in vain, who lost his head only in the presence of trains, who would drive his cousin down to an Arkansas drunk farm at the drop of a hat and write him letters of encouragement on hotel stationery. I might turn out to be an improvement on Harry, but I still didn't feel it was within me to aspire to what my father seemed to represent: sobriety, honor, loving-kindness. I didn't think I stood a chance of becoming like him.

I said, "Maybe we should pretend we don't know who he is—the robber. If it's him, I mean."

"We could do that," Uncle Louis said. "It might make dinner go more smoothly."

I'd opened the top drawer of the dresser, not quite absent-mindedly. It was a weakness of mine to want to open other people's drawers. In Uncle Louis's, I found a heap of thin silk-like socks, all of them dark, some plain and some patterned with faint little yellow clocks. This style of sock—which my father wore, too—seemed dandyish for a man who was so careless of his appearance. Perhaps it was all that was available at the downtown men's store where he and my father shopped. Or perhaps Uncle Louis felt tenderly about his feet and ankles. I'd heard it said that he was a homosexual. Martin, the foreign exchange student, had said, "Your dad's cousin seems like a poofter. Is he?" I wasn't uninterested in this aspect of Uncle Louis's life, and yet it seemed less interesting than some of the other things I knew about him.

Near the bottom of the drawer, I found a handful of bullets. I held them in my palm and felt their weight and purpose.

Uncle Louis lifted himself out of the tub, dripping, groaning. "I guess I should come meet the company."

I put one of the bullets to my nose. It had a cool pleasant smell.

"Goddamnit," Uncle Louis said. He'd hit his foot or leg against something.

"You all right?" I put the bullets back.

"I'll be fine as soon as I can get some real alcohol in me," he said.

• • •

While we waited for Uncle Louis to come to the table, my father told the story of how a horse Uncle Louis's parents had owned had wandered next door onto my grandparents' property and dropped dead. The horse, Isabelle, had remained in my grandparents' yard for several days, rotting in the summer heat, until somebody could be found to haul her off.

"Isabelle had two gaits," Uncle Louis said, entering the dining room. "One was standing still and the other was walking in the direction of food. I think she was hoping to eat some of your mother's flowers before she passed on."

My father laughed and said, "I think she was revenge for Cyril."

Uncle Louis was wearing a clean white shirt and khakis held up by suspenders. He'd shaved. His shaggy gray eyebrows flickered above the rims of his eyeglasses. He greeted Harry and Libeth. He asked after Libeth's mother, whom he used to see at the opera in the days when he went. Louisville, I realized, was just a small upper South town that sometimes pretended to be a big city.

Cora introduced Jay to Uncle Louis. She said, "This is my friend Jay Beckman."

Uncle Louis shook Jay's hand and said it was nice to meet him. Neither gave any sign of recognizing each other. But Uncle Louis excused himself and went into the kitchen and then out of the house. Maybe he was going to get a bottle he'd remembered he'd hidden in the garage some years ago. Or maybe he was going to drive down to the Pine Room and spend the evening there, without his relatives and without Cora and her ex-felon of a boyfriend. It would be simpler to sit on a barstool, having removed oneself from the complications of life, its idiotic coincidences and mean symmetries, having cast aside all ambition except that of drinking oneself senseless.

After a while, my father said, "Maybe I should go find Lou." He got up from his chair. His tie was still tucked inside his shirt. The white napkin he clutched in his hand suggested a small nightgowned figure, a puppet ghost.

engine pushing through smoke and hazy impressionist light. The engine was unmistakably an engine, but it was blurry, too, like some beast in a dream aiming to swallow you.

Dwight Allen is the author of *The Green Suit*, published in 2000. His stories have appeared in *The Southern Review*, *The Georgia Review*, *Shenandoah*, *New England Review*, and other magazines and also in *New Stories from the South 1997*. He was born and raised in Louisville, Kentucky, and now lives in Madison, Wisconsin, with his wife and son. His new book will be published in 2003.

NANCY HOLYOKE

I started this story in 1997, when my father was on the other side of eighty. He was a little wobbly at that point, though of sound mind. I'd written another story in which a character modeled on my father—a judge, a ailroad buff, a thin, bespectacled man with a cowlick or two—dies in an tomobile accident. If I killed him in a piece of fiction, wasn't that a kind of tection against his dying in actuality?

n "End of the Steam Age," it is the job of Judge Dupree to keep his dipso- iac bachelor cousin Louis alive. Judge Dupree, who drinks nothing r than Coke, loves his cousin in a more than dutiful way. The judge is ed man, but his reserve weakens when he's around Louis. Whom else tell about his crush on Ingrid Bergman? The affection he feels for is deep but it is also boyish and unworldly, not unlike his love for d in the end the judge, who is a little squeamish and no more inseling a drunk than he is at figuring out why a stalled car helpless to keep his cousin from going off the rails.

e "End of the Steam Age" appeared in a magazine, my father for almost two years and I was almost two years into writing a ge, of which this story had become a part. When I began the aid to myself, If I write a novel that has a character like my r of it, won't that keep him close?

"I'll get him," I said, looking at Harry, who had found something in the middle distance to gaze at. My father sat back down.

I met Uncle Louis coming back inside through the kitchen door. He had one of Jay's Sterlings in his hand. He looked confused. He said, "I can't remember where I hid my gun."

"You have a gun?"

I bought it at a truck stop near Covington. Don't tell your dad. He wouldn't approve."

"Maybe we should eat now. We can find the gun and shoot Jay later, if necessary."

"I suppose that would be more polite." He took his glasses off and inspected the crudely taped stem. "I used to have an extra pair, but I couldn't find them this morning."

When we returned to the table, Uncle Louis with his beer in a glass, my father said grace, the holiday version. When he was done, Harry, suddenly roused, said, "And while you're at it, God, how about stopping the war in Vietnam? *Merci beaucoup.*"

"Amen," Cora said. The "A" in "Amen" was soft as a pillow, as sweetly formed as the breasts beneath her peasant blouse.

"Right on," Jay said, not loudly, almost as if he were muttering to himself.

My father and his cousin were silent for a moment. I spooned yams onto my plate. I didn't want to discuss the war. My father always routed me when we argued. (He routed Harry, too, but Harry didn't recognize it.) I wanted to put Cora's yams into my mouth. I wanted Jay to disappear.

"As soon as we pull out," my father said somberly, "the Communists will gobble up the country like seven-year locusts."

"We're killing peasants in rice paddies while propping up a corrupt government," Libeth said. "It's shameful."

"It gives me a headache just to think about it," Uncle Louis said, rising from his seat. He'd polished off the beer and was heading to the kitchen for another. My father watched him go. Perhaps he'd decided that he couldn't keep his cousin from blinding himself and walking off the edge of a cliff. Perhaps he'd decided that all he could do was wait at the bottom for Uncle Louis to stop falling. And then maybe he could get him to go back to Arkansas.

Harry, who was warming to the subject, said, "Who cares if the Communists take over, Dad? It's their country."

"They're just a bunch of slopeheads," Jay said. "Fuck the war and fuck them."

My father stiffened. He had a long face, which became longer when vulgarities disturbed the air around him. I heard a hiss: Uncle Louis opening a can of beer.

"Jay!" Cora said. "God!" Her cheeks and throat had turned a deep and becoming pink.

Jay stared at the chunks of turkey on his plate. The middle of his face was knotted with anger, as if he knew Cora wasn't going to be able to save him from whoever he was. She'd dump him sooner or later, and then he'd just be an ex-felon trying to get a job as a welder if he could first pass the course at JCTC. He wasn't the kind of clay you could really work with.

Jay got up from his place and went toward the kitchen, his boots digging into the thin Oriental rug. Cora followed.

A draft from somewhere made the candle flames shiver. Uncle Louis's house wasn't exactly airtight.

Libeth said, "He's kind of scary. I wonder why she hangs out with him."

"Maybe she likes a challenge," I said.

Harry said, "Are you sure it's him, Morgan, and not just another homicidal maniac we get to have Thanksgiving dinner with? Or maybe it's his twin."

"What?" my dad said, breaking his silence. "Whose twin?"

In the kitchen, Cora said, "Where do you think you're going, Jay?" She sounded like my mother when she was furious.

"Do you like being around these rich people and listening to their dumb shit stories about goats and horses? This is too grand for me, Cora." He took a breath. "Maybe if you bang him, they'll let you be a member of the family."

Harry giggled.

My father got up from his seat, shooting a look at me. Had he assumed, as I had, that it was me Jay was talking about Cora banging?

Uncle Louis said, "You can't talk like that here. Please leave my house."

"Is that my beer? You can't drink my beer, you fuckin' alky faggot."

"Stop it, Jay," Cora shouted. "Don't do that."

My father went toward the kitchen with his napkin in hand. Harry and I got up from our seats and stood around like rubber-neckers. By the time our father reached the kitchen, Jay had gone out the door, with Cora right behind him. They yelled at ea other in the dark. Then they drove off in their cars.

Uncle Louis came back into the dining room. His shi soaked with beer, and there were spots on his trousers. me while I go change," he said. But he didn't come downs

One night in early January, before he was too far bourbon, Uncle Louis found his gun and shot hims

It was the next day when I heard the news. I with Ida, eating lunch (a turkey sandwich, I'd about returning to college for the winter ter

"Lord save his soul," Ida said, tipping cig tray I'd hammered out for her at summe

That night, I went outside to smoke. got in Kentucky. No dog barked, no to sit under the stars. I followed my I saw my father sitting in his offic from the pole lamp was dim a disorder of his desk. He'd ta whatever he could see with behind. Maybe my fathe would've written, had explanation. My fath wall before him, wh

William Gay

CHARTING THE TERRITORIES OF THE RED

(from *The Southern Review*)

When the women came back from the rest area, slinging their purses along and giggling, Dennis guessed that someone had flirted with them. He hoped they'd keep their mouths shut about it. He was almost certain that Sandy wouldn't say a word, but you never knew about Christy.

Well, we got flirted with, Christy said. She linked an arm through his and leaned against him, standing on his feet, looking up at him. The sun was moving through her auburn hair, and there were already tiny beads of perspiration below her eyes, on the brown, poreless skin of her forehead. She smelled like Juicy Fruit chewing gum.

Dennis unlaced his arm from hers and stepped back and wiped his wire-rimmed glasses on the tail of his shirt. He was wearing jeans and a denim shirt with the sleeves scissored out at the shoulders. He glanced at Wesley. He put the glasses back on and turned and looked at the river. Moving light flashed off it like a heliograph. I guess we need to get the boats in the water, he said.

Wesley had both of Sandy's hands in both of his own. Her hands were small and brown and clasped, so in Wesley's huge fists they looked amputated at the wrists. Who flirted with you? Wesley asked.

Sandy just grinned and shook her head. She had short dark hair, far shorter than Wesley's. Wesley was looking down into her sharp, attentive face. The best thing about her face was her eyes, which were large and bluegreen and darkly fringed with thick lashes. The best thing about her eyes was the way they focused on you when you were talking to her, as if she was listening intently and retaining every word. Dennis had always suspected that she did this because she was deaf. Perhaps she didn't even know she did it.

Sandy had once been beaten terribly, but studying her closely Dennis could see no sign of this now. Perhaps the slightest suggestion of aberration about the nose, a hesitant air that she was probably not even aware of. But her skin was clear and brown, the complex and delicate latticework of bones intact beneath it.

Nobody was flirting with us, she said, smiling up at Wesley.

If they did you flashed them a little something, Wesley said.

If I couldn't get flirted with without flashing them a little something I'd just stay at the house, Christy said. She was giggling again. The big one said his name was Lester, she told Wesley. But don't worry, he was ugly and baldheaded.

Lester? What the hell kind of redneck name is Lester? Was he chewing Red Man? Did he have on overalls?

You know, Wesley's not the most sophisticated name I ever heard, Christy said. Nobody's named Wesley, nobody. Do you know one movie star named Wesley?

It occurred to Dennis that Christy might be doing a little flirting herself, although Wesley had been married to Sandy for almost two years and he supposed that he was going to marry Christy himself, someday sooner or later.

I don't know any movie stars named anything at all, Wesley said. I'll make him think goddamn Lester. I'll Lester him.

Wesley wore cutoff jeans and lowcut running shoes with the laces removed. He was bare to the waist and burnt redblack from the sun so he looked like a sinister statuary you'd chopped out of a block of mahogany with a doublebitted axe. He'd been in the water, and his jeans were wet, and his hair lay in wet black ringlets.

Nobody was flirting with anybody, Sandy said carefully. She enunciated each word clearly, and Dennis figured this as well was because she had been deaf so long. Now she had an expensive hearing aid smaller than the nail of her little finger, and she could hear as well as anyone, but this had not always been so.

Are you all going to get the boats and stuff? Christy asked.

Let's get everything down from the camp, Dennis said. We can pick the girls up here.

Then let's go, college man, Wesley said.

They followed a black path that wound through wild cane, brambles, blackberry briars. It led to a clearing where they'd spent the night. On the riverbank were sleeping bags and a red plastic ice chest. Dennis began to roll up the sleeping bag he'd slept in with Christy. Sometime far into the night he had awoken, some noise, a nightbird, an owl. Some wild cry that morphed into Sandy's quickened breathing as Wesley made love to her. He wondered if Wesley still beat her. He looped a string around the sleeping bag and lashed it tight. When the breathing had reached some frenzied peak and then slowly subsided to normal, he had turned over, being careful not to wake Christy, and gone back to sleep. He turned now and tossed the sleeping bag into one of the two aluminum canoes tied to a hackberry depending out over the river.

When the canoes rounded the bend through the trailing willow fronds, Dennis saw that a red four-wheel-drive Dodge truck had backed a boat trailer down the sloping bank to the shallows. On it were two aluminum canoes that might have been clones of the ones Dennis and Wesley were rowing. Two men were in the bed of the pickup, two men on the ground. The man unbooming the boats did indeed have on overalls. He was enormous, thicker and heavier than Wesley. He wore the overalls with no shirt, and his head was shaved. The top of his head was starkly white against the sunburned skin of his face, as if he'd just this minute finished shaving it.

Son of a bitch, Wesley said.

This is by God crazy, Dennis said, but Wesley had already

drifted the canoe parallel with the shore and was wading out. Don't let this canoe drift into the current, he said over his shoulder. He went up the bank looking at Sandy and Christy. Sandy's face was as blank as a slate you'd erased, but a sort of constrained glee in Christy's told him what he wanted to know. He turned to the men grouped about the red truck.

Lester, I heard you were trying to hit on my wife, he said.

The bald man was turned away, but they were so close Wesley could smell the sweat on him, see the glycerinous drops seeping out of the dark skin of his back. The man had a malignant-looking mole the size of a fingertip between his shoulders, where the galluses crossed. The man fitted a key into a lock clasped through two links of chain securing the canoes. The lock popped open, and he freed the chain and locked the hasp through another link and pocketed the key. He turned. He looked up at the two men in the back of the truck and grinned. At last he glanced at Wesley.

This electronic age, he said, and laughed. I reckon it's been all over the news already. He wiped the sweat off his head with a forearm and turned to inspect the women. They'd seated themselves on the bank above, and they were watching like spectators box-seated before some barbaric show.

Which one'd be your wife? Lester asked.

Faced with the prospect of describing his wife or pointing her out like a miscreant in a lineup, Wesley hesitated. Sandy raised her arm. That would be me, she said.

Did I hit on you? Say anything out of the way?

No. You didn't.

The man looked Wesley in the eye. He shrugged. What can I say, he said.

Hey, loosen up, good buddy, one of the men in the truck called. He turned and opened an ice chest and began to remove cans of beer from it. He was bare to the waist, and he had straight, shoulderlength hair that swung with his movement when he turned from the cooler. He tossed a can to Dennis: Unprepared, he still caught it onehanded, shifted hands with it. One for the ladies, the man said, and tossed them gently, one, two. When he pitched a fourth to Wesley, Wesley caught it and pivoted and threw it as far as he could out over the river. It vanished without so much as a splash.

Lester looked up at the longhaired man and grinned. Not his brand, he said.

Don't try to bullshit me, Wesley said.

I wouldn't even attempt it, friend, Lester said. He turned to the boat, his back to Wesley, as if he'd simply frozen him out, as if Wesley didn't exist anymore. He unlooped the chain and slid the canoes off the sloped bed into the water. The two men leapt from the bed of the truck and with the third began to load the boats with ice chests, oars, boxes of fishing tackle. They climbed into the canoes and headed them downstream into the current. Lester turned to the women. He doffed an imaginary hat. Ladies, he said.

Wesley seemed to be looking around for a rock to throw.

Let it go, Dennis said.

I could have handled them, Wesley said. All that fine help I had from you.

Dennis turned and spat into the river. Hellfire. You didn't need any help. You made as big a fool of yourself alone as you could have with me helping.

I ain't letting them shitkickers run over me, Wesley said. Hell. I got a good Christian raising and a eighth-grade education. I don't have to put up with this shit from anybody.

But Wesley's moods were mercurial, and he seemed to find what he had just said amusing. He repeated it to himself, then looked toward the girls. Let's get organized, he said. As soon as Jeeter Lester and his family get gone we'll start looking for that Civil War cave.

He waded out to the canoe containing the red cooler. But first let's all have a little shot of that jet fuel, he said.

Dennis was watching Sandy, and a look like apprehension flickered across her face and was gone. No more than the sudden shadow of a passing cloud. Wesley had removed the lid from the cooler. He had somewhere come by an enormous quantity of tiny bottles of Hiram Walker. They were the kind of bottles served on airlines, and Wesley called them jet fuel. He was fumbling under sandwiches, dumping things out. Jet fuel, jet fuel, he was saying.

I'm sorry, Wesley, Sandy called. I left that bag setting on the kitchen table.

Wesley straightened. Well it'll do a whole hell of a lot of good setting on a table fifty miles from where I am, he said. He sailed the lid out over the river like an enormous rectangular Frisbee.

I said I was sorry. I really am.

Regret is not jet fuel, Wesley said. He hurled the cooler into the water. Everything went: cellophaned sandwiches, a sixpack of Coke, apples bobbing in the rapid current. A bottle of vin rosé.

Shit, Dennis said.

Wesley came wading out of the river. Sandy and Christy were buckling on life jackets. Dennis glanced sharply at Wesley's face. He stood up and put his folded glasses into the pocket of the denim shirt.

I don't think you're supposed to be throwing crap in the river like that, Christy said.

Oh no, Wesley said. The river police will get me.

Dennis was staring out at the lighthammered water. Lester and his cohorts had drifted out of sight around the bend. Now where is this famous Civil War cave? he asked.

Supposed to be somewheres close, Wesley told him, relaxing visibly. He turned to the women. Can you all handle a canoe?

I can row as good as you can, Christy told him. Maybe better.

You all check out one side of the river and me and this fine defender of southern womanhood'll look on the other. Check out every bluff, look for anything that might be a cave. It's supposed to be about halfway up. If you find a cave, sing out as loud as you can and we'll be there. OK?

OK.

And keep those life jackets on. If you have to take a leak or just whatever, do it with the jackets on.

I'm not sure I can do that, Christy said. She turned and gave Dennis a look so absolutely blank it could have meant anything. It could have meant, You showed common sense staying out of that argument he had. Or it could have meant, Why the hell weren't you backing him up?

Wesley was looking out across the river. Goddamn it's hot, he said. Did anybody see where that beer hit?

They drifted with the current, and Dennis shipped the oars, only using one occasionally to steer clear of trees leaning into the water. Huge monoliths of black slate and pale limestone towered above them, ledges adorned with dwarf cedars twisted and windformed. The river moved under them, yellow and murmurous, flexing like the sleekridged skin of an enormous serpent.

Snipes, Wesley said suddenly.

Dennis thought he meant some kind of bird. He was scanning the willows and cane; he had a mental picture of some kind of long-legged bird, one foot raised out of the water, a fish in its mouth.

Where? he asked.

Wesley by God Snipes, Wesley said. Ain't he a movie star?

Yes, he is.

I'll have to tell Christy about that when we catch up. They're done out of sight around that shoal yonder.

After a while Wesley told him again the story of the Civil War cave.

The guy always called it that, the Civil War cave, as if the entire Civil War had been fought inside it. He said it was where Confederate soldiers hid out one time. You can't even see it from the ridge; you have to find it from the river. He said there was all kinds of shit in there. Artifacts. Old guns, lead balls. And bones too, old belt buckles. He didn't even care, can you feature that? Said the guns was all seized up with rust.

In the lifetime he had known Wesley, Dennis had heard this story perhaps a hundred times. He had his mind kicked out of gear, coasting along, listening to the river mumbling to itself. He thought of the look on Sandy's face when Wesley had turned from hurling the cooler into the river, and he thought about gauges.

Once, long ago, on one of the few occasions when he had been blind, falling-down drunk, it had occurred to Dennis that life would be much simpler if everything had a gauge on it, the sort that on an automobile measure the temperature of the engine and so on. If the brain had a gauge you would know immediately how smart a certain decision was. You could start to act on it, keeping an eye on the needle all the time. You could proceed, pull back, try another approach. If the heart had one you'd know how in love you were with somebody. And if you could read their gauge . . . you could live your life with one eye on the needles and never make a foolish move.

Dennis had made several foolish movements in his life, but he had never wavered in the conviction that Wesley had a gauge in his head. It measured how close he was to violence, and went from zero into uncharted deep red, and every moment of Wesley's life the needle hovered, trembling, on the hairline of white that was all that stood between order and chaos.

Dennis had long ago quit going to bars with Wesley. At a certain point in his drinking, as if a thermostat had clicked on somewhere, Wesley would swivel his stool and survey the room with a smile of good-natured benevolence, studying its contents as if to ascertain were there inanimate objects worth breaking, folks worth putting in the hospital.

Six months after he married Sandy, he had eased into the bedroom of an apartment in the housing project and studied the sleeping faces of Sandy and a man named Bobby Joe Seales. He had slammed Seales full in the face with his fist, then turned his attention to Sandy. He had broken her arm and nose and jaw and shifted back to Seales. The room was a scene of carnage, folks said, blood on the floor, blood on the walls, blood on the ceiling. He had ripped the shade from a lamp and used the lamp base as a club, beating Seales viciously. Folks came screaming, cops. Dennis did not hear this story from Wesley, or from Sandy, but he had heard it plenty of other places, and Wesley stood trial for aggravated assault. The son of a bitch aggravated me, Wesley had said. So I assaulted him.

Seales had been on the Critical List. Folks always spoke of it in capital letters as if it were a place. A place you didn't want to go. Don't fuck with Wesley Deavers, folks said. He put Bobby Joe Seales on the Critical List. It looked like they'd been killing hogs in there.

Did you hear something?

Dennis listened. All he could hear was the river, crows spilling raucous cries from above them, doves mourning from some deep hollow he couldn't see.

Something. Sounded like yelling.

Then he could hear voices, faint at first, sourceless, as if they were coming from thin air, or out of the depths of the yellow water. Then he heard, faint and faint: Dennis. Dennis.

They've found it, Wesley said. He took up his oars and turned the boat into the swift current. Let's move it, he said. The voices had grown louder. If this is the right cave we'll map it, Wesley said. Make us up some charts so we can find it again.

The river widened where it shoaled, then began narrowing into a bottleneck as the bend came up. Dennis could feel the river quickening under him, the canoe gaining urgency as it rocked in the current.

Dennis. Dennis.

I wish she'd shut the hell up, Dennis said.

All right, all right, Wesley yelled. We're coming.

That must be one hellacious cave.

But the cliffs had been tending away for some time now on this side of the river, and when they rounded the bend they saw that the bluffs had subsided to a steep, stony embankment where Christy and Sandy were huddled. Dennis couldn't see their canoe. They were on their knees and still wearing life jackets, their hair plastered tightly to their skulls. Sandy was crying, and Christy was talking to her and had an arm about her shoulders.

Now what the fuck is this news, Wesley said, and Dennis felt a cold shudder of unease. He remembered something Dorothy Parker had purportedly said once when her doorbell rang: What fresh hell is this?

They tipped us over, Christy said. Now she began to cry as well. Goddamn them. They were waiting for us here and grabbed the boat. All four of them, two boatloads. They tried to get us into the boats with them and when we wouldn't go they got rough, tried to drag us. I hit one with an oar, and that baldheaded fucker tipped us over. They took the boat.

Wesley seemed actually to pale. Dennis could see a cold pallor beneath the deep tan. It seemed to pulse in his face. Sandy, are you all right? Wesley asked.

She can't hear, Christy said. When we went under it did something to her hearing aid, ruined it. Shorted it out or something. She can't hear a thing, I mean not a goddamned thing.

Oh, Wesley cried. He seemed on the threshold of a seizure, some sort of rageinduced attack. Eight hundred fucking dollars, he said. Eight hundred dollars up a wild hog's ass and gone. I'm going to kill them. I'm going to absolutely fucking kill them.

Wesley made twelve dollars an hour, and Dennis knew that he was mentally dividing twelve into eight hundred and arriving at the number of hours he had worked to pay for the hearing aid.

Where's the other oars?

I don't know. They floated off.

I'm gone. I'm going to kill them graveyard dead.

He turned the boat about to face the current.

Hey, Christy called. Wait.

Stay right here, Wesley said. And I mean right here. Do not move from that rock till we get back with the boat.

Let them keep the goddamned boat, Christy screamed, but Wesley didn't reply. He heeled into the current and began to row. He did not speak for a long time. He rowed like a madman, like some sort of rowing machine kicked up on high. I'll row when you get tired, Dennis said. Fuck that, Wesley told him. After a while he looked back and grinned. How dead am I going to kill them? he asked.

Graveyard dead, Dennis said.

Wesley hadn't missed a stroke rowing. After a time he said, There will be some slow riding and sad singing.

Trees went by on the twin shorelines like a landscape unspooling endlessly from one reel to another. A flock of birds went down the metallic sky like a handful of hurled slate. Dennis guessed by now the Lester gang was long gone, into the tall timber, their canoes hidden in the brush, laughing and drinking beer, on their way back across the ridges to pick up their truck.

What were you going to do, back there, kick my ass?

Dennis was looking at the sliding yellow water. What?

Back there at the camp when my jet fuel was missing. You got up and folded your little glasses and shoved them in your pocket. You looked for all the world like a schoolteacher getting ready to straighten some folks out. You think you can kick my ass?

I wouldn't want to hurt you, Dennis said.

Wesley laughed. How long have you known me, Dennis?

You know that. Since the third grade.

Third grade. Have I ever lied to you?

I don't know. How would I know that? Not that I know of.

I never lied to you. So I'm telling the truth now. I'm going to kill them. I'm going to kill them with an oar, not flat like I was paddling their ass, but sideways like I was chopping wood. I'll take their heads off. Do you want out? I'll ease over and let you out.

The boat hadn't slackened. The oars dipped and pulled, dipped and pulled, with no variation in their rhythm. The boat seemed to have attained its own volition, its own momentum.

No, Dennis finally said, and he knew with a cold horror that Wesley was telling the truth.

Do you really think I'd stop long enough to let you out?

You never lie.

No.

I can ask you the one right question and you'll lie.

Ask it then.

But before he could ask it, Wesley suddenly shouted. A hoarse cry of exultation. Dennis looked. They were aligned on a sandbar far downriver, three of them, the three canoes beached on the shore like bright metallic whales. Tiny dark figures in attitudes of waiting, watching them come.

Shouts came skipping across the water. Now he could see that Lester had his hands cupped about his mouth like a megaphone. It took you long enough, he yelled.

Wesley might not have heard. He was leaning into the oars, the muscles in the arms that worked them knotting and relaxing, knotting and relaxing.

They stood like the last ragged phalanx of an army backed to the last wall there was. They each held an oar. When the boat was still twenty feet from the shoreline Wesley bailed out. Oar aloft like God's swift sword. He seemed to be skimming the surface, a dark, vengeful divinity the waters would not even have. He knocked Lester's oar aside with his own and drew back and swung. The oar made an eerie, abrupt whistling. Blood misted the air like paint from an exploding spray can. Lester went to his knees clutching his face, blood streaming between his fingers. Wesley hit him across the top of his head, and a vulval gash opened in the shaven flesh. Dennis slammed the longhaired man backward, and he stumbled and fell into a thicket of willows and wild cane. He advanced on him, swinging the oar like a man killing snakes. An oar caught him across the bicep, and his left arm went suddenly numb. He turned. A man with a fright wig of wild red hair and clenched yellow teeth broadsided him in the shoulder with the flat of an oar just as Wesley broke his own oar across the man's back. Wesley was left with a section half the length of a baseball bat. The redhaired man was going to run through the cane, and Wesley threw the stub of the paddle at him.

The longhaired man had simply vanished. Dennis had driven him into the cane, and he'd just disappeared. Dennis was almost giddy with relief. It seemed over before it had properly begun, and it had not been as bad as he had feared it would be.

Lester was crawling on his hands and knees away from the river. He crawled blindly, his eyes full of blood, which dripped into the sand below him.

Wesley picked up a discarded oar and walked between Lester and the growth of willows. He had the oar cocked like a chopping ax. Lester crawled on. When his head bumped Wesley's knee he reared backward, sitting on his folded legs. He made a mute, armsspread gesture of supplication.

Wesley, Dennis yelled.

Kill this motherfucker graveyard dead, Wesley said.

Dennis crossed the sand in two long strides and swung onto Wesley's arm and wrested the oar from him. Wesley sat down hard in the sand. He got up shaking his head as if he'd clear it. He crossed the sandbar and waded kneedeep into the river and scooped up handfuls of water and washed his face. Lester crawled on. Like something wounded that just won't die. When he was into the willows he struggled up and stood leaning with both hands cupping his knees. Then he straightened and began wiping the blood out of his eyes. Dennis lay on his back in the sand for a long time and stared into the sky, studying the shifting patterns the clouds made. Both arms ached, and he was slowly clasping and unclasping his left hand. The bowl of the sky spun slowly clockwise, like paleblue water emptying down an endless drain.

He could hear Lester lumbering off through the brush. Wesley came up and dropped onto the sand beside Dennis. Dennis had an arm flung across his eyes. He thought he might just lie here in the hot weight of the sun forever. His ribs hurt, and he could feel his muscles beginning to stiffen.

I wish I hadn't quit smoking and I had a cigarette, Wesley said. Or maybe a little shot of that jet fuel. Chastising rednecks is hot, heavy work, and it does wear a man out so.

Dennis didn't reply, and after a time Wesley said, You ought to've let me kill him. I knew you weren't as committed as I was. I could see your heart wasn't in it. You didn't have your mind right.

He was dragging off like a snake with its back broke, Dennis said. What the hell do you want? Let it be.

We need to get these boats back to where Sandy and Christy are. Damned if I don't dread rowing upstream. Bad as I feel.

You reckon we could rig up a towline and pull them along the bank?

I don't know.

You don't think they'd go back to where the girls are, do you?

I don't know.

We better go see. No telling what kind of depravities those inbred mutants could think of to do with an innocent young girl.

Dennis suddenly dropped the arm from his eyes and sat up. He could hear a truck engine. It was in the distance, but approaching, and the engine sounded wound out, as if it were being rawhided over and through the brush. He stood up. The truck seemed to be coming through the timber, and he realized that a road, probably an unused and grownover logging road, ran parallel with the river. They know this river, he thought. The fourth man went to get the truck. Through a break in the trees chrome mirrored back the light, the sun hammered off bright red metal. The truck stopped. The engine died. Immediately Dennis could hear voices, by turns angry and placating. They seemed to be fighting amongst themselves, trying to talk Lester either into or out of doing something. A door slammed; another or the same door slammed again. When he looked around, Wesley had risen and gathered up two of the paddles. He reached one of them to Dennis. Dennis waved it away. Let's get the hell out of Dodge, he said.

We got to get the boats.

To hell with the boats. We got to move.

Something was coming through the brake of wild cane, not walking or even running as a man might, but lurching and stumbling and crashing, some beast enraged past reason, past pain. Wesley turned toward the noise and waited with the oar at a loose port arms across his chest.

Lester came out of the cane with a .357 Magnum clasped bothhanded before him. It looked enormous even in his huge hands. Lester looked like something that had escaped halfbutchered from a meatpacker's clutches, like some bloody experiment gone awry.

His wild eyes were just black holes charred in the bloody suet of his face. The bullet splintered the oar and slammed into Wesley's chest. Wesley's head, his feet, seemed to jerk forward. Then Lester shot him in the head, and Wesley sprung backward as if a springloaded tether had jerked him away.

Dennis was at the edge of the canebrake running full out. He glanced back. The pistol swung around. He dove sideways into the cane, rolling, and running from the ground up as the explosion showered him with sand, the cane tilting and swaying in his bobbing vision. The horizon jerked with his footfalls. Another shot, shouts, curses, men running down from the truck. He'd lost his glasses, and trees swam into his blurred vision as though surfacing at breakneck speed from murky water. Branches clawed at him; a lowhanging vine hurled him forward like a projectile blown out of the wall of greenery. He slowed and went on. He could hear excited voices, but nobody seemed to be pursuing him. He went on anyway, his lungs hot as if he moved through a medium of smoke, of pure fire. The timber deepened, and he went on into it. He fell and lay across the roots of an enormous beech. The earth was loamy and black and smelled like corrupting flesh. He vomited and lay with his face in the vomit. He closed his eyes. After a while the truck cranked and retreated the way it had come, fast, winding out. He raised his face and spat. There was a taste in his mouth like a cankered penny, and he could smell fear on himself like an animal's rank musk that you can't wash off.

When he finally made it back to the sandbar, the first thing he did was hunt his glasses. They were lying in the cane where he'd dived and rolled, an earpiece bent at a crazy angle but nothing broken. He put them on, and everything jerked into focus, as if a vibratory world had abruptly halted its motion.

Wesley was on his back with the back of his head and both hands lying in the water. He looked as if he'd flung his arms up in surrender, way too late. Dennis looked away. He took off the denim shirt and spread it across Wesley's face.

He dragged one of the canoes parallel with the body and began trying to roll Wesley into it. Wesley was a big man, and this was no easy task. He was loath to touch the bare flesh, but finally there was no way round it and he picked up the legs and worked them across the canoe and braced his feet and tugged the torso over into it. The boat lurched in the shallow water. By this time he was crying, making animal sounds he did not recognize as coming from himself. He threw in two oars and, running behind the boat, shoved it into deeper water. When he climbed in, he had to sit with a foot on either side of Wesley's thighs in order to row. In the west the sinking sun was burning through the trees with a bluegold light.

Twilight was falling when he came upon them, a quarter mile or so downriver from where they'd been left. They were straggling along the bank, Christy carrying what he guessed was a stick for cottonmouths. He oared the boat around broadside and rowed to shore. He waded the last few feet and dragged the prow into the bank, turned toward the women. They were looking not at him but at what was in the boat. All this time he'd been wondering what he could say to Sandy, but he remembered with dizzy relief that she was deaf and he wouldn't have to say anything at all. There didn't seem to be any questions anyway, or any answers worth giving if there were.

Christy's face was a twisted gargoyle's mask. Oh no, she said. Oh, Jesus, please no.

Dennis sat on the bank with his feet in the water. Rowing upstream had been hard, and he had his bloody palms upturned on his knees, studying the broken blisters. Sandy rose and climbed down the embankment, steadying her descent with a hand on Dennis's shoulder. She stood staring down into the boat. She knelt in the shallow water. Dennis stood up and waded around the boat and steadied it. He looked curiously like a salesman standing at the ready to demonstrate something should the need arise. He could hear Christy crying. She cried on and on.

Wesley lay with the bloody shirt still flung across his face. He lay like a fallen giant. Treetrunk legs, huge bronze torso. Sandy took up one of his hands and held it. The great fingers, thick black hair between the knuckles. She held the hand a time, and then she began folding the limp fingers into a fist, a finger at a time, tucking the thumb down and holding the hand in a fist with her own two hands. She sat and looked at it. Dennis suddenly wondered if she was seeing the fist come at her out of a bloody and abrupt awakening, rising and falling as remorselessly as a knacker's hammer, and he leaned and disengaged her hand. The loose fist slapped against the hull and lay palm upward.

He thought she might be crying, but when he looked up her eyes were dry and calm. They locked with his. Nor would she look away, as if she were waiting for his lips to move so she could read them.

We've got to get him out of here, Christy sobbed. A road somewhere maybe; somebody would stop.

Nobody answered her. Dennis wasn't listening, and Sandy couldn't hear at all. He wondered what it would sound like to be deaf. What you'd hear. From the look on Sandy's face across the body of her fallen warrior he judged it must be a calm and restful sound, the sighing of a perpetual wind through clashing rushes, a lapping of peaceful water that never varies or ceases.

ELIZABETH K. DERAMUS

William Gay is the author of two novels, *The Long Home* and *Provinces of Night.* His fiction has appeared in *The Oxford American*, *The Southern Review*, *Harper's Magazine*, and other magazines, as well as in previous editions of *New Stories from the South.* He is at work on new short fiction and a novel, *The Lost Country.*

I heard a story about canoeers on Buffalo River who'd had a confrontation with boat paddles. This seemed a curious but apt choice of weapons, and the story came to me with all the fictional artifacts intact: the hearing aid, the abuse, the Civil War motif. An early reader of the story told me there was no characterization, only violence. If characterization grows out of character, which I believed at the time, that sort of seemed the point.

Max Steele

THE UNRIPE HEART

(from *The Washington Post Magazine*)

for Rick Moody

Those old enough remember the summer of 1932 as the summer of the Lindbergh case. I remember it as the hottest time of my childhood, when I was not allowed to go out of the yard, not for fear that I would be kidnapped in that small Southern town but because I had done a thing to my mother too dreadful ever to be mentioned in my family, or by the neighbors, or by those people who slowed their cars that afternoon to look up at the porch roof, where my crime was committed.

Hot! The regular paperboy had had heatstroke and been sent off to camp by some rich subscribers. The new paperboy was too young to be carrying the huge canvas bag, packed tight with news of the kidnapping-murder of the Lindberghs' young son and the determination of New Jersey officials and the FBI to find the killer. The ugliest rumor was that the boy was in some way defective or retarded and the Lindberghs had killed him or had him killed. Neighbors, sitting on their porches or seeking a breeze in their side yards, waited for the afternoon paperboy. Eager for the news but also alert to see where the paper might land. The twelve-year-old boy had no aim at all. He threw papers into bushes, fishponds (the new craze) and even, as was the case with us that day, onto the roofs of porches.

First of all, you need to know that I was barely eight and my mother fifty that hot summer. She had been in a bewitched change of life since I was three and was to stay in it until I was thirteen. Nothing could be done to stop or ease the symptoms of panic and what she considered sheer defensive rage. Her feet never seemed to touch the ground. She blazed through the house giving orders, starting jobs, starting others; the world was falling to pieces before her very eyes. And there was no money for anything. My older brothers and sisters stayed away from home as much as possible. But since I was not allowed to cross streets, she always knew where to find me.

My father simply took me aside from time to time when he would find me hiding and say: "I know. Just stay out of her way as much as possible. But don't hide. It breaks her heart when she finds you hiding from her. Someday you'll see how much she loves you." And he was right, because by the time I was grown she was known as a charming woman, much admired for her calm demeanor and nurturing consideration.

But that afternoon she called me from the gazebo in the backyard where I was rolling the watermelon in a shallow tub of cold water, getting ready for the slicing after dark.

At the back door she seized my wrist and said: "The paperboy's thrown the paper on the roof." She was really reminding me that my father expected the paper to be unopened and still neatly folded on his chair where he would read it, drinking iced tea and waiting for supper to be set on the dining room table. Nothing in the world seemed more important than that my father be given during these Depression days whatever little things would make him happy. She marched me through the house and up the stairs and into a bedroom with a window that opened onto the porch roof. There she picked up a cushion from an old leather chair and put the cushion on the roof. "Sit on that," she said and pointed me out onto the roof, toward the paper, down near the gutter. "Be careful," she said, and at those words I forgave her all her morning voice, shrill as an untuned violin.

Out on the hot slate roof I edged on my bottom and heels down the steep slope toward the paper. When I looked back for her approval, she waved encouragement, I know now, but in one crazed moment it looked as if she were thumbing her nose at me. "She's got me out here to kill me," I thought. The dead Lindbergh boy was on the minds of everyone, especially children. Most of us had never thought of death before.

She apparently thought I was slipping, falling. Out through the window she came. I screamed, knowing she was going to push me off. She was sure I was falling and came crawling top speed.

I swung over the peak of the hip roof, ran back of her to the baked brick house and back through the window opening. I latched the screen, pulled down the window and locked it. I ran through the bedroom and down the stairs. I flipped the night lock on the front door and slammed it behind me. I sat for a moment in my father's chair listening to her on the roof. What to do? Then my father's voice came back to me: "Don't hide from her."

When my heart quit racing and my breathing slowed, I sauntered, I thought, down the curved brick steps and down the flagstones to the street, where an iron hitching post stood next to a granite block. I had been told ladies once descended in their long dresses from their carriages to the block. (My mother, brought up Victorian, still wore her dresses long, and her collar pinned with a cameo. More Gibson girl than modern.) Without looking at her on the roof, I swung with one hand round the hitching post, stepping up on the granite block and down on each turn.

Sweat was running down my legs, and my good white shirt was clinging to me. She had made me two, this short-sleeved one and a long-sleeved one for school, from two of my father's old ones that had split down the back. Before I could even try them on she had said: "Now, go tear them up like you do everything else." Someone had told me she didn't even hear herself but I heard her.

Gradually I would steal glances at the house and the porch roof where my mother was sitting on the leather cushion, her back to the bricks, the newspaper held stretched out in front of her. The black-and-white skirt of her voile afternoon dress tucked neatly around her ankles. It would never have occurred to her to call or shout over such a distance. Dying, she would have had more dignity than that.

When I started to wheeze from the jumping and from the heat, I moved cautiously to the shade of the pecan tree in the side yard. Few in those days had fences that Southerners would have considered hostile, and so the yards were tactfully separated by bushes and hedges. (The azalea craze had not yet hit the Carolinas and so between our house and the Athertons' next door was a rosebush on a three-foot retaining wall the length of the yard.) Mr. and Mrs. Atherton were sitting in their side yard, almost hidden by the wall and roses. I sat playing with pecan shells on the grass almost above their heads. They could not see me and I could not see my mother.

After a long while and much rustling of the paper, Mrs. Atherton said, "Is that what I think it is?" She was looking at our roof.

"It is," Mr. Atherton said, glancing discreetly over the top of his paper. He was from Charleston, not really even from Charleston, just the outskirts, some even said Summerville, and had married a woman from Pennsylvania and always acted as if he had married beneath himself.

"What is she doing up there?" Mrs. Atherton asked.

Mr. Atherton coughed, meaning lower your voice, and said, "Reading the paper, obviously."

For a long while Mrs. Atherton thought about what she had been told, then dared a reprimand by asking: "But why is she reading it up there?"

Mr. Atherton turned a page and said, "I'm sure she has her reasons."

Mrs. Atherton had to ponder that but finally said: "I wonder what they are."

"They think it may be the work of a foreigner. From the ransom notes."

"Oh," Mrs. Atherton said, befuddled by the mixture of national and local news. She began fanning herself with a palm-leaf church fan with a mortuary ad stenciled on it. "I hope she's found a little breeze up there." She sounded confident that that was why my mother was out on the roof. By then people walking home from work began slowing and looking up at our roof, then people in cars were beginning to slow, puzzled over the loitering pedestrians, and then they, too, were staring up at my mother.

"When are you going to quit trying to mind other people's business?" Mr. Atherton asked.

"I . . ." she began. "It just seems a little odd to me, her sitting out there on the roof . . ."

"It's her roof," Mr. Atherton insisted.

"And her paper," Mrs. Atherton agreed quickly, "I suppose."

At the moment, it didn't seem an especially safe place for me to be. A few people had stopped dead on the sidewalk and were looking up, whispering, then moseying along.

I dropped the pecan shell canoes and ran to the backyard and the watermelon. Some mornings I was given a nickel and it was my job to buy the biggest watermelon I could get for the money. I had made friends with an old black man who had a mule and a wagon full of straw and watermelons. He enjoyed my bargaining and would even tote the watermelon, too heavy for me, to the gazebo. Now, slapping the cool watermelon, I could feel it tremble and knew the heart held but was almost ready to fall out when sliced. I stood absolutely still and slapped my own chest to make it tremble and wondered when my heart would be ripe. The watermelon was the best bargain I'd got since the Fourth of July, huge and exactly ripe. It almost seemed that the day had not gone all wrong and crazy.

Ordinarily my father drove into the driveway and parked under the oak trees, but today I did not hear him. He had parked on the street and I saw him only as he came up the gravel drive. Trying not to run but swinging his arms in a fast pace. He didn't even stop to talk about the perfect watermelon. "Why is the front door locked?" We never locked it except when the circus was in town. He didn't wait for an answer but was up the back steps and through the screen door.

It didn't seem like an especially safe place here in the gazebo, either. So I played a bit until I was behind the four fig trees, which were covered with linen napkins drying in the sun. I was almost hidden from the house.

I lay in the itchy grass and listened as my brothers came home on bicycles and I could hear my sisters playing a duet on the piano, and the rattling of china and clinking of water goblets and ice through the dining room windows. I wanted to cry, wondering if I'd be allowed to have supper, or watermelon at least. Or if I would be allowed back in the house. Again I wished I had a collie dog to cuddle up to even if I would have an asthma attack. (Why did my brothers tease me and tell me asthma was "smother's love"?)

It was funny: Here I was dripping with sweat in the same spot where in the winter I had been lying on the ground "like a dunce" freezing. That February day Dr. Rutledge had made a house call and had brought a New York doctor with him because my mother had fainted twice. Once in the kitchen and once in the back hall, where I had found her. They could not stop her "flooding."

Dr. Rutledge had explained that "flooding" meant bleeding and that was why she was so white and needed to stay off her feet. Both said they had never heard of a case of menopause so obdurate or so corrosive. I did not understand what they were talking about but I did understand when they said someone needed to be with her every moment. She was no longer nervous and angry and I wanted to be the one to be with her.

I sat in the darkened room and held my breath so I could see if she was breathing or not. She was lying, her back to me, fully clothed, with my delivery blanket over her shoulders. I tried not to make a sound. But suddenly she was nervous again and said, "I can't stand all that hovering. I'm not going to die. Go on out and play. Anywhere." When I didn't move, she said: "Just please go. Get out!"

Now, sweating in the tall grass, I wondered if she were up on the roof bleeding. I wanted to sneak along the house to see if blood was gushing or even dripping out of the downspout from the porch. Would the blood turn the daisies red? Did people push up red daisies? I lay so still even a snail couldn't have seen me move.

Finally, feeling I had dozed off, I could hear my sisters on the back steps calling my name, and then my father's voice. I could see him ducking under the fig trees, coming to get me. I curled up on my side and shut my eyes, pretending to be asleep.

"It's all right," he said. He was stooping down beside me and his firm hand was large on my shoulder. "We won't ever mention it," he promised. "None of us." And no one ever did.

Max Steele's name appeared first on the cover of *Harper's Magazine* in 1944, and more recently on that of the December 1998 issue. Between those two dates the reluctant, reclusive author has, in his own words, published a few books, taught in a few universities, received a few honorary degrees and prizes, and taught more than a few now-published and famous writers.

He was head of the Creative Writing program at UNC from 1966 to 1987 and will return there in this, his eightieth year, to teach.

DIANA STEELE

Recently when I was Writer-in-Residence at Bennington I met up again with that great minimalist writer, Amy Hempel, and became fascinated again by short-shorts.

So when an editor from The Washington Post *phoned and asked if I would write a short piece for the magazine section about summer, I said "yes" instead of my usual "no." Before I put down the phone I had a vivid image of a watermelon in my head.*

From fifty years of writing I knew to follow any image, or character, or line of dialogue that presents itself at such a moment. So when I pressed the ripe piece of the imaginary watermelon to the roof of my mouth, the story was there, intact.

The Post *specified nonfiction.* New Stories from the South *contains fiction. I would swear in any court that "Unripe Heart" is nonfiction. I would swear in the same court that it is fiction. I would swear anywhere that I pay no attention to academic labels and distinctions in trying to tell the truth.*

Aaron Gwyn

OF FALLING

(from *Louisiana Literature*)

George Crider was seven when Freddie was born, fifteen before his brother grew big enough to sit a horse. In the summers, after their chores were done, the boys would ride bareback across the pasture to a persimmon grove, spend their afternoons climbing the thin trees for fruit.

One day the animal they were riding stepped in a sinkhole and bucked. George caught hold of its mane, but his brother was behind him and fell to the ground. The boy's arm broke the skin, and the bone jutted into dirt. He developed tetanus and in two weeks was dead. George blamed himself for this, as did his parents, and at the funeral, when he climbed into the grave and sought to open the casket, his father lost two teeth trying to retrieve him.

Two years later, grown to well over six feet, he slid a razor in his hip pocket, a change of clothes in his knapsack, and without saying good-bye, walked for forty miles through the Quashita forest until he came to Highway 3, hitching across Oklahoma in the back of a cattle truck. He went to work in the oil field and bought a new car, kept a shotgun underneath his seat, sawed at the stock and barrel. One night he left for Louisiana and came back a week later with a Cajun woman, named Hattie, whom he had taken to wife.

Everyone thought George unflappable. He was tall and lean,

with a hard, lean face, and expressionless eyes. He did not talk about himself, or his brother, or his parents back in Shinewell, pastors of a Pentecostal church. He was quiet and felt no need to speak. The men he worked with respected him, for they knew he was strong and stubborn, and they would not have wanted to face him in a fight, fair or otherwise.

Then, in 1933, working the eighth floor of a drilling rig in Pontotoc County, scaffolding gave way, and George fell 116 feet onto the bank of a saltwater pit.

He did not remember this. Not the fabric blowing against his limbs, or the girders moving past, or the platform where he had stood traveling into sky. It took him nearly four seconds to reach the ground, but he could not recall them. For him there was only the eighth floor and the earth.

Through the years that followed, he would recount the incident for his wife: the stares of the men who found him, the ambulance and hospital, the doctor who examined him from top to toe as if he were a puzzle. He would tell her about watching the clouds change to ceiling tile, the sun to bright lamps and mirrors. He would tell about sandstone pressing into his back like shards of bone, and then the cool of the sheets, the anesthetic.

Yet, stretched beneath the shadow of the derrick, George's first thoughts were not of family, or friends, the condition of his soul, or whether he would be able to one day move his legs. His thoughts were not of the porch standing unfinished, the clothesline needing repair, the foundation wall that had shown signs of flaking just the day before. His thoughts were not of what he would lose in this world, gain or lose in the world hereafter.

Lying there with the sky weighing down and the wind moving over and across him, George had considered only the boards that had snapped beneath his feet. With his lower lip clenched between his teeth, he watched himself walk to where they lay at the side of the derrick and kick them to splinters.

• • •

The fall had broken both his arms, his legs, six of his ribs at their connecting points. His skull was fractured and his sternum snapped in half. The doctor who admitted him said he would not live through the night.

He lived regardless. Through that night, and the night after, and the night after that.

The doctors said it was a wonder; they said it was a phenomenon. One stood in the middle of his hospital room and pronounced it a miracle. And though he said George would never walk, he thought he might, one day, have a life of some kind.

In two years George was walking. In two more he had returned to work. By the time he reached his mid-thirties, George was as spry as any roughneck in the state. He was promoted to foreman, and through the depression years, when many left to seek work elsewhere, George and his wife began to build a collection of antique glassware. If he chose, he could retire young, live comfortably off his pension and what he had invested in glass rarities.

George seemed much the same as before the fall. To see him pull to the curb in his burgundy Pontiac, step out and approach an antique shop—a tall, slender man, graceful as a dancer, with jet-black hair, and eyes like drops of oil—you would not have thought he had fallen in his life. Not even from the height of a chair.

It was along this time, along the time George stacked his crutches in the rear of the closet and poured his vial of laudanum down the sink, that the dreams came.

They were not, as one would think, dreams of falling, the body released from its federation with the earth and betrayed to gravity. Neither were they dreams of collision, of impact. The dreams that visited George after his fall were of stillness.

In them, he would be lying in a field, feeling drops of sweat run into his eyes and pool around the sockets. When he attempted to raise his hand and wipe them, he could not. His ears itched; his face and neck. His body burned. He lay among the blades of grass, blinking into sky.

Soon there was a cloud. It was small at first. If he had been able, George could have retrieved a quarter from his pocket, held it at arm's length, and eclipsed the cloud entirely. But as it grew, he would have needed a fifty-cent piece, a silver dollar, and then, even with both hands outspread and extended in front of his face, wisps of gray would have bled the edges of his fingers.

There was nothing about the cloud to warrant fear. It was not boiling and black, or streaked with light. There was no rumbling, and it gave no sound. This was not the type of cloud from which angels or prophets descend.

Only, lying there beneath it, George came to know death in the stillness of wide and all but empty sky.

He awoke screaming. He awoke on the floor. The doctors said such dreams were common among those who had fallen. They gave him pills of all sizes, but the dreams did not stop.

Then one night he awoke running through the house, glassware rattling on the mahogany furniture. Hattie watched him from their doorway.

"Crider," she called, "you'll break everything we own."

She was right; several vases lay broken already.

When he wakened and was asked what he had been dreaming, George went out to his car and fell asleep across the seats. The next morning, he was sitting on the front stoop of Sharp's department store when the owner unlocked the doors.

George purchased four belts, fastened each to the other, and threaded them between his mattress and box springs. Each night he brought the ends together and buckled himself beneath his quilts.

Years passed in this way, with George awaking early every morning strapped to his bed. His wife began sleeping across the hall, and when they stayed in motels, made him reserve nonadjoining rooms.

Visitors seldom came, but when they did, Hattie would take them on a tour of their home. By then every surface in the house—

sideboard, dining and coffee table, ottoman, divan—was covered in antique glass. Hattie had acquired the largest collection in Perser and was slowly overtaking Herbert Nasser and his wife, Vinita, who made claim of the largest in Oklahoma.

Her guests followed her through the small, dark house, through the smell of must and old wood. There were two bedrooms, a bath, a small kitchen crowded with dining table and stove. None of the window blinds or curtains were open; Hattie feared those passing on the sidewalk would see inside. The worth of her collection was estimated at over thirty thousand dollars.

"This piece is very old," she would tell her visitors, pointing to a candy dish. "I found it in a filling station outside Shreveport."

They nodded, ran their hands along its rim.

"And this piece," Hattie said, "I didn't think the man would part with it."

They nodded again, looked to their watches.

She would conclude her tour by showing George's room, the straps on his bed. The guests looked at her husband. They wanted to know how long it had been, if he would mind telling the story of his fall.

He would tell it. He knew it by rote: the platform, the derrick, the hospital, the dreams. It took him only fifteen minutes.

When he finished, his audience shook their heads. Often they reached to squeeze his hand or touch him on the arm. Sometimes they turned to Hattie and forced a smile.

She smiled back, gestured to George.

"This is what I have to live with," she would tell them.

It was then 1957, the year Oral Roberts took a tent across the Midwest, bringing his revival to the lost and infirm. Hattie heard on the radio testimonies of those treated by Roberts. Some who had never walked made claim to walk. Some who had never seen claimed to see. Katherine Kuhlman was carried into his tent on a sheet and soon thereafter began a ministry of her own.

Hattie told her husband of this, and they drove 120 miles to a small town outside Tulsa where, for the past week, Roberts had held a tent revival. They arrived late and sat toward the back.

George found much of the service consonant with what he had known from his childhood. There was a stage, and a choir upon it, men in folding chairs dressed in ties, and slacks, and white shirts. There were rows and rows of similar chairs for the audience; stapled pages containing a few hymns; sawdust on the floor; carpets down the aisles. At midway through, paper buckets with crosses stenciled on them were passed for offering.

After Roberts delivered a brief sermon, he asked those in need of healing to form a line to the left of the stage. He told them it did not have to be physical healing.

"There are three kinds of healing," he told them. "There is physical healing, and emotional healing, and healing of the spirit." He said God could perform all three.

Hattie leaned over, whispered to George. He shook his head. She made to lean again, and he rose from his seat and stepped in line.

Roberts sat at the edge of the stage with a handkerchief in one hand, a bottle of olive oil in the other. He was a young man: long nose, a long, smooth face. His hair was combed with tonic and laid back upon his head, as was the fashion. He wore a plain white shirt, a tie, gray slacks, polished black shoes. Between his legs, he straddled a microphone.

Folks came and stood in front of the stage, handed one of Roberts's assistants an index card upon which was written their names and the names of their afflictions. These were in turn handed to Roberts.

George examined the blank card and the pencil he had been passed moments before. He looked back to the evangelist, who was addressing an elderly woman with braces on her legs.

"How long have you had this, sister?"

"I been this way since I was twenty-two," the woman told him.

Roberts poured oil into the palm of one hand and told her to come close. He leaned over the edge of the stage, put the hand to her cheek, and lifted the other toward the ceiling, praying into the microphone.

"Lord," he prayed, "deliver her."

The woman began to shiver, and then her body became rigid, and she fell backward onto the ground. A man in a dark suit came and covered her legs with a blanket. Another approached the stage, handed up her card, and George watched all this feeling of a sudden as if someone had hollowed him.

He made to turn, but just then, one of Roberts's assistants happened down the line. He noticed George's card was blank, touched him on the elbow, and inquired after his affliction.

George shook his head, tried to step around the man, but found himself blocked by a row of card tables piled with books and pamphlets.

The man looked askance, leaned toward him, and George quickly told the story of his fall. When he finished, the other's face had an amazed look. He took George by the arm, parted the crowd, and led him onto the stage. They stood to the side while Roberts prayed, and then the man went to the evangelist and whispered something.

Roberts turned. He stood, took the microphone from its stand, and walked to George. The crowd quieted. Roberts's voice in the microphone was wet, and very loud.

"Tell these people your name."

George shifted from one foot to the other. He brought a hand from behind his back and scratched at his nose. "George Crider," he said.

"And you had an accident?" Roberts asked him.

"Yes."

"You fell?"

"Yes."

"How far?"

"One hundred sixteen feet."

Many in the crowd gasped; some called out to God.

"And you were hurt?"

"Yes."

"How many bones did you break?"

"All of them," George said.

The preacher put his hand on George's shoulder.

"And what did the doctors say?"

George paused, looked down. "They told me I would never walk again."

There were a few moments of silence. Then the crowd began to stir and then to applaud. They cried in loud voices, and most all raised their hands to the ceiling. One man left his seat and began to run up and down the aisles.

Roberts turned to face them. "Do you hear that?" he said. "The God that did this can do the same for you. The same God who caused this brother to walk after breaking every bone in his body, can grant you your deliverance."

More folk left their seats and stepped in line. The preacher stood above them like an auctioneer.

George was led from the stage. He saw Hattie waiting for him near the ramp.

As he was about to walk away, the man who had discovered him asked if he would return the next night to give his testimony. George shook his head, took his wife by the arm, and escorted her from the tent.

It was more than twenty years before he would see another faith healer. In this time George retired from his job and began collecting his pension. He and Hattie traveled most the year, visiting antique shows, conventions, fairs, and galleries. They acquired piece after piece, and, in the 1969 edition of the *Carnival Glass Anthology,* there was a black-and-white photo of his wife standing next to a bookcase full of Depression-era teacups.

But, however great Hattie's satisfaction, George's condition grew worse. His hands would often shake and occasionally his vision blur. The man slept only two or three hours a night and at times would go days on no sleep at all, walking through his afternoons with a glazed look. He did not talk about the dreams or the ailments that made him unfamiliar to his body. He refused to go back to the doctors or turn to the God of his father. He refused to take the shotgun from under the seat of the car and place the barrel in his mouth. Regardless, he found himself polishing the gun once or twice a month, breaking it over at the dining room table to check the shells.

In Denton, Texas, one night, Hattie forced him into a revival meeting held by the Reverend R. W. Shambauch. She told George that life with him had caused her to need healing of the spirit. George watched the woman leave her seat, walk the aisle, and take her place at the end of Shambauch's prayer line. Her husband retrieved a hymnal from beside his chair and began to flip the pages.

Shambauch was an older man from Baton Rouge, Louisiana, who clothed his enormous body in immense black suits. He had fat features and a kind face, bushed eyebrows, pale eyes, a sweep of gray hair. The preacher smelled of strong cologne and sweat.

He stood down from the platform with a microphone, laying hands on those that came through his line. In front of each, he would pray loudly, examining the ceiling as people fell away from his thick fingers to the arms of an assistant.

At one point, George could no longer watch. He walked to the lobby, found a restroom, and then a vending machine. He went to purchase candy, but the parcel caught in a loop of the wire that held it. When he came back to the auditorium, his wife stood before the massive preacher. George crossed his arms to him and watched from the wings.

His wife seemed small from the distance. She was a petite woman still, short and of Creole descent, with gunmetal-colored hair pinned in an intricate bun. He watched her eyes close as Shambauch's hand came near her forehead, watched both Hattie's arms rise. He continued watching as her body went suddenly straight and she fell backward into the arms of Shambauch's man. She was laid on the ground, covered with a blanket.

"Slain," Shambauch said over the swell of the organ, "slain in the Spirit."

The next night Hattie persuaded George to return to Shambauch's meeting, where she again approached the prayer line and soon lay sprawled on the floor.

A month later, in Biloxi, Mississippi, George would watch his wife fall from the hands of the Reverend Shambauch, and two months later in Little Rock, and six later in Atlanta. Hattie began keeping two schedules on her refrigerator, one of antique conventions, one of Shambauch's camp meetings. And several years later, when Hattie stepped from the prayer line in front of the man of God, he held the microphone away from his face and asked where he knew her from.

Hattie smiled, raised both hands, and braced herself for the fall.

Years passed. Numb years of sickness and pain. Hattie continued seeing Shambauch when the preacher came within driving distance of Perser. If George was too ill to take her, Hattie would phone a nephew to do so, and when he could not oblige, the woman closed the door to her bedroom and watched the broadcast on TBN.

In the past, George had been a quiet man; he was utterly silent now. He did not answer his wife's questions, and when visitors called, he would retreat to his work shed behind the house. He was in considerable pain but took nothing for it. His lower back had deteriorated, his shoulders and hips. Some mornings it would take him upward of an hour to rise from bed. The dreams, as ever, continued to shake him, and he spent much time weighing the benefits of life and death.

Then one evening Hattie fell from the back porch. The woman was putting out bread for squirrels, and she slipped, snapping her leg below the knee. From the shed, George heard his wife's screaming. He managed to position her in the backseat of the car, drive her to the hospital. When they sent her home with a cast and crutches, it was George who helped her to bathe, brought her meals, took her from place to place.

"George," Hattie would say. "I need to go."

George would trundle in, assist the woman across their home, stand outside the bathroom door waiting.

It was late that summer when the First Perser Pentecostal Church of God brought in Leslie Snodgrass, an evangelist of fifteen, already known across Oklahoma and much of Arkansas. People said amazing things of the boy. They claimed signs and wonders, miracles and healing and salvation of the lost. He played the piano and sang, preached of fire and Christ, prayed over the hopelessly ill. The young man came from a small town outside Tahlequah and had been preaching since the age of six. He was short and fair and very thin, but his voice was the voice of a man three times his years, and audiences watched him with an amazed look. The elders in the crowd would shout and sing, and sinners sat with whitened faces, sinking quietly down in their seats. When Snodgrass ended his sermons, old and young alike, all souls in various stages of deliverance and damnation, would fall into the altars to seek mercy. He knelt among them and, when moved, stood to his feet and walked about, laying hands on the sick and troubled of spirit.

Hattie heard of this. It was all over Perser, the same week as the town's annual celebration of the oil boom. She began asking George to take her to Snodgrass. She wanted to see her leg heal quickly.

This took much effort for George had decided some time before he could not endure another service. But his wife was persistent, and in a matter of nights George found himself sitting in the pew along the rear wall of the church, listening to the words of Leslie Snodgrass.

The man watched the evangelist with an expression no less amazed than those around him. It was indeed a sight to astonish. The boy moved about like one possessed, holding his eyes tightly shut, wads of tissue paper clenched in his fists. There were hard men who had seen him preach and could not return to lives of sin, but, by this point, George believed only in anguish, for that, he felt, was the certainty of the world, and though mesmerized by the boy pacing the platform above him, he did not recover his faith.

The boy's sermon ended with an altar call, and the altars were soon full. George sat with open eyes, staring over the bowed heads. People knelt, wrestling with their spirits. Occasionally, an elder among them would raise his voice in travail. All prayed for what seemed a very long time, and then Snodgrass rose, approached the platform, and asked those in need of healing to come forward. Hattie began tugging at George's sleeve, wanting him to help her there.

George quietly took her by the hand, helped her to her feet, placed the crutches beneath her arms. The couple paced out into the aisle and began inching toward the people arced across the front of the church. George and Hattie walked to the building's far right. He made sure of his wife and then leaned his shoulder against the wall beside him to take the weight from his back.

He watched Snodgrass make his way down the line. The boy had no microphone; no handkerchief or oil. He would stop and speak quietly with each, bow his head and whisper, sometimes laying a pale hand to the person's shoulder. He was exceeding calm, the boy.

George watched all of this surprised to see the people standing. They did not fall; they did not quake or run the aisles. They stood their places with broken looks, the wise looks of the condemned.

George noticed his wife, who was also watching the boy, but her face held a bitter expression, more so the closer Snodgrass came. She seemed to realize the evangelist would not lay hands to her forehead. He would not send her to the carpet, and no assistant would stand behind her waiting with arms and a blanket. Hattie would go home much the same as she came, and seeing this, George began to chuckle quietly.

The boy came closer, and Hattie's face grew harsher still, and as he was praying for the man next to her, she took up her crutches and spun from the line, casting George derision as she turned.

George watched his wife go up the aisle, past the pew where

they formerly sat, out the double doors into the lobby. A louder laugh escaped his lips. When he brought his eyes back around, his face was cracked from the smiling, and Snodgrass stood in front of him.

George's laughter died, and he watched the evangelist with a heavy expression. The boy was utterly ashen, and he walked sternly up, raised his hand, and placed it to the old man's chest, closing his eyes to mumble a few words. He did not catch them. Only, the moment they left the boy's lips, the audience beheld George Crider fall like lightning.

It did not seem so to George. To him his descent seemed to take a very long time. At first there was the feeling that his legs had given way, his limbs wilted to nothing. He sensed his arm go numb and a terrific burst go off in his chest just to the left of where the boy had touched him. He felt warm there and very still, and the air that buzzed about his ears was like fire.

There was time for George to consider many things before he struck the ground, to consider a time before dreams troubled his sleep, before an injury placed him in a hospital bed. He considered walking forty miles through the Quashita forest, under the pines and cedars of southeast Oklahoma, and then the time of his boyhood under the dense trees, before his brother had fallen, before he had a brother at all. He considered when it was only he, and his mother, and his father, when they would pick him off the ground, only a child of four years then, place him in the center of a patchwork quilt, and lift him, allowing the boy to leave the fabric for a moment before he sank back into its folds. They repeated this for what seemed like hours—though it could not have been so long—the thin child rising and falling, caught up, snapped into the air.

It was weightless, that sense, the stomach a rush, face and arms and legs prickling, the heart feeling as if it might split. Rising and falling, and again, and over. If it had always been like that, there would have been point in nothing else but to live in the instant when gravity first took hold and pulled you to its center.

George considered this of all things as he abandoned himself to the fall, unaware he would expire some sixteen inches above the shag carpet and that his body would strike the floor with a hollow sound.

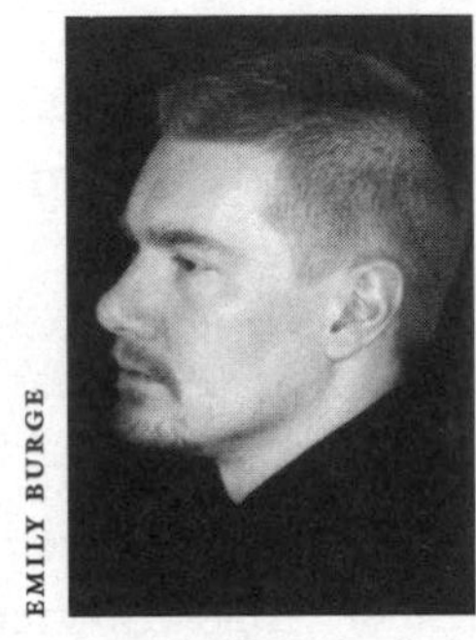
EMILY BURGE

Born in 1972, Aaron Gwyn grew up on a farm in south-central Oklahoma. He received a Masters in English from Oklahoma State University and is currently completing his Ph.D. at the University of Denver, where he teaches composition, literature, and creative writing. His stories have appeared in *The Chiron Review*, *Appalachian Heritage*, *Louisiana Literature*, and elsewhere, and he has fiction forthcoming in an anthology from Three Women Press. "Of Falling" is one of the stories in *Dog on the Cross*, a story-cycle he recently completed and for which he is presently seeking a publisher.

In a fashion fairly untypical for a writer as slow as myself, I wrote the initial draft of "Of Falling" in about a week's time. The story is loosely based on a great-uncle of mine, my grandmother's brother, who fell off an oil derrick at the age of sixty-one and experienced an almost full, and somewhat miraculous, recovery. Since fact was much stranger than fiction in this instance, I had to make the "George" character much younger than he actually was at the time of his fall so that his recovery would be believable. After the initial draft, I began to see the possibility of rendering a person's life by examining the repetition of certain actions that dominate it—in this context, falling. It was at this point that the story became much less about my uncle—no one's life being quite as pat as a short story—and much more about the external principles that shape our existence.

Dulane Upshaw Ponder

THE RAT SPOON

(from *The South Carolina Review*)

I met Minna and Harold," my great-grandmother told me, "on the very same November day my Mama died. I was eight years old. My Papa, then a Colonel in the Georgia Seventh, had been travelling down from North Georgia since April when the call came for the able-bodied to defend Atlanta. But there were Northern troops spread out through all the pine woods and mountains, and we didn't know if Papa was even alive. In June, Brown Sally left to go down to Jonesboro where her boys were. That left Mama and me alone. Mostly I remember being hungry and scratching the bloody rash that covered my arms and legs because we didn't have any vegetables to eat. All that summer, the Yankees burned Atlanta yard by yard. The sun rose and set behind a pall, and the black rains fell. One day a red twister cut along Peachtree Creek and the next day, fish fell from a green sky. Those lucky enough to get some of those trout before they rotted said they tasted like gunpowder. Once, thousands of brown rabbits ran in a sweep that covered half a mile, so many that the porch of the house creaked with them as they passed over. Mama got some in a pillowcase so we had meat for the first time in six months.

One morning when Mama and I were picking pine needles for tea, the trees began to whipsaw and the ground jumped up beneath us. During the darkness, Yankee artillery had drawn up behind

Hickory Ridge. Their guns were aimed at the Chattanooga railway three miles away but the Parrott guns couldn't find the range. A four-hundred-pound shell brought down most of the second story of the house and landed in the woodlot. That shell hole today is still there, but now it's Woodlot Pond. Only my bedroom on the end with the fireplace remained of the whole upstairs. During the shelling, we crawled into the trash pit where we spent all that day. There were snakes in the trash pit and other things that sometimes stirred. I wanted to scream but Mama said it's just the rustle of your petticoats. We shook and shook in that ditch but Mama held me until the guns stopped. It was early evening and the moon rose in the blue daylight sky. We waited for the soldiers to come. Mama began to cry and I did too when we heard the sound of rolling wagons. But it must have been a trick of the weather because the army never came. I later learned they passed to the West near Howell's Mill—so many horses, cannon, and men pounding the earth that what was left of the old Chapman place collapsed as they marched by. When we climbed out of the ditch, we noticed the smell for the first time. Something's dead nearby, Mama said, and we ran back fast to the house to get away from it. But the smell went with us; it was a part of us. That evening the last songbirds I would see for a season or more lay on the ground in the moonlight; they had been knocked from the branch as the shell passed over them. We ate them, too, a robin and a flicka bird with a nice fat breast. Nothing rustled, twittered, or squirmed outside that night and the air hung around us like damp laundry. It was the start of the silent time. After the guns stopped that day, we never heard a sound we didn't make ourselves. Except, of course, for the wind. It flew through the shattered trees, screaming like Charles Upton did in the barn when the doctor sawed off his right foot after the Battle of Kennesaw.

We were the last people in those parts. We stayed because Mama wanted to be there when Papa came home. When Brown Sally left, she tried to get us to go down south with her. But Mama wanted to stay. She gave Brown Sally a pound of meal, a black pot, and an iron spoon to stir it with. Tie that meal around your waist and hide it under your skirt, Mama told her. There are some who would kill you for it. Brown Sally gave Mama and me a green bead with yellow spots on it; then she walked off the front porch and into the sorghum field. We never saw her again.

Mrs. Carter came by in her wagon one afternoon on the way to Savannah. Her husband was one of the first to be killed in the War. He died when a man riding in front of him was hit by a mortar fragment. That man's teeth were blown from his jaw, striking Captain Carter in the temple. The day Mrs. Carter rode by our house for the last time, she told us of another tragedy. I'll never forget her face as she told us the fate of her two twin boys, Ethan and Peter. Just twelve years old and killed over at Westpoint in the fighting, ten days before. I still remember those boys today; they had dark red hair and matching chestnut ponies with blond manes and tails. A lot of little boys and old men died defending Atlanta; they were part of Joe Brown's Georgia Militia; they were all that was left of the Confederate army. That day, Mrs. Carter told Mama and me she'd set fire to her own house so no Yankee could ever step inside and defile the memories there. There's nothing left for me here, she told us. All the while Mrs. Carter was talking, Old Professor Carter sat in the back of the wagon on a stack of red leather-bound books, drinking whiskey and lecturing his class on Cicero. I never thought I'd ever be driving mules, she told us, but as you see I have no choice in the matter. And that was the last time we saw the Carters.

Mr. Bateman left that summer, too. He had a farm east of us where they mostly grew corn and raised pigs. We had a lot of good hams from the Bateman's in the early part of the War but toward the end, those pigs had all been slaughtered except for a few that went wild in the woods. One of those wild hogs came to the back of the house one day, and Mama tried to hit it on the head with a board while it was drinking in the creek. It turned on Mama and chased her back to the house. She hardly got the back door closed when it charged up the porch. Later I learned that one of the Bateman pigs ate a dead Confederate who'd been shot in a raid near the Chattanooga line. I also heard the Yankees ate that pig; I heard all kinds of stories, and now I believe that most of them were true. Mr. Bateman tried to persuade Mama to leave our home. But she wouldn't budge. Miss Mamie, he said, you are a very beautiful young woman; you shouldn't be up here all alone. Mr. Bateman, Mama said, I can't leave here until the Colonel comes. This farm is what he's fighting for. Thank you, but we are staying. And then Mr. Bateman gave Mama a little pistol and three bullets and said, there's one bullet for them and two for you, Miss Mamie. And then he said, good-bye Miss Mamie; good-bye Miss Lily. And he gave us a bushel of shelled corn and half a ham. I never saw Mr. Bateman again.

Strangers came along sometimes, too. I remember a lady who drove up one day in August dressed in a peach velvet gown. There was nothing in her wagon but a ten-foot tall chifforobe lying on its side. Inside the chifforobe was an old Master. One corner of the canvas had begun to blister from the heat. I drove here all alone from Marietta, she said, and I expect at some time soon to die because I have no food, no home or family. All I have left is this chifforobe and this painting by the Dutchman Frans Hals. My Mama had her over to the porch, where she gave her some water and a corn cake. Then we took the painting from the chifforobe and threw some cool water on the surface and the blisters collapsed. We cut the frame away. Then we covered the canvas with damp grass and rolled it up. I don't think that painting survived the War, though, because I never heard again of a Frans Hals with two cavaliers laughing against a blue ground.

Other strangers came. Some weren't friendly and we hid in the cellar as they rode by. We buried all our food in tins so if we were discovered in the cellar, we couldn't be robbed. When we hid, Mama always kept that pistol near. The last people we saw pulled up to the edge of the property in a fever wagon drawn by two black mules wearing black head plumes. Nobody drove those mules; they were led along on a twenty-foot rein held by a young black boy. We could hear children crying and a woman reciting the funeral service for the dead. That little boy came up to the porch to ask if he could wet some sheets to wrap his sick in. Mama said yes and helped him put the sheets down in the creek so the water could wash away the bloody flux. He told Mama, Those people are the Harrises, and they're going as far as they can get. I'm going, too, because they gave me this. And he showed us a gold and diamond stock pin that he'd sewn to the inside of his vest. If I don't die, he said, I'll be rich.

Now, in those days, even before the War, there were as many funerals as there were christenings. But once supplies were confiscated at the ports and the army had eaten up everything on the land, sickness and death marched through what was left of the South like the Devil's own brigade. And, of course, nobody knew why the fever might kill one and spare another. Malaria, yellow fever, tuberculosis, cholera, typhoid, dysentery, small pox—they took as many as the bullet and the bayonet, and maybe more. Some fled together, like the Harrises, who could still pray. Some stayed by their loved ones, and others denied them even a sip of cool water from a long-handled dipper. Some resorted to whiskey, others to bathing in their own urine, and some secretly carried mojos given to them by their black servants. But nothing really worked.

Well, Mama must have been sick for a long while before I noticed it. She was thin, and she was tired. But I was thin, too, and a child is always tired when asked to fetch something, make a bed, or stir the fire. I just couldn't see that Mama wasn't well. And when she would say, honey, I'm doing ten for forty today, I thought it was the natural state of things. We didn't have an easy life, being cold most of the time and being hungry. After the Yankee shell fell on the house, we had to move over to the cookhouse. All the windows in the house were broken. The big mirrors at the two ends of the parlor had come off the wall and the pieces were strewn like knives across the floor. The cut velvet on the divan rotted as the rain came in and the veneer cracked off the furniture. We stripped the highboy and put the veneer in the cookstove for kindling; it burned hot because of the French polish.

As I said, Mama must have been sick. I just didn't want to know. I wanted her to do for me the same as always. I wanted her to clean up the glass and sew up the sofa. I wanted chicken for dinner, and I wanted my doll still upstairs in my room, which was the only thing left above after the shelling. I wanted her to climb the swaying stairs and bring me the doll my Papa had given me. I knew those stairs were dangerous, but I didn't care. I wanted Mama to do what she'd always done for me, which was everything. I wanted her to do for me no matter what the cost. You know, anybody who says a child is a joy is a fool. A child thinks of nothing but itself. I know I did. As my Mama grew dull, for that's what she did, sitting and looking out the door of the cookhouse, I grew sharp with temper and a growing contempt for my Mama's lack of interest in pushing the world where I thought it should go.

Mama was sick. But it wasn't a fever or a pox or any of those other things that killed so many during the War. It was the awful tiredness Mama felt at just being alive during a time when so much happened that she'd never bargained for. She never imagined she'd wind up wearing a coat made from a Turkish rug. She never thought she would eat bitter green hickory nuts because she couldn't wait three weeks until they ripened. I hate this house, she would say. But I knew she meant I hate this house because it is broken and empty and I am alone. She wasn't, of course, alone. But she felt that way. She wanted somebody to give her what she'd always had—which was everything. We both wanted everything because we were used to it—at least before the War.

Mama got to the point where she didn't hear me most of the time. I would talk to her about Papa, how he was coming home to help us, how he would go out hunting with his rifle and we would have venison steaks—how he would rebuild the second story of the house, put in new windows, and cut enough hardwood to last for three winters. She would just sit in that ladder-back kitchen chair and watch the fire die down. I'm cold, she would say, put in some more of that pitch pine, but not so much that we burn what's left of the house down.

It was the first part of November when Mama started going to the smokehouse. She would say to me, eat your breakfast, what there is of it, so I can have some peace. And there she would go, down the path, carrying a little bag with her, down to the smokehouse where she would go in and put the big bolt up on the doors. I'd ask her what she was doing in there, and she would tell me to mind my own business and do my chores. But I could hear that shovel digging and digging. It would begin to get dark and she would still be in there. I'd call her—Mama, I made some corn pones and some dandelion stew. But she wouldn't come back to the cookhouse. Once I said to her, Mama it's so dark I had to follow the path in the moonlight. I knew it was blacker than coal itself in that smokehouse. But I still heard that digging. It's late, Mama. And she said, do you think I need light to do what I'm doing? Do you think time matters to me?

Days went by and Mama spent them shoveling dirt in the smokehouse. I stopped doing my chores. I stopped sweeping the cookhouse and shaking out the quilt. I left dishes dirty on the table and I only worked the pump when I was thirsty. I did the things I needed to do for me. I gathered dead wood and brought it in because I was cold. I made food because I was hungry. I went to the cellar and brought up the last sweet potatoes, and I roasted them. There were two of them, and I ate them both. I was proud of it. My Mama didn't care about me, so I had no use for her. She wouldn't come in until the moon had set and I was half asleep. She would sit in her chair and look out at the night. Her head would fall into her hands, and she would push back her hair over and over again. I couldn't talk to her, and she had nothing to say to me.

It went on this way for days until the afternoon when the music box began to play by itself. Mama went out the cookhouse door, which slammed behind her. Then the music box began to play 'When Johnnie Comes Marching Home.' Mama came in again and said to me, he's not coming back. Your Papa is never going to get back here. I can't forget him, Lily. But you can. You're young, and you should just get him out of your mind. I can't take it anymore, she said. I can't live my life just waiting and waiting while the house falls down, the food runs out, and the days get colder and colder. I'm twenty-six years old, and I look like a hag. Lily, she said, nobody ever told me it would be like this. I love you, but, you see, nobody ever told me. Then she took up that little bag she'd been carrying around with her and went down to the smokehouse.

I was glad to see her go. Being alone was easy. I could spin my dreams and turn my hopes to the day when Papa would come back to us. I remember getting the meal down from the shelf. It was the last ten pounds we had. I dug my hands into it and put some aside to hide away just for myself. I felt pleased that I could cheat my Mama that way. After all, she deserved it.

It rained hard that afternoon, and later the rain turned into sleet. I sat in front of the cookstove and tried to get wet wood to burn. Smoke seeped into the room, and the wood sizzled. It was very cold. It must have been about five o'clock when I heard the pistol shot. I ran out onto the smokehouse path. I called and called her as I went as fast as I could go. I pounded on the doors and called her again. The bar was up, and, of course, I couldn't break through. I stood there and listened to the sleet clatter like carpet tacks on the tin roof. Now, you might wonder why I didn't cry, why I didn't beat my head against the smokehouse doors and wail into the night. Well, by that time, just like my Mama, I was filled with a bitter wine. And a bitter wine moves you into a smoldering, dark place where your heart cannot speak. I never heard my Mama's voice again, but I can tell you that every day for the last ninety-some-odd years I have heard her saying to me, nobody ever told me it was going to be like this. I have cried about my Mama, cried and cried and still do, but I didn't cry that day or for a long time after that.

I didn't stay too long beside the smokehouse. I knew Mama was dead and there was nothing I could do about it. I went back to the cookhouse and decided right away to take all the things I would need and try to make it up those stairs to my room. I wanted to hold my beautiful doll and rock her in the little cradle my Papa had made for me. I went up the stairs to the landing ten times. Each time, I carried all that I could—the bag of meal, a sack of hickory nuts, a few candles and stubs, the little axe, the pail and cast iron pots filled with water, the wooden spoon, a china bowl and plate, two quilts, a box of matches, and the Bible, which I figured to use to start a fire by, tearing out the fragile pages as needed. On the tenth time up the stairs, I could hear the steps coming apart, and when I reached the landing, the whole staircase swung away over the downstairs hall. I knew then that I couldn't go back even if I wanted to. My fate was sealed. I lit one of the candles and opened the door to my room. It was cold. The big window was cracked, but it wasn't broken. Books had fallen from their shelves, and beneath them I found my baby doll. Her porcelain face was crushed. White dust circled her head like a halo. I tried to clutch her near, and a single blue eye rolled beneath the bureau. A kind of coldness came over me, colder than the room around me and colder than the night outside. I tried to walk over to the hearth though there was no fire. But I felt like I was walking in a freezing river, the current cutting around my skirts, my hands pulling back the icy waves. And then, I knew, just like Mrs. Carter, that I had to burn it all, everything that had been my life up to that time. I took the little axe, and I chopped at the legs of the bureau; I pulled out the drawers and emptied them on the floor. I chopped up the drawers too and ripped every bit of clothing into rags. I heaped everything into the fireplace and then I lit it. When the fire began to roar, I threw my doll baby in, and she burned until there was nothing left of her.

I guess something in me wanted to walk into that fire, too. But I was so close to my body then, being a child, that I couldn't do it. Couldn't do what Mama had done. I felt so tired and hungry that all I could hear was my stomach telling me to put something in it.

I knew I could do that—make something to eat, chew it up, and swallow it. So I made up some corn pone, put it in the skillet, and cooked it on the fire until it was brown. I ate all I could, which wasn't much, and put the rest aside on the hearth. I pulled the quilts over me and watched the fire as it worked around the curved mahogany feet of my dresser. I felt nothing inside of me but that cold river running around my heart. That is when Minna and Harold came to me.

It sounded like a little song being whistled a long way off and then a scratching like twigs against the windowpane. And then I saw them, two rats on the hearth. They were miserable-looking. Harold, which is what I named him, was a big fine rat about a foot long. But he was haggard. His amber brown fur clumped about his back and his tail was scaly and trembled as he tried to balance on it. Minna, his starving little wife, shook as she looked at me with her deep brown eyes. They raised their paws and groomed their whiskers nervously as they gazed at the skillet with the left-over pone. Now, I wasn't afraid because at that time I didn't feel anything at all. Or if I did feel anything, it was kinship with those two rats. I didn't move, and I stayed quiet, thinking those two will steal all they can get and they can have it, too. But I was wrong about Minna and Harold. Yes, they did help themselves to the little bit of dinner I'd made. But they were polite. They lifted up a bit of pone in their paws and nibbled it as they watched to see if I would try to chase them away. But I let them be because I was interested in them. I was interested because they were the only things alive in the world besides me. And in my world, I knew that things just happened to you no matter what you wanted or did. And so it happened that Minna and Harold came to me that night Mama died.

When I woke up the next morning, the sleet was still coming. Thunder pounded away somewhere far off and every now and then a lightning strike lit up my room in stripes through the louvered shutters. I surprised myself by being hungry and made up some more pone from the meal sack. Once the fire was going, I cooked my breakfast and waited. I was sure Minna and Harold would be back for their share, but they didn't come then. That day, the second day, I broke up more furniture with the little axe and fed the fire. I didn't wash because there wasn't enough water. I didn't drink any water for the same reason. Instead, I dipped my fingers into the bucket and sucked the drops off. Of course, I could have just hung that pail outside the window and let the sleet fall in. But I didn't think of it at the time. I guess I was just too young.

Well now, that day passed pretty slow, and most of it I spent trying not to think of anything that had happened. But at last the night began to come down, and I started cracking some hickory nuts. As you know, hickory nuts are not too meaty at best and getting those shells off took me some time. When I got a good handful of the edible parts, I did what I always did and made some little pones up, putting the nuts inside to roast on the fire. The smell of the meal was coming up nice, and those hickories added a little sweetness to the smell. By now it was true night outside. It was cold in spite of the fire. I don't know if it was the sweet roasting smell of the hickories, or whether it was the darkness or the cold, but I knew then on that second day that I had lost a piece of me and that I had an emptiness inside of me where once my Mama had been. I began to cry little tears that made such thin courses on my cheeks they felt like sewing thread. If I'd had any bourbon whiskey then, I would have drunk it until it filled every empty place in me. I suppose you could say that if a child could ever truly want to die, then I did at that time. But then, Minna and Harold came squeezing through that little gap between the bricks and the mantle. They sat down and they looked at me as the thin tears fell down my face. Their heads turned to the side; tiny fire reflections were mirrored in their black eyes. I broke off some bits of pone and placed them near me. They sat up and rubbed their paws together, and then they skittered closer to the meal. I stayed still the whole time until they were within a foot of me. Then I stuck out my hand and picked up the pone crumbs. They froze, and I was still again. I wanted them to touch me. I wasn't afraid. I wanted to feel their whiskers twitching against my hand. Minna was the first to eat from my hand. She reached for a bit and stuffed it into her cheeks. She backed up and stared at me to see what I would do. Harold chirped shrilly and held back. But when he saw that I held nothing against him, he came to me and had his share. When I had eaten my meal, I fed them the rest. They took each mouthful graciously, pausing afterward to watch what I would do. When the food was gone, they washed themselves by the fire and talked to each other quietly in their language of squeaks. When I fell asleep that night, Minna and Harold were still by the fire.

I don't really recall how many days I was up in that room. But the sleet kept coming. I would look through the shutters and I could see the grass standing up like silver needles while the hoar frost made little holes in the ground like shell shot. All that time, Minna and Harold came to me. Closer and closer we got until, one day, I coaxed Minna into my lap and she lay still while I used my hair brush to clear the dander from her coat. She was getting plumper and so was Harold, who never quite trusted me as she did. What happened to me during that time in the room, I can't really tell you. I know I must have done all the things I had to; I was alive, after all, when the Burkes found me. I just know that once I got into the room, Minna and Harold arrived, and the rest just happened. I watched them just like I watched a play. But I was in that play, too. And in the end, I got rewarded just like some heroine would. I didn't do anything special except that I took those two starving rats in and fed them and played with them because I didn't have anything else to do except die. And I guess I wasn't ready for that. That's how it is, you know. Life goes in fits and starts, hits a dead end and turns back again. And there's nothing you can do about it; it just happens.

The night before the Burkes came for me, I fed Minna and Harold as usual. They looked good. Their coats were smooth and shone in the firelight. Their eyes were clear and quick. When Minna finished her pone, she went over to the fireplace edge chirping to Harold to follow. It was the hidey-hole they always used, but this time they started to gnaw at the wood to make the space larger. When they had a hole about the size of a dollar, Harold went in and Minna followed. I never saw Harold again. But a few minutes later, Minna came out backwards tugging something she held between her teeth. She dropped it and came over to me and sat up on her hind legs. Her paws lifted up to me, and she cocked her head. Then she was gone, too.

The thing that Minna brought out of that mantelpiece was a spoon, a silver spoon. And when I took my little axe and opened that hidey-hole so I could stick a hand in, I found a lot more silver inside. It was a fortune, and even I knew it. Three silver salvers, big ones, too. Spoons and forks for twelve. And even knives, which had to be got separate then. And a bowl. And two large serving spoons. I was rich. And I kept thinking that I was rich. Not me and my Papa, but just me.

The truth is, honey, Mama was right. Papa never did come home from the War. After I'd spent all that time alone with Harold and Minna, I guess I believed I'd never see anybody again, much less my Papa. And that day the Burkes came for me, the sun finally shone, but I was a different person. I'd been through it, and I knew it. Mrs. Charles Burke drove up in a wagon just after the sun broke through and the circles of hoar frost began to melt into the ground again. She came with her three young boys and her escort, a Private who'd been assigned to guard them by the CSA. Charles Burke was a representative to the Confederate Congress. He'd always been a dear friend of Papa's. When I first heard the mules come into the yard, I was afraid. But I went to the shutters to look out through the slats because I had to know. I thought it might be Yankee foragers. But it was just the Burkes. I guess I had a philosophy by then, and didn't care much who it was. But I called out the window, and they seemed glad. I told them I couldn't come down, so they built a ladder from the broken stairs, and that's how

I came to meet them in the yard. I had my silver with me and the Burke boys helped me load it in the wagon. Where's your mother, Lily, Mrs. Burke said. And I told her, she's in the smokehouse and she's dead. I won't go down there, again, I said, but you can see for yourselves. And they did. They found her in the grave she'd made for herself with that spade. She'd done it with the little gun Mr. Bateman had given her. She'd climbed in and just done it with the earth piled all around. They covered her with her own till and said, may dust be to dust and ashes to ashes, but I had nothing to do with it. I'd had enough.

And when all that was done with, more bad news. My Papa, she said, had died on his way home. Someplace called Dahlonega, where a blister on his heel went septic on him and the limb had to be amputated. When they put the hot iron to the stump, it couldn't curb the bleeding which went on until he passed. So, there I was. I hadn't got anybody. But I had that rat spoon and everything that went with it. And I never told anybody about Harold and Minna. I lived with the Burkes, who cared for me as if I was their own. But, you know, there's a kind of glue people have that keeps them together. And even though the Burkes coddled me along and treated me like a little belle, I never could stick to them, and they couldn't stick to me. They were kind, and I was grateful. But, I guess, because of what happened to me, I just couldn't stick, and I could never love them.

Well, I got betrothed to a good man when the time came—your Great Grandfather. We married and the rat spoon and all the other silver made up my dowry. Now I still had title to that house where my Mama died and your Great Grandfather wanted us to settle there. But I told him. I'm never going back there. And so we didn't. But, you know, I still have that title, and your Grandfather and your Daddy both wanted me to go back. I said I never would. And I never have. I'm 103 years old now, and I haven't seen that place since. But I do know that everything that happened there is true. Minna and Harold came to me. I took care of them, and, in return, they gave me the rat spoon. It's right here with me, and I want you to see it now. See those little wedge marks on the bowl of the spoon. See there. That's where Minna pulled it out of the mantle to show it to me. That was the night the sleet kept on and on and the grass looked like silver needles standing up as far as you could see."

Dulane Upshaw Ponder is a writer living in New York City and the Hamptons, Long Island.

Mysteries and marvels. I still believe in them. In "The Rat Spoon," I tried to create a world in which the reader's understanding of historical fact would depend entirely on a willingness to accept the legitimacy of wondrous events. And, of course, there was the storytelling element. I wanted to use an oral-history style to capture all the musical and incantatory elements of Southern speech. I also wanted that mesmerizing flow of words reminiscent of the Biblical "begats," the old sagas and ballads. But mainly, I wanted to tell a good tale that might have happened but probably didn't.

Andrea Lee

ANTHROPOLOGY

(from *The Oxford American*)

My cousin says: Didn't you think about what *they* would think, that they were going to read it, too? Of course Aunt Noah and her friends would read it, if it were about them, the more so because it was in a fancy Northern magazine. They can read. You weren't dealing with a tribe of Mbuti Pygmies.)

It is bad enough and quite a novelty to be scolded by my cousin, who lives in a dusty labyrinth of books in a West Village artists' building and rarely abandons his Olympian bibliotaph's detachment to chide anyone face-to-face. But his chance remark about Pygmies also punishes me in an idiosyncratic way. It makes me remember a girl I knew at Harvard, a girl with the unlikely name of Undine Loving, whom everybody thought was my sister, the way everybody always assumes that young black women with light complexions and middle-class accents are close relations, as if there could be only one possible family of us. Anyway, this Undine—who was, I think, from Chicago and was prettier than I, with a pair of bright hazel eyes in a round, merry face that under cropped hair suggested a boy chorister, and an equally round, high-spirited backside in the tight Levi's she always wore—this Undine was a grad student, the brilliant protégé of a famous anthropologist, and she went off for a year to Zaire to live among Pygmies. They'll think she's a goddess, my boyfriend at the time annoyed me by remarking. After that I was haunted by an irritating vision of Undine: tall, fair, and callipygian among reverent little brown men with peppercorn hair: an African-American Snow White. I lost sight of her after that, but I'm certain that, in the Ituri Forest, Undine was as dedicated a professional who ever took notes—abandoning toothpaste and toilet paper and subjecting herself to the menstrual hut, clear and scientific about her motives. Never even fractionally disturbing the equilibrium of the Lilliputian society she had chosen to observe. Not like me.

Well, of course, I never had a science, never had a plan. (That's obvious, says my cousin.) Two years ago, the summer before I moved to Rome, I went to spend three weeks with my Great-Aunt Noah, in Ball County, North Carolina. It was a freak impulse: a last-minute addressing of my attention to the country I was leaving behind. I hadn't been there since I was a child. I was prompted by a writer's vague instinct that there was a thread to be grasped, a strand, initially finer than spider silk, that might grow firmer and more solid in my hands, might lead to something that for the want of a better term I call *of interest*. I never pretended—

(You wanted to investigate your *roots,* says my cousin flatly.) He extracts a cigarette from a red pack bearing the picture of a clove and the words *Kretek Jakarta* and lights it with the kind of ironic flourish that I imagine he uses to intimidate his students at NYU. The way he says *roots*—that spurious '70s term—is so shaming. It brings back all the jokes we used to make in college about fat black American tourists in polyester dashikis trundling around Senegal in Alex Haley tour buses. Black intellectuals are notorious for their snobbish reverence toward Africa—as if crass human nature didn't exist there, too. And, from his West Village aerie, my cousin regards with the same aggressive piety the patch of coastal North Carolina that, before the diaspora north and west, was home to five generations of our family.

We are sitting at his dining table, which is about the length and width of the Gutenberg Bible, covered with clove ash and Melitta filters and the corrected proofs of his latest article. The article is about the whitewashed "magic houses" of the Niger tribe and how the dense plaster arabesques that ornament their facades, gleaming like cake icing, are echoed faintly across the ocean in the designs of glorious, raucous Bahia. He is very good at what he does, my cousin. And he is the happiest of scholars, a minor celebrity in his field, paid royally by obscure foundations to rove from hemisphere to hemisphere, chasing artistic clues that point to a primeval tropical unity. Kerala, Cameroon, Honduras, the Phillipines. Ex-wife, children, a string of overeducated girlfriends left hovering wistfully in the dust behind him. He is always traveling, always alone, always vaguely belonging, always from somewhere else. Once he sent me a postcard from Cochin, signed, "Affectionately yours, The Wandering Negro."

Outside on Twelfth Street, sticky acid-green buds are bursting in a March heat wave. But no weather penetrates this studio, which is as close as a confessional and has two computer screens glowing balefully in the background. As he reprimands me I am observing with fascination that my cousin knows how to smoke like a European. I'm the one who lives in Rome, dammit, and yet it is he who smokes with one hand drifting almost incidentally up to his lips and then flowing bonelessly down to the tabletop. And the half-sweet smell of those ridiculous clove cigarettes has permeated every corner of his apartment, giving it a vague atmosphere of stale festivity as if a wassail bowl were tucked away on his overstuffed bookshelves.

I'd be more impressed by all this exotic intellectualism if I didn't remember him as a boy during the single summer we both spent with Aunt Noah down in Ball County. A sallow bookworm with a towering forehead that now in middle age has achieved a mandarin distinction but was then cartoonish. A greedy solitary boy who stole the crumbling syrupy crust off fruit cobblers and who spent the summer afternoons shut in Aunt Noah's unused living room fussily drawing ironclad ships of the Civil War. The two of us loathed each other, and all that summer we never willingly exchanged a word, except insults as I tore by him with my gang of scabby-kneed girlfriends from down the road.

The memory gives me courage to defend myself. All I did, after all, was write a magazine article.

(An article about quilts and superstitions! A fuzzy folkloristic excursion. You made Aunt Noah and the others look cute and rustic and backward like a mixture of *Amos 'n' Andy* and *The Beverly Hillbillies*. Talk about quilts—you embroidered your information. And you mortally offended them—you called them black.)

But they *are* black.

(They don't choose to define themselves that way, and if anybody knows that, you do. We're talking about a group of old people who don't look black and who have always called themselves, if anything, colored. People whose blood has been mixed for so many generations that their lives have been constructed on the idea of being a separate caste. Like in Brazil, or other sensible countries where they accept nuances. Anyway, in ten years Aunt Noah and all those people you visited will be dead. What use was it to upset them by forcing your definitions on them? It's not your place to tell them who they are.)

I nearly burst out laughing at this last phrase, which I haven't heard for a long time. It's not your place to do this, to say that. My cousin used it primly and deliberately as an allusion to the entire structure of family and tradition he thinks I flouted. The phrase is a country heirloom, passed down from women like our grandmother and her sister Eleanora and already sounding archaic on the lips of our mothers in the suburbs of the North. It evokes those towns on the North Carolina–Virginia border, where our families still own land: villages marooned in the tobacco fields, where—as in every other rural community in the world—"place," identity, whether defined by pigmentation, occupation, economic rank, or family name, forms an invisible web that lends structure to daily life. In Ball County everyone knows everyone's place. There, the white-white people, the white-black people like Aunt Noah, and the black-black people all keep to their own niches, even though they may rub shoulders every day and even though they may share the same last names and the same ancestors. Aunt

Eleanora became Aunt Noah—Noah as in *know*—because she is a phenomenal chronicler of place and can recite labyrinthine genealogies with the offhand fluency of a bard. When I was little I was convinced that she was called Noah because she had actually been aboard the Ark. And that she had stored in her head—perhaps on tiny pieces of parchment, like the papers in fortune cookies—the name of every child born since the waters receded from Ararat.

I was scared to death when I went down to Ball County after so many years. Am I thinking this or speaking aloud? Something of each. My cousin's face grows less bellicose as he listens. We actually like each other, my cousin and I. Our childhood hostility has been transmogrified into a bond that is nothing like the instinctive understanding that flows between brothers and sisters: It is more a deeply buried iron link of formal respect. When I was still living in Manhattan we rarely saw each other, but we knew we were snobs about the same occult things. That's why I allow him to scold me. That's why I have to try to explain things to him.

I was scared, I continue. The usual last-minute terrors you get when you're about to return to a place where you've been perfectly happy. I was convinced it would be awful: ruin and disillusion, not a blade of grass the way I remembered it. I was afraid above all that I wouldn't be able to sleep. That I would end up lying awake in a suffocating Southern night contemplating a wreath of moths around a lightbulb, and listening to an old woman thumping around in the next bedroom like a revenant in a coffin. I took medication with me. Strong stuff.

(Very practical, says my cousin.)

But the minute I got there I knew I wouldn't need it. You know I hate driving, so I took an overnight bus from the Port Authority. There isn't a plane or a train that goes near there. And when I got off the bus in front of Ball County Courthouse at dawn, the air was like milk. Five o'clock in the morning at the end of June and ninety percent humidity. White porches and green leaves swimming in mist. Aunt Noah picked me up and drove me down

Route 14 in the Oldsmobile that Uncle Pershing left her. A car as long and slow as Cleopatra's barge. And I just lay back, waking up, and sank into the luxurious realization that you can go home again. From vertical New York, life had turned horizontal as a mattress: tobacco, corn, and soybeans spreading out on either side. And you know the first thing I remembered?

(What?)

What it was like to pee in the cornfields. You know I used to run races through the rows with those girls from down the road, and very often we used to stop and pee, not because we had to, but for the fun of it. I remembered the exact feeling of squatting down in that long corridor of leaves, our feet sinking into the sides of the furrow as we pulled down our Carter's cotton underpants, the heat from the ground blasting up onto our backsides as we pissed lakes into the black dirt.

The last time before my visit that I had seen Aunt Noah was two years earlier at my wedding in Massachusetts. There she elicited great curiosity from my husband's family, a studious clan of New England Brahmins who could not digest the fact that the interracial marriage to which they had agreed with such eager tolerance had allied them with a woman who appeared to be an elderly white Southern housewife. She looked the same as she had at the wedding and very much as she had when we were kids. Eighty-three years old, with smooth, graying hair colored intermittently with Loving Care and styled in a precise 1950s helmet that suited her crisp pastel shirtwaist dresses and flat shoes. The same crumpled pale-skinned face of an aged belle, round and girlish from the front but the profile displaying a blunt leonine nose and calm predator's folds around the mouth—she was born, after all, in the magisterial solar month of July. The same blue-gray eyes, shrewd and humorous, sometimes alight with the intense love of a childless woman for her nieces and nephews but never sentimental, never suffering a fool. And, at odd moments, curiously remote.

Well, you look beautiful, she said, when she saw me get off the bus.

And the whole focus of my life seemed to shift around. At the close of my twenties, as I was beginning to feel unbearably adult, crushed by the responsibilities of a recently acquired husband, apartment, and job, here I was offered the brief chance to become a young girl again. Better than being a pampered visiting daughter in my mother's house: a pampered visiting niece.

Driving to her house through the sunrise, she said: I hear you made peace with those in-laws of yours.

Things are okay now, I said, feeling my face get hot. She was referring to a newlywed spat that had overflowed into the two families and brought out all the animosity that had been so dutifully concealed at the wedding.

They used excuses to make trouble between you and your husband. He's a nice boy, so I don't lay blame on your marrying white. But you have to watch out for white folks. No matter how friendly they act at first, you can't trust them.

As always it seemed funny to hear this from the lips of someone who looked like Aunt Noah. Who got teased up North by kids on the street when she walked through black neighborhoods. Until she stopped, as she always did, and told them what was what.

The sky was paling into tropical heat, the mist chased away by the brazen song of a million cicadas. The smell of fertilizer and drying earth flowed through the car windows, and I could feel my pores starting to pump out sweat, as if I'd parachuted into equatorial Africa.

Aunt Noah, I said, just to tweak her, you wouldn't have liked it if I'd married a black-black man.

Oh Lord, honey, no, she said. She put on the blinker and turned off the highway into the gravel driveway. We passed beneath the fringes of the giant willow that shaded the brick ranch house Uncle Pershing built fifty years ago as a palace for his beautiful childless wife. The house designed to rival the houses of rich white people in Ball County. Built and air-conditioned with the rent of dark-skinned tenants who cultivated the acres of tobacco that have belonged to Noah and Pershing's families for two hundred years.

They were cousins, Noah and Pershing, and they had married both for love and because marrying cousins was what one did among their people at that time. A nigger is just as bad as white trash, she said, turning off the engine. But honey, there were still plenty of boys you could have chosen from our own kind.

(You stayed two weeks, my cousin says, jealously.)

I was researching folkways, I tell him, keeping a straight face. I was hoping to find a mother lode of West African animism, pithy backwoods expressions, seventeenth-century English thieves' cant, poetic upwellings from the cyclic drama of agriculture, as played out on the Southeastern tidal plain. I wanted to be ravished by the dying tradition of the peasant South, like Jean Toomer.

(My cousin can't resist the reference. *Fecund Southern night, a pregnant Negress,* he declaims, in the orotund voice of a Baptist preacher.)

What I really did during my visit was laze around and let Aunt Noah spoil me. Every morning scrambled eggs, grits, country ham, and hot biscuits with homemade peach preserves. She was up for hours before me, working in her garden. A fructiferous Eden of giant pea vines, prodigious tomato plants, squash blossoms like Victrola horns. She wore a green sun hat that made her look like an elderly infant, blissfully happy. Breakfast over and the house tidy, we would set out on visits where she displayed me in the only way she knew how, as an ornamental young sprig on the family tree. I fell into the gratifying role of the cherished newlywed niece, passed around admiringly like a mail-order collectible doll. Dressing in her frilly pink guest room, I put on charming outfits: long skirts, flowery blouses. I looked like a poster girl for *Southern Living.* Everyone we visited was enchanted. My husband, who telephoned me every night, began to seem very far away: a small white boy's voice sounding forlornly out of Manhattan.

The people we called on all seemed to be distant relatives of Aunt Noah's and mine, and more than once I nearly fell asleep in a stuffy front room listening to two old voices tracing the spiderweb of connections. I'd decided to write about quilts, and that gave us an excuse to go chasing around Ball County peering at old masterpieces dragged out of mothballs, and new ones stitched out of lurid polyester. Everybody had quilts, and everybody had some variation of the same four family names. Hopper, Osborne, Amiel, Mills. There was Gertie Osborne, a little freckled woman with the diction of a Victorian schoolmistress who contributed the "Rambling Reader" column to the *Ball County Chronicle.* The tobacco magnate and head deacon P. H. Mills, tall and rich and silent in his white linen suits. Mary Amiel, who lived up the road from Aunt Noah and wrote poetry privately printed in a volume entitled *The Flaming Depths.* Aunt Noah's brother-in-law Hopper Mills, who rode a decrepit Vespa over to check up on her every day at dawn.

I practiced pistol-shooting in the woods and went to the tobacco auction and rode the rope-drawn ferry down at Crenshaw Crossing. And I attended the Mount Moriah Baptist church, where years before I had passed Sunday mornings in starched dresses and cotton gloves. The big church stood unchanged under the pines: an air-conditioned Williamsburg copy in brick as vauntingly prosperous as Aunt Noah's ranch house.

After the service, they were all together outside the church, chatting in the pine shade: the fabled White Negroes of Ball County. An enterprising *Ebony* magazine journalist had described them that way once, back in 1955. They were a group who defied conventional logic: Southern landowners of African descent who had pale skins and generations of free ancestors. Republicans to a man. People who'd fought to desegregate Greensboro and had marched on Washington yet still expected their poorer, blacker tenants to address them as Miss Nora or Mr. Fred. Most of them were over seventy: their sons and daughters had escaped years ago to Washington or Atlanta or Los Angeles or New York. To them I was the symbol of all those runaway children, and they loved me to pieces.

(But then you went and called them black. In print, which to people raised on the Bible and the *McGuffey Readers* is as definitive as a set of stone tablets. And you did it not in some academic journal but in a magazine that people buy on newsstands all over the country. To them it was the worst thing they could have read about themselves—)

I didn't—

(Except perhaps being called white.)

I didn't mean—

(It was the most presumptuous thing you could have done. They're old. They've survived, defining themselves in a certain way. We children and grandchildren can call ourselves Afro-American or African-American or black or whatever the week's fashion happens to be.)

You—

(And of course you knew this. We all grew up knowing it. You're a very smart woman, and the question is why you allowed yourself to be so careless. So breezy and destructive. Maybe to make sure you couldn't go back there.)

I say: That's enough. Stop it.

And my cousin, for a minute, does stop. I never noticed before how much he looks like Uncle Pershing. The same mountainous brow and reprobative eyes of a biblical patriarch that look out of framed photographs in Aunt Noah's living room. A memory reawakens of being similarly thundered at, in the course of that childhood summer, when I lied about borrowing Uncle Pershing's pocketknife.

We sit staring at each other across this little cluttered table in Greenwich Village. I am letting him tell me off as I would never allow my brother or my husband—especially my husband. But the buried link between my cousin and me makes the fact that I actually sit and take it inevitable. As I do, it occurs to me that fifty years ago, in the moribund world we are arguing about, it would have been an obvious choice for the two of us to get married. As Ball County cousins always did. And how far we have flown from it all, as if we were genuine emigrants, energetically forgetful of some small, dire old-world country plagued by dictators, drought, locusts, and pogroms. Years ago yet another of our cousins, a dentist in Atlanta, was approached by Aunt Noah about moving his family back to Ball County and taking over her house and land. I remember him grimacing with incredulity about it as we sat over drinks once in an airport bar. Why did the family select him for this honor? he asked, with a strained laugh. The last place anyone would ever want to be, he said.

I don't know what else to do but stumble on with my story.

Aunt Noah was having a good time showing me off. On one of the last days of my visit, she drove me clear across the county to the house where she grew up. I'd never been there, though I knew that was where it had all begun. It was on this land, in the 1740s, before North Carolina statutes about slavery and mixing of races had grown hard and fast, that a Scotch-Irish settler—a debtor or petty thief deported to the pitch-pine wilderness of the penal colony—allowed his handsome half-African, half-Indian bond-servant to marry his only daughter. The handsomeness of the bond-servant is part of the tradition, as is the pregnancy of the daughter. Their descendants took the land and joined the group of farmers and artisans who managed to carve out an independent station between the white planters and the black slaves until after the Civil War. Dissertations and books have been written about them. The name some scholars chose for them has a certain lyricism: Tide-water Free Negroes.

My daddy grew tobacco and was the best blacksmith in the county, Aunt Noah told me. There wasn't a man, black or white, who didn't respect him.

We had turned onto a dirt road that led through fields of tobacco and corn farmed by the two tenant families who divided the old house. It was a nineteenth-century farmhouse, white and green with a rambling porch and fretwork around the eaves. I saw with a pang that the paint was peeling and that the whole structure had achieved the undulating organic shape that signals imminent collapse.

I can't keep it up, and, honey, the tenants just do enough to keep the roof from falling in, she said. Good morning, Hattie, she called out, stopping the car and waving to a woman with cornrowed hair and skin the color of dark plums, who came out of the front door.

Good morning, Miss Nora, said Hattie.

Mama's flower garden was over there, Aunt Noah told me. You never saw such peonies. We had a fish pond and a greenhouse and an icehouse. Didn't have to buy anything except sugar and coffee and flour. And over there was a paddock for trotting horses. You know there was a fair every year where Papa and other of our kind of folks used to race their sulkies. Our own county fair.

She collected the rent, and we drove away. On the road, she stopped and showed me her mother's family graveyard, a mound covered with Amiel and Hopper tombstones rising in the middle of a tobacco field. She told me she paid a boy to clean off the brush.

You know it's hard to see the old place like that, she said. But I don't see any use in holding onto things just for the sake of holding on. You children are all off in the North, marrying your niggers or your white trash—honey, I'm just fooling, you know how I talk—and pretty soon we ugly old folks are going to go. Then there will just be some bones out in the fields and some money in the bank.

That was the night that my husband called from New York with the news we had hoped for: His assignment in Europe was for Rome.

(You really pissed them off, you know, says my cousin, continuing where he left off. You were already in Italy when the article was published, and your mother never told you, but it was quite an item for the rest of the family. There was that neighbor of Aunt Noah's, Dan Mills, who was threatening to sue. They said he was ranting: *I'm not African-American like they printed there! I'm not black!*)

Well, God knows I'm sorry about it now. But really—what could I have called them? The quaint colored folk of the Carolina lowlands? Mulattos and octoroons, like something out of *Mandingo*?

(You could have thought more about it, he says, his voice softening. You could have considered things before plunging into the quilts and the superstitions.)

You know, I tell him, I did talk to Aunt Noah just after the article came out. She said: Oh, honey, some of the folks around here got worked up about what you wrote, but they calmed right down when the TV truck came around and put them on the evening news.

My cousin drums his fingers thoughtfully on the table as I look on with a certain muted glee. I can tell that he isn't familiar with this twist in the story.

(Well— he says.) Rising to brew us another pot of coffee. Public scourging finished; case closed. By degrees he changes the subject to a much-discussed new book on W.E.B. Du Bois in Germany. Have I read about that sojourn in the early 1930s? Dubois's weirdly prescient musings on American segregation and the National Socialist racial laws?

We talk about this and about his ex-wife and his upcoming trip to Celebes and the recent flood of Nigerian Kok statues on the London art market. Then, irresistibly, we turn again to Ball County. I surprise my cousin by telling him that if I can get back to the States this fall, I may go down there for Thanksgiving. With my husband. Aunt Noah invited us. That's when they kill the pigs, and I want to taste some of that fall barbeque. Why don't you come too? I say.

(Me? I'm not a barbeque fan, he says. Having the grace to flush slightly on the ears. Aren't you afraid that they're going to burn a cross in front of your window? he adds with a smile.)

I'll never write about that place again, I say. Just one thing, though—

(What?)

What would you have called them?

He takes his time lighting up another Kretek Jakarta. His eyes, through the foreign smoke, grow as remote as Aunt Noah's, receding in the distance like a highway in a rearview mirror. And I have a moment of false nostalgia. A quick glimpse of an image that never was: a boy racing me down a long corridor of July corn, his big flat feet churning up the dirt where we'd peed to mark our territory like two young dogs, his skinny figure tearing along ahead of me, both of us breaking our necks to get to the vanishing point where the green rows come together and geometry begins. Gone.

His cigarette lit, my cousin shakes his head and gives a short exasperated laugh. (In the end, it doesn't make a damn bit of difference, does it? he says.)

Andrea Lee currently lives with her husband and two children in Torino, Italy. Her fiction has appeared in *The New Yorker* and *New York Times Magazine*, and she is the author of *Russian Journal* and the novel *Sarah Phillips*. "Anthropology" is part of the collection *Interesting Women*, which was published this past spring.

FILIPPO GALLINO

"Anthropology" came into being as an act of penance for a not-quite-crime that I nevertheless have always felt faintly uncomfortable about: a New Yorker *article I wrote long ago about some of my relatives down in Hertford County, North Carolina. The piece, entitled "Quilts," didn't actually hurt any feelings, but it had in its execution a kind of dashing carelessness—I wrote it in my early twenties—and an eagerness to relegate real people to picturesque types that bordered on callousness and nowadays makes me cringe. The only person to raise an eyebrow at the time was a cousin of mine in New York, but he never took me to task as the cousin does in the story—in fact, we have never really discussed it. So the dialogue is between me and me: a fleshing out of one of those fantasies of expiation we all have. In homage to "Quilts," I could have called it "Guilts." And I must say, entirely selfishly, that I did feel better after writing it.*

Doris Betts

ABOVEGROUND

(from *Epoch*)

She wanted—she demanded—to see her daughter's bones.

No, said the first funeral home she left, also the second, whose director would not even repeat her word. *Remains,* he said, very softly. *Closed casket.*

The third funeral home she tried served chiefly an African-American clientele and operated from a garish building with purple window panes in a part of town she'd never visited. But Whaley & Son was willing to collect what little was left of Jeannie Norwood, aged eighteen forever, from the county coroner and lay out that remnant under a white sheet in a clinical basement room that had other temporary sheets tactfully covering instruments and chemicals on surrounding shelves.

Mr. Whaley Senior stood to one side to let Martha Norwood enter the chilly room. After a motionless wait, she gently pushed aside his hand to lower the sheet herself. She already knew that Jeannie's body had lain for months in Uwharrie Mountain wilderness, that dogs or wild animals had made entry easier for later worms and flies, that all she would see now were the skull, some ribs, one partial leg, and a pelvis. Still, she drew down the sheet with slow ceremony, grateful that Mr. Whaley or his son had made a considerate attempt to reassemble the parts in order to suggest the whole.

The skull, not plastic-white like a sample for medical students, was a pale, creamy tan—almost flesh-colored, thought Martha, against her will. It had mellowed for six months under brown leaves and forest duff, rolled some yards away from crumbled vertebrae. It was intact; police said perhaps Jeannie had been strangled, which injury would not show. The teeth their orthodontist had so painfully aligned seemed unnaturally long, now that each root was visible.

And the soft tissues—those parts that had screamed, been raped, felt pain, were all gone, had fed crows and buzzards. Martha wrapped her mind in ice as these thoughts moved through it. She had outlived six months of hope, had slowly felt her full self going numb, by summer, cold; now in the fall she was frigid.

She cupped her hand over the shallow fontanel dent atop the skull. The sockets showed no hint of blue iris (her father's color); nose holes no longer revealed that the tip had been upturned, with freckles. And gone were the ears over whose decoration they had argued: one piercing or more. No silver earrings had been found.

Something low started in Martha's frosty throat that she prevented from rising to a moan.

But Mr. Whaley saw and cleared his own throat on her behalf, made a move to replace the sheet. She stopped him.

There between hipbones lay the bowl emptied of her grandchildren. Martha gave a last light touch with one finger to the curved pelvis that remained, rubbed lightly the jagged rib that had once shielded the heart, and at last pressed her finger square on her daughter's bony brow.

"I call down," she said in a low growly voice she did not recognize, "Hell on whoever did this to you."

Mr. Whaley said something like *aw* or *oh*.

Jeannie Norwood had disappeared the previous February, on Valentine's Eve, wearing a sweater and jacket but not her wool cap; it was found hanging in the employees' locker at One-Stop-Shop where she worked after school and some Saturdays. The next

October searchers and dogs found none of that winter clothing, not a thread. No bits of underwear or sock, not one shoelace. Of course the gold neck chain on which Jeannie had been adding real pearls on Christmas and birthdays, this year up to twelve, was missing, but no one thought a thief had killed her for that.

At first everyone, even Jeannie's parents, thought she had just run away. Martha and Gene had been quarreling so much back then. The cause seemed trivial now. Perhaps Jeannie had believed a shared anxiety would drive them close again?

Her disappearance almost worked. In the next weeks as they slowly gave up believing their daughter a runaway, Gene no longer took Valerie-the-dental-hygienist to outlying motels. Instead he sat with Martha by their telephone, where they waited in tense partnership for results from their posters, the latest TV appeal, the rising cash reward. They talked endlessly to each other of Jeannie. They reviewed the years back to pacifiers, toilet training. Often one memory would interrupt another.

Then in early June, when the high school closed for summer and Jeannie's classmates began planning for college, Gene Norwood suddenly gave up. At the end of a day just like the hundred before, without warning he almost banged his hands flat on each side of Martha's head in a thunderclap, then shook it left-to-right, side-to-side, making the negative move that matched his repetition: "No, no, no, let her go, Martha, you know she's dead, not coming back, not ever getting older," and on and on, hurting her neck.

"Stop talking," she whispered, "don't say it." She strained to pry his fingers loose; she caught both wrists, finally clawed at his knuckles.

He was relentless, louder. "No graduation, no wedding, no Jeannie, let her go, Martha. No Jeannie. You hear me? No Jeannie."

At last she'd been forced to kick his kneecap, hard, before Gene would drop both hands. He went into their bedroom to pack. By the next night he had moved into Valerie's apartment and by now, October, they had rented a larger place.

* * *

When Martha got home from Whaley Funeral Home and dropped her car keys by her lighted answering machine, she knew Gene must have phoned, so she crossed the kitchen to pour bourbon in a juice glass before playing his formal, careful voice.

"Hello, Martha. Yes, they called me and said they were sure. I guess you knew that. By the dental records. I said we'd be in touch about—about arrangements. However you want to do it. Martha?" Over his silence the tape whirred; then he added, "Except I think it should be soon and a private service. The newspaper is already calling."

Martha paused the recording and drank, as if making the real Gene wait until it suited her to hear him finish. Then his precise accountant's voice came on again to remind her of his parents' ample burial plot here, where they still expected to be buried in spite of their condo in Florida. Sure, said Gene, both of Martha's parents were buried in Michigan but it was already so cold there that, well?

Gene also suggested the Episcopal church where both were still on the roll—well, Jeannie, too—though he had never attended and last July Martha had quit as well.

When his voice had finished, she erased the next three messages from local reporters, looked up the number for Case and Stowe Dental Clinic, and asked for Valerie.

"It's Martha Norwood," she announced right away. "Got a pencil? Tell Gene the service is Wednesday at two. In the chapel at Whaley & Son. They're in the phone book. Tell him I bought my own burial plot this morning." She started to add that Valerie was not invited, but what was the point? She hung up.

Sipping her drink, she almost called down then a silent but suitable amount of Hell on Valerie and Gene, but just as afterthought; by now she had largely lost interest in both of them. His call had made her remember that hard trip home to Michigan, almost two decades ago. Martha's parents had died in a head-on collision before she could tell them she was pregnant. They had never known Jeannie was coming, much less how soon she was gone.

Martha lifted her glass as if toasting their good fortune.

In the springtime, when there were still occasional clues, reported sightings of Jeannie or her car, when Martha and Gene were making joint TV and radio appeals, after long days when they had cruised the streets to nail posters on telephone poles—back then she'd had the illusion that they had renewed their marriage vows before the more vivid gods of Grief and Terror. They clung bodily to each other, and not just in bed. Often in public they walked then holding hands, like politicians with their tame wives. They trailed police detectives to conduct their own interviews of Jeannie's friends, teachers, boyfriends, other workers at the One-Stop-Shop. All had spoken well of pretty Jeannie Norwood, yet the more strangers praised her, the less like their daughter she seemed. Only while they together kept sifting her possessions in Jeannie's room did her reality fill out her photographs. Here was the place where the real girl had lived. They wept over home videos where the real baby and child had been growing so smoothly and normally into real girlhood. They even unearthed from the attic her old report cards and faded Girl Scout vest with its embroidered badges.

And talk? They wore out each other's ears. If a single fact about Jeannie were allowed to fade, one word be lost, that would be giving up. Sometimes in the night Martha would wake her husband to remind him of Jeannie's first tap-dance recital, or the time they were afraid she had swallowed Clorox.

But April passed, and by May Gene was being out-talked. He began to stay late nights in the accounting office long after every tax form had been filed.

One midnight Martha drove to the apartment complex where she knew Valerie lived, but had to circle its parking lots twice before spotting Gene's car, out back, in the shadow of a Dumpster.

Instead of confronting him, for days afterward she heard herself speaking almost constantly of Jeannie, speaking alone. Babbling. Jeannie might have amnesia like that girl who had turned up blank-minded by a road in Florida? She would have ranked twelfth in her senior class. Jeannie: who had painted their mailbox with its ivy twining through white lettering, THE NORWOODS. "Remember how Jeannie laughed at people who couldn't tell plural from possessive?" An English major in the making. Then she had knocked the post sideways during her first driving lesson. One time Jeannie was baby-sitting and thought somebody was crawling through the front shrubbery, so Gene had to go with a flashlight to search. "But who knows, Gene, some man could have stalked her for years without—"

That was the very moment her mouth met the pressure of his fingers laid firmly across it, too firmly; if she had put out her tongue she could have tasted his wedding band.

And that's when he clapped both hands hard on her head in a vise, and began shaking it into denials that she could not endorse.

Martha had often relived that scene, even changed and improved her recollection. Was it her mouth he had covered first? Or did that come later, after she argued? Hadn't she argued? Had they just stood there, emptied of words like two balloons emptied of air?

Remembering, she often could reproduce words neither had actually spoken: should-have-saids, scriptwriter's talk. She outspoke him altogether, then.

But nothing could alter her other last words. The morning of February 13. Jeannie was headed out the back door in that red sweater so soon to become part of her last-seen description, wearing that brown jacket and cap. She would be driving to school in her eighteenth-birthday car, the one she would need in college, then going to work after class. Perhaps if they'd never bought her a car? If she'd always taken a bus or a cab? Or if Martha had driven her everywhere, or Gene, each of them always alert to danger?

Turning back from the door, Jeannie had called, and now kept on endlessly calling, "Mom, could you wash my sneakers this morning so they'll have time to dry?"

"Wash your own shoes," Martha said, and went on consolidating the leftover cereal milk from three bowls to one for Iris, the cat.

Wash your own shoes. Some final words.

Now it was fall and everything was long since washed and ironed, every dress and blouse, every winter garment dry-cleaned in mothproof bags and ready, the bedsheets fresh, her room well dusted and windows washed. Sometimes the cat, Jeannie's cat Iris, got in and settled herself on the pillow, and Martha would leave her there since cats were psychic—maybe this one sensed that today she was coming home.

Twice a week Martha would remove all Jeannie's photos from around the mirror frame, polish the glass, and replace them in the same order, lingering over the faces. This girlfriend, Shasta, had she told all she knew? And Ronnie: he looked so harmless with a chin that barely sloped into his skinny neck, not at all like a boy who—said Jeannie's diary— wanted his hand in her pants all the time, even at the movies.

Martha hated to know now what Jeannie had not confided then, that he'd enjoyed sex with her daughter. Martha (and Gene, of course) had been absolutely certain that Jeannie was saving it for marriage, especially after she did tell them that Shasta was not.

The day after Martha went to Whaley & Son to see the bones, she shooed the cat off Jeannie's bed, cleared all the photos of her friends, and dropped them helter-skelter in with bikini panties and bras, size 32-A. Except for Ronnie's picture. She put it low in the sock drawer.

It had always seemed likely to Martha that Ronnie must be the murderer, that Jeannie's diary made him capable, first, of teaching her to lie, so probably also of murder; but police had checked his whereabouts and said no.

Everyone agreed the killer, unless he'd been known to her, like Ronnie, must have been waiting in her car. Jeannie would never have picked up a stranger. Couldn't Martha and Gene recall dozens of times they had warned her? Week after week they repeated out loud their clear memories of this caution.

The One-Stop-Shop asked all its employees to leave their cars on the edges of the lot, so customers could park closer. Jeannie had said good night and signed her time card—so there would always be recorded the last good moments of her life—7:32. And then out into the dark.

A wake? How could they hold a wake over bones?

Instead, people gathered from way across town an hour in advance of the service and milled around on the grass outside Whaley & Son, especially men in dark suits from Gene's CPA firm, reluctant to go inside. Finally Gene led his group indoors to stand under a window that colored their heads like large, fat Welch's grapes, until Mr. Whaley gave a courteous nod toward the door marked Chapel Number 1. There was no Number 2.

They filed into the rows of chairs that faced the closed, dark coffin. Murmurs and coughs.

Martha picked from the uneasy crowd the plainclothes cop who had been so patient with her and who now mouthed silently to her raised eyebrows, "You never know," as he systematically surveyed the crowd. Then she spotted Shasta and Ronnie, a number of Jeannie's classmates, women from her former church, dozens of strangers who were unforgivably curious and—coming late—Gene's parents with bold Valerie, her arms hooked through their fragile ones.

But Mr. Whaley, who knew who was paying the bill, bent to ask Martha if it was time to start, then inclined his brindled head past the others to the overdressed Episcopal priest to come forward and read.

It was the standard Order for the Burial of the Dead from the older Prayer Book, and would have been no different a century ago, or if Jeannie were a grandmother, had been a judge, a banker, an athlete, if she had died hard or easy, repentant or terrified.

Although she bowed for prayer between mumblings, Martha watched the cop's flicker-fast eyes in case they might widen from sudden recognition that the killer had come into view. Only a local reporter trying to minimize his camera between his thighs aroused the policeman's interest.

Gene was seated on her same row, but not close. Beyond him, Valerie's hair in a tall permanent looked darker than it used to be.

After the regular service—no homily—Martha's former in-laws came to wrap her in two dry embraces. Their cheeks were cool and papery. Underneath, their own bones grated against hers.

Mother Norwood whispered, "I've been thinking about you."

Thinking what? That I've lost them both? That I let them go?

Gene's father said only, "Martha? Are you all right?"

Since he had a habit of breaking into other people's sentences, she said in a rush, "Not a bit, not at all, never worse, I'm—"

"Being very brave," he said, and then let someone else come shake her hand. She couldn't complain. From their retirement, the Norwoods had always been good to her, long distance, had adored Jeannie. Were surely grieving still.

"She's at rest now," Mother Norwood said, and after Martha's silence, repeated it to Gene who made a sour face.

Then Martha was riding in Whaley's white, extra-long hearse. Mr. Whaley had asked if her husband and other family would want to ride with her. She said no. She watched a series of small-town policemen take off their hats at intersections to wave the funeral procession properly on; and soon she was stumbling through uneven grass clumps to the tent (which was purple itself and had seldom bloomed in this particular cemetery). On all its four fringed sides, gold letters advertised the Whaleys.

This time the metal chairs were so arranged that Gene sat beside her. Not looking at him but straight ahead, Martha could almost see through the coffin walls at how little lay on its quilted satin, while Gene must be visualizing Jeannie in her full-fleshed girlhood; and she did not know which vision was the more unbearable. She could not take part when the priest cast earth inside the grave, promising that the corruptible bodies of those who sleep in Him shall be changed, and made like unto His own glorious body.

When it came time to repeat the Lord's Prayer, she allowed Gene's hand to take and squeeze hers, and by an effort made hers less limp, able to respond. She could not see Valerie but somehow sensed her looming behind them, like a tree trunk.

People she did not recognize spoke to her afterward, touched her too often, blocked her with hugs, became impediments between the grave and the long white hearse whose door Mr. Whaley had been holding open for quite some time. "I can drive you to your house, Mrs. Norwood."

Confused, she said, "But my car?"

"My son could bring that to you later."

"No, no, I can drive."

So he waited, motor idling, during the long delay while others leaned in the back window to murmur their sympathy.

One was the policeman, Davis Hall, who had worked with them for months. He stared uneasily around the interior of the big hearse, obviously surprised that she had it all to herself. Then he promised Martha the department would never close this case, that he personally would keep it open, that someday they'd find the man who did this—although a week ago he'd been saying it must have been a stranger passing through, maybe a drug user, and reminding Martha that the car had never turned up, might be repainted now and sold in Mexico.

But he'd been unfailingly kind. She managed to thank him for coming. He reached inside to press her hand, and close up she noticed for the first time that his graying eyebrows had curly hairs interspersed. She imagined that his body hair would match, and was shocked at herself.

Davis Hall let go her hand and moved off to speak to Gene, but briefly.

"Could we go, Mr. Whaley?"

"Of course." His voice was more resonant than the priest's. He began inching one fender into the narrow road that ran between rows of small pruned trees, just showing the first seasonal reds and yellows. In slow motion, people dodged aside.

Mr. Whaley said, "A very nice service."

She was looking in her purse at all the folded Kleenex she had brought but never used. After so many tears, there were now only beads of ice left way behind her eyes, but she wondered if black mourners made more noise and thus—to him—might register as more sincere. "It felt like a movie," she said.

"A dream, people used to say it was like a dream."

In silence they rode down wide shady streets, then between stores and offices, and finally among the more crowded frame houses where Mr. Whaley had his business. For the first time Martha realized that its façade with four skinny pillars only fronted a long building made of concrete blocks.

He pulled under a metal car shed to one side and was already opening her door before she realized they had stopped, saying, "Mrs. Norwood, would you like a cup of tea?"

She almost needed the Kleenex then. "Yes, and thank you."

He led her down the hall, past the office where they had negotiated terms, beyond the closed Chapel Number 1 door, beyond the room in which she had walked through his coffin display in search of something plain enough to choose. Then he unfolded plastic accordion doors that separated his home from funeral-home space. They stepped straight into a living room with crocheted spreads pinned onto every chair arm and headrest, covering end tables and draped over the top of an oversized television. On each side, doors stood open to small bedrooms, and straight ahead was a neat kitchen with a serving bar and stools. He seated her in a chair upholstered in sunflowers against a green field.

While he was in the kitchen, Martha strove to recall the word—*antimacassar*—that named all these lacy scarves and runners she had not seen on furniture since her grandmother's. She called, "Your wife crochets?"

"Myself." He brought in a tray with cups, cream, sugar. "I do it."

She tried to picture these same brown fingers, first sewing shut dead, lax mouths, and afterward forming these creamy thread stars and pineapples.

On his second trip he carried in the teapot and poured. "My wife is in the hospital."

"I'm sorry. Is it serious?"

He tapped the bristly hair where it made sideburns past his ears. "Crazy hospital. The one in Raleigh. Careful, it's very hot."

She dropped sugar cubes into her steaming cup while he took only cream, stirred the tea, watched her. "I'm sorry the newspaper sent that man," he said. "I told them not to."

"They don't listen. How long has Mrs. Whaley—"

Her voice was cut off by his quick response. "Years, many years. Everybody got troubles, Mrs. Norwood."

True enough, and though she could not absorb anymore, anyone else's, Martha nodded as if she might.

After they drank, resettled their spoons, looked around, he said, "Not many men crochet," to offer her some thin line of conversation.

"Oh no, my husband—"

"Never would. I could see that."

Martha couldn't imagine how but she felt uncomfortable; someone else used to cut off her sentences that way. Her father? Gene's. "Gene works with numbers. No hobbies at all," she said.

Completely neutral, he said, "It's a busy world."

They looked up when the younger Whaley came in to wash his hands at the kitchen sink. Martha realized that all along she had mistaken him for one of the gravediggers, and perhaps he was—his boots and trouser cuffs looked muddy. Where the father's graying hair made him look distinguished, like the gracious retainer managing some Delta plantation house, the son was too dark, too fat. A born day-laborer. Perhaps he only dug and filled graves himself to lower their costs; on Martha's side of town, small earth-moving machines did the job fast.

Mr. Whaley called, "Raymond, this is Mrs. Norwood."

"Sorry-fa-ya-loss," he muttered, then left by what must be the door and stairs down to the basement embalming room she had already seen.

Martha took a longer sip of the tea, which was good, slightly floral, not a grocery brand. "I couldn't do your line of work."

"My wife used to dress the ladies and curl their hair. She wouldn't do children, though." He caught himself. "I'm sorry. Your daughter?"

"Eighteen. No longer a child."

"Always," said Mr. Whaley, and he inclined his teacup toward the now-empty kitchen. "My Raymond." They were near the slight sediment in their cups before he said, "Surely they'll catch the man who did this thing."

"I hope so," Martha said, but felt her head slightly shaking no-no-no.

Somewhere a telephone rang. Afterward Raymond Whaley climbed the stairs and told his father they had a pickup.

"Who was it?" Mr. Whaley stood.

"The Oxford boy. At the hospital."

"But he was getting better! I'm so sorry, Mrs. Norwood, but it will take the two of us."

"It won't," said Raymond quickly.

"Since one has to speak to the family if they're still there."

Clearly Raymond had few words to offer mourners beyond his glib sorry-fa-ya-loss. Martha thanked them for the tea, for the service. She'd send the final check tomorrow.

Barely a block away the white hearse passed her, Raymond driving, and Mr. Whaley in the front seat, speaking rapidly to him, looking angry.

All that week Martha checked the obituaries until she found one for Jerome Torrance Oxford, thirteen, with unusually full details of how he had been playing with a .38 pistol belonging to Jason Wylie Fuller, thirty-two, of the home, and had accidentally shot himself up through the chin and brain and died, though his mother, Ramona Aleen Osgood, of the home, believed at the time that he was in South Oxford Middle School. At one time, undertakers themselves had written the newspaper death notices, but nowadays the family composed long paragraphs themselves, sometimes including rhymes.

In the snapshot, a boy in a team jacket from some other but unknown school posed against a brick wall, smiling but with no teeth in view. Jeannie had lived five years longer; maybe Jerome's mother would have swapped places with Martha to have those extra years.

One morning Mr. Whaley called to tell Martha that late flowers had come—should he just put them in place at the cemetery and mail her the senders' cards? She agreed. But when two more days had passed, and after a brief time of weeping over Jeannie's grave, she afterward made a stop at the A.M.E. Zion churchyard where the Oxford boy had been buried, and walked to where his funeral flowers (arranged just like Jeannie's, so white went in the center and colors formed a border) were also beginning to lean and wilt.

In the middle of the mound someone had driven in a metal stake and attached to it, sealed in a glass frame with the whole then wrapped in clear plastic, an enlargement of the boy's same photo from the newspaper. Now Martha could see that half his hair had been in cornrows, the rest cut very short with some design shaved in; and his smile was much more one-sided, especially in contrast to the straight lines of the brick wall, as if he had always felt off-balance and skewed to his right. In nearby gravestones, other portrait photos had here and there been embedded and somehow sealed, to notify passersby which particular faces were moldering underneath.

Several days later, having finished thanking everyone for flowers and excessive food, she stopped at the police station to ask Davis Hall precisely where they had found Jeannie, and who had actually found her. He said it was a bird club. He remained standing behind his desk so she could take this bit of information and depart.

"Is there a map? I want to go see."

"Oh no, ma'am. There's nothing at all to see. It's just woods on a hillside."

"Even so, I want to see."

He argued some more, and she insisted some more—having

seated herself without an invitation—until finally he looked through a file drawer and selected only one from maybe a dozen 8×10 photographs to show her a small heap of something under a cloth. In the woods. On a hillside.

"But I'm sure you have a map to the exact place."

"Mrs. Norwood." He took off his glasses and shook them in midair. "It's not as if your daughter was killed there. It's probably not the last thing she saw. If you've got some idea of spirit communion? No, she was carried there from someplace else so there's no real"—he waited—"atmosphere?" Again Martha asked firmly for a map. "You'll not pick up any messages, ma'am. I've been there. Believe me."

She bore down on insistence with a heavy, blown-out breath. He said he'd go with her, then. She shook her head.

After they'd argued some more—well, he argued; she simply went on doggedly requesting a map—he went to the same file drawer and got out a Stanley County map. He said, "I'll have to photocopy the section that applies, then show you how to find it." But he didn't move. He replaced his glasses, sighing. "All right, then."

"Thank you."

As soon as he'd left the room, Martha rushed to rummage in Jeannie's file, but the folders were packed with too many records of evidence and interviews, even false confessions there was reason to discount. She could only read snatches on this page and that—how a fractured hyoid bone would have proved strangulation if only it had been found, which candidates recently released from Central Prison with a suggestive history had all been checked and dismissed.

When the door opened again, Martha made it halfway back to her seat. Hall probably knew that she had been delving into his partly open drawer, but he only shook his head and showed her the park map, its roads, an X, and a photocopy of the enlarged quadrant where Jeannie had been . . . dumped?

He said, "Your husband will go with you?"

She shook her head.

Frowning, he ran his finger along the highways and past his spread left hand that flattened the map. No wedding band, she saw.

He told her the police had long since found everything there was to find. "I give you my word." He repeated that twice.

Later, as Martha drove west along Highway 64, she thought of him solemnly offering his word, one word, not a long speech. Davis Hall, she decided, might be the prototype of the man she should have married instead of Gene Norwood. Hall represented those stolid, beefy types who seemed content in their long marriages, within which husband and wife largely let each other alone. By contrast, Martha had in college been seduced by a vision of years of intimate conversations, and had visualized with Talker-Gene a future of ever-deepening understanding. A best girlfriend with a penis—that's what she had expected.

Yet it seemed to her now that the most faithful men she knew were all subverbal, gifted at woodworking, at car and house repair, always at home in the evenings but dozing off early. Such husbands went fishing or drinking with male friends; their wives socialized with other women. Separate lives. Joined, but separate. Even on golden wedding anniversaries, these husbands would still find women enigmatic and accept (prefer?) that mystery as affectionately and easily as they did the law of gravity.

Instead of a girlfriend, it would be like having a pet, she thought.

During the drive she wondered if Davis Hall, with or without a wedding band, was in such a marriage, was someone's domesticated spouse. And if Mrs. Whaley had gone crazy, not because of putting rouge on the dead, but from spending all those hours patiently discussing after dinner the funeral business with son and husband. Being a good listener. Saying the right loyal sentences. The way Valerie must now be pretending an interest in spreadsheets, and Gene in impacted wisdom teeth.

On the west side of Albemarle, Martha was suddenly into the Uwharries, oldest mountain range in America, now worn down to wooded hills. Then they had stood twenty thousand feet high, and dinosaurs had fed here; now most peaks, barely reaching a thousand, were the right size for lizards and snakes.

She stopped at a roadside café to eat barbecue while checking again the route Davis Hall had drawn on the map. The killer, doubtless at night, had entered Uwharrie National Forest on a regular trail, then struck off it on his own. Perhaps he knew the area? Every criminal record with any tie to Stanley or Montgomery counties had been unearthed and sifted. If he had parked Jeannie's car at one of the three trailhead lots near Troy or Ophir, he left no sign; and since other roads also intersected the trail, there were additional ways to enter and leave. She wondered if he had originally intended to throw the body into Badin Lake or one of its many feeder creeks, but then had tired of carrying her.

At that, Martha's lunch threatened to fight its way back up her throat.

The cashier told her how to get on Highway 24/27 and go west beyond Troy to the place Hall had marked. She found several cars parked in the trailhead lot; somehow she was not surprised to see the policeman's vehicle and Hall himself, smoking, sitting with his feet out its open front door. When she got out of hers, he called, "Better lock it," so she did. "You must be a slow driver," he said as he stepped on the cigarette and met her where a path was marked by a sign:

UWHARRIE NATIONAL RECREATIONAL TRAIL
FOLLOW WHITE BLAZES

"I stopped to eat."

"Good. You've got thin. But you'd never find the place by yourself," he added, sounding inconvenienced and long-suffering.

Martha did not answer, although secretly she still believed that instinct would have guided her.

He grumbled, "Mr. Norwood shouldn't have let you do this," as he led the way.

Davis had left his jacket in the car, so she was conscious of the gun in his shoulder holster, also a pedometer he clicked into action as soon as they stepped into the cool woods. "When I wrote down fifty feet, I meant fifty of *my* feet," he said with a tap to the small box on his belt, "so I could always retrace the route."

She followed on a path between pine and hardwoods, sometimes with evergreen laurel on the higher side. Mostly she watched his back, the undershirt showing through, a corolla of sweat spreading around the holster, a ridge of flesh blocked by his belt.

Past his prime, like me—thought Martha—but who ever knew when prime occurred; who starred the calendar to mark its peak? Wading through leaves, she decided hers might have come in the years when Jeannie was between three and eight, that safe and rewarding time when she and Gene had watched all their efforts bloom.

When Davis Hall muttered something under his breath, Martha realized he had been counting each white paint blaze they passed. He'd been right; she would never have found the exact point where they had to veer off the path, though here the leaves did look as if they had been scuffled through, and perhaps an Indian tracker could have found where twigs had snapped.

But now there was no path to follow, and soon her foot plunged into a hole concealed by leaves. With a grunt she dropped onto the other knee.

Hall got behind and lifted her by both elbows. "Turn your ankle?"

"It's not bad.

He steadied her until she could move easily, said they were almost there. The land had developed a sharper slant, gradual at first, but before long Martha was trying not to limp too fast down a slope that descended at the same angle as in the photo she had seen. Ahead of her, Hall climbed down more slowly. She didn't want to careen into him and braked herself by catching tree trunks on the way.

Now she became certain that shoes—big shoes, policemen's shoes—had trampled these leaves, that sticks and dead limbs had been churned up, collected, rearranged on the edge of the place where Davis Hall, stopped, was standing still between two oaks. He turned to watch her thrashing closer. "You all right, Mrs. Norwood?"

She reached him and heard herself say angrily, "I wanted to be alone."

Instead of answering, he took a few more steps into the center of the clearing, held out one arm and sighted along it to a maple, then looked back to his shoes. "About here," he said, and went on staring at the ground.

If the forest floor had ever showed the dark outline of a body, of its decomposition, there was nothing now. When she squatted, Martha realized that this layer of leaves and pine cones was recent and thin, that while investigators must have scraped down to bare dirt for yards around, the trees had recently been shedding a new cover of this season's weakest leaves, still pale-greenish and yellow. She picked up one to test its flexibility—sweetgum, purplish-red, the leaf that as a child Jeannie had liked because its five points seemed to fit her hand.

While examining the leaf, Martha suddenly realized her nylons were ripped from knee to ankle, with parallel threads glued to a bloody scrape down one shin.

She floundered upright and fell onto Davis Hall, wailing.

He didn't say a word but grabbed and held her almost too tight, as if by strength alone he could wring out all her tears at once, and the pressure did expel so much of her breath that sobbing grew difficult. Against his damp chest she groaned and sniffled. She felt his fingers slide into her hair as he moved her head slightly away from his holster. The hand stayed there, kneading lightly.

Time passed—a little or a lot—until she had quieted enough that both could hear a woodpecker drumming not too far away.

Now Martha tried to step away, but his arms squeezed harder so she lurched awkwardly off-balance, her feet in the wrong position with the rest of her leaning like a half-fallen tree (a widow-maker, she thought stupidly; they call them widow-makers). An ache spread through the small of her back, forcing her to step close again.

Suddenly she could feel him. Her whole body startled. Not since high school dating days had she been pressed against such obvious male arousal. Gene had often required coaxing.

She whispered, "Are you married?"

His arms relaxed. "Yes." It was his turn, with several side-steps, to move away until their bodies were no longer touching.

In fact, both their faces now came into view—overheated, embarrassed. His did not seem especially attractive to Martha nor, surely, could hers to him. She absently raked a hand down her whole front. Once she had been a size eight. She could smell his sweat. What on earth was she doing?

From the twitches in his face, Davis Hall seemed to be deciding what to say: *I warned you? I'm sorry? You asked for it?*

Martha turned aside and scanned the small clearing as if she might collect souvenirs instead of relics.

"You're hurt." He knelt and took her lower leg between his hands. She felt heat rush into it. "It's not deep."

He lifted his suddenly vulnerable face, staring. She stared back into his very dark eyes.

"Why did you bring your gun?"

"Habit." It was time for him to break off this too-intense gaze but he bore in like a hypnotist. "You ever thought of learning to shoot? I could teach you."

"No. I mean yes." There flew into her mind that photograph of the Oxford boy, who had received no gun-safety lessons. Perhaps after all Jeannie, too, had been shot, the bullet passing only through soft internal organs and into a floor someplace, or the empty sky. Perhaps before Martha died, she would have a chance to kill the man who had killed her daughter.

"I mean: no, I hadn't thought of it but, yes, perhaps it's a good idea."

"There's a law enforcement firing range. South of town."

"Okay, yes," she said again.

"Are we through here? This way, then." Now he directed her in front of him, out of the clearing, slowly up the hill that felt steeper this time. At the place Martha had fallen (she saw now she had blundered into the rotten roots of a stump) there was blood on the leaves. Without speaking they walked the trail through forest and were occasionally spattered with colored leaves that the wind discarded. At last the path widened and she could again see the sky and a western sun.

Behind her Davis said softly, "I'm married but I'm not dead yet."

She closed her eyes and hurried on blindly, unable to imagine anything less sensitive the man could have said. They were approaching the parking lot when Martha finally said, "I don't own a gun."

"I have several. Friday's usually a good day," came the voice behind her. "On Saturdays it gets crowded."

The journey had tired her. She stood at trailhead for a few deep breaths. "I can try this coming Friday. Thank you, Mr. Hall."

"Dave," he said.

After a long career teaching fiction at UNC-Chapel Hill, Doris Betts retired last year to her Arabian horse farm near Pittsboro to work on novels and stories herself. The recipient of the Medal of Merit in the Short Story from the American Academy of Arts and Letters, she has published nine books of fiction, most recently *The Sharp Teeth of Love*. A new novel, *Who Is Sylvia*, is in progress.

I'm a longtime reader of true crime and am always appalled by those grieving parents forced to identify their murdered children via bones and scraps. When I began this story, I was also deep in an awed rereading of Alice Munro's wonderful stories, which always seem less structured than organic. So I began "Aboveground" with no more than an idea of a mother identifying her daughter's bones, and then I let the story seek its own way. I'm trying to learn a looser narrative shape in this and in several other new stories due to appear in literary magazines.

R. T. Smith

I HAVE LOST MY RIGHT

(from *The Missouri Review*)

When we heard the horse we moved from the firelight by the ivied oak where we'd been bivouacked and stood to our mounts. It was coming right at us. Pistol aimed at the snapping brush, I called out a challenge. Virg was crouched beside me, his hackles stiff and fangs bared. Haemon Willis and Coates had their Sharps at the ready. Nobody was our friend; we couldn't be too careful.

"Name your Jesus or get misery and oblivion." I cocked the hammer.

"Gentlemen, my Jesus is the roaring boy Jeff Davis," the voice came back. "I smelled your smoke."

He could have been the worst foe, might have been our nightmare, and we couldn't allow him to go back and reveal us.

"Approach and be recognized. Come slowly, stranger."

The rider emerged from the copse astride a huge chunk of a horse, wide as a wagon, and Coates called out, "What in the black hell is that? Looks like you could have the whole Trojan army stowed in that thing."

I didn't like Coates. He was cross-eyed and ornery. I didn't trust his resolve, but I was stuck with him.

"It's a Morgan. My own sweet Caesar took some shrapnel down by the Wilderness Church. I had to put him down, and this monster was standing, drinking from the narrows of Scott's Run. He'd dragged a sledge with a man on it. That unlucky Christian must have caught some lead. His head was all caved in, what was left looking like a cherry cake. I'm Reeves Eason. Captain. I've been riding around all evening with these dispatches, and I am spent. Do you gents mind if I unlimber?"

An officer, but his outfit and accent were the right color to match us, so we stood down and offered him a cup of our rye coffee. At least he wasn't a danger right off, but Virg still acted cautious, slinking around the work horse, which paid him no mind and started tearing new grass.

Eason swung down from the stirrups and wrapped the strap of his pouch around the pommel a couple of extra loops.

"Some mastiff you have there. He wears his muscles like an acrobat."

"He's a dragon on people he don't take to. Who you with?"

"A courier out of Old Jack's staff. "

"You with him when he got popped?"

"As it happens, fate assigned me that sad vantage. The night was black as the inside of a musket, just a glint of moon. Boswell was reaching me a map when the idiots volleyed. He snapped to attention, said, 'Lordy,' and dropped stone dead. I think Old Jack was just hit in the hand, but then Little Sorrel ran him at the flashes. He got bucked about and branch-lashed across the eyes. Another round and he was hit bad."

Here he paused and squatted on his heels like a countryman.

"It should have all been over before that. We had the bluebellies fooled. We hit them at Talley's, at Dowdell Farm. Hazel Grove was an error, but we recovered. We knew the terrain and we had their right flank under. We were rolling them up, but it got dark. Then it was pure bedlam, skirmishers blazing away in all directions, taking down their own people. That was why he chose to scout it, to discover the right conclusion in person."

"We heard they took his wing, but he's strong and sure to come back riled."

"That's the current story. They're moving him over to Guinea Station to rest up. Hunter McGuire is a keen doctor, smart as a whip, no nonsense. Put him under the laudanum. They say Jack dreamed music while they sawed him, a sorrow song of a blade on bone. Might as well be our anthem now. I see by your caps you're from the Two Corps, Barton's. What mission are you pursuing so far off your unit?"

That was the one we were dreading, but we had a story. The confusion that had made it easy for us to slip off was a cool excuse for most anything. Willis was the one who worked it out, the one who suggested we should give the whole show up and see to our own private business. With the Stonewall Brigade out of action, he figured the end was coming, and I reckoned why not get back and put in some corn instead of learning up close what a Northern stockade was like. Besides, I had a premonition after Sharpsburg. That was the longest, reddest day I ever hope to witness. It was looking like the generals was working a contract to exterminate us all, and I'd commenced to believe "skulk" means "save your bacon." I wanted to go home and start over.

So I said, "Tell you the truth, we don't know. We were scouting up the Salem Church road when Hooker swung his batteries onto us. That was holy hell, worst I've seed. When the brimstone was over, Kyd Douglas sent a batch of us with intelligence to Early. I reckon you heard how that turned out. We were too late and met Dan Sickles's Yankees coming on from Fredericksburg. Some bluehorse boys chased after us for the better part of a day, like they thought we had some big secret. Everything that favored a path just vanished in the brush and hardwoods, and we was lost in the tangle. It was Virg, this dog, that showed us through the wilderness and back here. We're hoping to hook up with Douglas and the other scouts come first light."

We was hunkered down now about the fire, warming our hands on the sludge we were calling coffee, wishing words could make it so. The dog was pacing on the shore side of the tree, alert but not nervous, making little half-circles about that big horse. Virg kept sniffing the wind and cocking his head, his yellow eyes glowing like Jack O'Lantern. Wasn't any other sounds but the stream slipping by—branch of the Rappahannock, we reckoned—and ever so often an owl off to the north.

The captain didn't seem at ease. With red piping on the breast and pants, his uniform was good quality, a real contrast to our shoddy, and he'd give a tug here and there to make it neater on him. He wore a brace of big navy Colts in his belt, and he was a little soft-faced, I thought, young, but with old eyes. Everybody had old eyes by then. From the way he kept staring down the coffee pot like it might jump at him, I was sure he had somewhere else he wanted to be. In the darkness, with no flags and no generals, he seemed a man who might still believe in glorious war, but maybe it was just the same fear of being afraid we all felt.

"You ever knowed Old Jack up close?" Willis asked.

"On occasion. I have seen him close enough to know to be wary, but last Christmas I was with him helping serve up a dinner at the Corbin house. Jimmie Smith, his orderly, had come up with turkeys and white biscuit, a bucket of oysters, pie and wine pickles. Stuart was there in his ostrich hat, and General Jackson dandled a girl child on his knee."

"And what did you get?"

"A drumstick to myself and pone and a slough of beans. A warm cot, a safe place to shit. But even when he was cooing at that child, he scared me."

"How come?"

"Don't get me wrong; I reverence Old Jack, but he's got killer's eyes, and with Bible zeal mustered behind them. I can't get over how cold they can be, like they're looking at you from the moon. But the boys love him, they do, and if we ever have to figure out how to fight this crusade without him, well, I'm not convinced we could manage."

It was Coates's turn, and he took the sweetgum switch he'd been chewing out of his mouth.

"I heard what he said at Fredericksburg about the Yankees charging on the wall."

"What was that?"

"General said, or they say he did, 'Shoot them all. I do not wish them to be brave.'"

"That a fact?"

"They tell it for true. Name's Hob Coates. I mustered into the Rockbridge Artillery with Jimmie Smith in sixty-one. Didn't know he'd got himself on the easy wagon. Staff, by damn. We had us some serious times together, riding the caisson or swabbing a cannon by day, talking about home at the campfire. Likely the war's got to be a lark to him now."

I didn't like where this was going, so I said, "Coates, this hell ain't a lark for no soul. Boys started off with braid on their hats and shiny swords found out loving Minnie was no honeymoon."

The officer spooned some of our beans and sowbelly into his pan and asked, "Loving Minnie?"

"You know, the minié ball, song of the death angel, like a banjo string snapping."

"Yeah. You don't have to be at Bloody Lane to testify to that," said Willis. He was shuffling about the scrag for some wood sticks.

Coates kept going. "I knowed the general in Lexington, too. I mean, just to see. He wasn't no personality to speak of. Just a haughty professor kind of fellow. The VMI cadets said he . . . hush. Listen." His face had gone hard as a walnut mask.

At first we heard nothing, then the rattle of tack and gear clanging upwind on the road. Then we went into a quiet scurry. We got the fire covered with dirt from the pit and went to our horses to cover their nostrils. I was worried that clodhopper Morgan would whinny, afraid I wouldn't see my thirty acres or Luanne and Junebug again. It could be Federal scouts feeling out our lines or a straggle of graybacks aiming to reconnect with Lee. Or bummers out scavenging. Either way, we was dead for sure if they got wind of us. I thought about Jack's officer, about his not really knowing what you might call "our predicament." I touched the handle of my Bowie knife. I could feel the antler bone, rough in the dark. For ten minutes that seemed an hour there was nothing but the soft damp of Hector's nostrils and the tar of night and that sanded antler bone, my palm going back and across it, my mind thinking of cutting the new man's throat quick, just to narrow the possibles. I was drifting loose, everything I believe in turning to dust, all my secret plans falling away, trying not to think of home, the rich dirt, my old daddy's voice. I reckoned if we got caught it would serve us right, but I wasn't on right's side anymore. We had crossed into the valley of the shadow on our own steam.

Then I noticed the dog was leaning against me, his hackles sharped, muzzle thrust into the darkness. I knew his back lip was curled, excitement dripping from his tongue. I could feel him tensed up like a bowstring, and I prayed he wouldn't get a wild hair. In the year he'd been with me, his instincts had proved right every time I could judge. Hoping he'd stay smart, I was holding my breath past possibility.

Soon the moon came out of a cloud, and we could see some. Just woods, the clear space over running water.

Then somebody whispered, "Didn't hear us, didn't see."

"Was it Yanks?"

"Don't know," said the officer. "No sense taking a chance. Been enough night mistakes in this battle, everybody half asleep from loading and shooting, loading and shooting and trying to remember a prayer. If we just lay low, morning will set things right."

While Eason was unsaddling and gathering pine limbs to stretch his blanket on, he asked was I from Carolina, on account of my accent. I told him I was from the southside, farm country down below Roanoke, so he wasn't far off.

"And you've seen some action?"

"Hot work. Hot and bloody."

The dog was snuffling around him, not studying the horse no more.

"I never seen Virg to take a liking to anybody so quick. He ain't the world's most friendly cur."

But sure enough, Virg was nuzzling the captain's hand and licking it. It seemed to make the man nervous.

"We have a pack of Walkers back home," he said. "They're just frisky, like children."

"Where's that, home?"

"Kentucky. Two or three days west from here. Not far from the Virginia line."

"But your people voted to keep in? Why'd you join with the Southerns? I mean, you could as easy be riding with those bluebellies back yonder."

He laughed and said, "We don't know for certain they were Billy Blue, but yes, I suppose I could. And so could Jeff Davis, another son of Kentucky, you might recall. My uncle served with him down in Mexico, Buena Vista, and I appreciate his words. He said that if we're not free to pull out of something we joined, we're not very free in it, either."

Coates caught my eye then.

He finished, "Appears to me people have a right to live the way they want, and if somebody sends an army to change their mind, well, woe betide."

He was settling his gear and making a pillow out of his kit.

"I believe I'll try to sleep now. If you all will work out the sentry duty, you can wake me when it's my rotation."

He was a peculiar fellow for an officer, and I kept getting the feeling he had things he wasn't saying. I wondered did he really trust us, being as how we were, well . . . it might not of made such easy sense we'd be so misplaced after the fight. Maybe he swallowed our story, maybe he didn't, but he did pull his hat over his eyes and lay back like a man who meant to put hisself into our hands. I figured we'd just let him sleep, split the watch between the three of us and be ready to move come sunup. That was a long time off.

I woke to a general pandemonium, snarl and snuffle, horses snorting, the cries of men in the darkness. A shot monstrous close. Another one. Dawn was just getting started, a flitch of bacon in the eastern sky, and I could see Willis was laying across a log, not moving, his face bloody.

It didn't make no sense what I could see by the firepit. Virg had something he was dragging at, and Eason was smacking him across the back with a pistol. Coates had grappled Eason by the jacket and was trying to pull him away. Then I saw Coates's big stabbing knife move, but the officer twisted out and swung his pistol around, and it whoomed right against Coates's belly. His body jumped back, and Eason drew down on me, shouting, "Don't move, don't do it." Virg was a-scamper now, dragging something through the briars. He gathered speed and went past me at full skedaddle.

I could see what he had clamped in his jaw was chawed meat and bone. It looked like a arm.

"Call back that damn dog, sir, or I shall open you up."

I was still dazed and sleepy and discombobulated, so I couldn't understand him at first, but he repeated it.

"The dog. Call it back."

I hollered into the woods where ground fog was making the bloomed dogwoods even more ghostly, but I couldn't see hide nor hair of Virg. Then Eason was beside me, and I could see a terror in his eyes.

"We've got to get it back," he said, but then, "No, it will be too late. He is a dog, and the damage is surely done."

Tears were streaking into his sparse beard, and I asked what the hell was going on. He kept the pistol leveled at me as we stared into the woods.

"That was Old Jack's arm the dog stole."

"What're you telling me?"

"The general's arm. Now I have to work fast."

It had started up when Willis dozed off, and Virg got into the captain's message sack, drawn beyond any discipline he had to the grueful secret which had been luring and taunting him all evening. He must of got it out of the bag and the raincoat it was wrapped in before the noise woke Willis and Eason. Being as it was too dark to see clearly, Willis must have been afraid the commotion meant Eason was turning on us, had found us out for deserters, so he went to kill the man, but his Sharps just blowed up, ripping off his face and hands. Then Coates rose up and joined the general confusion, and that was when I come to. But then, whilst Eason was explaining to me, we heard a horse a-gallop and saw Coates was riding west like hell bent for leather, so he must not of been hit mortal.

"Why did those ape brains try to kill me?" he asked.

"But what are you doing with the general's arm that has been cut off?"

He had the pistol, so I told him our sorry story fast, not dwelling on the desertion part. I was desperate to hear his answer to my question. Willis was gone to the Kingdom for certain, and I didn't know what would come about next, but I was pretty sure old Coates would not be circling back to look after me, and that I might be headed for a rope.

His story turned out to be right simple, too. The doctor had told him to take the arm off into the woods and bury it proper, but Eason knew his chief would be up and on his feet in a few days and like any good Christian, he would likely want some say in what happened to his own parts. Since Eason had been sent on a scout —it wasn't no dispatches he had at all—he figured he could just spend a couple of days on a ramble while the army pulled itself together and Jackson come to his senses, after all the buckeye whiskey and chloroforms had done wore off. He was disobeying orders, too, and now he didn't have nothing to show for it but a story he might have trouble finding believers for. He had a new look of menace on his face, and I saw he was somebody who was capable of strange reasons.

I said, "Look here, Captain . . ." and that's when he told me to turn around.

When I woke up that time, I was in mortal pain. I was gagged with a stick and rag and tied, hand and feet, and I could see what he'd done. Then Eason was holding a whiskey flask in front of my eyes, and I couldn't breathe, couldn't raise spittle, the gag being tight and my body heaving and panting. The fire was burning bright just behind him, and morning was filling the sky. I think I heard some birds calling. I don't remember. The pain was just under my shoulder, and it hurt like lightning. He'd taken the better part of my arm.

"I noticed you favored your left hand, so I took the right one. I used the serrate edge of your hunting knife, and I believe it's a lucky cut, a clean job, considering. I have cauterized it, and when you're well enough to sit a horse, we'll get you to some corpsmen. I believe you'll fare well enough. Would you take drink?"

Of course, that was when he explained how this bold course had solved both our troubles, because now my war was over for good, and I could go back to the bosom of my family. He tied up his bundle again, and I saw my arm for the last time disappearing into the bloody rain slicker. All I could think about was the pain and would I live to see my front gate again. Ever so often I would look from the rawhide tight on me to the singed sleeve and the rusty blood showing around my wrapped-up stump, and I would go swoony.

Soon as I was able to sit Hector without everything going back to night, we lit out. He didn't bother to throw no earth on poor Willis, and now he had no face, I wondered if he'd get to Heaven, or if anybody would ever know who he was. The crows in the leaves over us wouldn't likely care.

The business went tolerable well back at camp. Considering. The captain told the sentries I was tied onto the horse for my own safety, and they bustled me straight to the doctor tent. All the surgeons was amazed at the story. The captain said he'd come in on the hindquarters of a skirmish, and I'd taken a ball in the wrist. Pretty soon Kyd Douglas himself was setting beside me saying I was a bold warrior and a lucky man. That captain was right about one thing: like so many busted rebels, I was headed home, nobody suspecting I had lit out on my own furlough without waiting for such a hard reason.

But he was wrong about Old Blue Light shaking it off, wanting his pieces back and hitting the Yanks all over again like an avenging angel. He caught the fevers, I heard later, and tried to move ghost troops to the front in his delirious raving. His wife was at his side, but even her nursing couldn't save him. He crossed over the dark river in a week, and there was general mourning and gloominess all across the South. Story is the arm got buried without much ceremony, and I have to wonder didn't they ever notice it was a right arm, and not the one where Jackson took minié balls on that black night after Chancellorsville. People say there is a marker there, and pilgrims still go to it to tear their duds and shed tears over the Lost Cause. I don't expect to make the journey.

I heard once that Reeves Eason saw the wildfire close up outside Gettysburg and did something heroic, following Old Pete this time, but he must of somehow missed catching the devil's eye up there by that graveyard in Pennsylvania because ten years after Appomattox I got this short letter from Richmond on fancy stationery paper, and all it said was, "Did you ever find that dog?"

SARAH KENNEDY

R. T. Smith's collections of poetry include *Trespasser, Messenger,* and the forthcoming *Brightwood.* His stories have appeared in *The Missouri Review, The Southern Review, Southern Humanities Review,* and other journals, as well as his collection, *Faith.* He edits *Shenandoah: The Washington and Lee Review* and lives in Rockbridge County, Virginia, with his wife, Sarah Kennedy.

Preparing to teach a course entitled "The Civil War in American Literature," I was reading Foote, Robertson, and Freeman, and found my mind circling back to the loss of Jackson's arm and then his life. I have visited the arm's cemetery plot, and thinking about the standard account, I began to imagine an alternative story. Because both Lee and Jackson are buried in Lexington (mostly) and revered, it's easy to start thinking about the Lost Cause in irreverent ways. Pretty soon I had my narrator and his squad of deserters and a voice I sympathized with and wanted to listen to. The title, of course, comes from Lee's comment that, as Jackson had lost his left arm, Lee had lost his right.

Brad Barkley

BENEATH THE DEEP, SLOW MOTION

(from *The Virginia Quarterly Review*)

Early morning, and Clarendon starts like a wind-up toy—cotton and rice farmers machining the Delta soil, jackhammers breaking the streets downtown. Bosco is talking, too much and too loud, finding no difference between nighttime talk and daytime, between drunk and sober. Along the shore, the streetlights blink out all at once. For the second time that morning, Bosco talks about killing Leo Myer.

"We could, Ray," he says, sober a moment. "You know we could."

Ray feels something shift when the words are said, feels that slow, familiar movement toward trouble.

"Always running off at the goddamn mouth, Bosco," Ray says, laughs it off. "Ought to wrap it with duct tape instead of this."

Ray waves his 12 gauge, its stock covered in greasy tape, then shoves the barrel under the river's surface and pulls the trigger. The muffled *whomp* boils downward, jarring his bones, the water exploding upward in a rain of mud and algae. Bubbles rise with the blood and mangled remains of a carp. Ray nets the fish from the water, tosses it in the cooler. Later, he will grill it over hardware cloth with potatoes wrapped in tinfoil, and they will pick out like bones from the flesh the tiny lead pellets, spitting them into the currents.

"You say that 'cause you know I'm right," Bosco says, his smile cutting thin, framed by the mustache that edges his mouth. They have been up all night, drinking beer and shooting carp. Ray switches off the lamps that float in the shallows. The carp move in shadows across the pebbly bottom. Bosco finishes his chocolate milk, drops the carton and stomps it, making Ray jump.

"About all I know is you're a kid, Bosco," Ray says. "A thirty-five-year-old goddamn kid." Bosco shrugs and drinks, his shirtless chest bony and sunken.

They stand on the deck of Bosco's houseboat, which once served as a repair barge and welding deck for BG Ironworks until it ran on a shoal in the middle of the Arkansas River, fifty yards downstream of the railroad trestle outside Clarendon. Permanent as an island now, the boat holds as the river washes around it. Red-wing blackbirds balance on the rope that connects the barge to shore, the same rope that Ray and Bosco shinny across for groceries, liquor, and generator fuel. When Bosco finds women from town they shinny across with him, legs scissoring the rope, skirts gaping, Ray shining his flashlight on the whites of their thighs. The women squeal and curse Bosco for where he lives, curse the light and the oily rope, drunk and laughing while Ray holds his breath, waiting for them to slip and disappear forever beneath the deep, slow motion of the river.

Bosco lifts another beer from the plastic bag hanging in the current. The white scar from his surgery looks fresh still, lines stitched across his shoulder where the Jonesboro doctors removed the cancer. The indentations there form notches in the line of his shoulder, the flesh gouged and ridged. Ray looks at it, winces. After the surgery was when he began to spend all his time on the barge—not just Saturday nights—helping Bosco tie his shoes, cook his food, and, for a time, button his pants.

Bosco takes the gun, his mouth hanging open as he scans the water. They will shoot until the sheriff's deputy drives down to the river bank and hollers for them to call it a day.

"We better quit soon," Ray says.

"How much you think them diamonds are worth?" Bosco asks. "How easy would it be to walk in there, off the son of a bitch, and get out?" He drinks his beer and elbows Ray, starts humming the *Jeopardy* theme. Riffing off game shows is a stage in Bosco's drunkenness, lodged somewhere between vomiting and blacking out. After they have caught a day's haul of oysters, he will watch the shows on his little five-inch black-and-white, the cord for the TV running off the generator inside the cramped cabin of the barge, where he keeps his mattress, refrigerator, and the back issues of *National Geographic* he finds on the library free table and uses for kindling. Nights they sit at the edge of the barge, occupying an old couch Bosco found on the roadside and floated across, left in the sun to dry. Bosco watches game shows and comedies, shouts at the screen, while Ray watches the river and thinks about the water flowing past them, all the bits of sediment carried to the ocean. They sit until the generator runs out of gas, then fire up lamps to shoot carp in the shallows, run trotlines for catfish.

"Just let the idea go, Bosco," Ray tells him.

"You don't think I'd do it?"

"Well, let's see. Last month, panning for gold was gonna make us rich and before that crystal meth and before that parting out cars. Now it's hauling oysters that's not making us dime one, so you're going to kill Leo Myer and take a stack of diamonds that might or might not even be there. Bullshit, Bosco."

Bosco takes back the gun, racks it, and fires beneath the water. Bits of gravel clink against the side of the rusted water heater that floats beside them, chained to the barge.

"One big difference this time, Ray," Bosco says. "I *need* the goddamn money." He blinks and looks away, tips up his beer can to hide his eyes.

The first time the doctor found the cancer in Bosco's shoulder was an accident, an X-ray done after some bar-fight soreness wouldn't work itself out. With no money or insurance, Bosco had worked out a payment plan that would see him through to old age, and if he skipped even one payment, Ray knew, the collection agency would be along to take his barge, his beaten-down truck, his little TV, his refrigerator, and his last pair of socks. Now he complains of new soreness in his shoulder, tiredness in his days, but his joke is that he can't buy anymore sickness until the last one is paid for. He has stopped smiling when he says it.

Bosco tosses his beer can into the river and fires at it. He racks and fires again, at the willow tree that tethers the shinny rope. Ray grabs the gun by the barrel and twists it from Bosco's fingers. He spits into the water and watches it float away, then ejects the empty shell.

"We won't ever be rich, Bosco, not in this life."

They cook and eat carp into the afternoon, putting off that day's haul of oysters, work which renders their only cash until the end of the month when Ray collects for his weekend motor route. He drives the same camper truck he sleeps in when he's not on the barge, muscling it down bumpy washouts in the dead of night, listening to radio baseball and talk shows, shoving the *Clarendon Gazette* into the green plastic tubes mounted at the side of the road. All day, while they eat and drink, while the river washes around them, Bosco talks of Leo's diamonds, how they are there for the taking, how that woman he met at the bar has seen them herself. He talks nonstop, nodding and jabbering, rubbing his ruined shoulder.

By early evening Ray lets himself be talked into a visit to Leo's place. Bosco says he wants to case it out, words he has lifted from some TV show. Ray agrees, wanting Bosco to stand there in Leo's apartment, work it through his brain, see the impossibility of it. They drive out County Road 10 toward Berryville, drinking beer, swatting mosquitoes. They come to the brick building that once held Sunshine Dairy, where Leo runs his business from a single room on the second floor. Out beside the road is Leo's hand-painted sign advertising his palm reading, tarot cards, and shiatsu massages, ten dollars each. The front windows are webbed by strips of masking tape and yellowed, curling posters for the Shriner's

Bar-B-Q and the Marv-L Circus. Inside, the old cream separators and capping machines sit rusting, covered in dust.

"So if Leo's rich, how come he lives in this hole?" Ray asks.

"You've heard the story," Bosco says.

"Yeah, I've heard it," Ray says. "That one and about a thousand others."

"Well, I guess we'll see then, won't we?"

The story seeps into the bars in the way of all rumor, through spilled beer and bullshit and games of eight ball and last call, places where Bosco has picked up the story and made it his own. The word is that Leo Myer once worked as a diamond wholesaler in Atlanta, that one afternoon he pocketed five pounds of rough stones off the plane from Barrons, that he picked Clarendon, Arkansas, off a road atlas and settled in to hide himself. Leo speaks with a New York accent, wears flowing caftans to the IGA in town, silver rings and ear hoops, tiny braids woven in his longish hair.

"That's right, Bosco," Ray says. "We'll see, and then you can drop this shit."

"Just keep his ass busy," Bosco says.

After a steep climb to the second floor, they ring the buzzer. The door opens with a tinkling of chimes and Leo yawns at them from behind his graying beard. Behind him, the TV plays a commercial for dog food.

"Visitors," he says. The room is thick with incense and yellow light, the walls pale green, hung with feathers and beads. "What can I do for you boys?" He is without his caftan and earrings, and wears instead sweatpants and a gray T-shirt.

"My buddy here would like his palm read," Bosco says.

"Is that a fact? Just what problem are you working through?"

Ray shrugs. "Whatever."

Leo smiles at them. "Why don't you fellows save your money. Go buy a few rounds at the Barbary Coast."

"No, we really want to know the future," Bosco says. "We can pay." He cuts his eyes at Ray as he unfolds a crumpled ten from his jeans and hands it to Leo.

Leo shrugs, opens the door to let them in. They sit down at a pocked wooden table in the kitchen while Bosco heads toward the sink.

"Mind if I get some water?" Bosco asks. Leo waves the back of his hand and slips on a pair of dimestore reading glasses. He uses the remote control to click off the TV.

"Why don't you tell me what you're thinking," Leo says to Ray. "That's our usual start."

"I was thinking how much this dump looks like a whorehouse," Ray says. He watches Bosco drink from a jelly jar.

"This anger toward me interests me," Leo says. He looks up, smiles, touches his beard. "Is that what you paid for? To come here and vent?"

"Ray's just nervous," Bosco says from behind Leo. "His first time."

Leo holds out his fingertips as if he's asking Ray for a dance. Bosco nods, and Ray offers his hand. Leo's fingers are warm and damp. He bends Ray's hand toward the light, caressing the palm. Bosco walks slowly around the room touching the strings of colored beads, the macramé wall decorations, the feathers hung from threads. Ray doesn't like a man touching him. He drinks with his left hand, downing his beer.

"Anger is bad for your heart, as bad as cigarettes," Leo says. "The Chinese call anger a weary bird with no place to roost."

Bosco slips to the back of the room and eases open a drawer on a rolltop desk. Ray imagines he hears it squeak. He watches Bosco riffle through papers with his thumb, then pull a wooden cigar box from the back of the drawer. Leo starts to look over his shoulder.

"That's me exactly," Ray says quickly. "All pissed off and no place to go."

"I see that in your lines, most of them broken, irregular. Our work then is to trace it back to its source, chase the riders back to the crimson palace."

Bosco frowns and mouths the word "shit," then tilts the cigar box for Ray to see the strings of cheap, plastic beads. He replaces the box and eases the drawer closed. In the corner of the room, a painted screen partially hides an iron bed and a chest of drawers. Bosco steps over and leans his hands against the chest of drawers. His shadow dips and angles against the opposite wall.

"Chase the riders? What the fuck are you talking about, Leo?" Ray says.

Leo lifts his hand to gesture, his rings flashing. "The riders are stray emotions, wants, unfulfilled dreams. They are sent out by the crimson palace—your heart." He smiles. "We're speaking metaphorically, friend."

Ray nods as if this makes some sense to him, and Bosco ducks behind the screen. Ray watches him in the mirror. Bosco slides open the top drawer.

Leo leans across the table, sending up wafts of cologne. His eyes are slate colored, bloodshot. He is no longer studying Ray's hand, only holding it. "What are yours?" he asks.

Ray draws back, tethered by his own hand. "What are my what?"

Bosco slowly lifts something out of the second drawer and sets it on top of the dresser. He looks back over his shoulder, catching Ray's eye.

"Your unfulfilled dreams, the empty areas of your existence," Leo says. He smiles like a cop, like he knows something. Ray closes his eyes, wanting this whole thing over with, wanting to be back on the barge, watching the water.

"Go on, Ray," Bosco says. Ray opens his eyes and Bosco is standing beside the screen, hands behind his back. Leo does not turn to look at him. Bosco grins. "Go ahead and tell old Leo about your so-called dream."

Ray feels the heat in his face.

"Yes, Ray," Leo says, "what is your so-called dream, as your friend puts it?"

Ray shakes his head. This is something he does not talk about. He only ever told Bosco because of a night of too many tequila shots and no moon, the river and the barge wrapped in nightfall, the generator out of gas, only the quiet and the drunken surges inside and his feet in the warm water, words spilling out into the darkness. And for the reason of their silent work together in the river hauling oysters out of the mud, thirty feet down, roped to one another, feeling their way through the dark murk of the river. Thinking of all that, loose and drunk, he let slip and knew right away how hollow it sounded, his dream of diving in the ocean, swimming through the warm currents, a kid wish he'd kept with him like some lucky penny left in a pocket and tarnished with age. But still he keeps it, fingering the notion, imagining it when he is driving his route and rain comes. Stuck on some back road, wipers burned out, waiting for the storm to pass, water washing sideways in faint ripples across his windshield, he will press his face to the glass and think of sharks and eels, of bright fish and coral reefs. He has never seen these things except on TV, which he knows is next to not seeing it at all, worse maybe, for how TV makes everything small.

"Well, goddamn, Ray," Bosco said that night. "Your truck's right there. Right *there.* Get in it and head south for twelve hours. You'll hit the damn ocean. Hell, if we could get the barge unstuck, we'd be there by breakfast."

Ray shook his head and shrugged, his awkwardness invisible in the darkness. "It ain't the ocean, really. The ocean is just a thing, like my head just picked it. I don't know."

"So you're all but dying to see the ocean but not really the ocean. Now we're making sense." Bosco threw a bottle out into the river.

Ray wanted to say then how after so much time the ocean meant nothing more than some new thing, how he wore the boredom of his thirty-eight years like a sickness, how his life ran past like the water past the barge—giving him only the trick of movement. He felt he was done with living, or it with him, and that apart from what he'd already been through—a handful of shit jobs, a year of marriage, a week in the county jail—nothing much else was left to happen.

"Give my word, Ray," Bosco said. "We'll get our asses on down to Biloxi as soon as oyster season's up."

Ray shrugged, pushed his bottle under the surface and let it sink.

Now Leo squeezes his hand and whispers. “You needn’t cling to sadness, son. Tell me your dream.”

“Yeah, tell him,” Bosco says, and smirks. “Tell him about the ocean.”

“The ocean?” Leo raises his eyebrows.

Ray’s face flushes. “Just shut the fuck up, Bosco.”

“You dream of leaving, of escape,” Leo says, nodding. “Water represents birth, renewal, baptism.”

“Don’t talk about it,” Ray says. He jerks his hand from Leo’s grasp. “Bosco, keep your goddamn mouth closed.”

Bosco shakes his head and smiles, then slowly withdraws his hands from behind his back and holds up to the light a large and imperfect diamond. He nods, grinning wildly.

Leo raises his hands in a gesture of mock surrender. “My young friend,” he says. “You show up here, you pay me ten dollars. What is it you want?”

Bosco steps behind Leo, makes a gun with his thumb and finger, and points it at the back of Leo’s head. They are like that for a moment—Leo awaiting Ray’s answer, his hands still in the air, Bosco with his phantom gun. The seconds play out this pantomime of robbery, until the realization opens within Ray: They *could* do it. Bosco is right. They could.

“This is a two-way street,” Leo says. “You come back when you decide how I can help you.” Ray does not speak, his mind still held by that brief flash in Bosco’s fingers. He looks again at Bosco, who hammers down his thumb trigger and mouths the word “pow.” Bosco grins again, tips his head toward the door.

“I’ll do that,” Ray says, standing, shaking. “I will come back.”

Early Friday morning, after his route, Ray drives out County Road 10 and pulls over beside Sunshine Dairy. The windows of the building reflect the dust-colored light of dawn. Ray thinks of Leo inside, sleeping, the strung feathers twisting slightly in the dark, the capping machines and cream separators below him, the diamonds shining and hidden, their value hoarded away. He sees it so clearly, Bosco yanking the .38 from his denim coat, jamming the steel against the back of Leo's skull, the blood and flesh and hair exploding like carp out of the river bottom. Ray watches the gray windows of Leo's apartment, his mind drawing the stillness of that death from out of this stillness, the one before him now, lit pale orange as the sun rises on the faint noise of radio static. As he watches, a light clicks on and the drapes part. A wedge of Leo's face appears in the gap between the curtains. Ray pushes back into his seat, guns the engine, and spins out, his fingers shaking. By the time he crosses into Clarendon, the town has started up again. Ray stops at the Quick-Mart for cigarettes and beer and donuts, two cartons of chocolate milk for Bosco. Today is for oystering, and Ray is relieved in this; beneath the river, there will be no talk of killing.

The night before, after they left Leo's, it was all Bosco could talk about, wound up like a kid on his way to the circus—breathless, bouncing in the seat of the truck.

"Hey, look at this," he said, drawing the stolen diamond from his pocket. The stone was milk white, irregularly shaped.

"Real smart," Ray said. "He's probably calling the cops right now."

Bosco shook his head. "Never miss it. Had fifty of these if he had one. An old Parcheesi box." He shook his head again. "Think I'd find a better hiding place for my stash." Bosco nudged Ray. "I think I *will*."

"We don't even know that's a real diamond," Ray said, though looking, he knew.

Bosco gripped the stone and drew a long, thin scratch across the width of Ray's windshield.

"Now what do you say?" Bosco asked. "Could write the fucking Declaration of Independence if I wanted to."

Ray kept driving toward the river without speaking, as he drives now through the early morning. Traffic is heavy going the other way, the men in suits and ties headed into Berryville, the women putting on makeup in their rearview mirrors, coffee cups steaming their windshields. The scratch on his own windshield catches the morning sun, making tiny prisms, needles of colored light.

In the river along the barge, two of their antifreeze jugs bounce, pulling under the surface and then popping up again. They haul up catfish thrashing onto the deck. Bosco tries to club them with the butt of his .38, missing each time, the metal deck of the barge clanging. He grabs the fish to hold it down, and the dorsal fin pierces the palm of his hand.

"Shit *damn,*" Bosco shouts. He falls back onto the deck, kicking the fish back into the river, still hooked to its line. His gun skitters across the barge.

"Can you think of any other ways to kill yourself?" Ray asks. Bosco sucks on his palm while Ray takes the gun, hauls up the antifreeze jug, lifts the fish into the air and shoots it through the head. He unhooks the limp fish and tosses it to Bosco.

"See if you can skin it and get it in the cooler without losing a limb. Then we'll get the heater in the water."

Bosco grins, his mouth wet with his own blood. "Yessir, bossman."

Ray retrieves from the cabin their plastic bucket of weights, most of them old iron window sash weights, along with scraps of steel they found on the barge. He fills the front and back pockets of his jeans, and with a length of rope makes a belt of sash weights to tie around his waist. The second belt he makes for Bosco, who is still struggling with the pliers, trying to skin the catfish. It will go bad before he finishes. Now fifty pounds heavier, Ray takes a pint of bourbon from the fridge and drinks. The bottom of the river is always cold, even in August. Ray walks out and ties the weight belt to Bosco, then stuffs his pockets full of iron while Bosco wipes off his hands. He holds up the bottle so Bosco can drink, spilling some down his shirt front. Finally, he uncurls fifty feet of clothesline and cinches either end to their waists.

Bosco drinks again. "Let us not forget our tithes and offerings, brothers," he says. "When the Lord has delivered into our hands those goddamn diamonds, let us give back to Jesus."

Ray stiffens at the mention of the diamonds. For the whole day Bosco has been planning how they will have the diamonds cut and sold in Little Rock, and how they will spend the money—fast cars and stereos and guns. He talks as if their lives are fairy tales, already written.

"So it's blasphemy now," Ray says. "We're trying something new."

"Listen, bud, if God was of a mind to strike me down, he'd of gotten me twenty fuck-ups ago."

Ray unchains the water heater from the side of the barge and floats it around to the front. The river currents lift and push it, banging it against the barge. Ray thinks that if it hit hard enough, it could knock them off their shoal and into open water. They tie it off to one of the cleats on the barge then grasp it on opposite sides, gripping it by its brass valves and pipe fittings. They draw deep breaths, readying themselves to strain against the weight of it. The old heater shell is lead-lined, industrial sized, nearly as heavy as a small car.

"All the way up," Ray says. "Nice big bubble for us." Words he repeats every time, a kind of incantation. They count three and lift the heater, the two of them grunting and spitting, until it is upright and flush against the surface of the water.

"Now," Ray says through his teeth, and they drop it, careful not to let it tip. They wait until it slips beneath the surface, thick rope coiling in after it. No bubble rises after the rope stops, and they know it has landed upright in the mud.

"We're good," Ray says. He draws five deep breaths, holds his clam rake tight to his chest and jumps in, the weights in his clothes pulling him down. The rope around his waist tightens until he hears the muffled *sloosh* of Bosco jumping in after him. He has learned to keep his eyes open underwater, and watches overhead as the filtered light shifts from murky yellow to dull brown, and then is gone almost completely. His feet settle on the bottom and he moves toward where he thinks the heater has landed, his boots sinking in, pulled downward. With his hands he finds the heater, and as his eyes adjust he can see it, faint white, slightly tilted. Ray gives two tugs on the rope and waits for Bosco to find him, hearing only the pounding of his heart in his ears. Three minutes he will last without a breath, the noise of his pulse like a clock reminding him. Bosco is there suddenly and they set to work, moving out from the heater like spokes from a hub, with or against the pull of the river. They rake the mud for oysters and clams, prying them out, saving them in burlap sacks tied to their belts. Later, sitting on the barge, they will sort them for size. Ray works quickly, his lungs feeling as though they too are weighted. His used-up air lets loose in quick, fat bursts as his muscles repeat their pattern—rake, dig, sack—like some song his body sings within itself. After twenty steps he turns back, lungs throbbing, the pulse of blood in the muscles of his face.

Ray is first beneath the heater, always, as Bosco seems able to hold his breath forever. He gives Ray a thumbs-up sign in the dark swirl of mud they have stirred. They lift the heater, and Bosco steadies it long enough for Ray to slide underneath and up in. Inside the heater is black as ink, the smell full of musk and rot, the curved walls sweaty, slick with moss and algae. There is no water down as far as his knees. Ray gulps mouthfuls of the trapped air, talks to himself to hear a voice, breathes again, then raps his knuckles on the wall and listens for the sound of Bosco lifting the heater for him.

For half a minute there is no sound, and Ray raps the wall again. *"Dammit, Bosco,"* he yells. He pushes up, without enough leverage to budge the heater. This prank is one that Bosco never tires of, one he will pull on Ray a couple times a week.

"Okay, fine," Ray shouts. "Stay out there and drown your sorry ass."

Finally there comes the squeak of Bosco's hands searching for a grip, then the suck of mud at the bottom. Ray takes one last deep breath and squirms out through the gap. He holds the heater for

Bosco to go inside. Looming up in Ray's face, Bosco grins and gives another thumbs-up, then disappears. They work this way for more than an hour, raking the spokes, filling their bags, taking their turns inside the heater. At the end of their work they turn the hot water valve at the top of the heater and let it fill, then climb the heater's rope back up to the barge, the weight belts and oyster bags hanging down, pulling at them.

They stand dripping on the deck of the barge, tossing off their weights.

"Had you that time," Bosco says, panting. "You thought I'd got washed away."

"Hell, yes, you fooled me. About twice as much as three days ago when you pulled the same trick."

"Well, this is near about the last time we have to dig oysters out of the shit. After we get those diamonds."

Ray nods, wipes mud from his face.

"Tell me this right now, Bosco. You gonna put the gun against his head? Pull the trigger? Stand there with pieces of Leo's brain down your shirt, blood on your hands, and then go digging through his shit? You can do all that?"

"Hell, Ray, you ever seen me handle a gun? I mean it—"

Ray shoves him hard against his good shoulder, staggering him. Bosco looks stung, his mouth open, dark water running in thin lines across his face.

"No more of your bullshit," Ray says. "Tell me here and now. You need that money or you might die, Bosco." Ray lightly taps Bosco's other shoulder, where the pain is, where the cancer has been. "No bullshit, just listen. I ain't dying, but I ain't afraid of good money either. So you tell me, Bosco. A gun in your hand, you raise it up, you fire into Leo's head. You shatter his skull. More blood than you've seen in your life. Think about that, Bosco, and tell me. You going to be able to do it?"

They stand facing each other, the puddles around their feet joining. Bosco's mouth works, his eyes dart to the side. He will not look at Ray.

"Go on, Bosco. You say the word, and we'll dump these fucking oysters back in the river and head over right now. Got your gun loaded? Just say."

Bosco looks off toward the water curling past the edge of the barge. His eyes well up, his face flushed. He slowly shakes his head, not speaking.

Ray points a finger at him. "That's it then, understand? Not another goddamn word about it."

They use up the afternoon parked at the juncture of highways 45 and 19, in the shade of a tree, selling the oysters out of a cooler in the back of Ray's pickup. They sell mostly to people from town headed back to their country houses, men with their ties loosened, women in convertibles with the tops up. Ray uses a scale he made to weigh more than true by taking it apart and stretching the spring. They charge six dollars a pound, a dollar cheaper than IGA.

When they have sold out or when what is left has gone bad, the shells opening, they will head into town, stopping at the liquor store on the way. By the time they get where they are going—usually the Lightbulb Club or the Barbary Coast—they are half drunk on bourbon. Today, though, Ray eases off a little, steering toward the fire station on River Road, for what he calls the best deal in town, all-you-can-eat fried chicken and barbecue for four dollars, with slaw and biscuits and lemonade on the side.

"Every damn body and their seven kids will be there," Bosco says. "Ain't worth it."

"It's worth it," Ray tells him. "I'm sick of hauling dinner out of that shit-hole river. Sick of all of it."

"Plus there won't be no women there," Bosco says. "Just housewives." He wipes his nose on his sleeve.

Ray nods, pleased that Bosco has found something to pout over, to distract him from the diamonds. He has not mentioned them since that morning. All afternoon, in the hot shade of the tree, Ray has seen Leo alone in his apartment, seen the small swirl of the feathers, has heard Leo's breath in the quiet room. He thinks of the cancer growing inside Bosco's shoulder, cells gone wrong and dark, growing there maybe even now, as Bosco drinks and wipes his mouth. He thinks of himself, shucking off his thirty-eight years like oyster shells. It would be two lives for one, he thinks. Two for one.

At the firehouse the men in their blue uniforms sweat over gas grills while the wind whips paper plates and napkins off the picnic tables and around the yard. Mothers and fathers sit on blankets spread across the grass. The bigger kids hurl water balloons at one another while the little kids crowd around a fat, panting dalmation —Sparky—who shows the kids how to stop, drop, and roll, put through his paces by a short fireman with a blond mustache.

The man taking money sits at a card table in the driveway. Ray pays for both of them and waits for his change.

"You boys aren't drunk, are you?" the man says. He gives them a smile with no humor in it. The man wants to find some excuse to keep them out, Ray thinks. Two river rats fucking up his nice family gathering.

"Not drunk," Ray says. "Just hungry as hell." Bosco laughs.

They stand in line for chicken and barbecue, cole slaw, biscuits, peach cobbler, and lemonade. Both pile their plates so high that some of the food teeters off into the grass. Bosco pulls his pint of bourbon from his pocket and refills their half-emptied lemonade cups. When they finish, Ray feels doubly drunk, from the whiskey and from his overly-fed stomach. He eats one last biscuit, not from hunger but just for the excess of it, sloshing it around in his mouth with a gulp of the spiked lemonade. He can't remember when he felt this happy, eating the way he did as a kid visiting his grandparents in Hot Springs, going a night without eating carp and mudfish from out of the dirty river and drinking half-warmed beer. Soon it will be fall again, oyster season over and back to little money, just what he makes from his route and whatever he and Bosco can throw together in the way of odd jobs. Last year it was helping businesses downtown string up their Christmas lights for four bucks an hour. For a man his age, nothing more than sympathy work.

He looks over at Bosco, who is still chewing and swallowing, bobbing his head in time with the bluegrass music that spills out of the loudspeaker mounted on the side of the firehouse. Every so often the music is interrupted by the crackle and chirp of the dispatcher radioing the sheriff's deputies. A couple of the young parents dance in a ring around their children, who laugh and giggle in the middle. Ray takes the bottle from Bosco and pours over the ice in his cup. He swallows, hardly tasting it now, his happiness climbing like some balloon he's released. He gets up and starts dancing too, Bosco tugging on his pant leg, telling him to sit down. He wanders around the yard, stepping on blankets, thinking how strange it is that all these people—his age, many of them, or younger—have ended up this way. They have nice, shining cars, nice, shining houses, nice, shining jobs.

"Nice, shining lives," Ray says aloud, not aware until he's said it that he has been thinking this. He laughs at the idea that these people have got where they are by following some simple plan, going to school, meeting the right people. That's all fine, he thinks. His real question is how they knew from the start that there was supposed to *be* a plan, how did they know to move in some direction and not another? He stops now at the outside edge of a ring of children, a new group gathered around to watch Sparky go through his paces. He can see their polished lives laid out before them. He remembers teachers, principals, counselors from high school, two decades past now, telling him that he needed direction. He can hear them saying it, see their faces. How was he to know that they only meant that his life would end up somewhere, and that automatic pilot brought you down low to stay? *I have direction,* he thinks, though the children turning to look at him tells him that he must be talking out loud again. His direction is down, the bottom of the river, then back to where he started, ready the next day to go down again. Down, down, Bosco behind or below him, tethered to him, the two ends of some finite thing, always down.

Sparky catches a Milk-Bone tossed by the fireman. The dog wags his tail and the children clap. For a better view Ray lifts himself onto the back of the ladder truck parked in the driveway, its doors open for display, the ladder extended into the air.

"Always tell mom and dad to test those smoke detectors," the fireman says. Sparky nods and the children laugh.

"Have a plan for getting out," the fireman says.

A plan. For getting out. The words fill Ray's mouth as he repeats them, resonate at the bottom of his cup as he drinks, burn at the back of his throat. The children stare at him, the fireman glares. He smiles at them. We have our plan, he wants to tell them. He and Bosco. For getting out. For getting off the bottom of the river. *Leo . . . Gun . . . Parcheesi box . . . Diamonds.* Ray tries to shake the idea from his head. Maybe they are done with it, and Bosco won't pull anymore. Maybe Ray's speech earlier has ended it, planting them forever at the river bottom.

"Why do you think we bring Sparky to the fires?" the fireman asks. Ray can tell this is the setup for some cornball joke.

"I know," Ray says, and they all turn toward him, sudden as a school of fish. "He pisses on it when the rest of you fuckers get wrung out."

The fireman's face darkens. "I think you need to get on home now, buddy, sleep it off."

Ray smiles. "I ain't your fucking buddy."

The fireman points his finger, raises his voice. "Now you listen—"

Ray whistles and snaps his fingers. "Here, boy. C'mon boy." Sparky jumps up and trots in Ray's direction, the show only half over. The children look around, confused. Bosco is there suddenly, pulling at Ray's pant leg, calling for him to come down. Ray likes this, the fireman flustered, everything mixed up. He has spoiled the plan. He sees this as the core of living in this world: plans made or not made, plans messed up. They have a plan for getting out and will not use it if Bosco will not talk about it, if Bosco will let himself die quietly instead.

"I think we're done here, Ray," Bosco says, pulling at him. Ray yanks loose from his grip and steps up on the ladder. He climbs about twenty feet and some of the children clap, thinking this is part of the show.

"What do you think you're doing?" the fireman yells. Sparky barks.

"Hey, Bosco," Ray shouts down, his tongue thick in his mouth. "What's your plan for next spring? What say we dive down to the river bottom, rake around in the shit, then do it again the next day, then a thousand more times after that."

Bosco shrugs. "Okay."

Ray climbs further up the ladder, feeling it sway under him. He can see the air conditioners on top of the firehouse, and, in the distance, a corner of the river. Other firemen leave their posts at the gas grills and trot over to surround the back of the truck. Ray turns and sits on the rung.

"Come down from there now," a fireman shouts. "We can't be responsible for your safety. The outriggers aren't extended."

"Careful, Bosco," Ray says. "You might want to check your calendar, make double sure about next spring." He laughs at his joke, then stands and looks a hundred feet up at the top of the ladder. He thinks of climbing all the way up, then decides against it. Just more up and down, going nowhere.

"I'm sure, Ray," Bosco says, sober with his embarrassment.

Ray climbs down to the platform then jumps to the pavement. The firemen tell him to get lost before they call the sheriff, and some of the children start clapping again.

"Okay, then," he tells Bosco. "We're set."

That night Ray makes an excuse of wanting tequila, which means a ride to the liquor store in Berryville, down the highway past Leo's place. Ray wants to feel the pull of the dairy, the thin stretch of lawn and plaster wall separating them from that other life. He wants to know if it is enough to draw murder from them. He thinks of little else as they ride into the early gray of night, the noise of I-40 rising on the near horizon. As they pass Leo's, the dairy is dark, Bosco is punching the buttons on Ray's radio, complaining that there are no decent rock-and-roll stations. In Berryville they buy their tequila, drinking as they head back toward Clarendon. All along the road are the mashed bodies of frogs, which appear on the highways in the late part of summer, signaling its end.

Ray takes a long swig, the tequila a burning rope through him. As they pass the dairy again he taps the brakes, slowing. Yellow light from Leo's window angles across the yard and gravel driveway. His curtains are open, a box fan on the windowsill. Leo stands shirtless in front of it. Faint music finds its way to the open window of Ray's truck.

Ray passes the bottle to Bosco. He can feel the tequila inside him, an invisible thumb pushing him down. "There it is," he says.

"There what is?" Bosco drinks, some of it spilling down his shirt. He wipes his mouth on his sleeve.

"Leo's place, what do you think I mean?"

"He's standing right there, probably giving himself a massage." Bosco smiles, wiping his shirtfront. He is so thin now, wasting away inside his clothes.

"Bet he's planning how to spend his money," Ray says. He cuts his eyes at Bosco, then looks at the slice of road lit by his headlights.

"He *don't* spend it, that's the damn waste of the whole thing. If that was me, I would . . . I don't know, find something to spend it on. I'd buy stuff." He sniffs, scratches at his tooth with a fingernail. Ray hits the gas and watches in the rearview as the yellow light recedes. They ride in silence, slowly killing the bottle.

"You were right on what you said," Bosco finally says. It is fully dark now, Ray cannot see his face.

"Right on what?"

"On not being able to do Leo the way we said. You were 100 percent on that one. Just not in me to pull that trigger."

Ray takes a long swallow, warmth and relief mixing inside him. Tomorrow is for oysters, he thinks. A few dollars in their pockets.

Near the river bridge they see the lights from downtown

reflected, the fluorescent glow off the Methodist church spire, the faint glow of their trotline jugs. The barge is further down, hidden in shadow. Later, they sit on the couch at the edge of the barge, drinking down toward the end of the bottle, chasing it with beer, drinking for hours. It is the way it was before Bosco's cancer, when Ray visited only on weekends. They talk of going into the Barbary Coast, trying to lure some women back to the barge. Bosco is happy, talking about game shows, asking Ray to name the top five things you buy at the grocery store. When the mosquitoes get bad, Bosco hauls out a quart jar of citronella oil and they wipe their arms and faces with it. The river washes around them. Their antifreeze jugs bob in the dark.

"You're a different story," Bosco says, out of the dark. He smokes, the orange of his cigarette moving.

"What are you talking about, Bosco?"

"I mean you could do it. To Leo. You're the one."

Ray tightens his hands on his beer bottle.

"You're drunk as hell, Bosco." His own drunkenness threatens to push him through the floor of the barge, down into the river bottom.

"Yeah, but I know you, Ray. You told me what you did today because you know me, and now I'm telling you because I know you just the same. You could kill Leo."

Ray's hands shake. "Don't talk about this shit, anymore, Bosco. We're done with it."

"After we finished, you know what? I bet you'd say it was the easiest thing you'd ever done," Bosco says. For a moment, Ray thinks of shinnying across to his truck, starting it, leaving all this behind. But without Ray, Bosco would not be capable even of diving in the river for oysters, of catching carp. He would be lost. Ray picks up the .38, hefting it, letting his fingers curl around it. He clicks the safety off and on and off and on.

Bosco coughs and winces, rubs his shoulder. The gas lantern hisses at his feet. "I bet you already made plans for your half. Of course you ought get more than half, you pull the trigger. I mean, that's only f—"

"Shut your goddamn mouth, Bosco." Ray raises the .38 to Bosco's head, clicks the safety off, pulls back the hammer.

Bosco smiles, looks at him. "Right now? You're just proving my point." Ray lets the hammer down and eases the safety back on. For a minute, neither of them speak.

"And you better listen," Bosco says, whispering above the sound of the water. "Without that money, Ray, I'll die. You ever stop and think about that?" He flicks his cigarette into the river, then pulls the diamond from his pants pocket and taps it nervously on the wooden arm of the couch. Ray looks at him, his face lit faintly by the light of early dawn, the grayness of disease on him like a second skin.

"You're talking about a man's life," Ray says. Already the town is waking up, cars moving across the bridge.

"You're goddamn right we are," he says. He wipes his mouth with his fingers, his hand shaking. The diamond glistens dully in his fingers.

Ray shakes his head. "We're done with it, Bosco."

"No we ain't," Bosco says. "You won't let me die, Ray. You won't."

Ray pushes himself up, stretches. "We should get this heater in the water." He has not slept, is still full of tequila and beer. He feels heavy, weighted down. He thinks of the cancer, thinks of it growing, cell by cell, in Bosco's shoulder.

"You'd just better hear me, Ray," Bosco says, slipping the diamond back in his pocket, "because I ain't finished. I ain't gonna finish."

Ray pretends to ignore him. He grabs the water heater and struggles with it alone until Bosco finally helps. They muscle it up, then stop to rest, breathing together, Bosco holding his chest with one hand.

"Everything is easy, Ray," Bosco says. "I'll load the gun and talk us inside. I swear I will. Hell, I'll drive if you want me to. Ray . . . you know you will."

Ray steadies the heater, leveling it on the water. "Nice big bubble for us," he says without thinking. He can feel Bosco staring at him. They release the heater, then wait to make sure their bubble does not escape and rise to the surface.

"We're good," Ray says. They silently pass the bag of weights, filling their pockets, stringing their belts. Ray uncurls the clothesline to tether them together.

They stand at the edge of the barge. Bosco grins. "Last time we'll have to—" he starts to say, before Ray leaps into the river, sinking fast, moved by the current. He feels the rope tighten, Bosco pulled in behind him. He settles in the gravel and mud. The water is clearer than usual, a light, murky gold. He walks until the heater looms up in his vision, white and blurry. He gives the two quick tugs on the rope and Bosco soon finds him. They work out from the heater in their long spokes. It is slow today, only a few oysters under their rakes. When it is time, they lift the heater and Bosco strains holding it while Ray slips underneath. The darkness of it always startles him, like instant blindness. He hears himself pant for breath, runs his fingers around the mossy sides. He holds his head in his hands, squeezes, breathes.

Ray taps the side of the heater and Bosco lifts it to let him out. Ray takes it from him to allow Bosco inside. Just before he slips under, Bosco holds up the diamond and gives Ray a thumbs-up. His face is drawn, desperate, searching Ray's eyes. He slips down and in. Without the money he will die, and without Ray he will not have the money. He believes in everything that Ray is to him, just as he believes that bullshit and stupid jokes are equal to cancer, that killing is some easy thing. He pulls his faith from TV shows. They are moving toward the things he believes in now, he is pulling Ray toward them, toward the explosion of brain and hair and blood, toward the shining box of diamonds. In the dark water and the throbbing of his lungs the scene repeats itself like memory. Bosco taps the side of the heater. He will reemerge, his eyes panicked and full of death. The taps on the heater grow louder—sharper and more distinct—and Ray realizes that Bosco is tapping with the diamond. The clicks resonate like gunshots through some distant wall, mixed in the noise of his pulse in his ears, of the slow push of water. He shakes his head, his lungs aching already, too soon, way before his time in the heater. His chest burns, the taps coming in sharp ripples of sound as his fingers work at the knotted rope around his waist, at the belt of weights holding him down. He unties them and rises slightly, Bosco's voice shouting from a thousand miles away as Ray twists the hot water valve atop the heater, letting in the water, the bubbles rising fat and bright, moving upward as the taps of the diamond quicken and then slow, as Ray gives himself to the current, following the bubbles, his lungs strained to bursting, his eyes held by a patch of greasy light above him. He rises, flailing through moments, as if all he could know of what would come next and next were held above him always, just beyond reach, in a layer of thin white air.

M. MORAN

Brad Barkley is a native of North Carolina. His first novel, *Money, Love,* made the "Best of 2000" lists selected by *The Washington Post* and *Library Journal.* He is also the author of *Circle View,* a collection of stories. His fiction has appeared in such places as *Glimmer Train, The Oxford American, The Georgia Review, Book Magazine, The Southern Review,* and *The Virginia Quarterly Review,* which twice awarded him the Balch Prize for best fiction. He has won fellowships from the Maryland State Arts Council and the NEA. He has two new books forthcoming, a novel entitled *Alison's Automotive Repair Manual* and a collection entitled *The Properties of Stainless Steel.* He lives and teaches in Frostburg, Maryland.

This was one of those stories that took a few years to find its rightful shape, frustrating my constant belief (renewed with every story) that I ought to be able to knock it out in a week or two. The idea grew in some cryptic way out of a trip I took across southeast Arkansas with another writer. We were lost, and it was one in the morning, and speeding along on some deserted two-lane road I turned off the headlights in the car, plunging us into the blackest night I'd ever seen, hundreds of miles away from anything that could be called a city. Something about the darkness of those moments, the creepiness of them, found their way into the story. But despite the surface grimness, the story was a pleasure to work on, especially the underwater scenes, which I wrote sitting at my computer, holding my breath.

Ingrid Hill

THE MORE THEY STAY THE SAME

(from *The Raleigh News & Observer*)

So the doctor is out. The old-fashioned sign in the window that faces the suburban New Orleans mall promenade says that, and it's true. If you come strolling past our store, checking out kiosks, admiring or reviling the new faux-northwoods-evergreen decorations with yellow and purple and green Mardi Gras ribbons, fingering credit cards deep in your pocket, you see this crazy anachronistic sign.

I'm a so-called "optician," which means the optometrist's girlfriend who can do a few things like adjust the sidepieces of glasses-frames, sort the orders, tend the front desk. I get to wear a white coat. Looks professional, hey. I'm the only female in the employ of Opti-Shop.

So my boyfriend (he's Doctor Bevalacqua to the public) is at lunch and also buying a pair of Rollerblades for himself so we can go blading this weekend even if he's almost thirty—he's going to bring back Chinese for me, spicy chicken cashew, from Panda Express in the food court. The lab tech who makes the glasses, Mordecai, who is black, is also at lunch, which he shouldn't be: he used up his lunch hour this morning buying virtual-reality game software down the promenade. The other optician, Lorenzo, who's Mexican, called in sick; I know he's not: he's just ticked at

Bev because he called him on the carpet about some numbers that didn't make sense, and Lorenzo's not fond of the carpet. The third guy, Chad, quit yesterday because he got a job at a drive-through espresso stand where he can sit and read sci-fi between customers. "Great!" growls Bev, rolling his eyes, Groucho Marx-y. "Super career move!" Chad just flips him off, so low-energy that Bev doesn't even see it.

So I'm all alone here, surrounded by seven hundred pairs of glasses-frames by twenty-three manufacturers, ranged in displays under their designer logos, pictures of Sophia Loren in huge googly goggles, and nobody-models looking vacant. I'm hearing my stomach growl, I'm thinking about whether I *should* be the only female employee, whether I *should* be holding the fort while these guys goof off, whether *anything's* changed since my mother —who went to jail overnight when she was my age for picketing something or other that she said was sexist—was right after all. She didn't wear a bra then, and her boobs sag now from that. She says, "Honey, that's what breasts do. That's not feminist politics: it's simple gravity." She keeps saying: *Nothing has changed since the seventies, Caro, I swear nothing's changed.*

So now this freak comes in. Hunting-camouflage jacket (there's nothing to hunt within thirty miles), Saints ballcap. A little spacey, bit of a shuffly walk. Maybe thirty-five, forty. He's got like a two-day beard, scruffy, not even cool. He tips his hat. Funny kind of tipping, theatrical, super-polite. He says, *Doctor is out means what.* He looks around the store. It sounds as if he has an accent, but I can't quite tell. I say, *Gone to lunch,* and I shrug. I say *What can I do for you? Would you like an appointment for an eye exam?* I'm way cheerful. He says *I am from Soviet Union.* He's skipping words as if he's really foreign but something about him is off-kilter. Like the accent seems to come and go. I think I'll try this: I say, *There is no Soviet Union.* I start to let him know I'm no dummy, I'm in college part-time, but I don't want to say anything that acquaints him with me. He looks at me funny. I say, *It fell.* He looks for a minute as if he's confused, or he's angry. I think of my mother talking about international politics when she was little, everyone scared of the Russian Bear. I think: this guy looks like a bear, I'm glad it's daytime and the mall is well-lit. He says, *Yes, well.* He says then: *I am from Georgia.* He's got this accent now that's wavering like the colors in the bottom of an old Wurlitzer jukebox. I say *Soviet Georgia?* He says something that sounds like *si. So do you have some glasses on order?* I say, redirecting. *I can look you up.* He makes a leer-like smile and echoes what I have just said. He says, as if he is a space alien trying to pass as an earthling by echoing me, *I can look you up.* I say, *Excuse me?* The echo sounds distinctly like a threat. I'm glad I don't have my last name on my nametag. *I like very much girls of America,* he says. *Very . . . sqvisshy,* he says. When he says squishy his accent sounds genuine. His eyes are on my chest, on the front of my lab coat. I say, *You are in the wrong store, sir.* I don't know what else to say. His eyes are small, dark, and animal-like. *No, in right store,* he says. *You would like to come home with me?* I kind of half-laugh, nervous ha-ha, and I sound like Mickey Mouse. Minnie. *To Soviet Georgia?* I say. It seems, the second it comes to me, to be the right thing to say, like to distance him as a looney, but when it comes out, it sounds just horrible. He says *Yes. My old mother love you like daughter. She sew you good apron.* His eyes are still on my chest. His accent is nowhere in evidence. *I think you need to leave,* I say. I am wishing Bev would come back, I feel like a wimp, and I wonder whether, my mother's politics notwithstanding, this gender stuff will ever change. I think of the Soviet Union, kaput, and Deng Xiao Ping dead and the map of the People's Republic of China dotted with KFCs. Then I look at Señor Soviet Georgia before me. I think—I take French—*"Plus ça change, plus c'est la même chose."* The more things change, the more they stay the same. My mom told me one day—big shrug—that when she was really little there were only blacks and whites in New Orleans, and after they desegregated in '54 her daddy and mamma moved her out to Metairie so she could be in an all-white school, but now there's all kinds of people. *Vietnamese shrimpers!* she says, with delight but as if extraterrestrials had landed. *I love it!* she says. *It's a whole new world*. Well, she's right. The acrylic nail place down the promenade has all Vietnamese manicurists. I tell Monsieur Soviet Georgia, "Really," I say, just as nice as can be. I say more firmly, "Go, now." I wonder how to say it in Russian. I feel cuckoo. "Scram," I say. *You look more sqvisshy than every American girl I have see,* he says. I pick up the phone. I call Security, real easy, real smooth. I watch his camouflage back as he shuffles away. I know he's a fake but I'm still really sad for his poor aproned mother back in the snow in Russia. Whoa! Here comes Bev, wafting Szechuan smells, grinning like a five-year-old, waving his Rollerblades. The doctor is in.

Ingrid Hill has published stories in *The Southern Review, The Michigan Quarterly Review, Shenandoah, North American Review, Louisiana Literature,* and *Story;* and a collection of fiction, *Dixie Church Interstate Blues.* She has held fellowships from Yaddo and MacDowell and is a two-time National Endowment for the Arts recipient. She grew up in New Orleans, and is the mother of twelve children, including two sets of twins. She lives in Iowa City with her family.

ANDREW SCHMIDT

The short-short story is not my natural metier. In the morning, first thing, I check in the mirror to see if I've turned into Alice Munro during the night, because my stories have been getting longer and denser, approaching the condition of novels. When the News and Observer *solicited a 1200-worder, my first thought was: don't even* go *there. I rolled my eyes. But do you remember that old Reese's peanut butter cup commercial (ha!! you do!!) in which the guy carrying the peanut butter bumps into the guy carrying chocolate, and, eh voilà, peanut butter cup? The request for the short short bumped into an anecdote my brilliant daughter gave me. Right about the time the request came in, my daughter Annika, a French major under-*

employed part-time in an optical shop, called me during the day and said, "Let me tell you about this guy who just came into the store." He appears verbatim. The other employees, of course, are figments of my fevered imagination. The dare I set myself (okay, Ms. Harry Houdini) was to show in 1200 words the astonishing cultural changes in ethnic diversity and tolerance in the New South, alongside the same old sexist attitudes, hard as a diamond but less sparkly-nice.

Kate Small

MAXIMUM SUNLIGHT

(from *Nimrod International*)

Hide," my mother says in Vietnamese, and, *"that is my ax."* I snatch these words. *"Father,"* she murmurs.

"More," I say, shaking her.

"No," she says in her sleep. Her voice makes a fog before her face.

She walks from work to the Vietnam Veterans' Memorial. I stay in the trees. Maybe he is there, his name too high for her to reach because she doesn't stretch up. She looks from her fingertips to the Wall. One hundred and twenty-seven steps from the Zero Mile Stone. Nine hundred and thirty-one steps from the salon where she does manicures.

I got arrested for sitting in Lincoln's lap.

It's 4 A.M. in Vietnam," I said to the cop.

"Good goddamn morning Vietnam," he said.

"You smell like bad weather," my mother hissed in Vietnamese when I got home. *"Like fish hanging in trees after a flood."* It sounded like water, but she slapped me when she said it.

In Georgetown there's a bar called The Tet Café where I serve drinks with vapors swirling out. My first night, a guy asks me where I'm from. Before I can say, he tells me how people called him baby-killer and spit in his face and that's what he got instead of a parade. Now when they ask where I'm from, I say, "Virginia," and they say, "no *really,*" and I say, "Virginia, really."

"A glass of milk! A plate of dog!" The same one always yells, in bad Saigon slang.

I dump the peanut shells out of their ashtrays. They complain about the noise from the arcade next door. "Goddamn kids," they say, "goddamn computers." I bring them Chex party-mix. They ask about my mother. "What kind of a girl was she?" they slur, but it's not a question. They rhyme *Nam* with *ram* and shove it down their own throats with gin and tonic. Still, they know more Vietnamese than I do.

The man at the tourism office is skeptical.

"This is the soil of the Constitution Gardens," I demonstrate for him. "The Potomac is a golden artery of commerce. The Zero Mile Stone is the rock from which all distances are measured." I am trying to get a job as a tour guide. I will be called "Hospitality Associate."

"What's your last name?" he asks. "What's your current employment?"

He wants to watch me talk. I tell him about how men draw in the palm-leaf tables with their thumbnails but the words don't stay so they use knives. I tell him about the parade they still want, how they play dog-tag hockey, how they switch their R's and L's for a "Charlie Chan" accent when they say, "hey li'l gal, get me one of them rare steaks!" I tell him how they watch the blood rise from the slit to the knife in their American-Sized Portions. That's how the menu describes things, I say. I tell him about the teenagers next door, vanquishing aliens and kung-fu turtles with virtual guns. I tell him how to make a Singapore Sling and about the coconut cans—how there is a smiling Cambodian girl on each of them, sixty smiling girls rattling in a box in the alley. A couple always roll to the drain and maggots nest inside, letters looping on the tin like a not-finished language for small people, people like frogs peeping under mushrooms, people sprayed and crushed in narrow places.

Tran is my last name I tell the employment man.

"You have to have a positive attitude," he says. We are alone, but I know I am a speck in a vast crowd of shadow-colored people, pouring through a street in Ho Chi Minh City.

"Mia is my first name," I say to his back. "M I A," I spell.

I saw a ticker-tape parade once, for a baseball player who won a big game. Balls of confetti unrolled around him like yo-yos. I was small, and a man standing near us started wrapping me in paper. Other people added their streamers to my shredded dress and I turned into the kind of girl-clown my mother hates. Her hands dropped to her pockets. I was spinning but I saw her mouth in a smear, her lips a hard, red almond. A boy raised a cigarette lighter but I was already the tip of a candle, the kind that burns the ceiling.

My mother grabbed my hair. *"Why are you always so hungry?"* she says in Vietnamese when I am something too much. I am the wig on a drag queen or a loud aunt in an attic. I am a piece of sweaty lingerie left in the wrong place, the finger you give to a cop when you know he can't catch you, the tongue through the crack in the school bus and the wing of spit to follow it.

The day after the parade it rained and the paper-dust made a gray paste on all the taxi windshields. For a week there were ribbons unwashed from the gutters. *Maytag the Dependability People* they said a thousand times in a row.

The famous baseball player moved to Japan.

The Vietnam Veterans' Memorial is as serene as a bomb shelter. People leave things here: boonie hats, flowers, candles, sandwiches, sometimes a single green beret. The rangers take the things gently, like temple monks.

I'm not the kind of Buddhist my mother wants. She says ancestors need a lot of attention or else they will float, lost in a swamp of ghosts.

"I'll say prayers and make rice when you're dead," I say, but she shakes her head.

"Only a son," she says in English. Even though she has a little shrine with fruit and carnations for a picture of a man with a cane and a chicken.

"Who is that guy anyway?" I ask.

She doesn't say. She serves him broth and papaya salad. She lifts his bowl and wipes his frame slowly. She moves like the men and women who leave bandoleers and canteens at the Wall; C rations, boots, socks, compasses, maps, binoculars, sandbags, mosquito netting, trip flares, bronze stars, purple hearts, prom dresses, letters, steering wheels, party hats, football helmets, mittens, baby shoes, teakettles, engagement rings, record albums, and boxes of soil.

I saw a whole uniform in cleaner's plastic. A note on the collar said, "Belonged to John N. LaSalle of Cincinnati." I found John N. LaSalle of Cincinnati in panel 19W. I have a dream about him, pressed down to the size of a bouillon cube, nested with others in a deep, hidden room. But drawers spring from the Wall. Fingers, feet, and braids pour out. Sap comes up. Flies struggle and crunch beneath the fists of mothers. I wake up and tell myself, *no,* because nothing sticks to it, not paint, lipstick, palms, or blood.

"We're looking for an upbeat approach," the employment man says. He says I can take a big test on all the monuments next week. I smile, including my teeth. "We have to think about 'sympathy fatigue,'" the employment man says. "Do you know what that means? Let's call you Mira, instead."

I am named after Mia Farrow of the movie *Rosemary's Baby.* My mother liked the kind of skin she has. How you can see the veins, and a nose that looks like it was pinched with pliers.

"Like beautiful French women," my mother says in English.

Like the kind of orchid, if you touch it, all the parts let go at the stem. My father was a white man but he must have been dark.

"Stay in less sunlight," my mother says. She pours extra bleach into my sheets.

* * *

When I ask, she says she can't remember his face. "They all look the same," she says.

I wonder how many makes *all*. And how many of me there are, sprung from the random plantings. Sometimes I pick out a white grandmother at the Wall, somebody named Edna or Doris or Thelma. But she already has bright yellow grandchildren with round pink heads and clothes. If I stood in a photo with them I would infect the film or disappear like the face of a black dog next to a blond cocker spaniel. These grandmothers wear blouses tucked into skirts and say prayers to their vinyl purses and leave flowers and recipes. Sometimes they come by twos and you know their men are dead. They whisper things like "live and let live," and "water under the bridge." Last week there was one screaming. "I sent you my son," she yelled, "now send him back." There wasn't an echo.

"American Boxwoods border the Rose Garden," I say, practicing when no one is there. "Generations of Americans have rolled Easter eggs under their limbs."

If you have someone here, you know the taste of the dust. I try reading blind and by touch, but the letters don't raise themselves to me. The engravings are too shallow and my hands can't make them shape into words. My fingers trace the elbows of V's and T's, hook on the G and know F, but not D versus P. The dust is the city: granite and skin. I leave it on my lip, like the mark of Ash Wednesday on a Catholic Vietnamese.

After me there was another baby. I waited for his spongy face to shape like mine since we were made of the same things: mother, plus white man. Not the same white man, but mother, and white. Which sometimes means, mother minus something, sometimes, mother, plus something else. Our fathers might have been Irish or Polish or Texan. It doesn't matter, because when you mix chocolate into vanilla pudding, you can't stir it back.

She thought milk would make us strong and pale. She thought our firm thick American skeletons would glow through our skin like the thousand-watt smiles of cheerleaders and toothpaste models. She named him Bryan because there can't be a more American name than that. She thought it would straighten out the leak in his heart and his too-soft bones, his ears barely there like other Agent Orange babies and My Lai leftovers who don't hear lullabies.

I talked to him while he slept. "Being Bryan will blond out the jungle tucked into you," I whispered. "A Bryan doesn't smell like coriander and temple incense. His palms don't close around a seaweed scent."

"Don't breathe into his face," my mother said. She motioned me away from the cradle.

His lids were shut tight, tiny Bryan dreams rolling beneath them, birds perched on wires strung four thousand three hundred and eighty miles from the Zero Mile Stone. "Listen to that," she'd say to him in English, to what's closer, buses, taxis, feet. "Brih-yaahn," she'd say, drawing him back in her long careful vowels, to us.

"Not all your brother," she still says in English when I do something disappointing like the parade or the night on Lincoln's lap. She'll jerk her head toward him even though he's not there: "*not* same as you," she says.

I used to imagine meeting my Dad.

"Hey li'l gal," he'd say. I'd forget I'd already gotten to America. I'd see myself meeting him at the airport, me short and dusty in an ugly plaid dress and carrying things: a fan, an oar, a fern. A television crew would film the whole thing. My father would sweep me up in his hairy pink arms and Peter Jennings would dab his eyes and shake my father's hand. I would be renamed Veronica or Debbie or Ashley, and Peter Jennings would send me money for college and buy the baby a wheelchair. But I started looking at the pictures of GIs people leave here, field photos glued onto cardboard and wrapped in plastic. I stole one, of a boy with ragged teeth, a belt full of bullets, and a dangling button. Who had the time to hold something like a needle, to bend the eye away from the horizon, shadows in ditches, or the motion of the trees? And thread is too clean, too much like women's fingers which smell like soap and roses. He must have let the button fall away. My stolen photo-boy stared like a man, but baby-white creases showed where dirt kept the sun out of his neck. His bayonet held a souvenir skull, front teeth chipped out like a child's. He must have boiled or rubbed it clean with sand. Even though my hand would fit that face like the curve of the moon, even though I am tied to the flesh by the karma of a female birth and must repay the parents in this life, I tore up the picture.

My mother says the mundane recollection of objects of the past is an obstacle to progress on the Buddhist path. But she saves things, like the deck of cards in the sleeve of a sweater beneath a bag of unstrung beads in a shoe-box behind a suitcase under the bed. The 6 of Clubs is on the top. The Queen of Diamonds has one breast propped in her own hand but no one bothered to draw fingers. The King rubs his sword. The Jacks have faces like babies. She saved these cards he played and cheated with, held in the same hands which ran over her laundry-soaped self, when *self* is a word he would never have recognized in Vietnamese, even if it sat feathered on her tongue, a bird not swallowed to the side of the yanking, she for him the flesh around *empty*.

I find a cracked plastic Avon compact inside a sock. *"I hate a mirror,"* my mother sometimes says in Vietnamese. But in it I see what she was: a beautiful girl covered in lice, flat-bellied, fragile and hard. I see the tires on the roof behind her, and behind that, a curve of workers in a field. She was a good runner.

In her sleep, she tells me there are big white-winged birds which know how to hide when choppers drown out their thick treetop conversation. In her sleep, she wonders if the sound returns as the smoke goes down, a little like a thousand poker chips falling on a hard dirt floor.

"You have to memorize the whole script," the employment man says.

I think of telling him the noble eight-fold path: the four cardinal facts, the three jewels, the five aggregates, the six precepts, the eight benevolent persons, the nine unwholesome courses of action, the ten fetters, but I figure this is too foreign, so in order to demonstrate my memory in a patriotic way, I say, "Eric S. Johansson, Miles V. Nathan, Doug A. Wilson, Morris P. Davies, Frederick R. Johnson, Thomas B. Eager, Eli C. Green, Edward B. Moss, Lyle G. Thomas, John H. Mercer, Bruce J. Hill, Stephen D. Phelan, Jerome L. Lee, William N. Del Simone, Rudolph I. Bennet, John W. Jones, Earl A. McMillan, Gary W. Cohen, Andrew S. Kelley, Jason P. Colfatti, Scott D. Edwards, Robert C. Monroe, Keith L. Sanderson, Jackson I. Flynn, Conrad G. Peters," and when I take a breath I don't finish July 5th, 1969, because the employment man is squinting at me, and I see I should have done the Sunday brunch specials. Eggs Benedict. Strawberry Waffle. Crab Quiche. Bottomless Bloody Marys.

There are seventy-three more names for July 5th, 1969, but I don't say them. "I don't forget things," I tell him. I walk to The Tet Café.

"Have gun will travel ho ho ho!" Dry ice curls up around ceramic tikki heads. Alcohol softens geography—it soaks to shreds the maps inside their heads. Pitchers of Mai Tais put Hawaii near Southeast Asia, next to Tokyo, alongside Bombay. China is a tiny blue island floating in a tsunami of 80 proof Hawaiian punch.

"Shotguns, silencers, bayonets . . ." I disappear. I fall between beads of soldier's pidgin. "Sayonara, aloha, kemosabe," jargon like blisters, on them, not me. The napalm their own bodies make, which never breaks on the surface to dry and scab but is reabsorbed into some black gash of shame. Their words clobber the Vietnamese I have collected, from the old people who sit behind the electric coffee pot at the Lau Family Center. *"Corn, cucumber, melon, eggplant, onion, sugar, blacksmith,"* the grandmothers slowly say for me. "C-4 explosives!" somebody shouts in the bar. "Feather hatchets, fragmentation grenades, tear gas!" Souvenir lingo flies through their talk with the grace of clay pigeons. "Jungle, yellow, red, clever whores, bony-assed." Knees and feet bounce. The floor vibrates like their tongues, littered with keepsakes to say like a broken rosary, to squeeze like fragments of some saint's body. "It's raining slants," one says, holding bourbon on his tongue, a gulp of communion.

"You will tell an American story," my mother says, when I say I have applied for the tour-guide job. She doesn't like The Tet Café.

She offers to do my nails. Her fingers are dry at the ends though they rub lotion into other palms. Candy-Apple, Four-Alarm, Reckless—these are her new names for red. My mother enamels the tips of lady senators and their secretaries who don't know how much their handshakes look like Thai girls on playing cards with tiny breasts and fallen kimonos.

"No thanks," I say. "Leave my nails plain, but help me get the coconut smell out."

My mother rubs my fingers with eucalyptus oil. *"Don't forget Buddha's second truth,"* she says in Vietnamese, spreading lotion into my knuckles.

That's the one about the thirst of the passions being a big fat trap.

"What kind of girl was she?" the employment man asks about my mother.

Suddenly I am tired of this place where all the buildings reach toward the sky because they think there is no place else to go.

"My mother is an American citizen," I say. I hold my face blank. Underneath it, I see myself going west. I see myself standing on the edge which faces the Pacific Rim, a place where my heart could crack open and the filth could spill out.

"Since when?" he asks.

"Vietnow," I whisper. It falls out of my mouth like a dead bird.

The employment man's pupils focus.

For a second I shut my eyes. In my dreams, we have an island covered with light white beds. Not Guam. A floating tablet full of clean blowing laundry. We gather on *Tet,* the celebration of the lunar new year. Pieces of moonlight spell songs in floating jars: *boat people, boat people, swim this way.* Fish cluster into arrows. My mother rests. The big white birds come, and the naked girl running, the naked girl screaming down a dusty road, sinks into a feather quilt. And babies. On the day of the mining of the harbor of Haiphong, lightning awakens whole bales of fish, lying in empty aluminum boats. The island, a raft, floats like a bandage. I swim out to sea and find Bryan poised in the tidal crack. Try to imagine a wall forty times the size of the one which is the Vietnam Veterans' Memorial. That is the size needed to include the names of all the dead Indochinese.

"I'm going to give you one more chance," the employment man says.

Again, my mother takes the bus to the Wall. She wears a red wool suit, her hair pulled tight, her feet in pumps like an American woman, her body narrow and tough, like mine. She is kneeling when a man with an instant Polaroid camera takes her picture. Gently he stretches the wet paper square toward her. She shakes her head. He leaves her alone.

"I gave you my boy," she says to nobody. She takes the bus back to work.

My mother casts no shadow in that photo, she is a thumb of gray. She is squinting. It is too bright, but letters etch up around her. *David, James, Philip, Douglas, Richard, Gary, Peter.* Fire-splashed nights, a harvest of young men, these crowd out the small survivors.

I think of the night Bryan stopped breathing. Then too, mother knelt by him, her back to me, her spine straight. I could not be still. I rode my bike down one-way streets, all the way to Lincoln's lap. Heat-seeking rain slicked my pumping legs like a chemical herbicide, and when I climbed up the slippery marble to print a hot stain of myself into those empty eyes, the cop arrived. Abe pitched me out, no uncle of mine, and I keeled down, my heels in the air, kicking nothing.

I put in my pocket the fresh photo of my mother the man left on the ground. I think of carving with hammer and knife Bryan's name in the Wall. And hers. And mine. But I realize my mother has taught me something much stronger: quietness. Maybe it is time to let myself be more than half *her.* Maybe I come from a single drop shot from the sky, a bullet of juice, a quick squirt of acid landing in her lap when she sat on her heels one day, to wipe the sweat from her neck. I am proud of my mother. She is the boss of the salon now. It used to be called *Miss Splendid,* but she has renamed it, *Maximum Saigon.* I put the small picture back on the Wall, where it belongs.

I sit at her feet, and tell my mother that when I go for my final tour-guide interview, I will put my hands behind my back. I will drop my eyes from employment man's face, and he will enjoy how tall he is. I don't say, *I will keep myself and my things safe, but where you store yours under the bed, I will mark mine in words, in a notebook.*

"Yes," she says, in Vietnamese. She teaches me the son's prayer. Together we chant for our ancestors. I imagine the rice, the white birds rising, the barbed wire, things I was too small to save on the back of my retinas, when Bryan was sorting himself in her belly. I imagine Hue's Forbidden Purple City, and Nam Giao Hill, with its staircases facing north, south, east, and west.

No, I'll say to the employment man, I don't have dead Cambodians bursting out of my pores, I will promise to talk about the cherry blossoms of the Potomac River. I won't describe how for years my mother has come here just to turn her back on the Wall, knowing they can't reach for the hem of her dress or the tail of her hair and yank her to the ground. I'll describe the trees planted around the promenade, and employment man won't have to worry about anything sneaky and lurking, like guerrillas in trees, or evil laundresses and peasant mothers who deal death from bicycle baskets. And no pitiful boat people washing up on beaches in leaky crafts and taking jobs from hard-working Americans, no emaciated victims rotting by the millions under the Khmer Rouge, spindly figures living forever in border encampments for long-forgotten reasons. These Yoshino trees furnish the setting for the annual Cherry Blossom Festival, I'll say, at the time of year when the men at The Tet Café file out of the grove by the Wall and stop short where the grass slopes, searching for their own names, wondering if there ever was, during the dinner hour, jungle and dust whipped to a frenzy for the camera by the blades of helicopters and full metal jackets. Even they will forget, confused by the fragrant blooms which last for ten or twelve days only. Amnesia comes, whether or not there are Kodachromes of disemboweled Vietnamese propped on the Wall, posed with beer cans in stiffened teenage hands. May you be comforted by the fact that so many of us tried to leave, hidden in wheel-wells and half-empty body bags. I won't describe the updrafts of blossom snow on the day my mother takes a photo of me, in my new tour-guide uniform, lunch-hour petals around me, carried by the first humid currents. It'll be 4 A.M. in Vietnam when she splits the camera's focus between my body and the writing on the Wall. Let my name be a smear. She'll catch me like that, in a slash of high-noon light. Together we shimmer like that kind of bug which spends the whole of its three days of life trembling fixed one inch above the skin of a pond. This is the picture we want, and we will walk away and into the cherry perfume. This is not *Miss Saigon,* I will say, and these are decorative trees which bear no fruit.

Kate Small's work has appeared in *Nimrod, The Boston Review, The Madison Review, Chelsea, Other Voices, Prism International,* and the anthology *Best New American Voices,* edited by Tobias Wolff. She is a recipient of a National Endowment for the Arts Fellowship, for 2002.

JEFF JOSLIN

Maximum Sunlight" was inspired by three days vigil at the Vietnam Veteran's Memorial in Washington, D.C. I am fascinated by the interrogative quality of Maya Lin's Wall: forced up against its polished surface, each visitor must confront his or her own reflection in granite. It occurred to me while standing there that I don't know of any English language literature that presses us to consider the insignificant role the Indochinese have played in the American debate over that war. During two generations of involvement with Indochina, most Americans have seen Southeast Asians as creatures to be killed, pitied, or saved, but rarely as human beings.

The story included here is part of a novel. I hope that Mia, its speaker, will put some pressure on the phenomenon of "compassion fatigue" in America.

George Singleton

SHOW-AND-TELL

(from *The Atlantic Monthly*)

I wasn't old enough to know that my father couldn't have obtained a long-lost letter from the famed lovers Héloise and Abelard, and since European history wasn't part of my third-grade curriculum, I felt no remorse at the time for bringing the handwritten document (on lined three-hole Blue Horse filler paper), announcing its value, and reading it to the class at Friday show-and-tell. My classmates—who would all grow up to be idiots, in my opinion, since they feared anything outside of Forty-five, South Carolina, thus making them settle down exactly where they got trained, thus shrinking the gene pool even more—brought the usual: starfishes and conch shells bought in Myrtle Beach gift shops, though claimed to have been found during summer vacation; Indian-head pennies given as birthday gifts by grandfathers; the occasional pet gerbil, corn snake, or tropical fish.

My father instructed me how to read the letter, what words to stress, when to pause. I, of course, protested directly after the first dry run. Some of the words and phrases reached beyond my vocabulary. The general tone of the letter, I knew, would only get me playground-taunted by boys and girls alike. My father told me to pipe down and read louder. He told me to use my hands better, and he got out a metronome.

I didn't know that my father—"a widower" is how he told me

to describe him, although everyone knew that Mom had run off to Nashville and hadn't died—had once dated Ms. Suber, my teacher. My parents' pasts never came up in conversation, even after my mother ended up tending bar at a place called the Merchant's Lunch, on Lower Broad, more often than she sang on various honky-tonk stages, waiting for representation by a man who would call her the next Patsy Cline. No, the prom night and homecoming of my father's senior year in high school with Ms. Suber never leaked out in our talks, whether we ate supper in front of the television screaming at Walter Cronkite or played pinball down at the Sunken Gardens Lounge.

I got up in front of the class. I knew that a personal, caring, loving, benevolent God didn't exist, seeing as I had prayed that my classmates would exceed their allotted time, et cetera, et cetera, and then we'd go to recess, lunch, and one of the mandatory filmstrips that South Carolina elementary school students watched weekly, on topics as tragic and diverse as Friendship, Fire Safety, Personal Hygiene, and Bee Stings. "I have a famous letter written from one famous person to another famous person," I said.

Ms. Suber held her mouth in a tiny O. Nowadays I realize that she was a beauty, but at the time she seemed just another seventy-year-old woman in front of an elementary school class, her corkboard filled with exclamation marks. She wasn't but thirty-five, really. Ms. Suber motioned for me to move closer to the music stand she also used on Recorder Day. "And what are these famous people's names, Mendal?"

Ricky Hutton, who'd already shown off a ship in a bottle that he didn't make but said he did, yelled out, "My father has a letter from President Johnson's wife thanking him for picking up litter."

"My grandma sent me a birthday card with a two-dollar bill inside," said Libby Belcher, the dumbest girl in the class, who went on to get a doctorate in education and then became superintendent of the school district.

I stood there with my folded document. Ms. Suber said, "Go on."

"I forget who wrote this letter. I mean, they were French people."

"Might it be Napoleon and Josephine?" Ms. Suber produced a smirk that I would see often in my life, from women who immediately recognized any untruth I chose to tell.

I said, "My father told me, but I forget. It's not signed or anything." Which was true.

Ms. Suber pointed at Bill Gilliland and told him to quit throwing his baseball in the air, a baseball supposedly signed by Shoeless Joe Jackson. None of us believed this, seeing as the signature was printed, at best. We never relented on Gilliland, and in due course he used the ball in pickup games until the cover wore off.

I unfolded the letter and read, "'My dearest.'"

"These are French people writing in English, I suppose," Ms. Suber said.

I nodded. I said, "They were smart, I believe. 'I want to tell you that if I live to be a hundred I won't meet another man like you. If I live to be a hundred there shall be no love to match ours.'"

The entire class began laughing, of course. My face reddened. I looked at Ms. Suber, but she concentrated on her shoe. "'That guy who wrote that "How Do I Love Thee" poem has nothing on us, my sugar-booger-baby.'"

"That's enough," Ms. Suber belted out. "You can sit down, Mendal."

I pointed at the letter. I had another dozen paragraphs to go, some of which contained rhymes. I hadn't gotten to the word "throbbing," which showed up fourteen times. "I'm not making any of this up," I said. I walked two steps toward my third-grade teacher, but she stood up and told everyone to go outside except me.

Glenn Flack walked by and said, "You're in trouble, Mendal Dawes." Carol Anderson, who was my third-grade girlfriend, looked as if she was going to cry.

Ms. Suber said, "You've done nothing wrong, Mendal. Please tell your daddy that I got it. When he asks what happened today, just say 'Ms. Suber got it.' Okay?"

I put the letter in my side pants pocket. I said, "My father's a widower."

My father was waiting for me when I got home. I never really knew what he did for a living, outside of driving within a hundred-mile radius of Forty-five, buying up land, and then reselling it when the time was right. He had a knack. That was his word. For a time I thought it was the make of his car. "I drive around all day and buy land," he said more than once, before and after my mother took off to replace Patsy Cline. "I have a Knack."

I came home wearing a canvas book bag on my back, filled with a math book and an abacus. I said, "Hey, Dad."

He held his arms wide open, as if I were a returning POW. "Did your teacher send back a note to me?"

I reached in my pocket and pulled out the letter from Héloise to Abelard. I handed it to him and said, "She made me quit reading."

"She made you quit reading? How far along did you get?"

I told him that I had only gotten to the part about "sugar-booger-baby." I said, "Is this one of those lessons in life you keep telling me about, like when we went camping?" My father taught me early on how to tell the difference between regular leaves and poison ivy, when we camped out beside the Saluda River, far from any commode, waiting for him to envision which tract would be most salable later.

"Goddamn it to hell. She didn't say anything else after you read the letter?"

My father wore a seersucker suit and a string tie. I said, "She called recess pretty much in the middle of me reading the thing. This is some kind of practical joke, isn't it?"

My father looked at me as if I'd peed on his wing tips. He said, "Now, why would I do something like that to the only human being I love in this world?"

I couldn't imagine why. Why would a man who—as he liked to tell me often—before my birth had played baseball for the Yankees in the summer and football for the Packers in the winter, and had competed in the Olympics, ever revert to playing jokes on his nine-year-old son? "Ms. Suber seemed kind of mad."

"Did she cry? Did she start crying? Did she turn her head away from y'all and blow her nose into a handkerchief? Don't hold back, Mendal. Don't think that you're embarrassing your teacher or anything for telling the truth. Ms. Suber would want you to tell the truth, wouldn't she?"

I said, "Uh-huh. Probably."

"Uh-huh probably she cried, or uh-huh probably she'd want you to tell the truth?" My father walked to the kitchen backward, pulled a bottle of bourbon from a shelf, and drank from it straight. Twenty years later I would do the same thing, but over a dog that needed to be put to sleep.

I said, "Uh-huh. I told her you were a widower and everything. We got to go to recess early."

My father kept walking backward. He took a glass from the cabinet and cracked an ice tray. He put cubes in the glass, poured bourbon into it, and stood staring at me as if I had told secrets to the enemy. "Did she say that she's thinking about getting married?"

I said, "She didn't say anything."

"I've gotten ahold of a genuine Cherokee Indian bracelet and ring," my father said the next Thursday night. "No BS here on this one. Your mother's father—that would be your grandfather—gave them to us a long time ago as a wedding present. He got them when he was traveling through Cherokee country. Your grandfather used to sell cotton, you know. Sometimes the Cherokees needed cotton. Sometimes they didn't have money, and he traded things for cotton. That's the way things go."

I said, "I was thinking about taking some pinecones." I had found some pinecones that were so perfect it wasn't funny. They looked like Christmas trees built to scale. "I was going to take a rock and say it was a meteorite."

"No, no. Take some of my Cherokee Indian jewelry, Mendal. I don't mind. I don't care! Hot damn, I didn't even remember having the things, so it won't matter none if they get broken or stolen. This is the real thing, Bubba."

What could I do? I wasn't but nine years old, and early on I'd been taught to do whatever my elders said, outside of drinking whiskey and smoking cigarettes when they got drunk and made the offer, usually at the Sunken Gardens Lounge. I thought, *Maybe I can take my father's weird jewelry and stick it in my desktop. Maybe I can stick a pinecone inside my lunch box.* "Yessir."

"I won't have it any other way," he said. "Wait here."

My father went back to what used to be my mother's and his bedroom. He opened up a wooden box he had fashioned in high school shop and pulled out a thin silver bracelet plus a one-pearl ring. I didn't know that these trinkets had once adorned the left arm of my third-grade teacher, right before she broke up with my father and went off to college, and long before she graduated, taught in some other school system for ten years, and then came back to her hometown.

I took the trinkets in a small cotton sack. My father told me that he'd come get me for lunch if I wanted him to, that I didn't need to pack a bologna sandwich and banana as always. I went to the refrigerator and made my own and then left through the back door.

Glenn Flack started off show-and-tell with an X ray of his mother's ankle. She'd fallen off the front porch trying to run from bees—something the rest of us knew not to do, seeing as we'd learned how to act in one of the weekly filmstrips. I got called next and said, "I have some priceless Cherokee Indian artifacts to show y'all. The Cherokee Indians had a way with hammering and chiseling." My father had made me memorize this speech.

I showed my classmates what ended up having been bought at Rey's Jewelers. Ms. Suber said, "Let me take a look at that" and got up to take the bracelet from my hand. She peered at it and then held it at arm's length and said, "This looks like it says 'sterling' on the inside, Mendal. I believe you might've picked up the wrong Indian jewelry to bring to school."

"Indian giver, Indian giver, Indian giver!" Melissa Beasley yelled out. It wasn't a taboo term back then. This was a time, understand, before we knew to use terms like "Native American–head penny" instead of "Indian-head penny," like I said before.

I said, "I just know what my dad told me. That's all I know." I took the bracelet from Ms. Suber, pulled out the ring, and stood there as if offering a Milk-Bone to a stray and skittish dog.

Ms. Suber said, "I've had enough of this" and told me to return to my desk. I put the pearl ring on my thumb and stuck the bracelet around the toe of my tennis shoe. Ms. Suber said, "Has your father gone insane lately, Mendal?"

It embarrassed me, certainly, and if she had said it twenty or thirty years later, I could've sued her for harassment, slander, and making me potentially agoraphobic. My desk was in the last row. Every student turned toward me except Shirley Ebo, the only black girl in the entire school, four years after integration. She looked forward, as always, ready to approach the music stand and explain her show-and-tell object, a face jug made by an old, old relative of hers named Dave the Slave.

I said, "My father has a Knack." Maybe I said nothing, really, but I thought about my father's Knack. I waited.

Ms. Suber sat back down. She looked at the ceiling and said, "I'm sorry, Mendal. I didn't mean to yell at you. Everyone go on to recess."

And so it continued for six weeks. I finally told my father that I couldn't undergo any more humiliation, that I would play hooky, that I would show up at school and say I had forgotten to bring my show-and-tell. I said, "I'm only going to take these stupid things you keep telling me stories about if it brings in some money, Dad."

Not that I was ever a capitalist or anything, but I figured early on that show-and-tell would end up somehow hurting my penmanship or spelling grade, and that maybe I needed to start saving money in order to get a head start in life should I not get into college. My father said, "That sounds fair enough. How much will you charge me to take this old, dried Mayan wrist corsage and matching boutonniere?"

I said, "Five bucks each."

My father handed them over. If the goddamn school system had ever shown a worthwhile Friday filmstrip concerning inductive logic, I would've figured out back then that when Ms. Suber and my father had had their horrific and execrable high school breakup, my father had gone over to her house and gathered up everything he'd ever bestowed on her, from birthday to Valentine's Day to special three-month anniversary and so on. He had gifts she'd given him too, I supposed much later, though I doubted they were worthy of monogamy.

But I didn't know logic. I thought only that my father hated the school system, had no trust whatsoever in public education, and wanted to drive my teacher to a nervous breakdown in order to get her to quit. Or, I thought, it was his way of flirting—that since my mother had "died," he wanted to show a prospective second wife some of the more spectacular possessions he could offer a needful woman.

He said, "I can handle ten dollars a show-and-tell session, for two items. Remind me not to give you an hourglass. I don't want you charging me per grain of sand."

This was all by the first of October. By Christmas break I'd brought in cuff links worn by Louis Quatorze, a fountain pen used by the fifty-six signers of the Declaration of Independence (my father tutored me on stressing "Independence" when I announced my cherished object to the class), a locket once owned by Elmer the glue inventor, thus explaining why the thing couldn't be opened, a pack of stale Viceroys that once belonged to the men who raised the American flag on Iwo Jima. I brought in more famous love letters, all on lined Blue Horse paper: from Ginger Rogers to Fred Astaire, from Anne Hathaway to Shakespeare, from all of Henry VIII's wives to him. One letter, according to my dad, was from Plato to Socrates, though he said it wasn't the original, and that he'd gone to the trouble of learning Greek in order to translate the thing.

Ms. Suber became exasperated with each new disclosure. She moved from picking names at random or in alphabetical order to always choosing me last. My classmates voted me Most Popular, Most Likely to Succeed, and Third Grade President, essentially because I got us ten more minutes of recess every Friday.

I walked down to the County Bank every Friday after school and deposited the money my father had forked over in a regular savings account. This was a time before IRAs. It was a time before stock portfolios, mutual funds, and the like. They gave me a toaster for starting the account and a dinner plate every time I walked in with ten dollars or more. After a few months I could've hosted a dinner party for twelve.

On Saturday mornings, more often than not, I drove with my father from place to place, looking over land he had bought or planned to buy. He had acquired a few acres of woodland before my birth, and soon thereafter the Army Corps of Engineers came in, flooded the Savannah River, and made my father's property near lakefront. He sold that parcel, took that money, and bought more land in an area that bordered what would become I-95. He couldn't go wrong. My father was not unlike the fool who threw darts at a map and went with his gut instinct. He would buy useless swampland, and someone else would soon insist on buying that land at twice to ten times his cost in order to build a golf course, a subdivision, or a nuclear-power facility. I had no idea what he did between these ventures, outside of reading and wondering. How else would he know about Abelard and Héloise, or even Socrates and Plato? He hadn't gone to college. He hadn't taken some kind of correspondence course.

We drove, and I stuck my head out the window like the dog I had owned before my mother took him to Nashville. We'd get to some land, puff down a dirt road usually, and my father would stare hard for ten or fifteen minutes. He barely turned his head from side to side, and he never turned off the engine. Sometimes he'd say at the end, "I think I got a fouled spark plug," or "You can tell that that gas additive's working properly."

He never mentioned people from history, or the jewelry of the dead. I took along Hardy Boys mysteries but never opened the covers. Finally, one afternoon, I said, "Ms. Suber wants to know if you're planning on coming to the PTA meeting. I forgot to tell you."

My father turned off the ignition. He reached beneath his seat and pulled out a can of beer and a church key. We sat parked between two gullies, somewhere in Greenwood County. "Hot damn, boy, you need to tell me these things. When is it?"

I said, "I forgot. I got in so much trouble Friday that I forgot." I'd taken a tortoise to show-and-tell and said his name was John the Baptist. At first Ms. Suber seemed delighted. When she asked why I had named him John the Baptist, I said, "Watch this." I screamed, "John the Baptist!" When he retreated into his shell and lost his head, I nodded. She had me sit back down. None of my classmates got the joke.

"The PTA meeting's on Tuesday. It's on Tuesday." I wore a pair of cut-off blue jeans with the bottoms cut into one-inch strips. My mother used to make them for me when I'd grown taller but hadn't gained weight around the middle. I had on my light-blue Little League T-shirt, with SUNKEN GARDENS on the front and 69 for my number on the back. My father had insisted that I get that number, and that I would thank him one day.

"Hell, yes. Do I need to bring anything? I mean, is this one of those meetings where parents need to bring food? I know how to make potato salad. I can make potato salad and cole slaw, you know."

"She just asked me to ask if you'd show up. That's all she said, I swear."

My father looked out at what I understood to be another

wasteland. Empty beer cans were scattered in front of us, and the remains of a haphazard bonfire someone had made right in the middle of a path. "Maybe I should call her up and ask if she needs anything."

Although I didn't understand the depth of my father's obsession, I said, "Ms. Suber won't be in town until that night. We have a substitute on Monday, 'cause she has to go to a funeral somewhere."

My father drank from his beer. He handed the can over and told me to take little sips at first. I said, "Mom wouldn't want you to give me beer."

He nodded. "Mom wouldn't want you to do a lot of things, just like she didn't want me to do a lot of things. But she's not here, is she? Your momma's spending all her time praying that she never gets laryngitis, while the rest of us hope she does."

I didn't know that my father had been taking Fridays off in order to see the school secretary, feign needing to leave me a bag lunch, and then stand looking through the vertical window of my classroom door while I expounded the rarity of a letter sweater once worn by General Custer, or whatever. When the PTA meeting came around, I went with my father, though no other students attended. Pretty much it was only parents, teachers, and a couple of the lunch ladies, who had volunteered to serve a punch of ginger ale and grape juice. My father entered Ms. Suber's classroom and approached her as if she were a newspaper boy he'd forgotten to pay. He said, "I thought you'd eventually send a letter home asking for a conference. I thought you'd finally buckle under." He said, "Go look at the goldfish, Mendal," and pointed toward our aquarium.

I looked at the corner of the room. My classmates' parents were sitting at tiny desks, their knees bobbing like the shells of surfaced turtles. My third-grade teacher said, "I know you think this is cute, but it's not. I don't know why you think you can re-court me however many years later after what you did to me back then."

My father pushed me in the direction of the aquarium. Ms. Suber waved and smiled at Glenn Flack's parents, who were walking in. I said, "Can I go sit in the car?"

Ms. Suber said, "You stay right here, Mendal."

"I might not have been able to go to college like you did, Lola, but I've done good for myself," my father said. I thought one thing only: *Lola?*

"I know you have, Lee. I know you've done well. And let me be the first to say how proud I am of you, and how I'm sorry if I hurt you, and that I've seen you looking in the window when Mendal does his bogus show-and-tells." She pointed at the window in the door. Mr. and Mrs. Anderson walked in. "I need to start this thing up."

My father said to me, "If you want to go sit in the car, go ahead." He handed me the keys, leaned down, and said, "There's a beer in the glove compartment, son."

Let me say that this was South Carolina in 1968. Although my memory's not perfect, I think that at the time, neither drinking nor driving was against the law for minors, nor was smoking cigarettes before the age of twelve. Five years later I would drive my minibike to the Sunken Gardens, meet one of the black boys twirling trays out in the parking lot, order my eight-pack of Miller ponies, and have it delivered to me without conscience or threat of law.

I pretended to go into the parking lot but circled around to the outside of Ms. Suber's classroom. I stood beneath one of the six jalousies, crouched, and listened. Ms. Suber welcomed the parents and said that it was an exciting year. She said something about how all of us would have to take a national test later on to see how we compared with the rest of the nation. She said something about a school play.

Ms. Suber warned parents of a looming head-lice epidemic. She paced back and forth and asked everyone to introduce himself or herself. Someone asked if the school would ever sponsor another cake-and-pie sale in order to buy new recorders. My father said he'd be glad to have a potato-salad-and-cole-slaw sale. I didn't hear the teacher's answer. From where I crouched I could only look up at the sky and notice how some stars twinkled madly while others shone hard and fast like mica afire.

By the time I reached high school, my mother had moved from Nashville to New Orleans and then from New Orleans to Las Vegas. She never made it as a country singer or a blues singer, but she seemed to thrive as a hostess of sorts. As I crouched there beneath a window jutting out above boxwoods, I thought of my mother and imagined what she might be doing at the moment my father experienced his first PTA meeting. Was she crooning to conventioneers? Was she sitting in a back room worrying over pantyhose? That's what I thought, I swear to God. Everyone in Ms. Suber's classroom seemed to be talking with cookies in their mouths. I heard my father laugh hard twice—once when Ms. Suber said she knew that her students saw her as a witch, and another time when she said she knew that her students went home complaining that she didn't spank exactly the way their parents spanked.

Again, this was in the middle of the Vietnam War. Spanking made good soldiers.

My third-grade teacher said that she didn't have anything else to say, and told her students' parents to feel free to call her up should they have questions concerning grades, expectations, or field trips. She said she appreciated anyone who wanted to help chaperone kids or to work after school in a tutoring capacity. I stood up and watched my friends' parents leave single file, my father last in line.

Fifteen minutes after sitting in the car, five minutes after everyone else had driven out of the parking lot, I climbed out the passenger side and crept back to Ms. Suber's window. I expected my father to have Lola Suber in a headlock, or backed up against the Famous Christians of the World corkboard display. I didn't foresee their having moved desks against the walls in order to make a better dance floor.

My father held my third-grade teacher in a way I'd seen him

hold a woman only once before: one Fourth of July he had danced with my mother in the backyard while the neighbors shot bottle rockets straight up. My mother had placed her head on his shoulder and smiled, her eyes raised to the sky. Lola Suber didn't look upward. She didn't smile either. My father seemed to be humming, or talking low. I couldn't hear exactly what went on, but years later he confessed that he had set forth everything he meant to say and do, everything he hoped she taught the other students and me when it came to matters of passion.

I did hear Lola Suber remind him that they had broken up because she had decided to have a serious and exclusive relationship with Jesus Christ.

There amid the boxwoods I hunkered down and thought only about the troubles I might have during future show-and-tells, I swear to God. I stood back up, saw them dancing, and returned to the car. I would let my father open the glove compartment later.

George Singleton's new collection of stories, *The Half-Mammals of Dixie*, will be published in fall 2002. A previous collection, *These People Are Us*, will be released in paperback, also in fall 2002. His stories have appeared in *The Atlantic Monthly*, *Harper's*, *Book*, *Zoetrope: All-Story*, *Playboy*, and *The Georgia Review*, among other magazines. He lives in Dacusville, South Carolina, with clay artist Glenda Guion and their eleven dogs and one cat.

GLENDA GUION

Back in 1963 my father took me out to a rocky beach in California, both of us armed with crowbars. We pried abalone from their resting spots. I don't know if we later cooked what muscled meat lived beneath the mother-of-pearl covering, but I do know that I got to keep the shells.

Jump to 1968 South Carolina. Fifth grade show-and-tell day. I brought my abalone and it got passed around. This new rich kid named Tony—and I've never trusted anyone named after an adjective, subsequent to this particular afternoon—peered inside and said, "It looks like something's written here. It looks like it says 'Made in China.'"

Well I stood there all embarrassed. I was one of those kids whose voice quaked and quivered during show-and-tell, or a book report.

I said, "I found this a long time ago, on a shore far, far away where crustacean-like invertebrates other than crawdads live." At least that's what I say now. And evidently—speaking of craws—this Tony guy stuck in mine until I forced the story out.

Julie Orringer

PILGRIMS

(from *Ploughshares*)

It was Thanksgiving Day and hot, because this was New Orleans; they were driving uptown to have dinner with strangers. Ella pushed at her loose tooth with the tip of her tongue and fanned her legs with the hem of her velvet dress. On the seat beside her, Benjamin fidgeted with his shirt buttons. He had worn his pilgrim costume, brown shorts and a white shirt and yellow paper buckles taped to his shoes. In the front seat their father drove without a word, while their mother dozed against the window glass. She wore a blue dress and a strand of jade beads and a knit cotton hat beneath which she was bald.

Three months earlier Ella's father had explained what chemotherapy was, and how it would make her mother better. He had even taken Ella to the hospital once when her mother had a treatment. She remembered it like a filmstrip from school, a series of connected images she wished she didn't have to watch: her mother with an IV needle in her arm, the steady drip from the bag of orange liquid, her father speaking softly to himself as he paced the room, her mother shaking so hard she had to be tied down.

At night Ella and her brother tapped a secret code against the wall that separated their rooms: one knock, I'm afraid; two knocks, don't worry; three knocks, are you still awake?; four, come quick. And then there was the Emergency Signal, a stream of knocks that kept on coming, which meant her brother could hear their mother and father crying in their bedroom. If it went on for more than a minute, Ella would give four knocks, and her brother would run to her room and crawl under the covers.

There were changes in the house, healing rituals which required Ella's mother to go outside and embrace trees or lie facedown on the grass. Sometimes she did a kind of Asian dance that looked like karate. She ate bean paste and Japanese vegetables, or sticky brown rice wrapped in seaweed. And now they were going to have dinner with people they had never met, people who ate seaweed and brown rice every day of their lives.

They drove through the Garden District, where Spanish moss hung like beards from the trees. Once during Mardi Gras, Ella had ridden a trolley here with her brother and grandmother, down to the French Quarter, where they'd eaten beignets at Café du Monde. She wished she were sitting in one of those wrought-iron chairs and shaking powdered sugar onto a beignet. How much better than to be surrounded by strangers, eating food that tasted like the bottom of the sea.

They turned onto a side street, and her father studied the directions. "It should be at the end of this block," he said.

Ella's mother shifted in her seat. "Where are we?" she asked, her voice dreamy with painkillers.

"Almost there," said Ella's father.

They pulled to the curb in front of a white house with sagging porches and a trampled lawn. Vines covered the walls and moss grew thick and green between the roof slates. Under the porte-cochère stood a beat-up Honda and a Volkswagen with mismatched side panels. A faded Big Wheel lay on its side on the walk.

"Come on," their father said, and gave them a tired smile. "Time for fun." He got out of the car and opened the doors for Ella and her mother, sweeping his arm chauffeur-like as they climbed out.

Beside the front door was a tarnished doorbell in the shape of a lion's head. "Push it," her father said. Ella pushed. A sound like church bells echoed inside the house.

Then the door swung open, and there was Mr. Kaplan, a tall man with wiry orange hair and big, dry-looking teeth. He shook hands with Ella's parents, so long and vigorously it seemed to Ella he might as well say *congratulations*.

"And you must be Ben and Ella," he said, bending down.

Ella gave a mute nod. Her brother kicked at the doorjamb.

"Well, come on in," he said. "I have a tree castle out back."

Benjamin's face came up, twisted with skepticism. "A what?"

"The kids are back there. They'll show you," he said.

"What an interesting foyer," their mother said. She bent down to look at the brass animals on the floor, a turtle and a jackal and a llama. Next to the animals stood a blue vase full of rusty metal flowers. A crystal chandelier dangled from the ceiling, its arms hung with dozens of God's-eyes and tiny plastic babies from Mardi Gras king cakes. On a low wooden shelf against the wall, pair after pair of canvas sandals and sneakers and Birkenstocks were piled in a heap. A crayoned sign above it said SHOES OFF NOW!

Ella looked down at her feet. She was wearing her new patent-leather Mary Janes.

"Your socks are nice, too," her father said, and touched her shoulder. He stepped out of his own brown loafers and set them on top of the pile. Then he knelt before Ella's mother and removed her pumps. "Shoes off," he said to Ella and Ben.

"Even me?" Ben said. He looked down at his paper buckles.

Their father took off Ben's shoes and removed the paper buckles, tape intact. Then he pressed one buckle onto each of Ben's socks. "There," he said.

Ben looked as if he might cry.

"Everyone's in the kitchen," Mr. Kaplan said. "We're all cooking."

"Marvelous," said Ella's mother. "We love to cook."

They followed him down a cavern of a hall, its walls decorated with sepia-toned photographs of children and parents, all of them staring stone-faced from their gilt frames. They passed a sweep of stairs, and a room with nothing in it but straw mats and pictures of blue Indian goddesses sitting on beds of cloud.

"What's that room?" Benjamin said.

"Meditation room," Mr. Kaplan said, as if it were as commonplace as a den.

The kitchen smelled of roasting squash and baked apples and spices. There was an old brick oven and a stove with so many burners it looked as if it had been stolen from a restaurant. At the kitchen table, men and women with long hair and loose clothes sliced vegetables or stirred things into bowls. Some of them wore knitted hats like her mother, their skin dull-gray, their eyes purple-shaded underneath. To Ella it seemed they could be relatives of her mother's, shameful cousins recently discovered.

A tall woman with a green scarf around her waist came over and embraced Ella's mother, then bent down to hug Ella and Benjamin. She smelled of smoky perfume. Her wide eyes skewed in different directions, as if she were watching two movies projected into opposite corners of the room. Ella did not know how to look at her.

"We're so happy you decided to come," the woman said. "I'm Delilah, Eddy's sister."

"Who's Eddy?" said Ben.

"Mr. Kaplan," their father said.

"We use our real names here," Delilah said. "No one is a mister."

She led their parents over to the long table and put utensils into their hands. Their mother was to mix oats into a pastry crust, and their father to chop carrots, something Ella had never seen him do. He looked around in panic, then hunched over and began cutting a carrot into clumsy pieces. He kept glancing at the man to his left, a bearded man with a shaved head, as if to make sure he was doing it right.

Delilah gave Ella and Benjamin hard cookies that tasted like burnt rice. It seemed Ella would have to chew forever. Her loose tooth waggled in its socket.

"The kids are all out back," Delilah said. "There's plenty of time to play before dinner."

"What kids?" Benjamin asked.

"You'll see," said Delilah. She tilted her head at Ella, one of her eyes moving over Ella's velvet dress. "Here's a little trick I learned when I was a girl," she said. In one swift movement she took the back hem of the dress, brought it up between Ella's knees, and tucked it into the sash. "Now you're wearing shorts," she said.

Ella didn't feel like she was wearing shorts. As soon as Delilah turned away, she pulled her skirt out of her sash and let it fall around her legs.

The wooden deck outside was cluttered with Tinkertoys and clay flowerpots and Little Golden Books. Ella heard children screaming and laughing nearby. As she and Benjamin moved to the edge of the deck, there was a rustle in the bushes, and a skinny boy leaped out and pointed a suction-cup arrow at them. He stood there breathing hard, his hair full of leaves, his chest bare. "You're on duty," he said.

"Me?" Benjamin said.

"Yes, you," the boy said. "Both of you." He motioned them off the porch with his arrow and took them around the side of the house. There, built into the side of a sprawling oak, was the biggest, most sophisticated treehouse Ella had ever seen. There were tiny rooms of sagging plywood, and rope ladders hanging down from doors, and a telescope and a fireman's pole and a red net full of leaves. From one wide platform—almost as high as the top of the house—it seemed you could jump down onto a huge trampoline. Even higher was a kind of crow's nest, a little circular platform built around the trunk. A red-painted sign on the railing read DAGNER! Ella could hear the other children screaming, but she couldn't see them. A collie dog barked crazily, staring up at the tree.

"Take off your socks! That's an order," the skinny boy said.

Benjamin glanced at Ella as if to ask if this were okay. Ella shrugged. It seemed ridiculous to walk around outside in socks. She bent and peeled off her anklets. Benjamin carefully removed his pilgrim buckles and put them in his pocket, then sat down and took off his socks. The skinny boy grabbed the socks from their hands and tucked them into the waistband of his shorts.

The mud was thick and cold between Ella's toes, and pecan shells bit her feet as the boy herded them toward the treehouse. He prodded Ella toward a ladder of prickly-looking rope. When she stepped onto the first rung, the ladder swung toward the tree and her toes banged against the trunk. The skinny boy laughed.

"Go on," he said. "Hurry up. And no whining."

The rope burned her hands and feet as she ascended. The ladder seemed to go on forever. Ben followed below, making the rope buck and sway as they climbed. At the top there was a small square opening, and Ella thrust both her arms inside and pulled herself into a dark coop. As she stood, her head knocked against something dangling from the ceiling on a length of string. It was a bird's skull, no bigger than a walnut. Dozens of others hung from the ceiling around her. Benjamin huddled at her side.

"Sick," he said.

"Don't look," Ella said.

The suction-cup arrow came up through the hole in the floor.

"Keep going," said the boy. "You're not there yet."

"Go where?" Ella said.

"Through the wall."

Ella brushed the skulls out of her way and leveled her shoulder against one of the walls. It creaked open like a door. Outside, a tree limb as thick as her torso extended up to another plywood box, this one much larger than the first. Ella dropped to her knees and crawled upward. Benjamin followed.

Apparently this was the hostage room. Four kids stood in the semi-darkness, wide-eyed and still as sculptures, each bound at the ankles and wrists with vine handcuffs. Two of the kids, a boy and a girl, were so skinny that Ella could see the outlines of bones in their arms and legs. Their hair was patchy and ragged, their eyes black and almond-shaped. In the corner, a white-haired boy in purple overalls whimpered softly to himself. And at the center of the room a girl Benjamin's age stood tied to the tree trunk with brown string. She had the same wild gray eyes and leafy hair as the boy with the arrows.

"It's mine, it's *my* treehouse," she said as Ella stared at her.

"Is Mr. Kaplan your dad?" Benjamin said.

"My dat-*tee,*" the girl corrected him.

"Where's your mom?"

"She died," said the girl, and looked him fiercely in the eye.

Benjamin sucked in his breath and glanced at Ella.

Ella wanted to hit this girl. She bent down close to the girl's face, making her eyes small and mean. "If this is so your treehouse," Ella said, "then how come you're tied up?"

"It's *jail,*" the girl spat. "In jail you get tied up."

"We could untie you," said Benjamin. He tugged at one of her bonds.

The girl opened her mouth and let out a scream so shrill Ella's eardrums buzzed. Once, as her father had pulled into the driveway at night, he had trapped a rabbit by the leg beneath the wheel of his car; the rabbit had made a sound like that. Benjamin dropped the string and moved against Ella, and the children with ragged hair laughed and jumped on the platform until it crackled and groaned. The boy in purple overalls cried in his corner.

Benjamin put his lips to Ella's ear. "I don't understand it here," he whispered.

There was a scuffle at the door, and the skinny boy stepped into the hostage room. "All right," he said. "Who gets killed?"

"Kill those kids, Peter," the girl said, pointing to Benjamin and Ella.

"Us?" Benjamin said.

"Who do you think?" said the boy.

He poked them in the back with his suction-cup arrow and moved them toward the tree trunk, where rough boards formed a ladder to the next level. Ella and Benjamin climbed until they had reached a narrow platform, and then Peter pushed them to the edge. Ella looked down at the trampoline. It was a longer drop than the high dive at the public pool. She looked over her shoulder, and Peter glared at her. Down below the collie barked and barked, his black nose pointed up at them.

Benjamin took Ella's hand and closed his eyes. Then Peter shoved them from behind, and they stumbled forward into space.

There was a moment of terrifying emptiness, nothing but air beneath Ella's feet. She could hear the collie's bark getting closer as she fell. She slammed into the trampoline knees first, then flew, shrieking, back up into the air. When she hit the trampoline a second time, Benjamin's head knocked against her chin. He stood up rubbing his head, and Ella tasted salt in her mouth. Her loose tooth had slipped its roots. She spit it into her palm and studied its jagged edge.

"Move," Peter called from above. The boy in purple overalls was just climbing up onto the platform. Peter pulled him forward until his toes curled over the edge.

"I lost my tooth!" Ella yelled.

"Get off!"

Benjamin scrambled off the trampoline. Ella crawled to the edge, the tooth gleaming and red-rimmed between her fingers, and then the trampoline lurched with the weight of the boy in purple overalls. The tooth flew from her hand and into the bushes, too small to make a sound when it hit.

When she burst into the house crying, blood streaming from her mouth, the long-haired men and women dropped their mixing spoons and went to her. She twisted away from them, looking frantically for her mother and father, but they were nowhere to be seen. Her throat ached with crying. There was no way to explain that she wasn't hurt, that she was upset because her tooth was gone, and because everything about that house made her want to run away and hide. The adults, their faces creased with worry, pulled her to the sink and held her mouth open. The woman with skewed eyes, Delilah, pressed a tissue against the space where her tooth had been. Ella could smell onion and apples on her hands.

"The time was right," she said. "The new tooth's already coming in."

"Whose is she?" one of the men asked.

Delilah told him the names of Ella's parents. It was strange to hear those familiar words, *Ann* and *Gary,* in the mouths of these long-haired strangers.

"Your mother is upstairs," Delilah said, her eyes swiveling toward some distant hidden room. "She felt a little swimmy-headed. Your dad just brought her some special tea. Maybe we should let her rest, hm?"

Ella slipped out from beneath Delilah's hand and ran to the hall, remembering the stairway she'd seen earlier. There it was before her, a curve of glossy steps leading to nowhere she knew. Her mother's cough drifted down from one of the bedroom doors. Ella put a foot onto the first stair, feeling the eyes of the adults on her back. No one said anything to stop her. After a moment, she began to climb.

In the upstairs hallway, toys and kids' shoes lay strewn across the floor, and crumpled pants and shirts and dresses lay in a musty-smelling heap. Two naked Barbies sprawled in a frying pan. A record player sat in the middle of the hall, its vacant turntable spinning. Ella stepped over the cord and went into the first room, a small room with a sleeping bag on the bare mattress ticking. In a cage on the nightstand, a white rat scrabbled at a cardboard tube. A finger-painted sign above the bed said CLARIES ROOM. Her mother's cough rose again from down the hall, and she turned and ran toward the sound.

In a room whose blue walls and curtains made everything look as if it were underwater, her mother lay pale and coughing on a bed piled high with pillows. Her father sat on the edge of the bed, his hands raised in the air, thumbs hooked together and palms spread wide. For a moment Ella had no idea what he was doing. Then she saw the shadow of her father's hands against the wall, in the light of a blue-shaded lamp. A shock of relief went through her.

"Tweet, tweet," Ella said.

"Right," her father said. "A birdie."

Ella's mother turned toward her and smiled, more awake, more like her real self than earlier. "Do another one, Gary," she said.

Ella's father twisted his hands into a new shape in the air.

"A dog?" Ella said.

"A fish!" said her mother.

"No," he said, and adjusted his hands. "It's a horsie, see?"

"A horsie?" said Ella's mother. "With fins?"

That made Ella laugh a little.

"Hey," her mother said. "Come here, you. Smile again."

Ella did as she was told.

"What's that? You lost your tooth!"

"It's gone," Ella said. She climbed onto the bed to explain, but as she flopped down on the mattress her mother's face contracted with pain.

"Please don't bounce," her mother said. She touched the place where her surgery had been.

Ella's father gave her a stern look and lifted her off the bed. "Your mom's sleepy," he said. "You should run back downstairs now."

"She's always sleepy," Ella said, looking down at her muddy feet. She thought of her tooth lying out in the weeds, and how she'd have nothing to put under her pillow for the tooth fairy.

Her mother began to cry.

Ella's father went to the window and stared down into the yard, his breath fogging the glass. "Go ahead, Ella," he said. "We just need a few minutes."

"My tooth," Ella said. She knew she should leave, but couldn't.

"It'll grow back bigger and stronger," her father said.

She could see he didn't understand what had happened. If only her mother would stop crying, she could explain everything. In the blue light her mother looked cold and far away, pressed under the weight of tons of water.

"I'll be down soon," her mother said, sniffling. "Go out and play."

Ella opened her mouth to form some protest, but no words came out.

"Go on, now," her father said.

"It fell in a bush!" she wailed, then turned and ran downstairs.

* * *

The other children had come in by then. Her brother stood in line at the downstairs bathroom to wash before dinner, comparing fingernail dirt with the boy in purple overalls. Hands deep in the pockets of her velvet dress, Ella wandered through the echoing hall into a room lined from floor to ceiling with books. Many of the titles were in other languages, some even written in different alphabets. She recognized *D'Aulaire's Book of Greek Myths* and *The Riverside Shakespeare* and *Grimm's Fairy Tales.* Scattered around on small tables and decorative stands were tiny human figurines with animal heads—horse-man, giraffe-man, panther-man. On one table sat an Egyptian beetle made of milky-green stone, and beside him a real beetle, shiny as metal, who flew at Ella's face when she reached to touch his shell. She batted him away with the back of her hand.

And then, just above where the beetle had fallen, Ella saw a shelf without any books at all. It was low, the height of her knees, with a frayed blue scarf pinned against its back wall. Burnt-down candles stood on either side of a black lacquer box, and on top of this box stood a glass filled with red water.

Ella reached for the glass, and someone behind her screamed.

She turned around. Clarie stood in the doorway, dress unbuttoned at one shoulder, face smeared with mud.

"Don't touch that," she said.

Ella took a step back. "I wasn't going to."

Clarie's eyes seemed to ignite as she bent down and took the glass in both hands. She held it near a lamp, so the light shone through it and cast a red oval upon the wall.

"It's my mother," she said.

For dinner there was a roasted dome of something that looked like meat but wasn't. It was springy and steaming, and when Mr. Kaplan cut it open, Ella could see that it was stuffed with rice and yams. Benjamin tried to hide under the table, but their father pulled him up by the arms and set him in his place. He prodded his wedge of roast until it slid onto the tablecloth. Then he began to cry quietly.

"The kids aren't vegetarian," their father said, in apology to the men and women at the table. He picked up the slice of roast with his fingers and put it back on Ben's plate. The other men and women held their forks motionless above their own plates, looking at Ella's mother and father with pity.

"Look, Ben," said Delilah. "It's called seitan. Wheat gluten. The other kids love it."

The boy and girl with almond-shaped eyes and ragged hair stopped in mid-chew. The girl looked at Benjamin and narrowed her eyes.

"I don't eat gluten," Benjamin said.

"Come on, now," their father said. "It's great."

Ella's mother pressed her fingers against her temples. She hadn't touched her own dinner. Ella, sitting beside her, took a bite of wheat gluten. It was almost like meat, firm and savory, and the stuffing was flavored with forest-smelling spices. As she glanced around the table, she thought of the picture of the First Thanksgiving on the bulletin board at school: the smiling Pilgrims eating turkey and squash, the stern-faced Native Americans looking as if they knew the worst was yet to come. Who among them that night were the Native Americans? Who were the Pilgrims? The dark old house was like a wilderness around them, the wind sighing through its rooms.

"I jumped on the trampoline," said the boy with ragged hair, pulling on the sleeve of the woman next to him. "That boy did a flip." He pointed at Peter, who was smashing rice against his plate with his thumb. "He tied his sister to the tree."

Mr. Kaplan set down his fork. He looked sideways at Peter, his mouth pressed into a stern line. "I told you never to do that again," he said. He sounded angry, but his voice was quiet, almost a whisper.

"She made me!" Peter said, and plunged a spoon into his baked squash.

Mr. Kaplan's eyes went glossy and faraway. He stared off at the blank wall above Ella's mother's head, drifting away from the noise and chatter of the dinner table. Next to him Delilah shuttled her mismatched eyes back and forth. Ella's mother straightened in her chair.

"Ed," she called softly.

Mr. Kaplan blinked hard and looked at her.

"Tell us about your tai chi class."

"What," he said.

"Your tai chi class."

"You know, I don't really want to talk right now," he said. He pushed back his chair and went into the kitchen. There was the sound of water, and then the clink of dishes in the sink. Delilah shook her head. The other adults looked down at their plates. Ella's mother wiped the corners of her mouth with her napkin and crossed her arms over her chest.

"Does anyone want more rice?" Ella's father asked.

"I think we're all thinking about Lena," said the man with the shaved head.

"I know I am," said Delilah.

"Infinity to infinity," said the man. "Dust into star."

The men and women looked at each other, their eyes carrying some message Ella couldn't understand. They clasped each other's hands and bent their heads. "Infinity to infinity," they repeated. "Dust into star."

"Matter into energy," said the man. "Identity into oneness."

"Matter into energy," everyone said. Ella glanced at her father, whose jaw was set hard, unmoving. Her mother's lips formed the words, but no sound came out. Ella thought of the usual Thanksgivings at her uncle Bon's, where everyone talked and laughed at the table and they ate turkey and dressing and sweet potatoes with marshmallows melted on top. She closed her eyes and held her breath, filling her chest with a tightness that felt like magic power. If she tried hard enough could she transport them all, her mother and father, Benjamin and herself, to that other time? She held her breath until it seemed she would explode, then let it out in a rush. She opened her eyes. Nothing had changed. Peter kicked the table leg, and the collie, crouched beside Clarie's chair, whimpered his unease. Ella could see Clarie's hand on his collar, her knuckles bloodless as stones.

Mr. Kaplan returned with a platter of baked apples. He cleared his throat, and everyone turned to look at him. "Guess what we forgot," he said. "I spent nearly an hour peeling these things." He held the platter aloft, waiting.

"Who wants some nice baked apples?" he said. "Baked apples. I peeled them."

No one said a word.

After dinner the adults drifted into the room with the straw mats and Indian goddesses. Ella understood that the children were not invited, but she lingered in the doorway to see what would happen. Mr. Kaplan bent over a tiny brass dish and held a match to a black cone. A wisp of smoke curled toward the ceiling, and after a moment Ella smelled a dusty, flowery scent. Her mother and father and the rest of the adults sat cross-legged on the floor, not touching each other. A low hum began to fill the room like something with weight and substance. Ella saw her father raise an eyebrow at her mother, as if to ask if these people were serious. But her mother's shoulders were bent in meditation, her mouth open with the drone of the mantra, and Ella's father sighed and let his head fall forward.

Someone pinched Ella's shoulder, and she turned around. Peter stood behind her, his eyes narrow. "Come on," he said. "You're supposed to help clean up."

In the kitchen the children stacked dirty dishes on the counter and ran water in the sink. The boy and girl with almond eyes climbed up onto a wide wooden stepstool and began to scrub dishes. Peter scraped all the scraps into an aluminum pan and gave it to Clarie, who set it on the floor near the dog's water dish. The collie fell at the leftover food with sounds that made Ella sick to her stomach. Clarie stood next to him and stroked his tail.

Then Benjamin came into the kitchen carrying the glass of red water. "Somebody forgot this under the table," he said.

Again there was the dying-rabbit screech. Clarie batted her palms against the sides of her head. "No!" she shrieked. "Put it down!"

Benjamin's eyes went wide, and he set the glass on the kitchen counter. "I don't want it," he said.

The boy in purple overalls squinted at the glass. "Looks like Kool-Aid," he said.

"She gets all crazy," said Peter. "Watch." Peter lifted the glass high into the air, and Clarie ran toward him. "You can't have it," he said.

Clarie jumped up and down in fury, her hands flapping like limp rags. Her mouth opened, but no sound came out. Then she curled her fingers into claws and scratched at Peter's arms and chest until he twisted away. He ran across the kitchen and onto the deck, holding the glass in the air, and Clarie followed him, screaming.

The ragged-haired brother and sister looked at each other, arms gloved in white bubbles. In one quick movement they were off the stool, shaking suds around the kitchen. "Come on!" said the boy. "Let's go watch!"

Benjamin grabbed Ella's hand and pulled her toward the screen door. The children pushed out onto the deck and then ran toward the tree castle, where Clarie and her brother were climbing the first rope ladder. It was dark now, and floodlights on the roof of the house illuminated the entire castle, its rooms silver-gray and ghostly, its ropes and nets swaying in a rising breeze. The children gathered on the grass near the trampoline.

Peter held the glass as he climbed, the red water sloshing against its sides. "Come and get it," he crooned. He reached the first room, and they heard the wall-door scrape against the trunk as he pushed it open. Then he moved out onto the oak limb, agile as the siamang monkeys Ella had seen at the zoo. He might as well have had a tail.

Clarie crawled behind him, her hands scrabbling at the bark. Peter howled at the sky as he reached the hostage room.

Benjamin moved toward Ella and pressed his head against her arm. "I want to go home," he said.

"Shh," Ella said. "We can't."

High above, Peter climbed onto the platform from which they had jumped earlier. Still holding the glass, he pulled himself up the tree trunk to the crow's nest. High up on that small, railed platform, where the tree branches became thin and sparse, he stopped. Below him Clarie scrambled onto the jumping platform. She looked out across the yard as if unsure of where he had gone. "Up here," Peter said, holding the glass high.

Ella could hear Clarie grunting as she pulled herself up into the crow's nest. She stood and reached for the glass, her face a small moon in the dark. A few acorns scuttled off the crow's nest platform.

"Give it!" she cried again.

Peter stood looking at her for a moment in the dark. "You really want it?"

"Peter!"

He swept the glass through the air. The water flew out in an arc, ruby-colored against the glare of the floodlights. Clarie leaned out as if to catch it between her fingers, and with a splintering crack she broke through the railing. Her dress fluttered silently as she fell, and her white hands grasped at the air. There was a quiet instant, the soft sound of water falling on grass. Then, with a shock Ella felt in the soles of her feet, Clarie hit the ground. The girl with the ragged hair screamed.

Clarie lay beside the trampoline, still as sleep, her neck bent at an impossible angle. Ella wanted to look away, but couldn't. The other children, even Benjamin, moved to where Clarie lay and circled around, some calling her name, some just looking. Peter slid down the fireman's pole and stumbled across the lawn toward his sister. He pushed Benjamin aside. With one toe he nudged Clarie's shoulder, then knelt and rolled her over. A bare bone glistened from her wrist. The boy in purple overalls threw up onto the grass.

Ella turned and ran toward the house. She banged the screen door open and skidded across the kitchen floor into the hall. At the doorway of the meditation room she stopped, breathing hard. The adults sat just as she had left them, eyes closed, mouths open slightly, their sound beating like a living thing, their thumbs and forefingers circled into perfect O's. She could smell the heat of them rising in the room and mingling with the scent of the incense. Her father's chin rested on his chest as if he had fallen asleep. Beside him her mother looked drained of blood, her skin so white she seemed almost holy.

"Mom," Ella whispered. "Mom."

Ella's mother turned slightly and opened her eyes. For a moment she seemed between two worlds, her eyes unfocused and distant. Then she blinked and looked at Ella. She shook her head no.

"Please," Ella said, but her mother closed her eyes again. Ella stood there for a long time watching her, but she didn't move or speak. Finally Ella turned and went back outside.

By the time she reached the tree castle, Peter had dragged Clarie halfway across the lawn. He turned his eyes on Ella, and she stared back at him. The sound of the mantra continued unbroken from the house. Peter hoisted Clarie again under the arms and dragged her to the bushes, her bare feet bumping over the grass. Then he rolled her over until she was hidden in shadow. He pulled her dress down so it covered her thighs, and turned her head toward the fence that bordered the backyard.

"Get some leaves and stuff," he said. "We have to cover her."

Ella would not move. She took Benjamin's hand, but he pulled away from her and wandered across the lawn, pulling up handfuls of grass. She watched the children pick up twigs, Spanish moss, leaves, anything they could find. The boy in purple overalls gathered cedar bark from a flower bed, and Peter dragged fallen branches out of the underbrush near the fence. They scattered everything they found over Clarie's body. In five minutes they had covered her entirely.

"Go back inside," Peter said. "If anyone cries or says anything, I'll kill them."

Ella turned to go, and that was when she saw her tooth, a tiny white pebble in the weeds. She picked it up and rubbed it clean. Then she knelt beside Clarie, clearing away moss and leaves until she found Clarie's hand. She dropped the tooth into the palm and closed the fingers around it. A shiver spread through her chest, and she covered the hand again. Then she put her arm around Benjamin, and they all went back inside. Drawn by the sound of the chanting, they wandered into the hall. All around them hung the yellow photographs, the stony men and women and children looking down at them with sad and knowing eyes. In an oval of black velvet, one girl in a white dress held the string of a wooden duck, her lips open as if she were about to speak. Her eyes had the wildness of Clarie's eyes, her legs the same bowed curve.

At last there was a rustle from the meditation room, and the adults drifted out into the hall. They blinked at the light and rubbed their elbows and knees. Ella's mother and father linked arms and moved toward their children. Benjamin gave a hiccup. His eyes looked strange, the pupils huge, the whites flat and dry. Their mother noticed right away. "We'd better get going," she said to Ella's father. "Ben's tired."

She went into the foyer and pulled their shoes from the pile. Mr. Kaplan followed, looking around in bewilderment, as if he could not believe people were leaving. He patted Benjamin on the head and asked Ella's mother if she wanted to take some leftover food. Ella's mother shook her head no. Her father thanked Mr. Kaplan for his hospitality. Somewhere toward the back of the house, the dog began to bark, a crazy, high-pitched bark, as if the world were ending. Ella pulled Benjamin through the front door, barefoot, and her parents followed them to the car.

All the way past the rows of live oaks, past the cemetery where the little tombs stood like grounded boats, past the low flat shotgun houses with their flaking roofs, Benjamin sat rigid on the back seat and cried without a sound. Ella felt the sobs leaving his chest in waves of hot air. She closed her eyes and followed the car in her mind down the streets that led to their house, until it seemed they had driven past their house long ago and were moving on to a place where strange beds awaited them, where they would fall asleep thinking of dark forests and wake to the lives of strangers.

Julie Orringer is the Marsh McCall Lecturer at Stanford University. She was a Truman Capote Fellow in the Stegner Program at Stanford, and she received her M.F.A. from the Iowa Writers' Workshop. Her stories have appeared in *The Yale Review, The Paris Review, Ploughshares, The Pushcart Prize XXV,* and *The Best New American Voices 2001.* She is completing a short story collection, *How to Breathe Underwater.*

RYAN HARTY

"Pilgrims" began with an image that has stayed with me over the two decades since my family lived in New Orleans: a glass of red water, and a little girl who insisted, mysteriously, that it was her mother. I met this girl at a macrobiotic Thanksgiving feast my family attended nearly a year after my own mother's cancer diagnosis. The girl's mother had died of cancer not long before that Thanksgiving. Through that girl, I felt as I were seeing something of my own family's foreign and terrifying future. I remember playing outside on a rickety play structure and trampoline, losing a tooth, and eating a faux turkey made of seitan. I remember, too, feeling very protective of my brother, who was too young then to understand the sense of dread we were both feeling.

While this story began as a revisiting of that Thanksgiving, it went in a direction I could not have expected. For a long time I resisted the idea of Clarie's death. Hadn't she gone through enough? Hadn't her father, and her brother, gone through enough? What kind of person was I to envision such an ending? But that ending remained through the story's subsequent drafts. Finally I came to understand it was a way of communicating the sense of disconnection I felt between the time before we knew my mother had cancer, and the time afterward. Something had changed irrevocably. There was no going back. All we could do was to become the people we would be afterward, people who understood loss.

Bill Roorbach

BIG BEND

(from *The Atlantic Monthly*)

That night Mr. Hunter (the crew all called him Mr. Hunter) lay quietly awake for two hours before the line of his thoughts finally made the twitching conversion to mirage and hallucination that heralded ease and melting sleep.

What had kept him awake was primarily a worry that he was being too much the imperious old businessman, the self he thought he'd conquered—even killed—in retirement, the part of himself that poor Betty had least admired (though this was the part that brought home the bacon). This area of worry he packaged with a resolution only to ask questions for at least one day of work—no statements or commands or observations or commentary, no matter what, to Stubby or anyone else; no matter what, questions only.

Stubby, who was now snortingly asleep in the next bunk of their nice but spare staff accommodations here at Big Bend National Park, was not hard to compartmentalize: Mr. Hunter would simply stop laughing or smiling at or even acknowledging Stubby's stupid jokes and jibes, would not rise to bait (politics primarily), would not pretend to believe Stubby's stories, especially those about his exploits with women. Scott was Stubby's actual name. He was fifty-three, an old hippie who had never cut his ponytail or jettisoned the idea that corporations were ruining the world, and who called the unlikely women of his tall tales "chicks" and "chiquitas." Strange bedfellows, Stubby and Mr. Hunter, who shared a two-bed room in the workers' quarters.

Another cause of sleeplessness was Martha Kolodny of Chicago, here in blazing, gorgeous, blooming, desolate Big Bend on an amateur ornithological quest. Stubby called her "Mothra," which had been funny at first, given Ms. Kolodny's size and thorough, squawking presence, but which was funny no longer, given the startling fact of Mr. Hunter's crush on her, which had arrived unannounced after his long conversation with her just this evening, in the middle of a huge laugh from Ms. Kolodny, a huge and happy, hilarious laugh from the heart of her very handsome heart. The Kolodny compartment in his businesslike brain he closed and latched with a simple instruction to himself: *Do not have crushes, Mr. Hunter.* He was too old for crushes ("sneakers" he'd called them in high school, class of 1944). And Ms. Kolodny was not the proper recipient of a crush in any case. She was under fifty and certainly over 150 pounds, Mr. Hunter's own lifelong adult weight, and married, completely married, two large rings on the proper finger, giant gemstones blazing.

Still other concerns, carefully placed by Mr. Hunter one by one in their nighttime lockers: the house in Atlanta (Arnie would take care of the yard and the gardens, and Miss Feather would clean the many rooms, as always, in his absence); the neglect of his retirement portfolio (Fairchild Ltd. had always needed prodding but had always gotten the job done, spectacularly in the past several years); the coming Texas summer, a summer he might rather miss.

Oh, but Betty, his wife, his girl, his one and only love, his lover, his helpmate, his best friend, mother of their three (thoroughly adult) children, dead of stroke three years. They had planned all they would do when he retired; and when he did retire, she died. So he was mourning not only the loss of her but also the loss of his long-held vision of the future, the thought that one distant day she would bury him. No compartment was large enough to compartmentalize Bitty (as he always called her), but he achieved a kind of soft peace, like sleep, when he thought of her. He no longer experienced the sharp pains and gouged holes everywhere in him and the tears every night. *Count your blessings, Mr. Hunter,* he had thought wryly, and had melted a little at one broad edge of his consciousness, and had soon fallen asleep in the West Texas night.

The National Park Service hired senior citizens, as part of its policy of not discriminating based on age and so forth, for pleasant jobs at above minimum wage. And because they didn't accept volunteers for the real, honest work that Mr. Hunter had decided to escape into for a salutary year, he signed on for pay, though he certainly didn't need the money. And here in Texas, Mr. Hunter, rich as Croesus and older, found himself shoveling sand up into the back of the smallest dump truck he'd ever seen, half shovelfuls so as not to hurt his back, and no one minded how little he did. He was old in the eyes of his fellows on the work crew—a seventy-something, as Stubby pointed out, working for $6.13 an hour.

The crew was motley, all right: Mr. Hunter, who was assumed to be the widower he was, and assumed to be needy, which of course he was not (in fact, the more he compared himself with his new colleagues, the wealthier he knew himself to be). Dylan Briscoe, painfully polite, adrift after college, who had wanted to go to Yellowstone to follow his ranger girlfriend but had been assigned here the previous summer. He lost his girl, met a new girl, spent the winter in Texas with Juanita from Lajitas, a plainspoken Mexican-American woman of no beauty, hovered near Mr. Hunter on every job, and gave Mr. Hunter his crew name—Mr. Hunter—because Dylan was constitutionally unable to associate the name Dennis with such an old geezer. Freddy was a brainy, obnoxious jock taking a semester off from the University of Alabama. He was leery of Mr. Hunter, disdainful of Stubby, horrible on the subject of women ("gash," he called them collectively), resentful of work, smelling of beer from the start of the day, yet well-read and decently educated despite all. Luis Marichal, the crew boss, about whom much was assumed (jail, knife fights, mayhem) but little was actually known, was liked by all, despite his otherness, for saying "Quit complaining" in a scary voice to Freddy more than once. He always had a gentle smile for Mr. Hunter. Finally, Stubby, short and fat and truly good-humored. Nothing needed to be assumed about Stubby, because Stubby told all: he had recently beat a drug habit, was once a roadie for the Rolling Stones, had been married thrice, had a child from each marriage, had worked many tech jobs in the early days of computers, had fallen into drink after the last divorce or before it, and then into cocaine, and then into heroin, had ended up in the hospital for four months in profound depression, had recovered, had "blown out the toxins," had found that work with his hands and back made him sane. And sane he was, he said. This work crew in Texas had made him so.

All of them earned $6.13 an hour, excepting Dylan, hired on some student-intern program with a lower pay scale, too shy to ask for parity, and of course excepting Luis, who'd been crew here many years though he wasn't thirty, and was foreman—Luis made probably nine bucks an hour, with four young kids to support. And in a way excepting Mr. Hunter, who in addition to his $6.13 an hour from the Seniors-in-the-Parks Program was watching his retirement lump sum grow into a mountain in eight figures.

Mr. Hunter shoveled sand with the rest of them, a wash of sand from the last big rain, which had made nearly a dune on the shoulder of the road for a hundred yards, a dune dangerous to bicyclists. The crew shoveled into the small dump truck, and Luis drove, if rolling the truck ahead a few feet at a time could be called driving. Mr. Hunter wore comfortable and expensive relaxed-fit jeans. He preferred shoveling to the jobs the other seniors got: cashier at the postcard stand, official greeter, filing associate, inventory specialist, cushy nonsense along those lines.

Mr. Hunter shoveled as lightly as anybody and did not laugh at Stubby's stories and thought of Martha Kolodny for no reason he could make sense of—her laugh from the center of her heart and soul, and her large frame that oughtn't to be alluring to him at all but was indeed, and her braininess. Intelligence always was sexy to him. She was as smart as Bitty and as quick, though Bitty would have called her noisy.

Big Bend here in April after a wet winter was in thorough bloom: prickly pear, cholla, century plants, scores of others, colors picked from the sunset and the sandstone cliffs and the backs of birds. Mr. Hunter, thinking to get some conversation started, asked his first question of the day, knowing the answer in advance: "Dylan, what can you tell us about the subject of love?"

Dylan blushed and said, "Juanita," with evident pride and huge love for his woman. And everyone at once said, "Juanita from Lajitas," which was fun to say and which had become a chant and which they knew Dylan liked to hear. Not even Freddy would say anything that might harm Dylan-boy's spirit.

"You are like me," Luis said. "A steady heart and a solid love."

And Stubby, damn him, said, "Mr. Hunter, what about you?"

"Have you noticed that I'm only asking questions today?" Mr. Hunter replied.

"But I saw you stalking Mothra," Stubby said. "Mothra, Queen of the Bird-watchers' Bus. She's a cute one, she is. Tall drink of water, she is. I'll bet she was one athlete in her day! Iron Woman! Anchor in the freestyle relay! Bench press two hundred pounds, easy. What do you say, Mr. Hunter? You were gabbing with her nearly three hours yesterday in the parking lot there. You were! No, no, sir, you were! You're a better man than I! More power to you! She won't give me the time of day; with you she's laughing and shouting and joking! And she was scratching her nose the whole time, which Keith Richards once told me is the sure sign you're going to get a little wiggle in."

All work (such as it was) ceased. Mr. Hunter made a game smile and smiled some more and enjoyed the breeze and the attention. He asked a question: "Do you know that Plato's *Republic* begins with a discussion of just this subject—of love and sex? And do you know that one of the fellows sitting around Socrates says something like 'I saw Sophocles'—the old poet, he calls him—'I saw the old poet down in town the other day, three score and ten, and I asked him: At your age, Sophocles, what of love?' And do you know what Sophocles told that man? Sophocles told that man, 'I feel I have been released by a mad and furious beast!'"

The crew stood with eyebrows raised a long time, absorbing this tale from the mysterious void of time that was Mr. Hunter's life.

After a long silence Stubby said, "Oh, fuck you."

Mr. Hunter knew what Stubby meant: the implied analogy was faulty. And Stubby was right. Martha Kolodny was certainly on Mr. Hunter's mind, Martha Kolodny of all women, and the mad and furious beast had hold of Mr. Hunter certainly. It wasn't as if he'd had no erections in the past three affectionless years—but the one he'd had this morning caught his attention surely. And it wasn't all about erections, either. It was that laugh from the heart and the bright conversation and something more: Martha Kolodny could *see* Mr. Hunter, and he hadn't been seen clearly in three years. Nor had his particular brand of jokes been laughed at, or his ideas praised, nor had someone noticed his hair (still full and shiny, and bone-in-the-desert white) or looked at his hands so, or gazed into his eyes.

At the Thursday-evening ranger's program a very bright young scientist lectured about Mexican fruit bats with passion, somewhat mollifying Dennis Hunter's disappointment. Oh, in the growing night the assembled travelers and rangers and tourists and campers and workers (including Stubby) did see bats, as promised. And among the assembled listeners were a number of birders from Martha Kolodny's bus. But Martha was not among them.

Dennis Hunter lurked on a back bench in clean clothes—Hong Kong–tailored white shirt, khaki pants, Birkenstocks (ah, retirement), eight-needle silken socks—trying to remember how long Martha had said her birding group would be here. Until April 17 was the date he remembered, almost his second daughter's birthday; his second daughter was, yes, about Martha's age. Five more days, only five.

Then he felt a sweeping presence and heard a suppressed laugh from deep inside the heart of someone's capacious heart, and Martha stood just beside him. "May I sit?" she asked. This was a whisper, but still louder in Dennis's ear than the ranger's lecture. She sat on his bench and slid to his side like an old friend; got herself settled, deep and quiet, her perfume expansile; put her chin in the air and raised her eyebrows, seeming to try to find her place in the stream of words as the passionate ranger introduced a film.

The heavy narration covered the same ground the lecture had, with less fervor and erudition, but the pictures of bats were pleasing to watch: the film employed all sorts of camera and lighting tricks and slow-motion tricks and freeze-frames and animation. Bats streaming out of Carlsbad Caverns, not eight hours from here. "Always wanted to see that," Martha said, leaning into Dennis. "Always, always."

"I thought for you it was birds," Dennis said.

Martha put a hand to her nose and scratched. "Whatever has wings," she said. Her other hand was on the bench close between them, and she leaned on it so that her head was not a breath away from Dennis's. He smelled her shampoo—coconut and vanilla. Her henna-red hair, braided in a thick lariat, her distinct chin, the strong slope of her nose, her deep tan, her wrinkles from laughing from the heart of her, her wide shoulders and loose white shirt—all of it, all of her, was in his peripheral vision as he watched the film, which was more truly peripheral though he stared at it, her many scents in his nostrils.

The night before, they had taken care of the small talk and more: Martha Kolodny was an arts administrator, which title Dennis pretended not to understand, though he knew well enough what it meant. She was the kind of person he had disdained in his years as a marketing wizard at Pfizer (years he had then told her about). Talking to Martha, he'd felt the truth of something Bitty had once said: he had really grown up after sixty-five. Martha had patiently explained that she ran a grants-writing office that helped to provide funding (not such huge figures as Martha seemed to think) for several arts organizations, the Lyric Opera of Chicago among them. She herself had once danced—modern dance—with high hopes. She was too *big,* she had said daintily. "My teachers always said I was too *big.*" And she had laughed that laugh that came from the heart of her heart and smote Dennis.

Her husband was a medical scientist at Northwestern, both a Ph.D. and an M.D. His first name was Wences. He was first-generation Polish. He was working on neuroreceptors, about which Dennis knew a thing or two from his years with the drug company. The couple had no kids; they had married late and had decided that at her age kids were not a good idea. Now she was forty-seven. Wences and she barely saw each other. For them the passion had fled. "I'm caught," she had said. "I'm caught in an *economic arrangement.*" Her eyes had been significant, Dennis thought.

The film ended abruptly. The ranger-scientist took the podium in the dark that followed. A spotlight hit his face. Martha sat up and looked at Mr. Hunter fondly; that was the only word for how she looked at him—like an old friend. She whispered, "One Batman joke from this boy and we're out of here!"

In a television voice the ranger said, "That's the Bat Signal, Robin."

"That's it," Martha said, feigning great shock. She rose and took Dennis's hand and pulled him ungently to his feet, and the two of them left the natural amphitheater and were soon striding along a rough path that led into the Chisos Mountains night.

"I knew you'd be at the talk!" Martha said.

"I'm not there now," Dennis said.

She said, "I can't get you out of my head!" She was breathless from the walk. They pulled up at the farthest end of a loop path that looked out over the great basin of the Rio Grande under brilliant, coruscating stars.

"I shoveled sand all day with the boys. Thinking of you."

"I love when you grin just like that," Martha said hotly.

But you are married, Dennis thought to say. He held the words back forcibly. What if she didn't mean anything romantic at all? What an awful gaffe that would be!

They looked out into the blackness of the valley and up into the depths of space and were quiet a long ten minutes. "Mexico over there," Dennis said.

"You know you can rent a canoe and paddle across the Rio Grande to Mexico for lunch? No customs inspection necessary."

He said, "Someone did say that. And at the hot springs, apparently, you can swim across pretty easily. But no lunch."

"Unless you brought your own," Martha said.

"And the hot springs are very nice, too, I hear. Nice to soak in, even in the heat, I hear." He'd heard all this from Freddy in the grossest terms. Freddy had said it was the place he'd bring a *bitch,* if there were anything but *stanking* javelinas around here.

"I would like to kiss you," Dennis said. He'd forgotten entirely how this sort of thing was done, knowing only that now (this he'd read), here in the twenty-first century, one got permission for everything, each step, before proceeding.

"I told my husband I wouldn't mess around with anyone while I was in Texas," Martha said. Then, less lightly, "That's the shambles our marriage is in."

"Well, Martha, darling, a kiss is certainly not necessary to a good friendship," Dennis said, glad he'd asked and not just invited rebuff and embarrassment, though he was embarrassed enough.

But Martha kissed him, full on the lips, and he was glad for the Listerine he had swilled and glad that life hadn't ended and glad to remember all the electrical connections and brightened cells and glowing nerves he was remembering from the bottom of his feet to the tip of his tongue as he kissed her and was kissed.

They talked and necked—no better expression for it—for an hour under the stars.

"Well," Dennis said, "I'm afraid, despite best intentions, you have kissed in Texas." He felt bad for Wences Kolodny.

"But I have not messed around," Martha said.

"On technicalities are the great cases won."

She said, "Do you want to take a little swim to Mexico tomorrow?"

"I'll unpack my swimming trunks."

"I said nothing to Wences about messing around in Mexico."

"That isn't funny to me," Dennis said.

But they kissed till near eleven, when the Chicago birders' bus loaded quickly and headed to the birders' hotel, on the outskirts of the enormous national park.

Dennis walked back to his room with feelings he hadn't had in fifty years, pain both physical and metaphysical, elation sublime. Ambivalence scratched and snarled like an enraged animal under his squeaky cot.

Mr. Hunter no longer had the physical strength of his estimable colleagues on the work detail, but they had not his old man's stamina. With his steady work all day he outperformed the college boys, though Stubby could do in a single hour more than the whole crew did in all of a typical day when he got inspired, which he did just before lunch on this day, Friday. Stubby worked like a dog and a demon and an ox, worked as if possessed—every cliché applied. He said, "We don't want Luis in trouble if this sand ain't up and off the road, boys!" They'd got about a quarter of it up the previous day, and already, by noon this day, two quarters more.

The crew stopped for lunch and ate in tired silence. Then, as they settled down into what should normally have been something like a siesta, Stubby turned to Mr. Hunter. He said, "Where did you and the bird lady go last night when you left the lecture so early?"

"Why do you ask?" Mr. Hunter said wryly, as the attention of the crew fell pleasingly upon him.

"I was only worried, is all," Stubby said, even more wryly.

After a long silence Luis grinned and said, "Tell us, Sophocles, old poet, what of love?"

"Love!" Stubby said. "You should have smelled our room in the night! What perfume! And perfume, my brothers, does not rub off without some rubbing!"

Still wryly—he could think of no other safe tack to take—Mr. Hunter said, "Do you imply that an old man should not seek romance?"

"Not s'long as it's with an old lady," Freddy said.

"She's not as old as all that," Stubby said. "She's not yet my age, and I'm a youth, as you can see."

"Is she over forty?" Dylan asked helpfully. Embarrassed, he bit into his burrito and looked out over the dry valley of the Rio Grande.

"Ah, forty!" Stubby said. "Forty is the youth of old age and the old age of youth!"

Freddy said equably, "How old are y'all, anyway, Mr. Hunter?" He leaned a long way, gave a short smile, reached and took one of Luis's tortillas.

"Three score and fourteen," Mr. Hunter replied. "Seventy-four. The youth of death, I would say, if pressed."

"What of love, Sophocles?" Luis said again.

Mr. Hunter could not help himself. He beamed. He said, "Do any of you really believe my private hours are any of your business?"

Stubby said, "Do we not have the right to learn from those older than us? And do you, Mr. Hunter, not have the duty to teach us?"

"Tay-ake her to Viagra Falls," Freddy said.

"Mr. Hunter has twice the cactus you have, hombre," Luis said.

"It's not all about sex," Dylan said.

"Hey, I don't know," Stubby said. "This woman, this bird-watcher, Mothra, obviously she's looking for something her marriage isn't giving her. She's taking power here. She's taking care of her needs. She's unfulfilled."

Dylan said, "But she made a promise."

"What is the nature of the promise we make in marriage?" Mr. Hunter said. He tried to sound wry, playing Socrates, but this was too close to the heart of his worry.

Dylan said, "That we should love, honor, and obey."

"The flesh is weak," Luis said opprobriously.

"The flesh has a job to do," Stubby said.

"I say go for it," Freddy said.

A long silence followed in the windless day, punctuated erratically by the squawks of Mexican jays.

"I don't see how," Mr. Hunter said.

Freddy said, "Well, the boy kisses the girl . . ."

And the crew laughed, except for Luis. He said, "And what of your wife in heaven? What will happen when you see her there?"

Only Mr. Hunter had seen Luis as religious before now. The air grew more serious. Everyone stared off, each in his own thoughts.

Then Stubby said, "Actually, there's probably more here than the moral question. You've really fallen for this chick, you know? How are you going to feel if it goes further and then—boom—she's back to her husband? Leaves you alone! That's going to be a blow!"

"When Tina broke up with me . . ." Freddy said. The others waited, but that was all he managed. Freddy looked off into the sky, and for the first time they could see his heart in his face and think of him as tender.

"There might be that kind of price," Stubby said.

"This is good advice," Mr. Hunter said. "I don't know if I could tolerate the aftermath of a one-night stand."

Stubby slid off his rock, leaned back against it, and closed his eyes. Dylan lay down, chewing a twig. Luis stood, stretched, patted Mr. Hunter's shoulder, and walked up the road to be alone. Luis prayed after lunch, Mr. Hunter knew. He might have thought Freddy was softly weeping if he didn't know what a tough customer Freddy was.

Mr. Hunter had made up his mind: no married woman for him.

Stubby had joked that Martha was an athlete, and so she was: forty-seven years old, Dennis Hunter's height and weight, she walked with the physical confidence of an athlete, looking in her shorts and stretch top as if she might jump up and fly at any moment. But in Dennis's little rental car her folded legs seemed delicate and soft. Her skin was beautiful to him, and her smell, and her voice.

"I couldn't sleep all last night," she said.

"I could barely work today," he said.

The rest of the talk on the hour's drive to the Hot Springs canyon was about the landscape of the park, and they didn't need to say much for looking at that landscape, the great buttes and cliffs and mesas miles away and unmoving. Martha read from her guidebook: "The park is eight hundred and one thousand one hundred sixty-three acres."

Dennis Hunter hadn't known that.

She read, "The Rio Grande was known to the Spanish conquistadors as the Great River of the North, and to the early pioneers as the River of Ghosts."

"I'm told this was Comanche territory," Dennis said. Luis had told him so.

Martha nodded her head, shook it, and then nodded it. "Comanche territory," she repeated, saying it from the heart of her heart where her laughter came from.

Oh, God. Dennis felt his heart flowing out to her entirely, yet not leaving his rib cage at all. They drove slowly through the great basin of the River of Ghosts, past the Chisos Mountains. A pickup truck with New Mexico plates zoomed up from behind, passed easily, zoomed out of sight. Dennis thought about how easily he could declare his love and ask dear Martha her intentions. Perhaps Wences was out. Perhaps a split was imminent. How ask? He said, "'Chisos' means something like 'ghostly' in the Apache language." Luis had told him that, too.

They were just quietly driving along, looking at the landscape. "Yes, it is," Martha said. "Ghostly, all right." She put her hands up in a gesture of amazement. She had taken off her rings. "Living things don't belong here. Not people, certainly."

Dennis felt himself and the car almost lifting off the pavement. Not that he was faint—not at all. If anything, he felt more present, floating car and all, with warm blood in his air-conditioned face and something humming in him, thighs to lungs. She'd taken off her rings. Dennis had never taken his ring off, not once for any reason, not since the night it went on his finger, June 11, 1947.

In the small canyon where the hot springs lay, they walked in the bright sun along seabed cliffs, striated layers of the ages thrown up by earth forces at odd angles. Martha immediately heard a great horned owl, and got it calling to her by hooting saucily. Dennis floated; he floated along the dry path and felt that Martha floated too.

Together they inspected the abandoned ruins of the old hotel and store there, the hotel and store about which Martha had read aloud from her guidebook. Together they found the petroglyphs she had read about, and walked along a Comanche path that had become a commercial enterprise's trail to the hot springs and was now a park path for tourists. Martha took Dennis's hand. He wanted to declare his love. How old-fashioned he knew he was! She would laugh at him, he thought, and this laugh would come from her teeth and not her heart.

The path descended between thick reeds and willows and the canyon wall. Soon Martha stopped and put a finger in the air. "Hear the river?"

Yes, Dennis heard it, a rushing sound ahead. Martha's hand was in his, their dry hands casually clasped, pressure of fingers in a small rhythm, a pulse of recognition: something profound between them.

Dennis couldn't find the words as the Rio Grande came into view: "Doesn't it . . . isn't it . . . doesn't this just . . . *tickle* you?" That was pathetic. He thought and tried again: "This little sprite of a muddy river, this ancient flow, this reed-bound oasis? That this is the famous border?"

"Dennis, I don't know what to do."

"That that is Mexico over there?"

"May I see you in Atlanta?"

They stopped on the plain and dusty rock—flat, polished sandstone, solidified mud. They stopped and held hands and looked at the river and could not look at each other.

She said, "What is this between us?"

Dennis could think of words for what was between them. It was passion, nothing less, on the one hand, and her husband, nothing less, on the other, both between them and no way to say a word at this moment about either. He let a long squeeze of her hand say what it could, and then he pulled her along. Brightly he said, "I expected gun turrets and chain-link fence and border stations."

"Well, there's nothing but desert for hundreds of miles. They just don't watch much here."

Pleasingly, no other soul occupied the hot springs, a steady gush of very hot water rising up out of a deteriorated square culvert built a century past. The buildings were gone—swept away by floods, they must have been. But one foundation remained, and formed a sort of enormous bathtub the size of a patio. In the hot air of the day the water didn't steam at all. Soft moss grew in the tub.

Martha sat on a rock and took her shoes off. Dennis liked her feet. He wondered if Wences liked her feet. He liked her knees very much. He liked that she was so strong and big, so unlike Bitty, who was a bone. He liked the fatty dimpling of Martha's thighs in her black shorts. She dipped her feet in. "Wow, hot," she said.

"Maybe too hot for today?" Dennis said.

"No, no, it's wonderful! And then the river will feel cold. A blessing." Then she said, "Well, no one's around." And she pulled off her shirt, just like that, and clicked something between her breasts to make her bra come loose, and shed it, and stepped out of her shorts and then her lacy panties (worn for him, he was startled to realize) and slipped into the hot water in a fluid motion, Dennis more or less looking away, looking more or less upward at the cliff (cliff swallows up there).

"I'm not sitting here alone," Martha said.

So Dennis tried a fluid kind of stripping like hers, but ended up hopping on one foot, trying to get his pants past his ankles. He stripped, and hopped, and slid into the hot water, self-conscious about his old body, the way his skin had become loose, the spots of him.

"It's love between us," he said, which was not the same as declaring love. "And that you are married."

"No touching in Texas," Martha said, far too lightly.

The water was shallow. She sat bare-breasted, up to her waist in the hot water, not exactly young herself. The water was gentle and very hot and melted them both, turned them red like lobsters.

"Swim," Martha said. She climbed out of the pool, down old steps into the river, and dropped herself into the current. Stroke, stroke, out of the current and she was standing on the bottom again, waist-deep. She was forty-seven, and married, and standing waist-deep and naked in the Rio Grande River, not twenty feet from Mexico. Dennis felt her gaze, considered Wences, heard Luis's stern voice, heard Freddy's *(go for it),* heard Bitty's funny laugh, thought of his three children, heard his daughter Candy *(Daddy, I know Mother would* want *you to date),* and followed Martha into the river, enjoying the relative cold of it after the scalding spring. Stroke, stroke, stroke, he was being swept away in the current; he pictured himself washed up on a flat rock dead and naked miles downstream. But Martha got hold of his hand, laughing, and they stood waist-deep together in the stream rushing past, silty, sweetly warm water.

"I'll get our stuff," Martha said.

She swam back and bundled everything—large towels, clothes, binoculars, bottle of wine—and easily swam with one arm in the air till she was back by Dennis's side, holding the bundle all in front of her chest, dry. And if not absolutely dry, what difference? It would dry in seconds in the sun and parched air.

Suddenly she said, "The American Association of Arts Administrators conference is in Atlanta this year." They stood in the flow of the river. "I could stay a week with you," she said. "Maybe more. It's June. Only two months from now."

"After that?" Dennis said.

Solemnly she said, "We shall see what we shall see." Then she laughed from the heart of the heart of her, and Dennis laughed and stumbled, and they made their way through the water to Mexico.

"I hope no one shoots us going back," Dennis said.

They made the rocky shore in Mexico and walked, not far, walked in Mexico until they were out of sight of the hot springs across the river, and right there under the late sun she spread the blanket and right there hugged him naked and the two older Americans in Mexico kissed and Dennis Hunter was a young man again—no, really—a boy in love, a tanned and buff shoveler of sand, a repairer of trails, a knower of animals, a listener to birds, anything but a widower alone in Atlanta the rest of his miserable days, miserable days alone.

Bill Roorbach, a 2002 NEA Fellow, is the author of five books, including the Flannery O'Connor Award–winning collection of stories, *Big Bend.* Other books are *The Smallest Color,* a novel; *Into Woods,* essays; *Summers with Juliet,* a memoir; *Writing Life Stories,* instruction. A sixth book, *Temple Stream,* is forthcoming. The story "Big Bend" was featured on the NPR program "Selected Shorts," as read by actor James Cromwell.

JULIE KARELSEN

Big Bend" got started in a funny way: I wanted to write a story about an older fellow, and I wanted to write a story set in the Big Bend country of West Texas, one of my favorite places on the planet. I put the two wishes together one morning and pretty soon Dennis emerged, and I just really liked him and wanted the best for him after all his sorrow. The rest is all him—he arrived and took over, the way retired executives will. Oh, and it had to be a love story, so I put Martha in there. And any control over the story that Dennis might have had was gone. He's a sweet old guy—I think about him all the time, about what might happen next.

Russell Banks

THE OUTER BANKS

(from *Esquire*)

The man pulled the RV off the road and parked it in a small paved lot, the front bumper kissing the concrete barrier, the large, pale-gray vehicle facing the sea, and his wife said, "Why are we stopping?" The rain came in curtains off the Atlantic, one after the other, like the waves breaking against the sand, only slower, neither building nor diminishing, passing over them rhythmically. They watched through the wide, flat windshield. There were no other vehicles in the lot and none in sight on the coastline road behind them. It was late fall, and the summer houses and rental cottages and motels were closed for the season.

"I don't know why. I mean, I do know. Because of the dog." He relighted the cold stub of his cigar, and for a long while the couple sat in silence, watching the rain come in.

Finally she said, "So these are the famous Outer Banks of North Carolina."

"Yeah. I'm sorry about the weather," he said. "'Graveyard of the Atlantic.'"

"Yes. I know."

"Joke, Alice? Joke?"

She didn't answer him. A moment passed, and he said, "We've got to do something about the dog. You know that."

"What've you got in mind? Bury her in the sand? That's a real cute idea, Ed. Bury her in the sand and drive on our merry way, just like that." She looked at her hands for a moment. "I don't like thinking about it either, you know."

He eased himself from his chair, stood uncertainly, and walked back through the living area and the tidy galley to the closet-sized bathroom, where he got down carefully on his knees and drew back the shower curtain and looked at the body of their dog. It was a black-and-white mixed breed—lab and springer, they'd been told—grizzled, lying on her side where Ed had found her this morning, when, naked, he'd gone to take a shower. He studied the dog's stiffened muzzle. "Poor bastard," he said.

"Maybe we should try to find a vet!" she called to him from the front.

"She's dead, Alice!" he hollered back.

"They'll know how to take care of her, I meant."

Ed stood up. He was seventy-two; the simple things had gotten very difficult very quickly—standing up, sitting down, getting out of bed, driving for longer than four or five hours. When they left home barely a year ago, none of those things had been difficult for him. That was why he had done it, left home, why they both had done it, because nothing simple was especially difficult for them, yet they were old enough to know that whatever they did not do or see now they would never do or see at all, ever.

It was her idea, too, not his alone—the romance of the open road, see America and die, master of your destiny, all that—although the actual plan had been his, to sell the house in Troy and all their furniture, to buy and outfit the RV, map and follow the Interstate from upstate New York to Disney World to the Grand Canyon to Yosemite to the Black Hills—man, he'd always wanted to see the Black Hills of Dakota, and Mount Rushmore was even grander and more inspirational than he'd hoped—then on to Graceland, and now the Outer Banks. He hadn't once missed the hardware store, and she hadn't missed the bank. They'd looked forward to retirement and, once there, had liked it, as if it were a vacation spot and they'd decided to stay year-round. There were no children or grandchildren or other close family—they were free as birds. "Snowbirds," they'd been called in Florida and out in Arizona. When they left home, their dog, Rosie, had been old, ten or eleven, he wasn't sure, they'd got her from the pound, but, Jesus, he hadn't figured on her dying like this. It was as if she had run out of air, out of life, like a watch that had run down because someone forgot to wind it.

He dropped his cigar butt into the toilet, looked at it for a second, and resisted flushing—she'd scowl when she saw it, he knew, because it was ugly, even he thought so, but he shouldn't waste the water—and walked heavily back to the front and sat in the driver's seat.

"Vets are for sick animals. Not dead animals," he said to her.

"I suppose you want to leave her in a Dumpster or just drop her at the side of the road somewhere."

"We should've found a home for Rosie. When we left Troy. Should've given her to some people or something, you know?" He looked at his wife as if for a solution. She was crying, though. Silently, with tears streaming down her pale cheeks, she cried steadily, as if she had been crying for a long time and had no idea how to stop.

He put a hand on her shoulder. "Alice. Hey, c'mon, don't cry. Jesus, it's not the end of the world."

She stopped and fumbled in the glove compartment for a tissue, found one, and wiped her face. "I know. But what are we going to do?"

"About what?"

"Oh, Ed. About Rosie. *This,*" she said and waved a hand at the rain and the sea. "Everything."

"It's my fault," he said. He stared at her profile, hoping she would turn to him and say no, it wasn't his fault, it wasn't anybody's. But she didn't turn to him; she said nothing.

Slowly, he rose from his seat again. He walked to the bathroom and pulled back the shower curtain. He kneeled down and gently lifted the dog in his arms, surprised that she was not heavier. Lying there, she had seemed solid and heavy, as if carved of wood and painted, like an old merry-go-round horse. He carried the dog to the side door of the RV and worked it open with his knee and stepped down to the pavement. The rain fell on him and he was quickly drenched. He wore only a short-sleeved shirt and Bermuda shorts and sneakers, and he was cold all of a sudden. He carried the dog to the far corner of the parking lot, stepped over the barrier to the beach, and walked with slow, careful steps through the wet sand toward the water. The rain blocked his vision and plastered white swatches of his hair to his skull and his thin clothes to his body.

Halfway between the parking lot and the water, he stopped and set the dog down. He was breathing rapidly from the effort. He wiped the rain from his eyes, got down on his hands and knees, and started scooping sand. He pulled double handfuls of it away, worked down through the wet, gray sand to the dry sand beneath, and kept digging until finally he had carved a large hole. Still on his knees, he reached across the hole and drew the body of the dog into it. Her hair was wet and smelled the way it had when she was still alive. Then, slowly, carefully, he covered her.

When he was finished and there was a low mound where before there had been a hole, he turned around and looked back at the RV in the parking lot. He could see his wife staring out the windshield from the passenger's seat. He couldn't tell if she was looking at him or at the sea or what. He turned his gaze toward the sea. The rain was still coming steadily in curtains, one after the other.

He stood and brushed the crumbs of wet sand from his clothes, bare legs, and hands and made his way back to the parking lot. When he had settled himself into the driver's seat, he said to his wife, "That's the end of it. I don't want to hear any more about it. Okay?" He turned the ignition key and started the motor. The windshield wipers swept back and forth like wands.

"Okay," she said.

He backed the RV around and headed toward the road. "You hungry?" he asked her.

She spoke slowly, as if to herself. "There's supposed to be a good seafood place a few miles south of here. It's toward Kitty Hawk. So that's good."

He put the RV into gear and pulled out of the lot onto the road south. "Fine," he said. "Too bad we have to see Kitty Hawk in the rain, though. I was looking forward to seeing it. I mean, the Wright brothers and all."

"I know you were," she said. The cumbersome vehicle splashed along the straight, two-lane highway, and no cars passed. Everyone else seemed to be inside today, staying home.

MARION ETTLINGER

Russell Banks is the author of fourteen books of fiction, including the novels *Continental Drift*, *Rule of the Bone*, and *Cloudsplitter*, and five collections of short stories, most recently *The Angel on the Roof: New and Selected Stories.* Two of his novels, *The Sweet Hereafter* and *Affliction*, were made into award-winning motion pictures. His work has received numerous awards and has been widely translated and anthologized. He is a member of the American Academy of Arts and Letters, and is the president of the International Parliament of Writers. He lives in upstate New York with his wife, the poet Chase Twichell.

The story came out of puzzlement. I bought a house in a small town in upstate New York from a childless couple in their late sixties, both retired, who had decided to sell everything they owned and buy a big RV and see America—while they still could, as the husband put it. I kept wondering what would happen to them once they had "seen" America, and in the lawyer's office at the closing of the sale I had a vision of them coming to the edge of the sea on a cold rainy day and realizing what they had done. Whom would they blame? Indeed, who was to blame? They moved me, this husband and wife with their willed fantasy of the open road, their dim but growing awareness of an approaching end-of-the-road. And they puzzled me, their apparent rootlessness, their willingness to let go of their past, and their inability to see the inevitable end of their journey, and I felt guilty, ashamed almost, to find myself buying their house.

Corey Mesler

THE GROWTH AND DEATH OF BUDDY GARDNER

(from *Pindeldyboz*)

I saw the best minds of my generation rock.
—*The Fugs*

You know Buddy "Slipshod" Gardner from his later solo work, the early seventies stuff when he latched onto the singer/songwriter craze begun probably by Sweet Baby James. You know him for his albums *Rain and Other Distractions* or *I Was a Child When Smaller*. But this is the story of headier days, days when the Overton Park Shell was a magical place, the later rainbow implied—when Buddy played lead guitar and sang for Black Lung, a blues rock band with a loyal Memphis following. The late Lee Baker, a guitar god himself then, said about Buddy, "He was the best of us. He was a seer, a prophet. That later acoustic stuff is crap, of course, but with Black Lung, Buddy was tapped into something *other*."

Back then, Black Lung played the Shell regularly, maybe opening for Johnny Winter, or teaming up with Mudboy and The Expanding Head Band for a minifestival that would start at dusk and stumble into the early morning hours like a dreamer looking for paradise. Lot of medicine passed about in those days. Lot of prescriptions from the hoodoo man. It was the sixties, people, and in Memphis that meant The Strip, The Shell, The Bitter Lemon.

Buddy was known all those places. Hell, Buddy was known everywhere in the River City.

This is the story of Buddy's taint, the story of Buddy and his pact with the devil. But Buddy had in him a black spot, fed by his desire to make it big, fed by ambition and greed and the sort of misdirected thinking which took *Rolling Stone* from the hands of the movement and placed it in the hands of the oppressors. The commodifying of the sixties, if you will, as embodied by the soul of Buddy Gardner. Buddy "Slipshod" Gardner, Memphis's answer to Jerry Garcia, Memphis's gift to the world, from integrity and precocity to sellout.

So much is lost now, so little written down, so little recorded. For those with the stamina to search it out, Black Lung made one album, released on the Pepper label, a little Memphis soul mixed in with their own acid-blues. It was called *Turntable Poison*. Some say it sounded like The Rascals crossed with Hot Tuna. One cut comes to mind, a piece they played in every set at The Shell, the ballad, "Mr. Handy and Hakel-Bärend." On the LP they insisted on the extended version with Buddy's long, side-handed solos, slick as molten lead, and the twelve-minute drum solo by Skippy Quetzalcoatl, effectively killing the album's potential sales but ensuring the group a spot in infamy alongside the lost tapes of Mudboy and the Neutrons and the missing five hours of von Stroheim's *Greed*.

There was also the shorter "Blues for Wendy Ward," with its plaintive chorus, "Thank you for at least that sweet ache," a phrase Buddy made sound like a supplication to the gods. "Wendy Ward" got some airplay around the country on the late-night FM stations, a minor flickering fame which only whet Buddy's appetite for more, for larger radio audiences, larger followings, more groupies, better food backstage. He wanted it all, Buddy did. No one asked him, What is all? If they had, he might be here today. Who can say? Pigpen's gone. Jim, Abbie, sweet Timmy Hardin. Was it the same spirit in the night that whisked away all these mortal souls? Can we ever know?

Buddy got his first musicmaker, a ukulele, when he was a sapling, six years old, a first-grader at Idlewild Elementary. He hung onto that uke as if it was his lifeline, time and time again having it taken from him on the playground while he serenaded a few curious classmates with his bewailing renditions of old Hank Williams songs. The end of most schooldays found little Buddy in the principal's office explaining why he should get his instrument back and vowing never to bring it again. Until tomorrow.

At twelve Buddy had graduated to electric guitar, a gift from his father, Al Gardner, who had played clarinet with a dance band called Dick Delisi and the Syncopators, at the Vapors Supper Club in his own misspent youth. Buddy's mother, Elise, could only pull at her hair and clap dishpan hands over her ears when the noise emanating from Buddy's room began. To her it sounded like the can opener on warp speed.

Buddy drew from everywhere, listening with equal fervor to Woody Guthrie, Odetta, Hoagy Carmichael, Django Reinhardt, Coleman Hawkins, Bill Haley, Lonnie Donegan, Howlin' Wolf, Eric Dolphy, Skip James, Shostakovich. Music fed Buddy the way most of us grew up on oatmeal and peanut butter; he absorbed it all, filtering it through his sensitive system to come out his delicate fingertips as liquid electricity, a sound many guitarists cannot duplicate and few can even explain.

By thirteen he had his own band, made up of less-skilled classmates at Snowden Elementary. They called themselves Regulation Footwear and soon were playing gigs at high school dances and other social occasions, at Clearpool, even at an end-of-school-year rally at the Overton Park Shell, foreshadowing later triumphs. Clearly, it was Buddy people came to see, Buddy who garnered them engagements with older audiences. Regulation's drummer, poor Gyp Leach, could barely keep time on his Sears drum set, taking lessons after school at Guitar & Drum City, just progressing past a four-four beat. But word was spreading about this precocious guitarist who sounded like a *coup de foudre,* this scrawny, pimply 8th-grader with licks like a junkyard dog: Buddy Gardner.

It was Jim Dickinson who dubbed Buddy "Slipshod," not because Buddy was a sloppy player but because he put together such sloppy groups around him. It mattered not to Buddy who was playing behind him. He was lost in the ether, playing for his own private gods, letting the Lydian reverberation carry him away, the sound coming from his own self. Oh, of course, he knew when the bassist was faking it, or the drummer was tripping over himself to keep up, or the rhythm guitarist was playing the same three chords over and over, hoping his stroking would be lost in the thunder. Buddy knew it, but he didn't care. He was soaring. He was making music, Memphis music, as sacred a calling as one could imagine.

Eventually, Buddy found his grounding, a group almost as flexuous and capable as Buddy, though few could approach Buddy's genius for the ineffable, that secret other place he could go with his music. Black Lung was born in the mid-sixties in an abandoned gas station when a bass player named Crafty Connor was introduced to Buddy through the coagulant Sid Selvidge. Memphis music bred Memphis music, is how Sid describes it today.

Crafty, who had a face like moits in wool, attended East High, where he had picked up the bass guitar (and put down his flügelhorn, much to his parents' disfavor) when he first heard Jack Bruce play. He wanted to be part of a power trio. He wanted to be part of the best power trio Memphis could build, and he wanted to build it. He called Sid, who said, "Well, you could do a lot worse than hooking up with this young guitar kraken, Buddy Gardner." Crafty called Buddy. Buddy called Skippy Quetzalcoatl, who had a drumming lineage like no one else's. His father had been a drummer, and *his* father before him, and back and back. Beale Street whispers the name Quetzalcoatl, late nights when the horns have died down and the wind sloughs around shop corners and up alleyways. It whispers the name like a mojo, a bit of song never transcribed, a bit of the *old* magic.

The abandoned gas station stood on a corner in midtown Memphis like a sepulcher, but it was soon to be transmogrified into a holy place, a place where anything could happen so beware. A place as bright as Sun, as holy as Stax. It is where Black Lung was born. Today it is a Taco Bell. But some know. Some still pass it by and cross themselves, harken back to the days of divination, the days when music could save a dying nation, a nation bent on its own self-immolation.

That was the sixties. Even in Memphis, an outpost planet. A tributary, if you will.

That first session, so it is told, was as if energy itself had been created in that empty concrete shell, where grass pushed through the floor, straining to catch these new vibes, this new electrical Jubal. Buddy cut loose as if he had been formerly playing in a straightjacket. And Skippy and Crafty—later rechristened Castor and Pollux—created a bottom like a Sheol torture chamber, like Thor and Loki at war. The crash and thunder coming out of that old Sinclair station was music from the beginning of time, the music the apes heard which made them men. Music, soul-deep. Collective unconscious–deep. They cohered, they veered away and came back, like the trajectory of stars. Buddy's solos were like fluid silver; he was reinventing the electric guitar.

It was around this time that Buddy began writing songs. He was shy about it. No one knows how many he wrote before he brought the first one to the group, the one that would later be their most requested song, "I Love My Aunt Jemima." Soon, though, he was bringing in songs in coacervations, as if he had eons of them bubbling up. That first acceptance by the group opened the floodgates and Buddy Gardner became something of a songwriting machine. Other artists recorded many of his best things, a blessing, and he became a regular at Hi Studios, at Sun, and later at Ardent. He was covered by many of the mid-South's biggest stars. And later by some of the country's: Elvis Costello did "Lemmy Caution's Incubus." Van Morrison made "Blues for Sid and Shirley" a staple of his live performances. Led Zeppelin, for God's sake, did "Procapé All Night," Jimmy Page being an early fan, as is written.

Just for the record Buddy wrote these hits for other stars: "Buttermilk Thighs," "Blues for Sandra Leathers," "Wrong for the Right of Way," "Arcade Late-Night Blues," "Open Channel D," "The Sins of Monk Cassava," "They Bribe the Lazy Quadling," "Patience Hell, I'm Gonna Kill Something," "The Nice and the Good," "Strawberry Fields for Only a Little While," "Take Me for Granted, Please," "Surfing the Big Muddy," "The Rules for Hide and Seek," "Young Avenue Blues," "Picnic in Overton Park," "Chin-Chin in Eden," "Turn on Your Love Lights but Turn that Damn Stereo Down," and on and on.

Buddy and the boys were off and running. Soon they were one of the most sought-after acts, playing gigs everywhere the area offered, in clubs, at outdoor festivals (happenings), and, of course, their famous half-aborted rooftop gig on top of the Sterick Building downtown. Officer Mike "Mooncalf" Milton, one of the arresting officers, recalls to this day how polite Buddy and the band were as they were being ushered into police cars while the mob roared. "Buddy Gardner was a gentleman in a jerk business," Officer Milton remembers.

This mildness, this Southern gentleman perception, follows Buddy to this day. It's hard to find someone to speak ill of him, even those he later abandoned or stepped on on his way to the top. He is often compared to courtly photographer Bill Eggleston, a friend of Buddy's from those acme days. The cover photograph of Black Lung's Pepper Records album, *Turntable Poison,* is an unaccredited Eggleston photograph (it is, of course, a weathered Sinclair sign, imbued with the enchantment Mr. Eggleston brought to all his work, a divergence quite inexplicable). Buddy was loved, revered. He was not held to the same rules as everyone else. So it goes with the great. And when Buddy started using drugs, mixing bennies, reds, and laxatives in dangerous quantities, no one was there to question him.

Of course, drugs were part of the scene then. They were everywhere. In the back of every minibus, in the bathroom of every nightclub, at practice sessions, in the homes of every groupie.

And Buddy had his groupies. The twins used to joke that Buddy played for scrimption and blow jobs. This has some truth to it—the money wasn't great in those days, asking for more money was seen as bourgeois or worse—but the women were wonderful. Buddy, though, let it be said, played for one pure reason in those halcyon days. He played for the rush, for the approach to the godhead. It was religion to Buddy. He sought the perfect note, the one that would bring about rapture.

One night, after a triple billing at the Shell (Black Lung was the middle act that night, sandwiched between the lesser talents of Rubdown and Barry and the White Panthers), Buddy wandered backstage after his set, still in that trance he seemed to enter when he played, and was greeted by a statuesque blond with eyes the color of the Wolf River at Sunset. She stepped into his path like a gunfighter.

Buddy looked deeply into her. She was an equation he could not quite decipher. Her eyes stayed on his. She was bewitching him, and even Buddy, already high from making music, was not immune.

Today people still talk about Lorelei Enos with a wary reticence. "Not much is known about her," people say. "She came in on a bad wind and left on another," one roadie told me. "Lori was beautiful, a beautiful person, a beautiful body, but she was half siren. She couldn't help it," another groupie remembers. "She was Satan's mistress," a musician, who wishes to remain anonymous, summed her up.

That first night Buddy went home with her. What happened there is shrouded in mystery, except Skippy recalls Buddy saying, "She had the most beautiful sex I've ever seen. It tasted like mushrooms and ginger ale. And its musk stayed on me for days, like it had gone subcutaneous, like it had replaced my own body odor."

Perhaps this was her hex: Ruthah, the perfume of Immortality. Others talk about the size and welcoming essence of Lorelei's breasts. Buddy was mothered; he fed there like a suckling, like a child. It wasn't love, but it was something between the sacred and the profane.

Some say Lorelei was responsible for the beginning of the slide downward for Buddy, filling his head with ideas of stardom, of leaving the backwash of Memphis and making it in a real town like L.A. or Boston. Buddy listened to Lorelei, for better or worse.

A happier image now: a small recording studio. A three-piece band, occasionally four when Jim Dickinson stops by and plays a little keyboards. A 20 × 20 room covered in egg cartons. The preternatural silence beforehand. The prelude. The creation of something new. From where there was nothing something now exists: songs, recordings, an album.

The making of *Turntable Poison* was a liminal time, a time of congruity, or grand passion. The melding of the three (sometimes four) musicians was synchronicity. It can happen more than once but it happened at least once for Black Lung. It's there on that vinyl circle, waiting for the needle like a junkie.

And for anyone lucky enough to find that masterpiece in someone's garage sale, in some second-hand record shop (where it can go for upwards of a hundred dollars or more), at some friend's apartment, there is knowledge passed. Because anyone who hears *Turntable Poison* hears right away what could have been, what should have been. What was. The album smokes. It tears down ceiling tiles. It disrupts fish in their blue aquarium lives. It calls like a squonk in the wee hours, in the time between sleep and dawn. It disrupts phone lines, dials up old girlfriends and makes them want you again. It stirs mud and makes bouillabaisse. Black Lung fashioned alchemy, friends, at least once, in that small studio, over a period of 72 straight hours without sleep, so the story goes. They laid down 43 minutes of catalytic reverb love. Some of you understand.

(And, an aside: they did not feel it necessary to include that one song on the LP by the drummer: an uncommon display of wisdom for the times but a good thing. Skippy could no more sing or write a song than fly.)

Listen to "Blues for Wendy Ward." Listen to "In Real Time Nothing Happens." Listen to "A Marriage of Rue" or "Hayley

Mills' Underpants." It's there. Under the surface like a chthonic river. Memphis Mojo. The only kind of magic that matters.

So, why would Buddy turn his back on the band after that triumph?

There are as many theories as theorists. Buddy wanted success, bigger success. He tasted perfection with *Turntable Poison* but it was local perfection. The album, though notorious today, an insider's treasure trove, a collector's grail, did not sell outside of Memphis. No major label bought the rights to it. Still, even this late, one wishes, with the advent of the compact disc revolution, that it would be reissued.

But now, Buddy wanted to be Hendrix, Clapton, Erik Brann, Zappa. That he settled for being Livingston Taylor is the story's twist, what gives it verisimilitude. Life is unpredictable, like a chemistry experiment. Like The River.

Skippy and Crafty were not even angry with Buddy, to hear them tell it today. Skippy works at Ardent and Crafty is a driver for UPS, but they recall those grand days with Buddy with something like ardor. "He was way ahead of all of us," Skippy says. "His energy came from someplace else."

At any rate in early 1970, having witnessed the death of some of the gods, Buddy Gardner turned his back on Memphis, and moved to L.A. with Lorelei, who then just as suddenly disappeared like a genii whose work is done. Some say she turned to making porno films. Some say she works in television. Some say she went back to perdition from whence she came.

But it was in L.A. that Buddy transformed himself into a folk artist, a singer/songwriter with a heart on his sleeve and an ace up it. He was as mellow as yellow, as smooth as California sunshine. And as empty as a bird's nest in December.

His two albums, *I Was a Child When Smaller* and *Rain and Other Distractions,* were mega-sellers. Buddy made it. He made it big.

For a price, yes.

Those last songs, dripping with feigned self-pity, seem apocalyptic in retrospect. "Allison All Gone" and "Goodbye to the Shell" especially appear to comment on Buddy's desire to burn his bridges, leave his Memphis past behind, forget his roots. And, of course, then there's "Burn My Bridges" and "Forget My Roots" off the second album. Even Buddy's skillful acoustic playing can't save those albums from their own wallowing, from their stooping to the lowest common denominator.

Of course they sold. They were huge. Buddy played with Carole King, with the L.A. Session, with Linda Rondstadt. He was revered, honored (Grammy for "Song for L. Enos," 1971), patted on his self-satisfied back.

But it was all so vacuous. And what for a Memphis musician is worse, so soulless. Buddy had gone to hell, many in Memphis thought, though no one said so. There was, for a homegrown prodigy, still respect, pride, a sort of sweetly sad valediction.

When Buddy was buried in L.A., that was the final blow. His parents flew out for the interment but no one else from Memphis went. It is said there were many celebrities there: Jack Nicholson, Susan Anspach, Donald Sutherland, Larry Hagman, Candice Bergen, Dennis Hopper, Jagger, Ringo. Some said Dylan was there, in disguise. It was Dylan who was later quoted widely as saying, "Buddy could have been bigger than me. He had Old Harry on his side."

With bigger success came more drugs, more women, more more. Death.

The official ruling was death by asphyxiation, choking on his own vomitus. It began to seem coroners handed this out to rock stars by rote. Janis and Jimi set the standard; anything less would be unseemly, not up to snuff. Next to his naked body were the cliché syringe, bottle of Jack Daniels, and a sheet of lyrics, a half-finished song to be called, apparently, "Wendy Ward Redux," as if at the end he tried to return to past glories and died trying. The penultimate line read, "You left your coppery skin behind." The final line, though difficult to decipher, seems to say, "Come back to me—" and the last word is either "you" or "youth."

Either way a sad epitaph.

But Buddy's gone gone. It's a sure thing. He burned brightly once but then seemed to just peter out like the Sixties itself, like a wind-up thing of wonder, a mechanical play-pretty. He ran down. Signposts to Gehenna: Altamont, the violent deaths of Jimi, Janis, Reverend King, and Bobby Kennedy. Nixon.

Ironically, Buddy "Slipshod" Gardner died on the same day, January 27, 1973, that Nixon officially ended the war in Southeast Asia.

I miss Buddy.

So *much* is gone, so many rainbows have faded away, and so many brightly painted faces now show the skull beneath. As John said, "The dream is over."

But he (who is gone gone, too) also said, "Love is all you need."

Both are true.

And, dreamers, lovers, children, both are lies.

CHERYL MESLER

Corey Mesler is the owner of Burke's Book Store in Memphis, Tennessee, one of the country's oldest (127 years) and best independent bookstores. He has published poetry and fiction in numerous journals including *Yellow Silk, Green Egg, Black Dirt, Thema, Mars Hill Review,* and *Poet Lore.* He has also been a book reviewer for *The Memphis Commercial Appeal, The Memphis Flyer, Brightleaf,* and *BookPage.* His novel, *Talk: A Novel in Dialogue,* has recently been published, and he is now at work on a collection of stories. Most important, he is Toby and Chloe's dad and Cheryl's husband.

My story, "The Growth and Death of Buddy Gardner," is part of a larger cycle of stories and poems entitled Chin-Chin in Eden: A Story Sequence Set in the Sixties on an Outpost Planet Called Memphis. *It is my own idiosyncratic, recondite rendition of the sixties, a decade that ended when I was a callow and unenlightened fourteen-year-old. Hence, it is built from poorly remembered history, manufactured legends, and bent mythology. "Buddy Gardner," in particular, is the result of my attempt to shoehorn into the book the eternally fulminating Memphis music scene and, at the same time, parody the overly sober music criticism industry. While Buddy is made of gossamer and Scotch tape, the case surrounding him is as authentic as a toothache.*

David Koon

THE BONE DIVERS

(from *Glimmer Train Stories*)

There had been rain somewhere to the north and east, and the Yazoo was bloated for that time of year, full of silt and streaked with mud at the center of the channel. The surface of the river crawled with swirls and eddies like the skin of an animal splayed out in the sun, and the air was full of dragonflies that swooped to taste the water then spiraled back up into the haze. Every so often, a sparrow would dive or rise from a branch on the waterline, seize one of the bottle-green dragonflies, and swallow it in midair.

The boat lay thirty feet off the muddy bank, its deck only a foot and a half above the water, like the step-up to a stage. A boom pole arched out from it, and a winch cable curved through the pulley at the apex before disappearing into the river. There was a compressor bolted aft of the barn-iron pilothouse, and it chugged in the silence: *chunka-chunka-chunka.* A stripe of grease was described on the plates below its pulley. An air line snaked away from the compressor and overboard, into the current that made the boat turn and creak against its anchor.

Curtis Pyle was in the pilothouse at the front, in a wooden chair backed up against the wheel. He was seventeen, lithe as a stem, his back overlaid with muscle. He had the face that was the blessing of his father and his grandfather before him, smooth yet mannish, soothing to women and horses and children. His nose would have been fine-boned and aquiline had it not been broken at some time in the past and left to set badly. With his flattened nose and tan that barely faded in winter, some mistook him for an Indian. His father, Pap, sometimes claimed to tourists who came into their museum from the road that Curtis's grandmother had been full-blood Seminole, a warrior-priestess, banished to the care of Pap's grandfather for the crime of religious conversion. But there was, in actuality, only a speck of Quapaw in them, contributed some time in the far distant past and then diluted by a troop of Germans, Irish, French, Scottish, and English. His father liked to say they were the product of a long line of shiftless men and reckless women—liars, con artists, cowards, adulterers, drunks, and thieves. As he sat staring at the letter in his hand, his whole blood-history seemed to lie focused like a pinprick of heat somewhere between his shoulder blades. He turned the letter in his hands as he sat and waited. On the corner of the envelope was a postage stamp that pictured the American flag, and he alternated between studying the stamp and listening to the whine of the cicadas in the kudzu at the edge of the river. He had heard somewhere that a misprinted stamp was worth money, so he sometimes held the envelope close enough to his face that anyone seeing him doing so, from a distance, might have thought him half blind.

He ran his finger over the ring of stars on the seal that had crossed the flap of the envelope. In the middle of the ring was a letter *T*. *T* for Tibidoux. Martha had bought *500 Embossed Gold Letterseals for Only Fifty Cents!!* from an ad in the back of a magazine, and now she used them anytime she mailed anything anywhere. She said in her letters that it was the little, old-fashioned touches like embossed gold letterseals that separated the great majority of women from the true ladies of the world, and that she was going to go on to be a true lady. In her last letter, the letter before the one he now held, she told him how she was going to have to give the rest of her seals to her little sister and send away for more, this time with a *P*. *P* for Pyle. In the margins of the letter, she had practiced writing what would be her new name over and over in a looping hand: Martha Jean Pyle. He looked at the name, and understood that a chain of dishonor either could or would not be broken here; might or might not be severed here, and well, and for good. Curtis pressed the envelope to his nose, and it smelled like peppermint, and like the perfume she had worn. He opened it and read the letter again.

They met at a dance, while he had been over for a month in the neighboring county visiting his cousins. The first thing he had seen when he drew close to her as she sat alone at the edge of the dance floor on a bench, staring at the planks between her feet, and the first thing he remembered when he thought of her now, was her skin. It immediately reminded him of his mother.

His mother had been a different kind of human being than Pap. Even as a boy, Curtis had no idea where she had come from, and could not conjure up a scenario in which his shrunken, cursing father might have wooed her away from her family and the life she had led. So he had satisfied himself with a tragic fantasy in which she had been carried off by force from a house on a tree-lined avenue in the city. Every morning when his mother rose, even when she was only going to the scrub board or to the ironing board, she never failed to dust her face and throat with a sweet-smelling powder taken on a puff from a box that sat on her dresser. To buy it, she sold butter and canned jellies to the woman who ran the stand at the roadside a mile from their house. Every night she sang to Curtis, even the nights when his father raged and spat curses, drunk, in the next room. She told him to grow up and be a different kind of man, and had explained to him as best as he could understand what being honest meant, that it was the kind of thing good men did. In the years since his mother died, she had become a shimmering myth to him, beautiful in the way only beautiful things glimpsed as a child and then lost forever can be beautiful.

Like his mother's, her skin was a startling near-white like cream, and seemed lit from within by candlelight. Her throat and hands and arms and the glimpse of flesh between the hem of her skirt and the tops of her shoes reminded him of the paper that Bibles always seemed to be printed on. Four days later—after he had told her he loved her and not meant it, and been gripped with a cool, creeping guilt that surprised him with its coming—when they were together for the first time in the hayloft of his cousins' barn, he risked fire to light a lamp he had brought, so that he could see his fingers against the backdrop of her skin. Now, nearly everything else about her seemed suddenly terrible. Her eyes were tiny and black, as lifeless as shot, just close-set enough to make her face remind him of some small animal that might nip if provoked. Her breasts and hips were cushionlike and flared sharply from shoulders and waistline and knees, so that her shape approximated that of a potbelly stove. She had been raised Pentecostal, and even though her family had fallen away from that faith, she wore her hair long enough to touch her ankles. She was still in the habit of keeping it up in public, and it mounded over her forehead like a heap of leaves.

But her voice was nice, he reminded himself, thin and still as the titter of a bird. When she spoke that first night while the dancers revolved slowly on the dance floor, after the first clumsy introductions, it was of flowers and lace and fabric on bolts in the Blind River Mercantile, and films she had seen and wept through. And later, after he had her, she spoke ceaselessly of what she knew of England and books she had read in which lovers tramped after one another through gardens where every leaf had been transformed into a silver coin by the moonlight. She carried somewhere on her person at all times a tiny book of poetry, and was always ready to produce it and read aloud. Some nights, after they had been together in the hayloft or on a pallet of feedsacks spread on the floor of the caved-in gin, she would read to him from that delicate book by the light of the moon, or by the harsher glow of the G.I. flashlight she had taken from her daddy's dresser drawer, and her voice would lull him into a wary sleep.

The brass bell above the pump rang three times before Curtis heard it. He folded the letter on its crease and stuffed it back into his pants pocket, then went to the winch and kicked the clutch lever to *On* with the heel of his boot. The winch wheezed and began spooling cable through the boom pole, and the air was filled with the grey scent of the electric motor. The pole groaned, and the rear of the boat sank under until the deck was only a foot above the waterline. Curtis put one hand on the boom pole and leaned out over the water to look down. The shape of the dredge defined itself, and then broke the surface of the water and was lifted clear, smelling earthy and wet as a catfish. Droplets fell in a shower from its edges and made rings fan into the shadow of the boat.

The brass dome of Pap's helmet rose beside the corner of the hull; the windows set into it fogged with his breath. He boosted himself up, wallowing aboard like a fish. As Curtis swung the load of mud around, Pap undid the seal of his suit with a whoosh. Curtis could hear the compressor hissing air into the helmet as Pap lifted it clear of his head. He dumped the dredge into a screen-bottomed box that stood on the deck, took the firehose off the reel by the pilothouse, and began rinsing the mud into the river, where it turned the water a creamy brown for a moment before the current swirled it away. Pap went in his diving suit and sat in the shade of the pilothouse and smoked, staring out at the trees on the far side of the river.

The things started appearing quickly. A sword pommel with the blade broken cleanly off at the hilt. A china cup with a missing handle that said *U.S. Army Qtrmstr's Corps* on the bottom. A cluster of minié balls, frozen blackly together, still holding the shape of the pouch they had been lost in. A handful of uniform buttons.The smashed carriage of a cavalry pistol. Half of a machine gear as big as a dinner plate. A flattened tin harmonica. A copper coin that had a wound taken out of its edge like a bite. Nothing was ever intact. Everything they found bore the marks of a sudden and incredible violence. Three times, the jet of the hose uncovered bits of bone, shot through with a delicate lattice of holes, and once the complete, hollow joint of a finger. As always, the sight of bone among the relics gave him a liquid feeling in the pit of his stomach, and he tossed these quickly over the edge and back into the water, where they swayed from side to side in the current as they sank.

They had a museum on Highway 61 that caught traffic out of Memphis, heading south toward the naval yards in New Orleans and Mobile. The museum was in a Pure Oil station that went bust during the years before the war, when the flow of trucks up from the Gulf had slowed almost to a dead stop and grass had grown in the cracks of the highway. It was the most successful of their schemes. Before this, there had been fortune telling, a water-witching service, trash collection, and folk-art painting on old sawblades. Pap and Curtis put up a sign on the side of a cotton wagon in a field five miles up the road that said, in red, terrible letters:

SEE THE U.S.S. BENJAMIN FRANKLIN &
CIVIL WAR NAVY MUSEUM!
WORST SHIPSINKING EVER!
1600+ MEN MET THEIR WATEREY DEATHS!

They had knocked out the walls between the three bays of the garage and filled them with things they had dredged up from the river: a black-iron bell, a silver teapot missing its lid, the fluted top of one of her funnels, a plaque with *U.S.S. Benjamin Franklin, 1858. Fitzhugh & Sons Steamship Co., Baltimore, Md.,* inscribed in whiplash script, as well as plates and butterknives and corkstoppered medicine bottles. Out behind, leaned against the wall of the station and inside its own enclosure, was their prize, and the last stop of every tour: one side of the frame of the Franklin's paddle wheel, twenty-five feet across, warped, and the braces twisted and split by the explosion that tore her apart. In the back was their room, cell-like, two Army cots and a potbellied stove. It had been the storeroom of the garage in the old days, and could never be rid of the smell of motor oil, and their sheets were always full of metal filings. Pap kept a blue pistol under his pillow. Some nights when he was drunk, he chased Curtis away with it, to sleep in the cinderblock building out back that had once housed the trucker's showers, or under the bridge a hundred yards up the road.

For a quarter a head, Curtis and Pap took through soldiers and their girls, salesmen who came in off the road, and the occasional family. In the gift shop set up in the station's old office, they had postcards showing the wheel frame with Pap's rusty pickup parked in front to give an idea of scale. A professional photographer had driven up from Vicksburg and taken the picture, and the cards had arrived six weeks later in a pasteboard box. Each one had *U.S.S. Benjamin Franklin Museum, Blakely, Miss.* written across the bottom in gold, and nice scalloped edges. On the back, in tiny letters, was printed: *The Sternwheel of the U.S.S. Benjamin Franklin, a steamboat serving as a hospital ship which exploded in January 1863 near the junction of the Yazoo and Mississippi Rivers, killing over 1,500 wounded Union Soldiers. Worst Naval Disaster in History. (Truck for purposes of scale.)* You could also buy minié balls for fifty cents, a brass uniform button for a dollar, and a belt buckle embossed with a bald eagle for ten. In the summer, the money was fairly steady. Pap, though, when he prayed, prayed for the big payoff. He had convinced himself of the existence of a strongbox in the hold of the ship, filled with a seized horde of Confederate gold. When he was on the bottom, that was what he felt for, the edges of the iron box that would take all his troubles away. At first, the lost horde had only been a possibility, something they laughed over while smoking. But in the months that followed, Pap brought it up more and more often. Finally, it had become plain that his father had convinced himself of the truth of it, as if he had brought it into existence, down in the murk and mud, by his will alone.

Curtis sat at the back of the building on a bucket in the shade of the wheel. He had the letter in his hands again, and folded and unfolded the corners until they were thin and black with grease from his fingers. Pap came out after a while and sat beside him in the shade. The cinderblock wall was cool against their backs. The old man had skinned off the rubberized canvas wetsuit, and wore only jeans with a hole that gaped open at the knee like a mouth.

His chest hair was the grey of steel wool. They heard a motor, and both leaned out to see if it might be a customer, but it was only a red moving van, and it moaned as it passed. Curtis heard a barge-boat whistle hoot forlornly over on the river.

"What you got?" Pap asked as he shook out a cigarette and lit it.

"Letter."

"Well done, Sherlock Holmes. I can see that fucking much." He puffed his smoke. "Who from?"

"This girl I met," he said, "when I went to visit Billy Wayne on Easter." Pap stared through the web of the wheel.

"Pregnet, is she?" Pap said.

Curtis turned to him, amazed.

"Ain't hard to figure out," Pap said. "You get a letter from a girl you hardly know, makes you act all pissy. Had to be."

Curtis stood and walked to the board fence that surrounded the wheel, built to keep people from sneaking around and taking pictures without paying. There was a knothole in one of the boards no bigger than a dime, and he put his finger in it. It made him think of the story his mother told him as a child, about the boy who put his finger in a hole in a dam and saved his town.

"She's coming into Vicksburg on the train Saturday," Curtis said, without turning around. "That's what the letter says, anyway."

"Well," Pap said, after a long pull on his smoke, "there's only two things you can do. You either marry her or you don't. Marry her, bring her up here, buy y'all a double bed and move her in the station till y'all can get someplace else to stay—and she might end up making a good wife, or might not. Or, you don't marry her."

"There's more to it than that."

"What's more to it? Two is all the choices you got. You pick her up when she comes into Vicksburg, or you leave her standing there. One or the other." Pap flagged his hands as if each solution might be held in a space no bigger than an apple crate.

"What I mean is, I got to marry her. I done wrote her and told her that I would."

"You love her?" Pap asked. "Love her enough to get up ever day for the rest of your life and look at her?"

"I don't think so."

"Then don't be stupid," Pap said, and huffed a little laugh under his breath. "There is women you fuck and women you marry. Sound like you found yourself one of the first type."

"She's got my baby inside," Curtis said. "I got to marry her."

"So swear up and down it ain't yours, dummy," Pap said. "She humped your ugly ass, didn't she?"

"It was her first time to. I was her first."

"So the only ones that know that is you and her and God up above. Man gets a woman pregnet all the time and don't get married. Nothing wrong with that. Been happening a hell of a lot longer than me or you been around." He paused and smoked. When he continued, his voice was low and reverent.

"We're close now, Curtis. Real close. I can feel it. I need your help for a while longer. When we find that box, we can both marry whatever we want."

"Good men don't run off on a woman like you said," Curtis said. "That ain't what a honest man does." Pap straightened on his bucket.

"Oh. Honest," he said. "Now you're a good man. Let me tell you something. Honest ain't good for nothing. You can't eat it, you can't drink it, and you can't fuck it. Likes of you and me are too goddamn poor to be honest."

"Well," Curtis said, "I ain't that way. Momma raised me different than that."

"Your momma!" Pap said. "Your momma—" Curtis balled his fingers into a fist, and cut an eye in his direction. Pap hunkered back down on his bucket and puffed his cigarette thoughtfully.

"I guess you're down to one choice then," he said, "Mister Honest."

The days seeped by, the hours hanging on him like a haze. He would wake, sure that it was near dawn, wondering why he couldn't hear Pap making coffee, and find that he had been asleep only two hours. He sat in the shade of the wheel and drew pictures in the dirt with a stick, watching the clouds dragged across and ripped to shreds by the wind off the river. In the evenings, he would go down to the levee and watch the barge boats pass under steam, chugging upriver. The fish hawks keeled and turned against the sunset, tucking their wings and plunging straight down into the water to emerge sometimes with a silvery shad. He convinced himself and reconvinced himself. The problem was a trap. Any time he thought of her, his mind turned in on itself like two evilly conjoined animals that hated nothing so much as each other. Finally, he came to a kind of conclusion, at first as soft and wavering as bottomland. He would do it. It was what his mother would want him to do. He had loved Martha enough to take her, and now he could love her enough to live with what he had done. Once he made the choice, he felt freed, as if a shame that had long hung over his head had suddenly been lifted.

Wednesday morning, it was his turn to dive. The silt on the bottom of the river was thick as pudding, and the only sensation was the sound of the current chattering against his helmet. His mind worked, and sometimes Martha's face rose before him, and other times the face of a sleeping infant that could be either a boy or a girl. He worked stiffly, scooping the mud up by the double handful and tilting it over the side of the dredge, feeling the edges of hidden things inside. Twice he felt the ribs of the ship, lying on the bottom like the bones of an animal, and they disintegrated at his touch. The air that hissed in at the back of the helmet smelled like grease gone bad in an iron pot. The river pulled and looped around him. The rains had come again in the north and east, and the Yazoo seethed with ribbons of cold and warm water that made his bones ache. That day, when he rose from the water into the blessedly hot air, the hose had turned up three gold coins the size of nickels, stacked neatly as plates in a cupboard, but stuck so tightly that Pap splintered the blade of his jackknife trying to pry them apart at the edge. Pap yelled, loud enough to send a yelp back to them from the bluffs on the other side of the river, and told him that this was only the first of it; that soon, they'd be turning up double-eagles by the bucketful. Even this couldn't melt the heaviness still caught in the middle of him like a chunk of ice.

On Thursday at dawn, they took the truck up to Memphis to sell the coins they had found to a pawnbroker three blocks off Beale Street. Not even the throng of people, streetcars, lights, police sirens, and automobile horns that had thrilled him as a boy could clear his head. On the sidewalk outside the dealer's shop, they split the money, and Pap disappeared toward the waterfront with his share, to get drunk and light whores' cigarettes with his Zippo lighter, and reappear the next morning at their hotel room, hung-over, stone broke, with a crescent-shaped bruise under his eye. Once he and Pap parted company, Curtis spent the day wandering from storefront to storefront, in and out of shops, looking for a gift to have in his arms when he met her at the train. Some trinket to hand her the moment she lighted from the car. He wanted to make her smile and tell him that she loved him and that she would never leave him. He believed that if he could do that, he would be all right. In a store on Poplar Avenue, he found it, on the head of a wax dummy: a silk hat, broad brimmed, blue, turned up on one side, topped with a cloud of sheer fabric. It was a strange, misshapen thing, but there also seemed to be something right about it in all its flowing silk, something he couldn't name, but was very close to the thought of the tiny book of poetry she secreted at all times next to her skin. The hat made him imagine a large, crepe-winged butterfly, just lit silently on a leaf in one of the moonlit gardens she had read to him about, lush and deep as true love. He walked back to the hotel, carrying the hat in an oval box with a label printed all in French pasted to the lid. He clutched it to him. He had spent the bulk of his money on it, and the expense calmed him somehow, as if he had made an irrevocable investment in his new marriage. On the way back to the hotel, he had seen a family—mother and father, pushing a baby in a buggy—and he stared, smiling at them, until they darted under the awning of a bank.

By the time he unlocked the door and lay down in his room with the box standing on the dressertop nearby, he knew that to marry her was the right thing. It was more than the right thing: it was the best thing.The son she would bear would be an important man someday, he thought, and he would be there. He could almost feel the pall of dishonor that had been passed to him slip from his shoulders, now no more than a cobweb that might drift down on a man walking from room to room in a haunted house. He imagined them, a man and his wife, walking arm in arm on the river levee, himself an old gentleman with an ivory-topped cane and a white mustache, who had refused to become the coward his father had been, married fifty years or more, and his wife never knowing of the time when as a foolish boy he had doubted his love for her. He thought of her voice as she read to him, like the song of a bird, and of her flesh, so smooth under his palms. He thought of going home and shining his boots, so they would be bright when he met her at the station. Staring at the box on the dresser, for the first time in days, he closed his eyes and really slept.

On Saturday, he rose at three, the night still flush against the windows like liquid. They had returned from Memphis the previous night, and on the other side of the room, Pap moaned between snores. A sliver of moon hung over the horizon, and by the time Curtis had put on his clothes and walked out of the station with his shined boots in his hand for silence, only the point of it shone above the trees like a monstrous tooth. In his other hand, he cradled the hatbox.The dark was moist and chill. He sat on the running board of the truck, put the box down beside him, and began pulling on his boots. One of Pap's hounds emerged from behind the station, tail thumping, and walked toward him a few steps. Then the dog yawned, and dropped in the dirt in a near-sprawl with his snout on his paws. Curtis's eyes had adjusted, and the yard was greys and blacks and near-blues like faded denim. He stood, opened the door of the truck, and pushed the box across the seat before pulling the transmission out of gear. He put his hands on the doorframe and began to push, the truck heavy and then rolling. When he was fifty feet from the station, he jumped in and pulled the door shut behind him until it clicked shut on its latch. The pedal sank under his foot, and he put the transmission in first gear and popped the clutch. The motor wheezed and started. When he turned on the headlights, they were weak and yellow, as if the darkness sucked the brightness from them like juice. He ratcheted through the gears, then sat back in the seat and listened to the chugging drone of the engine. The road was born from the darkness twenty feet off the nose of the pickup. The old, cracked highway seemed to have been laid across the face of the world with no more thought than a length of ribbon.

Vicksburg was silent in the dawn, full of a mist that had crept up the clay hills from the Yazoo, promising heat. On the docks of the city, the day laborers sat back on crates and mud-smelling nets, drank watery coffee, smoked cigarettes, and relished the chill so they could recall it delicious on their skin in the glare of noon. The sun came at 5:15, first orange on the courthouse then sifting down through the streets. Red and yellow on the Jefferson Hotel, the police station, the columned houses that stood in a line above the river, last to the leaning shacks at the water's edge. The night mist lifted from the city in the space of ten minutes like a net of fine mesh, then every alley and window was drenched in the greenish light of a summer morning.

The train station was brick, squat, and staffed by a man in a vest who had been asleep with his head down on the blotter the whole time Curtis had sat in the waiting room. The walls were lined with timetables, and a blackboard by the door had been scrawled across: *6:00 A.M.—Pass. Serv. from Ft. Smith, Little Rock, Blind River—ON TIME.* A railroad company calendar hung beside the board. It was printed with a picture of a locomotive just emerged from the mouth of a tunnel in some rocky, snow-covered place.

Curtis held the hatbox on his lap and stared out at the tracks that lay just outside the windows, gleaming blue in the new morning. Twice, he had gone out onto the dock and smoked, staring up the rails expectantly, only to come back inside and sit in his same place before the wood had grown cold. He felt excited and anxious for his life to begin. He could not get comfortable. He leaned on the arm of the bench, then straightened, then shifted his feet over one another. A redcap stuck his head in once, glanced around, then slammed the door again without a word. The room was still as midnight, the silence broken only by the occasional, dreamy whimpers of the clerk. A clock big as a barrelhead, its face yellowed with age and roman numerals around its dial instead of numbers, tick-tick-ticked over the clerk's window. Curtis had heard of Purgatory, the place where a soul might wait a thousand years before going on to Heaven, and he thought that it must be much like this room, full of benches and dust and ticking clocks.

Three times before the dawn, freights barreled past in the darkness. He felt them first, rumblings that seeped up through the soles of his feet. Then the engines exploded past the window in front of the bench where he sat, the light from their cabs seeming to stretch out like foxfire. Then the slab-sides of the cars would flicker past the platform, shadowy and haunted in the light thrown by the one tin fixture above the doors. It was like watching a line of animals stampede through the glow thrown by a lantern. Each time one of the trains blasted by, Curtis had the image in his head of one of the rails out by the platform wavering, then buckling under. He imagined the train keeling over like an earthwork and smashing the depot as easily as a man will crush a mosquito with the flat of his palm, and Martha running up the tracks in the dawn to find his body among the rubble. He thought of one of his hands, white as a fish belly, jutting out into the light from a jumble of bricks, a drip of blood from the tip of his longest finger.

Now he heard a rumble and a hiss of steam, and held his breath. A locomotive coasted past the depot like a black beetle hunched low to the earth. He began to rise, thinking it might be Martha's train, but it was going the wrong direction. Once it was by, he could see it was pulling a line of splintery boxcars that had faded pink and light green and sky blue under the suns of a thousand cities.The cars clamored to a stop on the far set of tracks, the cinder-bed of the yard between the train and the depot. The squeal of brakes made the clerk behind the desk jerk awake and almost fall off his stool. He grabbed a stack of paper and began shuffling it noisily, blinking away sleep. Curtis walked to the window and looked out. Up the line, two engineers in coveralls and pillowtick caps were jumping down from the train, heading across to a diner that stood on the same street as the depot, its back to the railyard. Curtis stood and waited for them, almost expectantly, to pass the time. Heat rose from the sides of the engine's boiler in a shimmer. He counted the cars back from the rear of the locomotive to as far back as he could see: thirty-two.

Standing at the window then, he thought of his son or daughter, tried to imagine their life and the things that child would see and know. The thought was too big for his head, so he left it there at the back of his mind, the great, unknowable, boundless future of his child, hanging somewhere in the coming years like a haze of blue smoke. He thought again of Martha and himself, an old married couple, an old gentleman and his wife, strolling arm-in-arm on the levee. This time however, walking with them, there was a handsome, upright woman with a fine-boned nose and fair skin that reminded him of the paper of Bibles. The woman wore a dress the color of watery ink, and was easy in it, and looked like she would have been as easy anywhere, in any sort of finery. Every so often, she would reach up and touch Old Curtis gently on the shoulder, or laugh out loud at the comments her mother made to her in the cool air, her laughter like the titter of a bird. Ahead of them, a boy and a girl ran breathlessly down the face of the levee, and Old Curtis called to them good-naturedly, gesturing with his cane, telling them not to go too near the edge of the river; that there could very well be anything in there, waiting to drag them in by a scaly paw. He resolved to tell them later of the explosion of the *Franklin*. How he himself had once dived on the wreck in search of treasure.The fantasy swam in his mind like a fish, glimpsed in the shallows.

From the diner down the line, the engineer and his fireman reemerged, one carrying a sack with a grease-stained bottom, each with a paper cup in his fist. They crawled up into the cab of the train, and it reminded Curtis of movies he had seen in which men climbed warily onto the backs of elephants. After a second, there was a hiss of steam, and the clang of engaging pins. Then the train was rolling, the wheels grinding the track under inch by inch. He turned and stared up the line. In the distance, an old drunk weaved between the rails in a pair of army-fatigue pants and a yellowed dress shirt. After a second, he stooped to pick up something from the cinders; a piece of glass, Curtis saw. Immediately, it was cast back down to shatter, as if it were just another of a thousand disappointments the drunk would be forced to endure before he was dead. He turned and headed south, into the cool shade between the buildings, and Curtis watched him until he was gone. Then he thought of Pap, even though he had kept the old man out of his head the entire morning.

The thought of Martha came to him then, and though it brought him joy to think of her now, and of the child she would bear, he found himself frowning at his reflection in the window. Curtis knew it was only a matter of time before his father would drive the two of them away from the station in a rage, waving the blue pistol above his head like a religious man will sometimes wave a Bible, and probably at the worst possible time. Then he had to think of her giving birth to his child among the soot-smelling pylons under the bridge. How would it break him to look in her eyes that day? He shook his head, tried to stop himself, to push the thoughts out of his mind, but couldn't. He had never in his life wondered about the question of fate, but he did then. He had the sudden terror that his was inevitable, and felt it now inside himself like an ache: He was sure he would do worse than think like Pap some day. In the heat of coming summers and the bone chill of coming winters, he saw himself become Pap: a drunk, a liar, a thief and robber of graves. Before, he had been able to believe in the power of his will over the blood in his veins, but now his faith wavered. Again, he thought of a chain, stretching far back through the shroud of years, and saw himself for the first time as a link in that chain, and saw another and another added in his passing. He saw the years to come. Watching the boxcars almost sliding up the tracks, gaining speed, he understood like he never had before. Violently, he knew the hearts of all the men that had poured out their seed in sheds and hovels and hay-mows and dirt lots to make him. They had lived their whole lives waiting for the moment when everything would be set right in the world, and it was the waiting for it that made them crazy, charged them with hate, sucked the souls from their bodies. They threw themselves against their fate until they were broken, as if there was anything they could do about it. Anything at all. They were as helpless to change as a child's tin ape, wound with a key. Fate was the thing. It was like the current in the deepest part of the river, a dark thing that would sweep him coldly along before it. He loved his child, even now as he was about to abandon it; loved it more than he had ever loved anything in his life. He did not love it for its blood, the way Pap might have loved him. The love of blood was a greedy man's love, a secret wish to live forever even though no one did. No, he loved his child wholly, sinew and muscle and bone, what it was and what it would become. What he had never known in all his dives on the wreck, with the hidden bones of dead men all around, he understood then for the first time: The end of all life was death, and the only valuable thing left over, the only thing which made you immortal, was what you left behind. He himself would be despised, and would disappear soon from their thoughts and into the darkness. But his son or daughter, and their sons and daughters, and theirs after them, would live on forever.

Then, up the tracks, he saw it, a boxcar, the green of an elm leaf. It stood ajar, three feet of blackness, open as a door. He knew sadly he had been waiting for it all along, and knew that the second he stepped toward it, he was damned. His mother's face seemed to hang before him, and he imagined that, somewhere, he could feel her hating him. He turned away from the window, and shouldered up the weight of his damnation. Curtis went to the desk and spoke to the clerk, then slid across a careful stack of money he fished from his wallet and told him her name. Then he fled on to the platform, ran across, and jumped down, his boots puffing up the cinders, their shine ruined. He trotted after the boxcar, and his lips were pressed into a line that could have either been a smile or a frown. And as he ran, another thought came to him: It was years in the unknowable future. A Saturday. A tall, upright man will leave his house with his children, a house on a quiet avenue of the city. And watching them from the shadows as they went would be a smiling old man, his body scarred and tattooed, looking as if all the dust and years of the earth had seeped into the creases of his very skin.

Twenty minutes later, the Blind River Express coasted into the station. The stairs were put down by the conductor, and a girl in a white dress and sunhat descended the steps. A bag was lowered to the platform behind her, and then the train was pulling away as it had slowed, the engine wheezing with its load of cars and the passengers' faces captive in the windows. The old porter, Tiger Millow, sat on one of the handtrucks in the shadow of the depot, smoking, his red cap over his knee. (The blue hat he found that day inside the station, he would take home to his wife. She would wear it to church the next morning, where the other ladies would call it grand, and pronounce her as beautiful as the Queen of Sheba.)

He saw lots of people in his day, coming and going: north, south, east, west. He prided himself on being able to tell a person's whole life story with one look at them. His *grandmère* had been a gris-gris woman, and told him a person's fate hung off their bones like an extra skin. He saw all kinds: rich and poor, businessmen and farmers, athletes and cripples. But it was ones like this girl that he liked to see most. As she walked across the platform, smiling, and then disappeared into the depot, he realized what it was he liked about somebody like her, that got off the train wearing that looking-around, expectant, so-happy-to-be-here face: A face like that didn't let on. He could tell nothing about her from it, other than she had been somewhere, had decided to leave that place, and had now come here. Looking at someone like that was like looking at blank paper. That kind of face made you think the person wearing it could turn out to be anybody. Anybody at all.

ELIZABETH KOON

David Koon is twenty-eight years old, and a graduate of the Iowa Writers' Workshop, where he was James Michener/Copernicus Fellow in Fiction. His stories have previously appeared in *Crazyhorse* and *The Arkansas Literary Forum*. This fall, he begins teaching creative writing and literature at his alma mater, the University of Arkansas at Little Rock. He lives in Little Rock with his wife, Lisa, and his son, Sam, and is currently working on a novel, *The Unrepentant Son of Don Juan*.

My wife says this is the most "manly" of my stories—a story only a man could or would want to write. I suppose it's like that because it is one of the stories I wrote while my father was dying—part of what I used to work through that. It took me a while to figure out what the story really meant, and it wasn't until I got my contributor's copies from Glimmer Train, *where the piece was originally published, that I did. I had gone home to Arkansas for his funeral, and when I got back to Louisiana, there they were in my mailbox, twenty, packed in cardboard. I laid them out on my coffee table, and my wife and I began looking them over. Anyone who's ever seen the magazine knows that in the back, they give the contributors for each issue a page to do whatever they want with—to print a childhood snapshot or a picture that interests them, a poem or just a short note about their lives. I sent in a photo of my father. In it, he is almost exactly the same age as I am now, holding my brother on his lap and—strangely—a breakover shotgun. "The Bone Divers" confounded me when I wrote it, but there, looking at that picture, thinking about the funeral, I understood why Curtis did what he did. Sometimes, you have to be brave enough to simply get out of the way and let someone go.*

Lucia Nevai

FAITH HEALER

(from *The Iowa Review*)

There are things you will automatically do for an ex no matter how many years you've been divorced. Eppie had me figured to the penny. She had the amount down. She had the frequency. I enjoyed that aspect of giving her money. She knew me when no one else knew me. It gave me pleasure to listen to her ask in her familiar little voice for the right amount for the right thing. One year it was $600 to have our German shepherd put down and properly buried in a pet cemetery because her hips went (the dog's). Another year, it was $2,000 for root canals. Things like that.

When I was still married to Jacquelyn, boy did that burn Jacquelyn up. *What does she want now? Are you going to give it to her? You treat your ex better than your spouse. Maybe you want two exes.* She stayed mad for two weeks when I gave Eppie money. It wasn't about money—money wasn't a problem for Jacquelyn and me. Not like it was when Eppie and I were married and sometimes didn't have the sixty bucks to pay the fuel bill or the thirty bucks for a new carburetor. It was the knowledge Eppie had about how to handle me, how much to ask for and when to ask. And the way I always said, *No problem.* After we divorced, Jacquelyn and I, she tried it, same trick, asking for money above and beyond what I'd agreed to, and I said no. Boy, was she surprised.

It was March—back to Eppie—when I took care of a legal fee,

$1,200 for a suit to stay in her apartment because they were trying to illegally evict her. So imagine my surprise when she called me in April from a pay phone at a rest stop on I-79, asking me to do her a favor. She usually paced her requests.

"A favor," I said. "What kind of favor?"

She asked me to drive her to a faith healer in Pikeville.

"Pikeville. Where's Pikeville?" I said because I was afraid something was wrong with her and I didn't want to know what.

"In Tennessee," she said. We both live in Pittsburgh. I live outside Pittsburgh on a lake and she lives downtown.

"Tennessee," I said, cool as a cucumber. "When?"

"Now."

"Where are you?" I asked.

And she told me the name of the rest stop. I listened to the truck traffic for a moment, gathering my courage. "What's wrong?" I asked.

"I had a ride set up, but he turned out to be a psycho." Her voice was brave and matter-of-fact, so mine was too.

"That's what's wrong with the world," I said. "I want to know what's wrong with you."

She paused. I knew what she was going to say because that kind of cancer ran in her family. I said it for her. "It's the liver, isn't it."

We got our first taste of spring in Virginia. The dogwoods were out and the redbud trees were in bloom. There was a Civil War battlefield behind the gas station and a souvenir store next door where Eppie bought a good-sized painting of John Wayne, oil on velvet. I watched her bargain with the fellow. He started out wanting twelve dollars for John Wayne. She got him down to two. Standing there in that Virginia souvenir store, she looked like any woman, not necessarily a sick one. She was wearing a little blue cotton dress and a bulky white cardigan sweater with big machine-embroidered flowers on the two front pockets. On her feet, she wore her little yellow flip-flops. Her face was as round and blank and sweet as a sugar cookie with her two little no-color eyes not quite looking at you. Her hair was still that wispy pale brown color, falling about her shoulders every which way. She burped a lot. That was the only change I could see in her. And every time she burped, she said, "Excuse me all to pieces," as if it was the first and only time that day—that year even—that she'd burped.

There was a 7-11 next to the souvenir store where I wanted to have a quick cup of coffee before getting the 4×4 back on the interstate. "What *now?*" I called to Eppie because although I was hightailing it in the direction of the 7-11, she was standing stock still with John Wayne under her arm.

So much of our marriage had taken place at that distance—roughly 26 feet—me always half turned away as I charged off in a direction I assumed to be our mutual goal, though I hadn't put it into words, Eppie always standing stock still at home plate, the point where my assumptions and hers parted ways. And nine times out of ten, you-know-who went sulking back to home plate with his tail between his legs. For a sweet little blank-faced woman, Eppie always got her way.

"Let's have coffee where we can meet real Virginians," she said. God, I missed her. Jacquelyn was not one-tenth the fun. I followed Eppie past the hardware store, past the church to a little luncheonette still serving breakfast. A ginger-colored cat was sleeping in the bay window next to a big African violet. It's funny. You hear the words *African violet* all your life without ever picturing the continent of Africa full of violets. We went inside and sat in a booth. A few regulars were lounging at the counter, drinking coffee. NO FOUL LANGUAGE read a stained sign over the coffee pot.

"Give us two breakfast specials," I said to the waitress without asking Eppie. I knew what she wanted.

"Yes sir," the waitress said with a sweet little obedient twang. She looked to be about ten years old. She went into the kitchen and waved a wand over two plates, piling them up with sausage, cheese grits, hash browns,and freshly fried eggs. Here I'd been going to Friendly's every morning, thinking THAT was breakfast, that frozen, reheated, overly manufactured stuff they cook the same from New York to California.

"Faster next time," I said. She laughed.

"Y'all looked so hungry!" she said. "I said to myself, *They are hungry—I bet they've been on the road traveling*. I wouldn't have known how hungry you can get traveling except I just got back from driving my three kids to Florida and it was real hard."

"Three kids," I said. "How old are you?"

"Nineteen," she said. "See, I met my husband at fifteen and got pregnant right away. But I told him I didn't want to get married if he was already thinking about getting a divorce. I wouldn't put my kids through what I went through."

"What's that," I said.

"Well, my stepdad, he used to beat me like a dog," she said. She said it descriptively, no blame attached, like the way you'd say *my stepdad used to teach me arithmetic*. "But first I was raised by my father," she said, "because my mother was *unfit*." She said unfit as if it were a State word, part of some proclamation. "See, the strange thing is my dad and my stepdad used to be best friends and drink together. And my mom and my stepmom, they used to be friends. Because my stepmom used to be married to my stepdad!" Her voice was joyful as if she felt important to be part of such a coincidence.

"See, one night my stepdad said to my dad when they were out in a boat, fishing, *I'm tired of the fat lady*—'cause my stepmom, she's real fat. So he says, *I'm tired of the fat lady. Do you want to switch?* And my dad thinks and he says, *Yeah, let's switch*. Now my stepdad beats my mother like a dog. She doesn't admit it, but he does. Like a dog. He beat all of us, me, my little brother and my little sister. My little brother, he got the worst of it. And now he's in the orphanage. But my stepmom—I love her to death. Bless her soul! She taught me everything I know. Ain't I lucky?"

We crossed the border into Tennessee. "Did you tell the god-damn kids?" I said. We had been driving in silence since Virginia after arguing briefly about where John Wayne was born. She said California. I knew damn well John Wayne was born in Winterset, Iowa, because my mother was born in Winterset, Iowa, and that's all they ever talked about there. It's not the kind of thing you get wrong.

I was mad at Eppie for not eating her breakfast. All she ate was one hashbrown and part of one egg. I had to eat the rest for her while that gal told us her life story. It made me feel terrible that Eppie was too damn sick to eat the things she used to enjoy so much.

Eppie went into her mute phase. She pressed her lips tightly together like a nun hearing a dirty joke and stared straight ahead as if I wasn't there.

Nothing I ever said about those kids was good enough for Eppie. For God's sake, they're children, she used to say to me ten times a day. I couldn't spank them. I couldn't even talk to them. It was because of them we got the divorce. And it hadn't helped them any. If anything, it hurt them. Charles, our son, still lived with Eppie. He was a sneaky, whiny little mama's boy. Deeana, our daughter, lived in Egypt. Deeana, she was a kid you could be proud of. But she liked blacks. Eppie and I were damn lucky she married an A-rab instead of a black. In high school, that's all she went out with, blacks, because we lived in a neighborhood where the blacks were taking over and the only good-looking, strong, healthy smart boys with a future in front of them were all black.

I kept looking at Eppie's profile out of the corner of my eye, applying the one thing I had learned in our marriage: if you ask a nasty question, ask it only once and then wait for a reply, don't repeat it over and over, saying each time, *I said blank, now answer me.* I waited and watched. Her little eyes drifted down to her lap. Her lips relaxed. She was about to speak. "No," she said.

I was floored. It was the closest she'd ever come to saying straight out, Clark, I was wrong all those years, keeping those selfish little brats away from the strong hand of their father.

As soon as I got the lump out of my throat, I said, "I never loved nobody but you all my life."

"Me too," she said.

We drove for a while. "How'd you find this place we're going?" I said.

Eppie reached into her purse and pulled out a crumpled piece of newspaper. She laid it on her thigh and set about flattening it, smoothing it with her palm over and over. I had not thought about her thighs for a long time. After blocking it out of my mind for many years, I could now remember exactly how we used to go about making love. She was the kind of gal who started out all stiff and unsure, but once you got her going, she didn't want to stop. I wondered if the good Lord was going to let me fuck her again.

"Faith Healer," she read from the classified section of *The Pittsburgh Telegraph*. "Willie Mae Dupray. One mile south of Jo-Jo's BBQ near Pikeville. I am waiting for your call. 315. 555 1772." She felt guilty. She wouldn't look at me.

"Jesus Christ, one mile south of a barbecue place?" I said. I put my foot on the brake and pulled the 4×4 onto the shoulder. I saw something on *60 Minutes* about bogus healers who prey on innocent victims and take their life savings. In this case, *my* life savings. "How much does this Willie person charge?" I noticed my voice was condescending. I learned that from Jacquelyn, that I'm condescending. Once Jacquelyn pointed it out to me, instead of me giving it up and speaking to her respectfully, I began to do it more often and enjoy it even more. It's kind of fun. It's as if you have rights and powers and can see the obvious when others can't. It's not true, of course, and that's what makes it fun.

"There's no charge," Eppie said.

"How does she pay for that advertisement?" I touched the ad on her thigh.

"She said people make donations. She said one lady from Dallas gave her a million dollars when she cured her son of leukemia."

"Well, all right then," I said. I took the truck back up to the limit. "What," I said because she was looking at her lap in that way she had when she couldn't accept the hard part of life. "What, hon," I said, a little bit softer and more gentle.

"I wanted her to cure me over the phone."

"Jesus Christ," I said. "These people can't cure over the phone. Christ himself couldn't cure over the phone. Did she say she could?"

"She said to come in person. She said to call you."

I straightened up. I looked at myself in the rearview mirror. "Did she call me by name?"

"She said a man who lived on the water still loved me and would do anything for me."

I almost drove off the road. I had only lived on the lake for three months. Score one for Willie Mae Dupray. "How'd you end up with the psycho, then?" I asked.

"I didn't believe her."

At the Knoxville rest stop, Eppie put a quarter into a vending machine where you fish for toys with a mechanical set of claws designed to drop anything of value before you win it. Somehow she held on tight and beat the machine, winning a little stuffed yellow duck worth at least fifty cents. "What the hell are we going to do with a duck," I said.

"Put him next to the Duke," she said. God, I loved her.

"Is there anything but Baptists here?" she said at 10 P.M. when we finally found a motel. In our search for something fairly clean with the AAA seal of approval sign on display, we had passed maybe 800 churches and all were Baptist.

"Guess not," I said. "You first." I indicated the bathroom. We each had a double bed to ourself. I sat on mine and listened to the rhythm of the water running in the sink as she gave herself her nightly sponge bath the same way she had for years. Left side of her face, right side. Neck, left and right. Shoulders, arms, breasts. *Why,* I wondered. *Why did we divorce? Why did we marry? Why were we born?*

What in the hell she did all night long I do not know, but it was not sleep. Six times she woke me up with her rustling around, pawing through her damn suitcase, trips to the bathroom, water running, more trips to the bathroom, sitting up to read, belching and burping. I got two winks, no more, and she got none.

"How'd you sleep?" she asked in the morning as we headed west on I-40.

"Fine," I said. "You?"

"Fine."

We had breakfast at the Kingston rest stop. I spread out the map of Tennessee and studied it over my third cup of coffee, looking for the fastest way to Pikeville. The restaurant was empty except for one other table, a family of sorts. The old man saw my map and came over. "Are you lost?" he asked, hoping we were.

I didn't feel like talking to this old man, so I just said, "No." And I pointedly looked back at my map.

"Have you been to Gatlinburg? If not, you should go," this old man said. "You'll love it." While he was talking about how great Gatlinburg was and how when he went there someone he hadn't seen since high school recognized him, his middle-aged daughter came over and stood by his side, talking up the Blue Ridge Parkway. They had a way of alternating sentences, of looking at me, then at each other just as they were about to pass the baton.

"You're right up *in* the mountains . . ." she said. "You can see for miles. . . . You'll think you are in heaven. . . . You can feel the presence of God everywhere."

Next the old guy's wife came over with her address book, going through it page by page with big slobbery licks of her thumb, until she found the name of a cheap motel to stay at outside Gatlinburg. It was an Irish name.

Finally the granddaughter came over. She was a cross-eyed little thing about eight years old. She elbowed her way in between her mother and her grandmother and proceeded to jump up and down and ran her fingers over my spread-out map in itsy-bitsy spider fashion.

These people were literally surrounding us, all talking at once, giving us instructions, seeming to agree yet constantly gently correcting each other.

Eppie, God bless her, vomited a little tiny bit right on the yolk of her fried egg and they left.

"Look at that goddamn thing," I said when we passed the Tennessee River dam they had made such a big stink about years back. They were right not to want it. It looked inhuman. "What a monstrosity," I said. "What an outrage. A dam doesn't have to look like that goddamn thing. A dam can be a work of art." And in the process of explaining it to her, I missed the turn to the bridge.

"Goddammit," I said. I hate to backtrack so we kept going. "There's got to be another goddamn bridge." I said it every mile.

Eppie turned on the radio to drown out my cursing. Every station either had a Bible-thumping Baptist promising you you'd go to hell or a fast-talking furniture salesman selling you suites of all sorts, bedroom, living room, dining room, on the installment plan. Furniture for who? All we saw was tarpaper shacks with rusted-out trucks parked in front.

I went up to one of these shacks to ask where the next bridge was across the Tennessee River. The screen door was wide open. The television was on. No one was home or if they were home, they were hiding. *Recipe No. 387,* read the television screen. *One navel orange. One bunch cilantro.*

We were a stone's throw from Georgia by the time we got over. I was following the backroads toward Pikeville when we came to a little wooden State Park sign with yellow letters. *Fall Creek Falls,* it read, *2 mi*. "Clark," Eppie said. "I want to see that waterfall."

We turned at the entrance. Do you think I could find that goddamn waterfall? By the time we parked and found the trail and I got Eppie up there, I was ready to kill. She hardly made it. I had to carry her the last hundred yards. She put her feet in the pool at the base of the falls and watched it nonstop for an hour. Then I carried her back. And do you think I could find my way out of there?

When I finally saw a ranger rolling toward us in his Jeep, I parked the 4×4 in the middle of the road and walked up to give him a piece of my mind.

Well, it was a her. That threw me off. That smoke-glass driver's-side window went gliding down with its brand-new hum and there is a gal with bright red spiky hair and that kind of orange lipstick that makes a man want to bite a woman's lips to see if they are real or artificial. She's got her little wrist resting on the steering wheel and here, she's wearing a big new diamond engagement ring. Her whole fuckin' life's in front of her.

"What's up?" she said—in a goddamn New York accent. No way was I asking *her* directions.

"Your signs are very misleading," I said. "You'd be well advised to correct them. You've caused two people a lot of hardship today. And that's not a good advertisement for Tennessee if you catch my drift."

"Which signs are those?" she asked.

"Your signs to the falls. Beginning out on the route there." And of course I pointed in the wrong direction because the road into the parking lot winds like a bastard, this way and that way.

"There's no sign there."

"Well, wherever the signs are, they are wrong," I said. And I explained it. While I laid it out for her piece by piece, she was looking over my shoulder at the traffic piling up behind my truck. "Nobody else has complained," she said.

"You goddamn little bitch," I said, "My wife almost died getting to your fucking falls."

"Don't you curse at me, sir," she said and she whipped out the walkie-talkie. "I'll write you up in a second." She clicked her monitor on and said, "Zero two niner, this is forty-six." I let her have it. I said some things I shouldn't have. I knew it at the time, but I couldn't stop myself. "White male, late fifties," she said into the CB, "six feet four, two hundred and thirty pounds, sandy gray hair, glasses, driving a Dodge 4×4, dark green, female passenger. Pennsylvania license plate NZ442D."

There were four or five cars lined up behind us. The drivers were all frowning and scowling at me. One guy called me an asshole. Here he was dressed in Eddie Bauer from head to toe, driving a metallic gold Lexus version of a jeep. I walked over and opened his car door. "You got a problem, pal?" I said. At least I got the satisfaction of seeing that shit-in-the-pants look on his face before we both heard the siren and saw the flashing red light.

Jo-Jo's BBQ was right where that girl ranger's superior said it would be. He told me not to pay any mind to her. She's a New Yorker, he said. He said she's a good egg but she's a little sensitive about the guff she gets from men in this state. He offered me a chew from his little tin of Red Dog and pointed me in the right direction. He weighed three hundred pounds if he weighed an ounce. His name was Randy Bright. If he had not given me flawless directions, I would have passed right by Jo-Jo's. I would never have dreamed that this tiny little unpainted roadside lean-to had the best barbecued pork and Southern fried chicken in Tennessee.

"Two of those," I said to the gal, pointing to the sign over the door: *Southern Fried Chicken. Fried to your order. Please allow 45 minutes.*

"Now it does take the full forty-five minutes, sir," she said, all apologies.

"We were told to order it by Randy Bright," I said.

Her face turned all smiles and sunshine. "Do y'all know Randy? Ain't he fun?" she said.

This gal brought us our ice tea, then she took the slip of paper with our order on it and walked up the hill to a ranch house. Out came Jo-Jo himself, a happy, fat, red-faced man wearing a clean white T-shirt and madras bermuda shorts and carrying a cast iron skillet as big as an automobile tire.

"You watch," I said to Eppie. She looked a little vague. Her eyes were glazed over and she was bone tired. I realized later instead of getting mad like I did with the lady ranger and showing off like I was doing now with Jo-Jo, I probably should have just shut up and got Eppie to the faith healer. But I didn't see that then. It was still all about me and what I needed to prove.

Jo-Jo went to town. He cut up a whole chicken and fried it for us and while he fried he talked. "Bless you Yankees," he says to us. "I cannot get my own next-door neighbor to wait forty-five minutes for my chicken. Everybody has got the Kentucky Fried mentality. They want everything right now. Well, they don't know what they're missing."

"Did you learn this recipe from your mama?" I asked.

"No sir," he said. "They made me a cook in the Army. Then when I got out, I worked my way up through Restaurant Associates. My first big hotel restaurant was in Chattanooga. I ran that restaurant for nine years. I had a black woman there who was the best restaurant manager I'd ever had. She did the work of three people. And she never forgot anything. That woman was smart.

"One day I noticed she was kind of down. And this woman always had a smile on her face. So I said to her, what's wrong. She said she'd been down to the furniture store to buy some furniture on the installment plan and even though she'd had a steady job with me for nine years, they wouldn't sell her a stick of furniture.

"I'll be a goddamn son of a bitch, I said. So I went down there with her and I co-signed the papers and she got the furniture and she never missed a payment.

"Now listen to this. A few years later when my sister was in the hospital with some problems and she needed a big operation, the doctors told me to have all my friends come to the hospital and give blood—because they had to have lots of blood on hand in case she needed a big transfusion. I made about five calls and I told my friends how important this was to me. Well a few days went by and the doctor called and said to me, Jo-Jo, we've got to do better than this. We've only got five pints of blood.

"Five pints of blood. I thought I had friends. So I was kind of down about that and here this black lady noticed this and she said to me, what's wrong. And I told her. And wouldn't you know, by that afternoon, a hundred black people were lined up at that hospital to give blood for my sister. And she needed it too. She needed a lot of blood. And do you know what? That Negro blood improved her. She was nasty before the operation and much better afterwards."

"What a story," I said to Eppie. She just stared straight ahead. I didn't know then how bad she was feeling.

"I had nigger friends all over Chattanooga," Jo-Jo said. "They'd come to the back door of the restaurant and I'd give them free food. I could never get them to come to the front door. Even though I invited them to. Many a night, I'd play cards with them. See that trophy?" Jo-Jo pointed to a Rook championship trophy on a little wall shelf over my head. I'd forgotten about Rook. "Many a night I'd play cards with them down on Nigger Street. They used to call it Nigger Street. Now they call it Martin Luther King Street. Well, there you are, folks. Taste that and tell me if you ever ate a better piece of fried chicken."

I ate straight through mine and Eppie's. I thanked him. I promised him we'd see him again. And then when I went to pay—he wouldn't let me. He said, "This is on the house. I enjoyed talking to you two so much, it wouldn't be right to ask you to pay."

I hugged that man. He was so fat, he was hard to hug—but I did my best. And when we got back in the car, I was so happy I thought I was drunk. "Wasn't that funny," I said to Eppie, "the way he said nigger so freely? Nigger this, nigger that. How long has it been since we could say nigger? Over twenty years, I believe."

"This is it," Eppie said. And I hooked a left into a little mud driveway next to a purple rural route mailbox. And out of this purple trailer comes the biggest, fattest old black woman either of us have ever seen.

"Hold on here," I said. "Did you know she was black?"

"Yes," she said.

"Hold on," I said. "Did you just make me drive you 1,200 miles to a black woman's house?"

"Clark," she said. "I just want to live."

I felt sick to my stomach. "I'm waiting here," I said. "This is as far as I go."

The black woman was stepping down off her stoop and waddling out to the truck. She was wearing a big old black-and-white polka-dot dress with a big clean white collar and three big black shiny buttons down the chest, the kind of dress I haven't seen on a woman since I was seven years old.

"Roll your goddamn window down," I said to Eppie after a few minutes because Eppie was staring at her lap while the black woman looked through the window at her. Eppie rolled it down.

"Are you Eppie?" she asked.

"Yes I am."

"Then you must be Clark."

I wouldn't answer.

"Well, I am Willie Mae," she said. "Won't you please come inside!"

Inside. The way she said the word hit me like a ray of light shining through the bars of a man serving a life sentence. I got out of the truck and opened Eppie's door for her like a gentleman. We went inside. Everything in the living room was purple. Somehow that made it easier.

"Would y'all like a cool drink?" Willie Mae said. She clasped her hands before her big chest.

Eppie said, "Yes, please."

Willie Mae brought us both a long, cool glass of ice tea with a purple crocheted sock ring around it so you can hold your cold drink without your damn fingers going numb. I took mine and put it on the purple rug.

"Look, miss," I said to Willie Mae. "I would not have driven all this way if I knew you was black—nothing against blacks."

Willie Mae smiled at me. Not a smile with the lips but a smile with the whole face. She smiled so long I reached down and drank some of her ice tea just to break the tension.

She bowed her great big head and clasped her hands delicately together in front of her big white collar and she closed her eyes. "Let us pray."

I don't pray. I never have prayed and I didn't intend to start. So while she and Eppie prayed, I sipped my drink and looked at the white undersides of Willie Mae's heels spilling out over the backs of her shoes as if with all the scrubbing and washing, the black color was starting to rub off her skin.

Her voice went up. Her voice went down. I don't know what all she said, but when she said, "A-men," Eppie was crying a little. "She needs you to comfort her when she cries," Willie Mae said to me. I don't much like anyone telling me what to do, let alone a woman. I'm a bastard of the first water who never did anything he was told to do except in Korea. And I wished I hadn't done it there. I wished I'd had the balls to say the hell with you and let them just court-martial me.

I looked at Eppie, sniffing and sighing, and something came over me. I did what Willie Mae said. I put my arms around her and she leaned into me and cried a little more. Not the big wailing stuff, because she didn't have enough life left in her for that. *Son-of-a-bitch,* I thought to myself, because it felt so good to have her all soft and sweet in my arms like that, *you could have been doing this when she cried for the last thirty years!*

"Where are your children?" Willie Mae asked me.

"Ask *her,*" I said as if it was Eppie's fault.

"I will," Willie Mae said. "But first I'm asking you."

"Deeana, she's in the foreign service in Cairo, Egypt. And Charles, he lives with Eppie."

"Do they know their mama is not well?" Willie Mae asked Eppie.

"No, ma'am," she said.

"Well, *why the hell not?*" Willie Mae said it with one of those great earthy gospely growls that makes you feel the presence of the truth, the whole truth and nothing but the truth. I was starting to like this woman.

"Charles, he's a basket case," Eppie said. "And Deeana, she has a job as a schoolteacher over there in the American school. They have finals about now."

"Thank the *Lord Above* for ex-husbands," Willie Mae said. I sat up straight. I wished to hell we'd have come here when we started having trouble. I would have comforted Eppie whenever she cried and she would have learned she was a damn pushover and a doormat with these kids.

"Let's invite these children into the room with us," Willie Mae said. She sat back in her big purple chair, rested her arms on the armrests with her white palms facing up, and let her head fall back a little. Her eyelids fluttered and I could see the whites of her eyes. I got a chill in my spine.

"Come in, Charles," she said, just as if a real person had knocked on the front door. I could feel a little wispy curl of hate in my gut. I never liked my son once he turned five.

"Come in, Deeana," Willie Mae said. I couldn't feel Deeana come in, but Eppie could. Eppie started to twitch a little. Her daughter could lie straight to her face and Eppie never knew.

"Children," Willie Mae said with a little bit of a reprimand. "Your mama is dying."

A noise filled the room. It sounded like a wolf who'd been shot in the side and was running around in circles, dragging its back half by the guts. It took a moment for me to realize the noise was coming out of me.

"Children," Willie Mae said, taking Eppie's hands in hers. "God is calling your mama home. Can you let your mama go home to God?" More wailing. "She *needs* you to release her. Her body is *wracked* with disease." She put that gospely growl in for emphasis. "She is sick from her *throat* to her *knees*. And she needs to shed this little body that's tying her to this earth and *join* the Lord as a beautiful spirit. Are you with me children?"

The wailing stopped. Eppie's eyes were closed, her face as still and calm as if she were asleep. The two of them were holding all four hands. Eppie started to glow. I mean glow. I loved that woman. I loved her more than life itself.

Willie Mae asked the children, first one, then the other, to give their mama a special message filled with details that were new to me, things that made me realize they'd had a whole life together, Eppie and the kids, that I had never been a part of and didn't know anything about. And I forgave her for letting them take advantage of her. You love your kids to death and they need to push you to the limit and you think it's love to give in.

I must have fallen asleep. All I know is when I woke up, I was alone in the living room. I snooped around the trailer, wondering how that woman found everything in purple, purple toilet seat cover, purple toilet brush, purple soap, purple mini-blinds, purple bedroom slippers, a purple Bible.

I walked out back. Eppie was in the hammock with a little quilt over her and Willie Mae was sitting in a metal lawn chair at her side, rocking her gently to and fro.

I killed her. That's what it comes down to. I got Eppie the morphine she asked me to. And I gave her the overdose she asked me to. You wouldn't think a thing like that would bring a man and a woman closer, but it *made* my life, having her whisper personal things right into my ear when her voice didn't have any noise left. She told me it was the most beautiful experience in her entire life, having me pick her up and carry her up to the lovely flat stone lookout over the waterfall. "Because of that," she whispered into my ear, "my life is complete." And hearing her say that, I knew mine wasn't and never would be.

And then she couldn't even whisper. All she could do was answer questions by squeezing my hand twice for yes and once for no. My last question was, *Now?* Meaning the overdose. She squeezed twice.

I killed her there in Tennessee and I buried her there. And the kids flew in and they got into a big fight and wouldn't speak to each other and they blamed me for not letting them help decide the details of her treatment. I just smiled at them with my whole face like Willie Mae had smiled at me and I forgave the little shits for everything.

I tried to go home. I really did. I gassed up the truck, set the alarm for 4:30 A.M. and took off. I got as far as the Tennessee border, but I couldn't bear to leave the state. The name itself, Tennessee, had a hold on me. It was only 10 A.M., but here I was, looking for a motel where I could spend the night. I found one, the Shamrock.

Shamrock, Shamrock, it sounded familiar. As I sat in the little aluminum lawn chair in front of my room, number 39, looking at the blackbirds swirling through the sky with the door wide open behind me and the television on inside so I wouldn't feel too lonely, I remembered. This was the motel *outside* Gatlinburg the old woman in the rest stop told me to stay in. Life was becoming pure magic now. Imagine that, magic coming to an old bastard like me.

Lucia Nevai's stories have been published in *The New Yorker*, *Zoetrope: All-Story*, *The Iowa Review*, and other publications. She is the author of two short-story collections, *Normal*, and *Star Game* (winner of the Iowa Short Fiction Award). She lives in upstate New York, where she writes screenplays.

NANDOR NEVAI

"Faith Healer" began as the voice of an unloveable, unredeemable bastard in my ear, trying to make his point to me. When it became clear he was a racist, I didn't want to sanitize him. I wasn't sure how he'd make out down South, but I wasn't going to help him. I will say I was pleased when he came around. I suppose as long as a person has love in their heart for someone or something, God can get to them through that love.

APPENDIX

A list of the magazines currently consulted for *New Stories from the South: The Year's Best, 2002,* with addresses, subscription rates, and editors.

Agni
Boston University Writing Program
236 Bay State Road
Boston, MA 02215
Semiannually, $15
Askold Melnyczuk

Alaska Quarterly Review
University of Alaska Anchorage
3211 Providence Drive
Anchorage, AK 99508
Quarterly, $10
Ronald Spatz

The Antioch Review
P.O. Box 148
Yellow Springs, OH 45387-0148
Quarterly, $35
Robert S. Fogarty

Apalachee Review
P.O. Box 10469
Tallahassee, FL 32302
Semiannually, $15
Laura Newton

Arts & Letters
Campus Box 89
Georgia College & State University
Milledgeville, GA 31061-0490
Semiannually, $15
Martin Lammon

The Atlantic Monthly
77 N. Washington St.
Boston, MA 02114
Monthly, $14.95
C. Michael Curtis

Black Warrior Review
University of Alabama
P.O. Box 862936
Tuscaloosa, AL 35486-0027
Semiannually, $14
T. J. Beitelman

Boulevard
4579 Laclede Ave., PMB 332
St. Louis, MO 63108-2103
Triannually, $15
Richard Burgin

The Carolina Quarterly
Greenlaw Hall CB# 3520
University of North Carolina
Chapel Hill, NC 27599-3520
Triannually, $12
Fiction Editor

The Chariton Review
Truman State University
Kirksville, MO 63501
Semiannually, $9
Jim Barnes

The Chattahoochee Review
Georgia Perimeter College
2101 Womack Road
Dunwoody, GA 30338-4497
Quarterly, $16
Lawrence Hetrick, Editor

Cimarron Review
205 Morrill Hall
Oklahoma State University
Stillwater, OK 74078-0135
Quarterly, $24
E. P. Walkiewicz

Columbia
415 Dodge Hall
2960 Broadway
Columbia University
New York, NY 10027-6902
Semiannually, $15
Kelly Zavotka

Confrontation
English Department
C.W. Post of L.I.U.
Brookville, NY 11548
Semiannually, $10
Martin Tucker, Editor

Conjunctions
Bard College
Annandale-on-Hudson, NY 12504
Semiannually, $18
Bradford Morrow

Crucible
Barton College
P.O. Box 5000
Wilson, NC 27893-7000
Annually, $6
Terrence L. Grimes

CutBank
Dept. of English
University of Montana
Missoula, MT 59812
Semiannually, $12
Elizabeth Burnett and Keith Dunlap

Denver Quarterly
University of Denver
Denver, CO 80208
Quarterly, $24
Bin Ramke

The Distillery
Division of Humanities and Social Science
Motlow State Community College
P.O. Box 8500
Lynchburg, TN 37352-8500
Semiannually, $15
Inman Majors

Epoch
251 Goldwin Smith Hall
Cornell University
Ithaca, NY 14853-3201
Triannually, $11
Michael Koch

Esquire
250 West 55th Street
New York, NY 10019
Monthly, $15.94
Adrienne Miller

Fiction
c/o English Department
City College of New York
New York, NY 10031
Quarterly, $32
Mark J. Mirsky

Five Points
GSU
University Plaza
Department of English
Atlanta, GA 30303-3083

Triannually, $20
Megan Sexton

The Florida Review
Department of English
University of Central Florida
Orlando, FL 32816
Semiannually, $10
Pat Rushin

Gargoyle
P.O. Box 6216
Arlington, VA 22206-0216
Semiannually, $20
Richard Peabody

The Georgia Review
University of Georgia
Athens, GA 30602-9009
Quarterly, $24
Stephen Corey

The Gettysburg Review
Gettysburg College
Gettysburg, PA 17325-1491
Quarterly, $24
Peter Stitt

Glimmer Train Stories
710 SW Madison St., #504
Portland, OR 97205
Quarterly, $32
Susan Burmeister-Brown
and Linda Burmeister Davies

Granta
1755 Broadway
5th Floor
New York, NY 10019-3780
Quarterly, $37
Ian Jack

The Greensboro Review
English Department
134 McIver Bldg.
University of North Carolina
P.O. Box 26170
Greensboro, NC 27412
Semiannually, $10
Jim Clark

Gulf Coast
Department of English
University of Houston
Houston, TX 77204-3012
Semiannually, $12
Mark Doty

Harper's Magazine
666 Broadway
New York, NY 10012
Monthly, $16
Ben Metcalf

High Plains Literary Review
180 Adams Street, Suite 250
Denver, CO 80206
Triannually, $20
Robert O. Greer, Jr.

Image
3307 Third Ave., W.
Seattle, WA 98119
Quarterly, $36
Gregory Wolfe

Indiana Review
465 Ballantine Ave.
Indiana University
Bloomington, IN 47405
Semiannually, $12
Laura McCoid

Inkwell
Manhattanville College
2900 Purchase St.
Purchase, NY 10577
Annually, $10.50
Steven Kerneklian

The Iowa Review
308 EPB
University of Iowa
Iowa City, IA 52242-1492
Triannually, $18
David Hamilton

The Journal
Ohio State University
Department of English
164 W. 17th Avenue
Columbus, OH 43210
Semiannually, $12
Kathy Fagan and Michelle Herman

Kalliope
Florida Community College
3939 Roosevelt Blvd.
Jacksonville, FL 32205
Triannually, $14.95
Mary Sue Koeppel

Karamu
English Department
Eastern Illinois University
Charleston, IL 61920
Annually, $7.50
Olga Abella

The Kenyon Review
Kenyon College
Gambier, OH 43022
Triannually, $25
David H. Lynn

The Literary Review
Fairleigh Dickinson University
285 Madison Avenue
Madison, NJ 07940
Quarterly, $18
Walter Cummins

The Long Story
18 Eaton Street
Lawrence, MA 01843
Annually, $6
R. P. Burnham

Lonzie's Fried Chicken
P.O. Box 189
Lynn, NC 28750
Semiannually, $14.95
E. H. Goree

Louisiana Literature
SLU-10792
Southeastern Louisiana University
Hammond, LA 70402
Semiannually, $12
Jack Bedell

Lynx Eye
c/o Scribblefest Literary Group
P.O. Box 6609
Los Osos, CA 93412-6609
Quarterly, $25
Pam McCully, Kathryn Morrison

Meridian
University of Virginia
P.O. Box 400121
Charlottesville, VA 22904-4121
Semiannually, $10
Ravi Howard

Mid-American Review
106 Hanna Hall
Department of English
Bowling Green State University
Bowling Green, OH 43403
Semiannually, $12
Michael Czyzniejewski

Mississippi Review
University of Southern Mississippi
Box 5144

Hattiesburg, MS 39406-5144
Semiannually, $15
Frederick Barthelme

The Missouri Review
1507 Hillcrest Hall
University of Missouri
Columbia, MO 65211
Triannually, $22
Speer Morgan

The Nebraska Review
Writers Workshop
Fine Arts Building 212
University of Nebraska at Omaha
Omaha, NE 68182-0324
Semiannually, $11
James Reed

New Delta Review
English Department
Louisiana State University
Baton Rouge, LA 70802-5001
Semiannually, $8.50
Andrew Spear

New England Review
Middlebury College
Middlebury, VT 05753
Quarterly, $23
Stephen Donadio

New Millennium Writings
P.O. Box 2463
Knoxville, TN 37901
Semiannually, $12.95
Don Williams

New Orleans Review
Box 195
Loyola University
New Orleans, LA 70118
Semiannually, $12
Christopher Chambers, Editor

The New Yorker
4 Times Square
New York, NY 10036
Weekly, $44.95
Bill Buford, Fiction Editor

Nimrod International Journal
The University of Tulsa
600 South College
Tulsa, OK 74104-3189
Semiannually, $17.50
Francine Ringold

The North American Review
University of Northern Iowa
1222 W. 27th Street
Cedar Falls, IA 50614-0516
Six times a year, $22
Vince Gotera

North Carolina Literary Review
English Department
2201 General Classroom Building
East Carolina University
Greenville, NC 27858-4353
Semiannually, $17
Margaret Bauer

Northwest Review
369 PLC
University of Oregon
Eugene, OR 97403
Triannually, $20
John Witte

The Ohio Review
344 Scott Quad
Ohio University
Athens, OH 45701-2979
Semiannually, $16
Wayne Dodd

Ohioana Quarterly
Ohioana Literary Assn.

274 E. First Avenue
Columbus, OH 43201
Quarterly, $25
Kate Templeton Hancock

Ontario Review
9 Honey Brook Drive
Princeton, NJ 08540
Semiannually, $14
Raymond J. Smith

Other Voices
University of Illinois at Chicago
Department of English (M/C 162)
601 S. Morgan Street
Chicago, IL 60607-7120
Quarterly, $24
Lois Hauselman

The Oxford American
P.O. Box 1156
Oxford, MS 38655
Quarterly, $24.95
Marc Smirnoff

The Paris Review
541 E. 72nd Street
New York, NY 10021
Quarterly, $40
George Plimpton

Parting Gifts
March Street Press
3413 Wilshire Drive
Greensboro, NC 27408
Semiannually, $12
Robert Bixby

Pembroke Magazine
UNC-P, Box 1510
Pembroke, NC 28372-1510
Annually, $8
Shelby Stephenson

PEN America: a Journal for Writers & Readers
PEN American Center
568 Broadway, Ste. 401
New York, NY 10012
M. Mark

Pindeldyboz
25-53 36th St.
Astoria, NY 11103
Semiannually, $20
Jeff Boison

Ploughshares
Emerson College
120 Boylston St.
Boston, MA 02116-4624
Triannually, $22
Don Lee

Prairie Schooner
201 Andrews Hall
University of Nebraska
Lincoln, NE 68588-0334
Quarterly, $26
Hilda Raz

Puerto del Sol
Box 30001, Department 3E
New Mexico State University
Las Cruces, NM 88003-9984
Semiannually, $10
Kevin McIlvoy

Quarterly West
200 S. Central Campus Drive
Room 317
University of Utah
Salt Lake City, UT 84112-9109
Semiannually, $14
Stephen Tuttle

River City
Department of English
The University of Memphis
Memphis, TN 38152-6176
Semiannually, $12
Thomas Russell

River Styx
634 North Grand Blvd.
12th Floor
St. Louis, MO 63103
Triannually, $20
Richard Newman

Santa Monica Review
Santa Monica College
1900 Pico Boulevard
Santa Monica, CA 90405
Semiannually, $12
Andrew Tonkovich

Seattle Review
Padelford Hall, Box 354330
University of Washington
Seattle, WA 98195-4330
Semiannually, $15
Colleen J. McElroy

Shenandoah
Washington and Lee University
Troubadour Theater
2nd Floor
Lexington, VA 24450-0303
Quarterly, $22
R. T. Smith

64
Shine Publications, Inc.
1435 West Main Street
Richmond, va 23220
10 times a year, $29.95
Lorna Wyckoff

The South Carolina Review
Department of English
Clemson University
Strode Tower, Box 340523
Clemson, SC 29634-0523
Semiannually, $18
Wayne Chapman

South Dakota Review
Box 111
University Exchange
University of South Dakota
Vermillion, SD 57069
Quarterly, $22
Brian Bedard

Southern Exposure
P.O. Box 531
Durham, NC 27702
Quarterly, $24
Pat Arnow, Editor

Southern Humanities Review
9088 Haley Center
Auburn University
Auburn, AL 36849
Quarterly, $15
Dan R. Latimer and Virginia M. Kouidis

The Southern Review
43 Allen Hall
Louisiana State University
Baton Rouge, LA 70803-5005
Quarterly, $25
James Olney

Southwest Review
307 Fondren Library West
Box 750374
Southern Methodist University
Dallas, TX 75275
Quarterly, $24
Willard Spiegelman

Sou'wester
Department of English
Southern Illinois University at Edwardsville
Edwardsville, IL 62026-1438
Semiannually, $10
Fred W. Robbins

StoryQuarterly
431 Sheridan Road
Kenilworth, IL 60043-1220

Annually, $10
M.M.M. Hayes

Sundog: The Southeast Review
Department of English
Florida State University
Tallahassee, FL 32311
Semiannually, $10
Jarret Keene

Tampa Review
The University of Tampa
401 W. Kennedy Boulevard
Tampa, FL 33606-1490
Semiannually, $15
Richard Mathews

Texas Review
English Department Box 2146
Sam Houston State University
Huntsville, TX 77341-2146
Semiannually, $20
Paul Ruffin

The Threepenny Review
P.O. Box 9131
Berkeley, CA 94709
Quarterly, $20
Wendy Lesser

Tin House
P.O. Box 10500
Portland, OR 97296-0500
Quarterly, $39.80
Rob Spillman

TriQuarterly
Northwestern University
2020 Ridge Avenue
Evanston, IL 60208-4302
Triannually, $24
Susan Firestone Hahn

The Virginia Quarterly Review
One West Range
P.O. Box 400223
Charlottesville, VA 22904-4223
Quarterly, $18
Staige D. Blackford

West Branch
Bucknell Hall
Bucknell University
Lewisburg, PA 17837
Semiannually, $7
Robert Love Taylor

Wind Magazine
P.O. Box 24548
Lexington, KY 40524
Triannually, $15
Charlie G. Hughes

Yemassee
Department of English
University of South Carolina
Columbia, SC 29208
Semiannually, $15
Lisa Kerr

Zoetrope: All-Story
1350 Avenue of the Americas
24th Floor
New York, NY 10019
Quarterly, $20
Adrienne Brodeur

ZYZZYVA
P.O. Box 590069
San Francisco, CA 94159-0069
Triannually, $36
Howard Junker

PUBLISHER'S NOTE

The stories reprinted in *New Stories from the South: The Year's Best, 2002* were selected from American short stories published in magazines issued between January and December 2001. Shannon Ravenel annually consults a list of about one hundred nationally distributed American periodicals and makes her choices for this anthology based on criteria that include original publication first-serially in magazine form and publication as short stories. Direct submissions are not considered.

PREVIOUS VOLUMES

Copies of previous volumes of *New Stories from the South* can be ordered through your local bookstore or by calling the Sales Department at Algonquin Books of Chapel Hill. Multiple copies for classroom adoptions are available at a special discount. For information, please call 919-967-0108.

New Stories from the South: The Year's Best, 1986

Max Apple, BRIDGING

Madison Smartt Bell, TRIPTYCH 2

Mary Ward Brown, TONGUES OF FLAME

Suzanne Brown, COMMUNION

James Lee Burke, THE CONVICT

Ron Carlson, AIR

Doug Crowell, SAYS VELMA

Leon V. Driskell, MARTHA JEAN

Elizabeth Harris, THE WORLD RECORD HOLDER

Mary Hood, SOMETHING GOOD FOR GINNIE

David Huddle, SUMMER OF THE MAGIC SHOW

Gloria Norris, HOLDING ON

Kurt Rheinheimer, UMPIRE

W. A. Smith, DELIVERY

Wallace Whatley, SOMETHING TO LOSE

Luke Whisnant, WALLWORK

Sylvia Wilkinson, CHICKEN SIMON

New Stories from the South: The Year's Best, 1987

James Gordon Bennett, DEPENDENTS

Robert Boswell, EDWARD AND JILL

Rosanne Caggeshall, PETER THE ROCK

John William Corrington, HEROIC MEASURES/VITAL SIGNS

Vicki Covington, MAGNOLIA

Andre Dubus, DRESSED LIKE SUMMER LEAVES

Mary Hood, AFTER MOORE

Trudy Lewis, VINCRISTINE

Lewis Nordan, SUGAR, THE EUNUCHS, AND BIG G. B.

Peggy Payne, THE PURE IN HEART

Bob Shacochis, WHERE PELHAM FELL

Lee Smith, LIFE ON THE MOON

Marly Swick, HEART

Robert Love Taylor, LADY OF SPAIN

Luke Whisnant, ACROSS FROM THE MOTOHEADS

New Stories from the South: The Year's Best, 1988

Ellen Akins, GEORGE BAILEY FISHING

Rick Bass, THE WATCH

Richard Bausch, THE MAN WHO KNEW BELLE STAR

Larry Brown, FACING THE MUSIC

Pam Durban, BELONGING

John Rolfe Gardiner, GAME FARM

Jim Hall, GAS

Charlotte Holmes, METROPOLITAN

Nanci Kincaid, LIKE THE OLD WOLF IN ALL THOSE WOLF STORIES

Barbara Kingsolver, ROSE-JOHNNY

Trudy Lewis, HALF MEASURES

Jill McCorkle, FIRST UNION BLUES

Mark Richard, HAPPINESS OF THE GARDEN VARIETY

Sunny Rogers, THE CRUMB

Annette Sanford, LIMITED ACCESS

Eve Shelnutt, VOICE

New Stories from the South: The Year's Best, 1989

Rick Bass, WILD HORSES

Madison Smartt Bell, CUSTOMS OF THE COUNTRY

James Gordon Bennett, PACIFIC THEATER

Larry Brown, SAMARITANS

Mary Ward Brown, IT WASN'T ALL DANCING

Kelly Cherry, WHERE SHE WAS

David Huddle, PLAYING

Sandy Huss, COUPON FOR BLOOD

Frank Manley, THE RAIN OF TERROR

Bobbie Ann Mason, WISH

Lewis Nordan, A HANK OF HAIR, A PIECE OF BONE

Kurt Rheinheimer, HOMES

Mark Richard, STRAYS

Annette Sanford, SIX WHITE HORSES

Paula Sharp, HOT SPRINGS

New Stories from the South: The Year's Best, 1990

Tom Bailey, CROW MAN

Rick Bass, THE HISTORY OF RODNEY

Richard Bausch, LETTER TO THE LADY OF THE HOUSE

Larry Brown, SLEEP

Moira Crone, JUST OUTSIDE THE B.T.

Clyde Edgerton, CHANGING NAMES

Greg Johnson, THE BOARDER

Nanci Kincaid, SPITTIN' IMAGE OF A BAPTIST BOY

Reginald McKnight, THE KIND OF LIGHT THAT SHINES ON TEXAS

Lewis Nordan, THE CELLAR OF RUNT CONROY

Lance Olsen, FAMILY

Mark Richard, FEAST OF THE EARTH, RANSOM OF THE CLAY

Ron Robinson, WHERE WE LAND

Bob Shacochis, LES FEMMES CREOLES

Molly Best Tinsley, ZOE

Donna Trussell, FISHBONE

New Stories from the South: The Year's Best, 1991

Rick Bass, IN THE LOYAL MOUNTAINS

Thomas Phillips Brewer, BLACK CAT BONE

Larry Brown, BIG BAD LOVE

Robert Olen Butler, RELIC

Barbara Hudson, THE ARABESQUE

Elizabeth Hunnewell, A LIFE OR DEATH MATTER

Hilding Johnson, SOUTH OF KITTATINNY

Nanci Kincaid, THIS IS NOT THE PICTURE SHOW

Bobbie Ann Mason, WITH JAZZ

Jill McCorkle, WAITING FOR HARD TIMES TO END

Robert Morgan, POINSETT'S BRIDGE

Reynolds Price, HIS FINAL MOTHER

Mark Richard, THE BIRDS FOR CHRISTMAS

Susan Starr Richards, THE SCREENED PORCH

Lee Smith, INTENSIVE CARE

Peter Taylor, COUSIN AUBREY

NEW STORIES FROM THE SOUTH: THE YEAR'S BEST, 1992

Alison Baker, CLEARWATER AND LATISSIMUS

Larry Brown, A ROADSIDE RESURRECTION

Mary Ward Brown, A NEW LIFE

James Lee Burke, TEXAS CITY, 1947

Robert Olen Butler, A GOOD SCENT FROM A STRANGE MOUNTAIN

Nanci Kincaid, A STURDY PAIR OF SHOES THAT FIT GOOD

Patricia Lear, AFTER MEMPHIS

Dan Leone, YOU HAVE CHOSEN CAKE

Karen Minton, LIKE HANDS ON A CAVE WALL

Reginald McKnight, QUITTING SMOKING

Elizabeth Seydel Morgan, ECONOMICS

Robert Morgan, DEATH CROWN

Susan Perabo, EXPLAINING DEATH TO THE DOG

Padgett Powell, THE WINNOWING OF MRS. SCHUPING

Lee Smith, THE BUBBA STORIES

Peter Taylor, THE WITCH OF OWL MOUNTAIN SPRINGS

Abraham Verghese, LILACS

New Stories from the South: The Year's Best, 1993

Richard Bausch, EVENING

Pinckney Benedict, BOUNTY

Wendell Berry, A JONQUIL FOR MARY PENN

Robert Olen Butler, PREPARATION

Lee Merrill Byrd, MAJOR SIX POCKETS

Kevin Calder, NAME ME THIS RIVER

Tony Earley, CHARLOTTE

Paula K. Gover, WHITE BOYS AND RIVER GIRLS

David Huddle, TROUBLE AT THE HOME OFFICE

Barbara Hudson, SELLING WHISKERS

Elizabeth Hunnewell, FAMILY PLANNING

Dennis Loy Johnson, RESCUING ED

Edward P. Jones, MARIE

Wayne Karlin, PRISONERS

Dan Leone, SPINACH

Jill McCorkle, MAN WATCHER

Annette Sanford, HELENS AND ROSES

Peter Taylor, THE WAITING ROOM

New Stories from the South: The Year's Best, 1994

Frederick Barthelme, RETREAT

Richard Bausch, AREN'T YOU HAPPY FOR ME?

Ethan Canin, THE PALACE THIEF

Kathleen Cushman, LUXURY

Tony Earley, THE PROPHET FROM JUPITER

Pamela Erbe, SWEET TOOTH

Barry Hannah, NICODEMUS BLUFF

Nanci Kincaid, PRETENDING THE BED WAS A RAFT

Nancy Krusoe, LANDSCAPE AND DREAM

Robert Morgan, DARK CORNER

Reynolds Price, DEEDS OF LIGHT

Leon Rooke, THE HEART MUST FROM ITS BREAKING

John Sayles, PEELING

George Singleton, OUTLAW HEAD & TAIL

Melanie Sumner, MY OTHER LIFE

Robert Love Taylor, MY MOTHER'S SHOES

NEW STORIES FROM THE SOUTH: THE YEAR'S BEST, 1995

R. Sebastian Bennett, RIDING WITH THE DOCTOR

Wendy Brenner, I AM THE BEAR

James Lee Burke, WATER PEOPLE

Robert Olen Butler, BOY BORN WITH TATTOO OF ELVIS

Ken Craven, PAYING ATTENTION

Tim Gautreaux, THE BUG MAN

Ellen Gilchrist, THE STUCCO HOUSE

Scott Gould, BASES

Barry Hannah, DRUMMER DOWN

MMM Hayes, FIXING LU

Hillary Hebert, LADIES OF THE MARBLE HEARTH

Jesse Lee Kercheval, GRAVITY

Caroline A. Langston, IN THE DISTANCE

Lynn Marie, TEAMS

Susan Perabo, GRAVITY

Dale Ray Phillips, EVERYTHING QUIET LIKE CHURCH

Elizabeth Spencer, THE RUNAWAYS

NEW STORIES FROM THE SOUTH: THE YEAR'S BEST, 1996

Robert Olen Butler, JEALOUS HUSBAND RETURNS IN FORM OF PARROT

Moira Crone, GAUGUIN

J. D. Dolan, MOOD MUSIC

Ellen Douglas, GRANT

William Faulkner, ROSE OF LEBANON

Kathy Flann, A HAPPY, SAFE THING

Tim Gautreaux, DIED AND GONE TO VEGAS

David Gilbert, COOL MOSS

Marcia Guthridge, THE HOST

Jill McCorkle, PARADISE

Robert Morgan, THE BALM OF GILEAD TREE

Tom Paine, GENERAL MARKMAN'S LAST STAND

Susan Perabo, SOME SAY THE WORLD

Annette Sanford, GOOSE GIRL

Lee Smith, THE HAPPY MEMORIES CLUB

NEW STORIES FROM THE SOUTH: THE YEAR'S BEST, 1997

PREFACE *by Robert Olen Butler*

Gene Able, MARRYING AUNT SADIE

Dwight Allen, THE GREEN SUIT

Edward Allen, ASHES NORTH

Robert Olen Butler, HELP ME FIND MY SPACEMAN LOVER

Janice Daugharty, ALONG A WIDER RIVER

Ellen Douglas, JULIA AND NELLIE

Pam Durban, GRAVITY

Charles East, PAVANE FOR A DEAD PRINCESS

Rhian Margaret Ellis, EVERY BUILDING WANTS TO FALL

Tim Gautreaux, LITTLE FROGS IN A DITCH

Elizabeth Gilbert, THE FINEST WIFE

Lucy Hochman, SIMPLER COMPONENTS

Beauvais McCaddon, THE HALF-PINT

Dale Ray Phillips, CORPORAL LOVE

Patricia Elam Ruff, THE TAXI RIDE

Lee Smith, NATIVE DAUGHTER

Judy Troy, RAMONE

Marc Vassallo, AFTER THE OPERA

Brad Vice, MOJO FARMER

New Stories from the South: The Year's Best, 1998

PREFACE *by Padgett Powell*

Frederick Barthelme, THE LESSON

Wendy Brenner, NIPPLE

Stephen Dixon, THE POET

Tony Earley, BRIDGE

Scott Ely, TALK RADIO

Tim Gautreaux, SORRY BLOOD

Michael Gills, WHERE WORDS GO

John Holman, RITA'S MYSTERY

Stephen Marion, NAKED AS TANYA

Jennifer Moses, GIRLS LIKE YOU

Padgett Powell, ALIENS OF AFFECTION

Sara Powers, THE BAKER'S WIFE

Mark Richard, MEMORIAL DAY

Nancy Richard, THE ORDER OF THINGS

Josh Russell, YELLOW JACK

Annette Sanford, IN THE LITTLE HUNKY RIVER

Enid Shomer, THE OTHER MOTHER

George Singleton, THESE PEOPLE ARE US

Molly Best Tinsley, THE ONLY WAY TO RIDE

NEW STORIES FROM THE SOUTH: THE YEAR'S BEST, 1999

PREFACE *by Tony Earley*

Andrew Alexander, LITTLE BITTY PRETTY ONE

Richard Bausch, MISSY

Pinckney Benedict, MIRACLE BOY

Wendy Brenner, THE HUMAN SIDE OF INSTRUMENTAL TRANSCOMMUNICATION

Laura Payne Butler, BOOKER T'S COMING HOME

Mary Clyde, KRISTA HAD A TREBLE CLEF ROSE

Janice Daugharty, NAME OF LOVE

Rick DeMarinis, BORROWED HEARTS

Tony Earley, QUILL

Clyde Edgerton, LUNCH AT THE PICADILLY

Michael Erard, BEYOND THE POINT

Tom Franklin, POACHERS

William Gay, THOSE DEEP ELM BROWN'S FERRY BLUES

Mary Gordon, STORYTELLING

Ingrid Hill, PAGAN BABIES

Michael Knight, BIRDLAND

Kurt Rheinheimer, NEIGHBORHOOD

Richard Schmitt, LEAVING VENICE, FLORIDA

Heather Sellers, FLA. BOYS

George Singleton, CAULK

New Stories from the South: The Year's Best, 2000

PREFACE *by Ellen Douglas*

A. Manette Ansay, BOX

Wendy Brenner, MR. PUNIVERSE

D. Winston Brown, IN THE DOORWAY OF RHEE'S JAZZ JOINT

Robert Olen Butler, HEAVY METAL

Cathy Day, THE CIRCUS HOUSE

R.H.W. Dillard, FORGETTING THE END OF THE WORLD

Tony Earley, JUST MARRIED

Clyde Edgerton, DEBRA'S FLAP AND SNAP

Tim Gautreaux, DANCING WITH THE ONE-ARMED GAL

William Gay, MY HAND IS JUST FINE WHERE IT IS

Allan Gurganus, HE'S AT THE OFFICE

John Holman, WAVE

Romulus Linney, THE WIDOW

Thomas McNeely, SHEEP

Christopher Miner, RHONDA AND HER CHILDREN

Chris Offutt, THE BEST FRIEND

Margo Rabb, HOW TO TELL A STORY

Karen Sagstetter, THE THING WITH WILLIE
Mary Helen Stefaniak, A NOTE TO BIOGRAPHERS REGARDING FAMOUS AUTHOR FLANNERY O'CONNOR
Melanie Sumner, GOOD-HEARTED WOMAN

New Stories from the South: The Year's Best, 2001

PREFACE *by Lee Smith*
John Barth, THE REST OF YOUR LIFE
Madison Smartt Bell, TWO LIVES
Marshall Boswell, IN BETWEEN THINGS
Carrie Brown, FATHER JUDGE RUN
Stephen Coyne, HUNTING COUNTRY
Moira Crone, WHERE WHAT GETS INTO PEOPLE COMES FROM
William Gay, THE PAPERHANGER
Jim Grimsley, JESUS IS SENDING YOU THIS MESSAGE
Ingrid Hill, JOLIE-GRAY
Christie Hodgen, THE HERO OF LONELINESS
Nicola Mason, THE WHIMSIED WORLD
Edith Pearlman, SKIN DEEP
Kurt Rheinheimer, SHOES
Jane R. Shippen, I AM NOT LIKE NUÑEZ
George Singleton, PUBLIC RELATIONS
Robert Love Taylor, PINK MIRACLE IN EAST TENNESSEE
James Ellis Thomas, THE SATURDAY MORNING CAR WASH CLUB
Elizabeth Tippens, MAKE A WISH
Linda Wendling, INAPPROPRIATE BABIES